It began on Freak Day—that day no one could explain, when strangers and family members alike went crazy and started biting one another. Some thought the outbreak was caused by a flu shot, others that it was a diet drug gone terribly wrong. All anyone knew is that once you were bitten and went to sleep, you woke up a freak.

Kendra, Terry, and the rest of the crew—having survived the freak attack at the abandoned barracks and the Siskiyou pirates—made it safely to the only town they could find that would have them: Domino Falls, aka Threadville.

Domino Falls has food, shelter, and a well-armed militia to fight off roving freaks . . .

But something doesn't seem quite right about the town's charismatic leader, Josey Wales—a B-movie actor who now has legendary status as the leader of a cultlike community that calls itself Threadies. Is it true that he predicted Freak Day? And what horror is lurking in the catacombs beneath his mansion?

What they find in Domino Falls threatens the fragile oasis of family they have created and everything they thought they knew about this strange and terrible new world. Kendra, Terry, and their band must decide if it is worth trading their freedom for survival.

Or should they risk the four-hundred-mile trip further south to the imagined safety of an island called Devil's Wake?

DOMINO FALLS

A Novel

Steven Barnes
and Tananarive Due

ATRIA PAPERBACK

New York   London   Toronto   Sydney   New Delhi

ATRIA PAPERBACK
A Division of Simon & Schuster, Inc.
1230 Avenue of the Americas
New York, NY 10020

First Atria Paperback edition February 2013

ATRIA PAPERBACK and colophon are trademarks of Simon & Schuster, Inc.

For information about special discounts for bulk purchases, please contact Simon & Schuster Special Sales at 1-866-506-1949 or business@simonandschuster.com.

The Simon & Schuster Speakers Bureau can bring authors to your live event. For more information or to book an event, contact the Simon & Schuster Speakers Bureau at 1-866-248-3049 or visit our website at www.simonspeakers.com.

Designed by Jacquelynne Hudson

Manufactured in the United States of America

10 9 8 7 6 5 4 3 2 1

Library of Congress Cataloging-in-Publication Data is available.

ISBN 978-1-4516-1702-3
ISBN 978-1-4516-1703-0 (ebook)

For our children, Jason and Nicki:
The future is yours.
May that future be as bright as the light
you have brought to our lives.

It was on the street outside. It was coming through your windows. It was a virus, an infection . . . By the time they tried to evacuate the cities, it was already too late. The infection was everywhere. The army blockades were overrun, and that's when the exodus started. The day before the TV stopped broadcasting, there were reports of infection in Paris and New York. You didn't hear anything more after that.

—*28 Days Later*

DOMINO
FALLS

One

Bainbridge Island, Washington
Snug Harbor Motor Court

Snow falls lightly as two motorcycles the color of arterial blood
cross the threshold of the Snug Harbor Motor Court: a Kawasaki
Ninja 250R and a Honda Interceptor, driven by two nut-brown
young men with long black hair, Darius Phillips and Dean Kitsap. Behind them rolls the school bus they call the Blue Beauty,
although the blue paint is flaking and the bus is far from beautiful. Windows are shattered, the body tattooed with bullet holes.
They have been at war, and will not have long to rest.

Bainbridge Island is the ancestral home of Dean and Darius's
people, the Suquamish Indians, fisherfolk for generations
before the first white traders appeared. Now . . . the Suquamish
own homes and businesses and fishing fleets and casinos and
restaurants. Those who can't afford better, like Dean's family,

huddle together in places like the Snug Harbor Motor Court. Nearly four hundred people share a hundred seventy trailers.

Dean, who leads the way, was born here. His mother and father and six brothers and sisters still live here, while an older brother is in the army, protecting strangers in a strange land. It is the only true home Dean has known. Still, somehow he cannot remember which way to turn.

There, at the central court—the cleared area houses a barbecue pit and a couple of weather-beaten picnic tables. Normally, children fill the narrow lane, playing in the snow, laughing and waving at the motorcycles and cars as they pass. Today, no one.

But the ground is cluttered with children's clothes, as if they are fresh from the laundry. Laid out in sets. So strange . . . pants, shirts, shoes . . . and footprints in the snow leading off toward the common play area.

A removable steel-frame barricade blocks the Blue Beauty from going farther. The bus's doors wheeze open.

First out is Terry Whittaker. Tall, dark-haired, wiry. Then Kendra Brookings peeks out and steps down, her nutmeg-colored, heart-shaped face pinched and cautious. Small, fragile-looking, but with a hidden strength that still surprises Dean. A survivor.

When had Dean learned about her strength? He isn't sure. And . . . she wasn't one of the Round Meadow Five, who had been sentenced to a summer of counseling kids at camp as punishment for their sins. How does he know her?

Sonia Petansu follows Kendra—thin, pale, angular. Long black hair with a vertical white streak. Cynical protectee of the largest of them, the big black guy everyone calls Piranha, Charlie Cawthone. Last off the bus is Corporal Ursalina Cortez, alert and serious, watching everything, missing nothing.

Dean moves toward the commons as the others follow him, silent, floating above the new snow, barely leaving footprints.

Dean finally hears an old woman's voice. Then he sees the children. They sit in the snow, dressed as they might have been to take a dip in the summer ocean, bare brown skin glimmering in the shimmering flecks, which seem to glide around them without touching. Why aren't the children shivering in the cold?

The old woman is telling stories, as she always has, from the time Dean was small. Everyone calls her Storyteller, and perhaps he once knew her real name, but he cannot remember. Storyteller has always been old. Dean's grandmother once told him that when she herself was a girl, Storyteller had spun her tales, and even then, she had been old. Storyteller has lived there since before the first trailer was towed to its berth.

Dean sits on the bench near the barbecue pit, where in the summer they roast salmon and beef ribs and enjoy the smell of lush green pine drifting from the Columbia Forest. A boy sitting there looks back and smiles, beckoning him over. His little brother, Raymond. Had Raymond been sitting there a moment ago? Why hadn't he seen him? Everything seems so strange.

"Years ago," Storyteller says, "before your grandparents were born, we knew things that you have forgotten, or pretend to have forgotten."

The children listen, rapt. "We knew not to let the children wander. The old ones would say, 'If you aren't careful, children, Kalkalilh will come and take you all away.'

"You have forgotten now, but if we forget, Kalkalilh will return. She is a giant, a huge woman who hides in the woods. Her home is far up in the mountains. In the evening or even in the daytime, but mostly in the evening, she will come prowling around the villages looking for disobedient children playing outside instead of doing their chores. Kalkalilh always has a great big basket strapped on her back, and can you guess what the basket for? She grabs children, throws them into the basket,

3

and scurries as fast as she can back home, up in the mountains. There, she boils them alive and sucks the marrow from their bones."

The children gasp, frightened. Perhaps Dean gasps with them. Fear whispers across his skin. Has he heard this story before? Has he seen the old woman with the basket with his own eyes?

"Since the children of the village did not want to die, they obeyed their parents, as good children did in those days . . ."

Dean looks down at his brother Raymond, whose hand slips into his. The fingers are small and cold. Dean rubs Raymond's hand to try to warm him, but Raymond's skin feels like a block of ice.

"But Kalkalilh was clever, and lured the parents away, so that the children were hungry and crying. Bigger children had been left to watch over the smaller ones, boys who were nearly men, and one of those older children was Dean. He was a great carver. He always had a sharp knife in his possession."

She looks at him when she says the words, and Dean's fingers touch his belt. There is indeed a knife there. He doesn't remember carrying a knife.

He looks around, and doesn't see the others who followed him here. His cousin, Darius, is gone. And the motorcycles, and the battered bus. No Kendra. No Terry. None of them. All gone. Only he remains with the children in the snow.

"A strange old woman came out of the woods, and in her hands were strips of dried salmon. 'Come, children, take this jerky.' And when the smallest girl reached to take the food, the cannibal woman grabbed her and threw her into the basket strapped to her back. And then grabbed up all the other children and headed off to her home in the mountains. Even Dean was trapped in the basket.

"But Dean was clever, and used his knife to cut a hole in the basket's straw, and one at a time, he pushed out the others and told them to go home. As each child thumped onto the ground, Kalkalilh said, 'What was that, Dean?' and Dean would say, 'Nothing, Gramma. It is only the sound of your feet on the ground.' And she believed his lie, so she continued walking until she arrived at her home. Dean tried to free all of the children, but a few remained trapped in the basket with him.

"Kalkalilh started a fire in her hearth, melting pitch to seal the eyes of the children, so that they would be unable to see if they dared try to escape.

"And Dean whispered to the children: 'As she starts to smear the pitch on your eyes, look down so that it smears on your foreheads and will not blind you.' And they agreed to do as he said, although they were very scared.

"When the cannibal woman finished smearing the pitch onto the children's foreheads, believing she had blinded them, she laughed while a bleached skull rolled on the ground. Then she sat down and started to paint her face in preparation of dancing to celebrate the succulent feast.

"While she danced on the opposite side of the fire from the children, Dean said, 'Come closer to us, Grandmother, as you are dancing.' And she did. When she came between the children and the fire, they all jumped on her and shoved her into the roaring hot flames. As soon as her hair hit the fire, she screamed as the lice on her head went up like a big puff of smoke. Dean used the fire tongs and kept pushing her further into the fire, saying, 'I am trying to help you.'

"And she screamed, and the children laughed and laughed . . ."

At the trailer park, Dean and the children laughed at the thought of the old woman dancing in the flames. Dean laughed until tears ran down his face while snow drifted to the earth and never touched him.

But Raymond's hand was so cold that it burned his skin, so he let his brother go. And when he glanced at Raymond's face, his brother's eyes were bright red.

The color of blood.

Two

December 19
Central California coast

The choking burr of the bus's engine had lulled Kendra to sleep, but a voice muttering about something called a *"Kal-kal-il"* eating children woke her. She saw Dean twitching in the seat in the row across from hers, both arms wound around his face as if to keep out the sunlight.

"Raymond . . ." he whispered. She had heard the name before. His brother?

Dean was the only one of them who had been home since Freak Day, and he'd never talked about what he had seen. Kendra decided that any dream about his brother couldn't be a good one.

She leaned over him, shaking him to wake him. His long jet-black hair was wound around his face like a veil.

"Dean?" she said, touching him gently on the elbow. He

opened his brown eyes warily, blinking. She recognized his confusion well; each day felt like you were waking into a dream. Which dream was worse?

"You were talking about someone eating children," she said.

He stared at her blankly, still trying to place her. "Snug Harbor," he said.

Piranha leaned over the seat, big brown hands clutched on the safety rail raised above each seat. "Where your parents lived?" he asked in his basso voice.

"Yeah," Dean said. He was stretching and twisting, almost like a snake shedding its skin.

"Never told us what happened there, man," Piranha said.

"No." Dean's eyes narrowed. "I didn't."

He stood and walked up to the front of the bus. He had begun his nap an hour ago, chaining his Honda to the back of Blue Beauty, leaving his cousin Darius to scout ahead of the bus on his bike alone.

"Pull over, Terry," Dean said. Terry was driving, as usual; as busted up as the Blue Beauty was after the pirate attack, Terry might be the only one of them who could manage the bus. Kendra usually sat in the seat behind Terry, but she'd moved closer to the supply boxes in the rear when she realized she couldn't stop staring at the back of his head, replaying their crazy, wonderful kiss on the beach in McKinleyville. If she distracted him as much as he did her, he might not be able to keep his eyes on the road. They didn't have the luxury of a high school crush.

Terry pulled over. They were on a stretch of farmland along the 101, maybe twenty miles south of Ukiah. Stalled cars were scattered along the road, but they didn't expect to run into real blockages until they got closer to San Francisco.

They heard Dean shift his bike down off the rack. Darius,

who had ridden up ahead of them, had circled back around to his side. Kendra watched Dean sadly, wondering what he had seen in his dream. She had nightmares too, and the images felt anything but harmless. Sometimes her dreams felt more real than the waking world, even if she didn't know which was more horrible. She was glad she didn't see her parents, or her grandfather, in her dreams—even though she missed them so much it was sometimes hard to breathe. But how could she select a handful of people to miss when the whole world might be gone?

Kendra watched Dean and his cousin talk through her window, wondering what they were saying. They were cousins, but so alike that everyone simply called them the Indian Twins.

"Hope he'll be okay," she said as he boarded his bike, giving the starter a confident thrust with his scuffed boot. But she was really talking about herself.

No one answered Kendra. Maybe no one had heard her over the radio. Maybe none of them would be okay.

The radio was loud; a persistent nattering from a man who called himself Reverend Wales, from a town ahead called Domino Falls. *". . . looked upon the burden, folks, and I said, YES, I can help build a haven. YES, I can give people hope. YES, the threads that bind us all can weave a new world from the wreckage of the old . . ."*

Domino Falls. It sounded more like a game of chance than true sanctuary.

The Twins gave Terry the thumbs-up sign. Then they rode off ahead of the bus, together.

At times the 101 was a broad clear stretch of freeway, and at others, when winding through one of the abandoned coastal towns, it was little more than a two-lane road dotted with interstate signs. Here, just on the outskirts of a town composed of a pair of gas stations, a convenience store, and a motel, it was the latter. Doors were ajar, windows shattered. The empty towns always creeped Terry out. He didn't know what had happened here, but it was just more evidence of bad news.

Up ahead, the two cherry-red motorcycles had pulled over to the side of the road. Darius waved to Terry to slow down. Terry cursed under his breath. They had agreed that they had enough gas to keep going without stopping. They'd been lucky at the last checkpoint, but stopping could always lead to trouble.

"Something's up," Terry said, keeping his voice even. He didn't want to panic the others, especially Kendra, but they had to be ready. Behind him, the familiar scurrying and clicking of metal told Terry that his little army was indeed prepared for anything.

"What's up?' Piranha said.

"Not sure yet."

"If that's a freak, it's my shot," Ursalina said.

Had Terry seen him all along? A few yards ahead of the bikes, a short, stout stranger in a gray shirt and a conical birthday hat was waving his arms at the bus.

Did freaks wave? Why were Dean and Darius letting him get so close? Any stranger was a freak or a pirate until proven otherwise. Both were deadly, but the pirates were worse. Pirates laid traps—like this fool in a birthday hat.

The Blue Beauty creaked to a halt. The man didn't seem to be armed, but that didn't mean there wasn't a sniper hiding nearby. Or a band of pirates out of sight. At the Siskiyou Pass, pirates had blocked the road and nearly killed them all. As Terry thought about it, phantom gunfire crackled in his ears.

"Why'd the Twins stop?" Piranha said. "So what if there's a dude in the road? We said we'd keep going."

Ursalina checked her rifle's action. "Some people never learn," she muttered.

Terry shrugged, sighing. "Maybe it's the birthday hat," he said, and slipped the gear into Park. The engine growled disapproval. He didn't dare kill the engine, or the Beauty might not start quickly enough when they needed to go. Hell, she might not start at all. "Everybody stay close. Watch for movement."

After the bus stopped, they all slowly climbed down, weapons ready.

Hipshot was the last, but the black terrier mix they'd inherited from Camp Round Meadow seemed reluctant to dismount. Not good. But Hippy wasn't barking a warning either. That . . . was telling. The man in the road wasn't infected. Hippy would know. Ursalina had told them that the soldiers at her base had called dogs PAWS—a Predator Advance Warning System. Dogs could smell the freak in people even before they turned.

Once they reached Dean and Darius, Terry gave them an irritated look.

"What can I say?" Darius said, grinning. "I can't pass up a chance to party."

"Tweedledee and Tweedledumber," Ursalina said, just loudly enough for them to hear. By silent vote, Terry was elected the one to make the initial approach. Protective coloration. Even Ursalina, the only one of them with military training, seemed satisfied to let him lead. Maybe she reckoned that hanging behind was safer than walking out front.

Terry walked within ten yards of the man, and stopped short. The man's wide grin was unnerving, and Terry couldn't quite read the look on his face. He seemed happy to see survivors, but there was something disturbing in his eyes. *So what if he's a little crazy? We're all bugnuts by now,* Terry thought. The man looked well-fed; in fact, he could stand to eat a little less. His clothes were grimy, but his skin and face were clean. He had somewhere to bathe. He didn't stink.

If he was just a survivor, like them, they might have to vote on whether or not to let him ride with them to Domino Falls. Terry, Piranha, Sonia, and the Twins had started out as only five, but they'd picked up Kendra and Ursalina since they'd left Camp Round Meadow. Now they might end up with more. But could they trust this guy?

"You out here by yourself?" Terry said.

"Merry Christmas!" he said. "No, it's me and my family. We don't see many people, and I need some people today. Would you follow me back to the house?" He was already turning to walk up the road.

"Need people. Why?"

The man stopped and turned. He winked. "Come on. It's Christmas! Well, it's almost Christmas, anyway. Can't fault folks for wanting company at Christmas."

Christmas! Terry knew it was late December, so Christmas must be less than a week away. He'd felt a lack of holiday spirit in years past, but this year it felt ridiculous, maybe even irreverent, to think about Santa Claus.

"Ho, ho, ho," Sonia said sarcastically. "Wonder what I'll steal *this* year."

Ursalina snickered. "I could use some hair conditioner. Big-time."

"Yeah, grab me that new iPad," Piranha said. "The one with the freak alarm."

"Shhhhh," Kendra shushed them. Kendra was the youngest in their group, only sixteen, but she already sounded like their

mother. She moved closer to Terry, curious about the stranger. Terry held his arm out, rigid, to keep her from getting too close.

"I'm sorry, sir," Kendra said. "We'd forgotten all about Christmas."

The man's grin vanished, and he suddenly looked grave. "Well, you can't forget Christmas. No, sirree. Not in our house. Always been a very special day. Come on! We were just about to cut the cake, but I heard your engine. You're the best gift of all. Guess you could say you're what I've been praying for."

His grin came back, brighter than before. He turned and began walking again, expecting them to follow.

For a moment, they all stood in silence, watching.

"You heard the man," Darius said. "There's cake."

As if that settled everything. In a way, maybe it did.

"Okay, we'll follow him," Terry said. "But we're getting back on the bus."

The bus trundled along behind their guide and the Twins' motorcycles down the empty road to a narrow path, where the stranger veered east. All joking had stopped once they were back on the Blue Beauty, and Kendra was glad. Jokes felt like bad luck. She wasn't afraid of the man, not exactly, but something gnawing at the edge of her awareness made her wish they had ignored him and driven on.

A two-story white-frame house stood at the end of the road, its blue and white trim well-maintained, the front steps a bit weathered, almost ratty. The man stopped to make sure they were still following, then he opened the unlocked door and walked inside. Kendra could hardly imagine leaving a door unlocked now, even for a short time.

"Honey, we're home," Terry said, slowing to a crawl in front of the house. No one laughed. Hippy backed up in the Beauty's stairwell, shivering.

"See that?" Piranha said, nodding toward Hipshot. "That's mutt language for keep your butts moving."

If they took a vote, Kendra wasn't sure what she would say.

"This is California," Terry said. "Maybe we should play by their rules. Be good neighbors. We've had nothing but hospitality since we crossed the Siskiyous. Let's ride our good luck."

The Blue Beauty sighed to a stop outside the house near the waiting motorcycles. Hippy lay in the aisle, looking at them. Not budging. Nothing quite right, nothing quite wrong. The Blue Beauty shivered enough to rattle the windows, the engine coughing.

"All right, *muchachos*," Ursalina said. "We'll go in, but we'll be careful. Only two at first. We do a sweep—make sure there're no ugly surprises. If it's clear, we all go."

"Keep the bus running, T," Piranha said. "We're burning gas, so we can't stay long."

"And if he's telling the truth?" Terry said. "What if there's a family and they want to come with us?"

They all looked at one another, except for Ursalina, who stared away. She probably didn't want to pick up any survivors, but she'd been the last in, so she couldn't complain.

"I guess they can come," Sonia said reluctantly. Kendra noticed that she was holding Piranha's hand. Since the night they'd spent with sanctuary on the beach, Sonia and Piranha no longer behaved as if they were hiding. "Especially if there's kids."

"Let's ask the Twins," Piranha said, "but Sonia's right. As long as we have room, why not? They can ride as far as Domino Falls, anyway. No promises after that."

There are no promises for any of us after that, Kendra thought, but she didn't have to say it aloud. They all knew that Domino Falls might be a trap. Ursalina was right: radio signals were a lure. Things that sound too good to be true usually were. If not for the beachfront paradise a hundred fifty miles back, they'd have had no reason to believe in the promise of Domino Falls and its claims of safety and normalcy. Just like they wouldn't have any reason to believe the word of a stranger standing in the road.

But they had to believe in something. Didn't they?

"Who's first in?" Terry said.

"I'll go," Ursalina said. "I'll take Dean with me."

They disembarked, stepping over Hipshot, and approached the house, walking no farther than the edge of the porch. Kendra tried not to be worried that the dog didn't want to follow them, but it couldn't be a good sign.

Silver cut-out letters were strung together on the front porch, reading Merry Christmas. They twisted gently in the wind, winding back and forth. Kendra heard happy holiday music from inside the house, and maybe the sound of laughter. *Grandma got run over by a reindeer* . . .

"Where's Hippy?" Dean asked.

"Won't get off the bus," Terry said.

"PAWS in action. Smarter'n the rest of us combined," Ursalina told Dean. "Come in with me. We're sweeping the house for pirates."

Dean looked from the bus to the house, weighing the matter. Then he nodded, his 9mm Hi-Point rifle at the ready.

The wait outside seemed interminable. The Christmas music changed to the Chipmunks singing about hula hoops, one of Kendra's favorites when she was young. The high-pitched revelry made her eyes sting with tears. She and her parents had sucked helium from balloons and sung along to that song every year. The sudden memory was so vivid that her knees went wobbly and the sky seemed to dim.

After what seemed like forever, Ursalina and Dean came back out, trailed by the portly stranger. Only the stranger was smiling. He proudly held out a cake cutter he might have retrieved from the kitchen.

"Clear," Ursalina said. "No one in the house. Looks like the family's out back. We saw them through the window."

"Kids?" Sonia said, anxious.

Ursalina nodded.

"Just like I told you," the stranger said, and waved them all along the side of the house. "Come on around. They're waiting."

The little man bounced ahead of them to a backyard gate that lay open, walking lightly on the balls of his feet. Happy happy, joy joy. Could it be contagious?

They followed him. First they passed a play set that looked almost new: swings and a small slide. Next to that, a tree house with both wood-slat ladders nailed into a bare-limbed apricot tree, and a knotted rope that looked an inch and a half thick, now swaying in the breeze. All of it looked like it might have been constructed since Freak Day.

Past the tree, Kendra finally saw the stranger's family. Three of them sat at a large red cedar picnic table that had been draped with a gaily-colored tablecloth; two small girls and a woman with frizzy yellow hair. "One . . . two . . . *three* . . ." the girls were saying in piping unison, and dissolving into giggles. "One . . . two . . . *three* . . ."

The others didn't see their approach because their backs were to them, all of them wearing identical birthday hats, oblivious to the world around them. A small evergreen beside the table was strung with tinsel and candy canes, and topped with a silver star. The table was piled with gaudily wrapped boxes and what looked like mailing tubes.

How had this family created an oasis when everything else was gone? The girls were laughing and eating cake with their fingers, not waiting for their father to cut it.

Kendra was close enough to Terry to hear him draw a startled breath. "I don't know if I want to laugh or cry," he whispered to her. Kendra wanted to do both. Her hand sought his, their fingers twining together. Everything seemed so . . . normal. As if the devastation that had touched the rest of the world hadn't quite penetrated here.

But not quite. What was it? Suddenly, Kendra knew, and felt a chill: Why were they celebrating outside the house? The December air was cold, and only the father was wearing a jacket. The others were barely dressed, practically in rags. What the—

The sudden sound of Hipshot's urgent barking made Kendra jump, startled. The dog had followed them after all, standing between them and the picnic table.

"I knew it . . ." Ursalina said, taking a step back. If not for the tremor in her voice, she'd have sounded triumphant.

Now that she was only twenty feet from the table, Kendra was close enough to see the cords wound around the family's feet.

Dean swung his rifle up. "What the hell is going on?"

"Just a party," the little man said, and when he turned, he seemed too bright, too happy. Why hadn't they seen it? "Every day, we have a party. Can't wait for Christmas."

Their kids and the mother turned toward them, their private party disturbed. Their eyes were reddish, their faces threaded with tiny vines, like rogue veins, growing where no veins should grow. All three tried to lunge to their feet, but they were held in place by cables fastened to their waists. They hissed and

thrashed, but the girls made laughing sounds. "One . . . two . . .
three . . ." they said in unison, twins even now.

The girls might have been pretty once, but no more.
Their round cheeks and matted blond hair were ghoulish.
Kendra stood behind Terry, who had pulled out his Browning
9mm. Sometimes freaks could talk! After the way she'd lost
Grandpa Joe, Kendra didn't think she could ever forget it, but
those girls had fooled her. What if one of them had been too
close?

Everyone who'd brought a gun had it trained on a member of
this bizarre family. Terry's was on the stranger. "What do you
want from us?" Terry said, raising his voice to be heard over
Hipshot's ferocious growling and barking. "Why'd you bring us
back here?"

"The girls were born on Christmas Day," the man said.
Now Kendra could hear his pain, grief, shock. "We've always
celebrated all month, so they wouldn't feel cheated. Can you
help me give them their present? I know it's what they'd want."

Terry backed up a step, and Kendra gladly retreated with
him. Piranha cursed, and they formed an instinctive half-circle
to protect themselves, ready to fire and flee. His family was
straining at the end of their ropes now, mouths stretched wide,
yearning, fingers questing.

"What present?" Terry said, his voice unsteady. "Man,
you're crazy. You can't help them. Let us make sure you're not
bit, and you can come with us. Leave them here."

The man shook his head, insistent. "I need you to help me
give them their present," he said, and his voice broke. "I can't
do it. Can't you see? Look at them! Listen to my girls laughing!
They sound exactly the same. I want to, but . . . I can't."

Those might have been his sanest words yet, Kendra realized.
Her throat swelled with grief for a family she'd never known.

"Let's get the hell out of here," Sonia said, tugging on Piranha.

But Piranha didn't move. He was staring at Terry. And Ursalina. For the first time Kendra could remember, they didn't have a plan. They didn't know what to do.

"She's right," Kendra said. "Let's go. We shouldn't have stopped."

Terry shook his head, taking another step back. "I'm sorry," he told the pleading man. "We can't help you."

But Kendra's eyes were drawn to Ursalina, who was gazing at the kids with curled lips and dead eyes. Then Ursalina looked toward Dean, and their eyes locked with a spark of communication. A pair of barely perceptible nods between them, in a secret tongue only they seemed to know.

Ursalina, after all, had fought in a war when her National Guard had fallen to an army of freaks. And Dean's war had followed him to his dreams; the war he'd fought at home.

"I can do it," Dean said.

Ursalina nodded. "Yeah. We can handle this."

Dean looked at Darius, who shook his head. All jokes were far from Darius's face. "Not me, bro," Darius said. "I'm going back to my bike."

"Go on," Dean said, nodding. "You and the others wait for us."

"Sir?" Terry said gently to the man. "Step around front with us, please. You don't want to be here right now."

Kendra dared to hope that if she made it back to the bus fast enough and covered her ears, she could pretend she'd never seen the bizarre Christmas scene in the backyard. But she never had the chance.

The stranger didn't come toward Terry. Instead, he rushed to the picnic table, toward his wife and children, his arms wide to embrace them. All Kendra saw was the ecstatic grin on his face. "I'm sorry, Melissa," he said. "I'm sorry, Caitlin and Cathy. Merry Christmas, angels. Happy birthday!"

For an instant, Kendra thought they were only trying to hug him too; they were all wrapped in an iron embrace, a tangle of frantic limbs.

But Kendra closed her eyes when she saw their teeth.

By the time the gunshots finally came from Ursalina and Dean, she had been praying for the sound of death.

Three

For two miles, they drove along a body of water labeled the Domino Falls Reservoir. Then, just as the map said, they were entering the town itself; a hand-painted sign read WELCOME TO THREADVILLE.

Terry's hope surged, pushing aside the recent, toxic memories. Was it actually possible that this was a real town? Mostly dry, brown farmland spread out on either side of them, not much visible from the road. And everything was fenced in, a triple barrier. Strings of barbed wire gleamed like silver spiderwebs in the sunlight. Terry thought the fencing was great, as long as it wasn't a cage.

"Guess we better like it here," Piranha said.

They passed a large white pickup truck parked between the barbed rows, and six hard-faced men busy burning freaks off the fence with flamethrowers that resembled back-mounted insecticide sprayers. Terry kept the Beauty moving so he wouldn't press his luck, but he couldn't help slowing down to watch the freaks slowly twisting in the concertina wire. One was almost cocooned, his labors ensnaring him more deeply in the razored strands. The three men spoke to one another without cheer.

From the bus, they all watched the flames like kids hypnotized by fireworks. The freaks twitched and twisted, the motions mild at first and then frenzied as the fire climbed their bodies and finally enshrouded them.

"*That's* what I'm talking about," Piranha muttered.

The freaks moaned loudly, more in confusion than pain. Terry doubted that freaks could feel pain the way humans did; they ignored their injuries too readily during a chase. But they seemed to know when they were dying. He could *hear* that they knew it. A . . . sadness? As if they were apologizing to someone or something for not fulfilling their proper function. A flesh-creeping sound. Then they were twitching, smoking marionettes.

Behind him, the others whooped and high-fived.

"Yep—I like it here," Piranha said. "It's got a real homey feel."

"Hallelujah," Ursalina said.

Terry caught Kendra's eyes in the mirror just as she was looking for his. They both knew there was nothing joyful about burning flesh, infected or not.

He wasn't about to shed any tears, but still . . .

Hell, that could be *his* body burning up there. Any of theirs. Any of them could.

The men backed away from the fence, and one of them turned around and saw the Blue Beauty. Terry slowed their vehicle to a crawl to demonstrate peaceful intentions. He waved to them, his expression sober. Ursalina gave them a thumbs-up through the window, but they didn't return it. Kendra waved at the men, then Darius and Dean on their bikes. No one seemed surprised to see newcomers or the condition of their bus. As if they were part of an official procession, they continued down the road.

Further on, at least two hundred people were crowded on both sides of the asphalt, ragged tents clumped around cook fires. Heads turned to watch the arrival of their bus. A couple of dogs yapped, racing to snap at their rear bumper. A man who looked at least eighty leaned on a twisted makeshift crutch as he scooped a cup of water out of a rusty barrel. He glared at Terry as they rumbled past. Would any of them be allowed inside?

A man in a bright yellow shirt waved them on, and Terry was relieved. The camp was better than nothing, but he'd expected more—and he definitely wanted to camp inside the fences, not outside. Terry kept driving.

They passed two barbed-wire gates, guarded by three-man rifle teams. The guards were polite but firm, all of them decked out in identical black jeans and golden shirts buttoned to their collars. There were no grins or "How can I help yous," and Terry figured there would be no "Have a nice day" when they were through.

They had finally reached the outskirts of Domino Falls . . . the place people called Threadville.

Beyond the fence, a rusting metal office desk was shadowed by a rippling canopy. The man at the desk was wrinkled and sun-beaten, probably at least seventy, with short-cropped white hair. The purple tattoo on his tautly muscled bicep read ONLY THE STRONG SURVIVE, and his eyes were like a marine sniper's. He wore a bright copper shirt, almost the color of gold.

Dean and Darius were drawing a crowd. Four guys in the

same bright yellow button-down shirts circled the Twins with sawed-off shotguns resting across their shoulders. Three of the men wore cowboy hats, which gave the picture an unpleasant light. The Twins sat astride their bikes with their jet-black hair and a long history written all over their faces, ignoring the men in the yellow shirts. *Never seen Native Americans before?*

A busty redhead in a tattered denim jacket stared holes through the Twins, caressing the butt of a Magnum worn in a sun-cracked leather holster slung low on her ample hips.

Other men in yellow shirts waited in the distance, all of them wearing guns in holsters, some carrying rifles or shotguns—they stood by the fences or lined the road farther beyond the checkpoint on the way to town. Kendra wondered who they were, what the yellow shirts meant. Kendra's father had loved talking about mob mentality, and that prison experiment at Stanford where the students who were given authority over their classmates morphed into Nazis. Why should this be any different?

Hipshot bounded out of the bus, heading for the nearest shrub to raise his leg. Without a vote or a conversation, Terry became their official spokesman. The old guy at the gate asked rapid-fire questions.

"Your business?"

"Trade and shelter," Terry said. "We've been on the road for—"

The gatekeeper didn't wait for the rest. "Anybody else on that bus?"

Terry shook his head. "Just us."

The old guy gestured, and one of the men in the yellow shirts went to the open bus door and climbed inside without an invitation. They saw him walk up and down the aisles. He

24

emerged a moment later, climbing out with a curt nod toward the gatekeeper. The old guy was satisfied.

"You have trade?" the old guy said. "Skills?"

"We're willing to work. Whatever it takes. We have food and some tools."

"Can any of you shoot?"

"Hell, yeah," Piranha said, and they all chimed in. Kendra knew more about shooting than she'd ever imagined.

"Weapons?" the man said.

"We have rifles, pistols, and ammunition," Terry said.

"What else you carrying on this wreck?"

Kendra bristled. The Blue Beauty might be a wreck, but she was *their* wreck.

"Canned and dried food, mostly," Terry said. "MREs. A couple drops of gas."

If Terry had won the old guy over, it didn't show in the Grim Reaper set of his jaw. He scanned them one by one, his gaze lingering on their eyes.

"Anyone bit?" he said. "Scratched? Broken skin? You look tired, son." His eyes had come back to Terry, resting there.

"I've been driving a bus ten days straight, and you can see we got shot all to hell . . . so yeah, I'm tired."

"We're all tired," Ursalina said, impatient.

The guy shot her a *Was I talking to you?* look that curled her lips, but she shut up.

Hipshot bounded back up to them and licked the back of Terry's hand. "See? No freaks here," Terry said.

"You'd be surprised," the man said. "I've seen 'em turn right where you're standing. One gal'd been bit and nobody in her party knew. So don't think I'm asking 'cuz I've got nothing better to do."

"No, sir," Kendra said, pouring on the politeness in her

little-girl voice. "We don't think that. We're just looking for somewhere safe."

Darius snickered.

"I'll let you in," the gatekeeper said finally. "But you're on probation, which means there's a zero tolerance policy for B.S. No one in your party is under fourteen, so tomorrow you'll all work. No exceptions. No free rides in Domino Falls. And you'll have a *very* thorough search—take me at my word. You surrender all weapons until after quarantine. After that, sidearms only unless you're part of a street or fence patrol."

There's always a catch, Kendra thought. She hadn't been armed long, but she'd gotten used to it. They looked at one another, fidgeting.

"Quarantine?" Piranha said, suspicious. "What's that for? We've got a dog. You'd know if we were infected."

The gatekeeper looked like he was up to his tonsils with questions, so the redhead with the huge handgun spoke up. "Dogs don't always pick up a fresh bite," she said. "We've learned that the hard way. You'll be quarantined for twelve hours. My advice? Get some sleep. You sniff all right after that, you're in."

"Or we hit the road?" Terry said.

The woman gave them a nasty grin. She had shaggy chestnut hair and a slight chip in one of her front teeth, made more noticeable by the gleam in her eyes. Otherwise, her teeth seemed cosmetically white. Maybe Threadville had a good dental plan.

"You belong to us now," the woman said. "If you're bit, you're dispatched."

"Dispatched where?" Kendra said. She imagined a concentration camp for the infected . . . until she remembered the burning freaks on the fences. She glanced at the men in yellow shirts again, noting their guns.

"To a shallow grave, *chica*," Ursalina said, chuckling.

"Before they've turned?" Kendra said, horrified.

The woman shrugged. "Consider it a favor."

"Got that right," Ursalina said. "This is war."

The gatekeeper and the woman both glanced at Ursalina appreciatively. One of the yellow shirts bumped Ursalina's fist, although he didn't crack a smile.

"Your dog kennels with us," the woman said. "Me and my brother will escort you to the quarantine site. Name's Jackie Burchett."

She glanced toward the Twins again, and for the first time Kendra noticed the intrigue twinkling in her eyes. They smiled at her, whipping off their sunglasses, both of them rising from their bikes.

"Darius Phillips." He tipped an imaginary hat, winking.

"Dean Kitsap."

Jackie's grin glowed. They all introduced themselves, but her eyes stayed on the Twins. Kendra doubted Jackie had heard anyone else or cared about their names.

"One thing, though," Terry said. "Is there a mechanic?"

"I figured her for a junker," Jackie said, assessing the bus. "You might be better off scrapping her for barter. Think she'll start back up?"

"It'll take some sweet talk, but she'll start. Just don't know for how long."

Jackie and the burliest of the other men headed toward a massive white pickup truck parked near the intake desk. "Yeah, we can swing by Myles's place. It's on the way, he's honest, and he'll take good care of you," Jackie said. "Just follow us."

Kendra didn't want to follow them. The woman's presence made it doubtful that they were being led to a slavers' trap, at least, but nothing soothed the alarm bell that had been sounding in her head since she'd first seen the yellow shirts.

But Kendra tried to ignore the alarm, following her friends back into the bus.

Terry was ready to feel good. More than ready. But he wasn't there yet.

The Blue Beauty could barely push fifteen miles per hour as he tried to keep up with their escorts' white pickup truck. Terry had never liked chaperones. He had to admit that Domino Falls seemed like a dream come true so far—they hadn't found any other settlement with a fraction of D.F.'s organization, and they'd been luckier than the people stuck outside the fences—but the rules bothered him. Had they really just spent months watching one another's backs to just suddenly start trusting strangers?

He checked out Kendra in the rearview, since she was in her usual seat behind him, and her forehead was furrowed with clear worry. Ursalina, as usual, was in her own world, staring at nothing out of her window. Sonia was sitting so close to Piranha, she was practically in his lap. Everyone looked ready to jump.

At least no one from Domino Falls had insisted on riding with them. The Twins were out of reach on their bikes, but the rest of them had a last chance to talk.

"Quick Council," Terry said. "Are we okay with all this?"

"Do we have a choice?" Piranha said. "I didn't want to mess it up for everybody, but hell no, I'm not down with anything that sounds like lockup."

"Yeah, and what's up with their sniff test?" Sonia said. "They shoot us if one of their dogs doesn't approve?"

"I sure hate giving up the firepower while they make up their minds," Ursalina said. "Maybe it's good policy for them, but it bites hard for us."

"I don't like it here," Kendra said, so quietly that Terry barely heard her.

Terry sighed, wishing he disagreed. "We have to be realistic, though," he said. "We can't turn around and take off, even if we knew where else to go."

"Don't even try it," Ursalina warned. "Those guys in the yellow shirts are former cops, military. I can smell it. Don't make any sudden movements. Maybe this place is legit, maybe not. But gun or no gun, if anything goes down, I'm busting heads. I'll take at least three of them with me."

Terry sighed. Unlike Ursalina, the blaze-of-glory routine didn't comfort him the way it might have once, at the Barracks where they had rescued her.

"Let's not separate," Kendra said. "Let's ask to stay together."

Terry cringed at the word *ask*. The minute you asked anyone for permission, you gave them the power to say no. Then what? Say *pretty please*?

But they all agreed that they wanted to stay together. Nobody was going to pick them off one by one or molest one of the girls when she was alone.

But would they be allowed to stay together? And for how long?

It was a ten-minute drive from the checkpoint to the rest of Threadville, on a two-lane road that branched from the I-5. The town was hidden by hills and trees except for fenced farmhouses, where teams of people worked in the neatly planted groves. Some workers stood on platforms picking ripe winter oranges. Terry couldn't identify the other trees and crops, but he thought he saw broccoli in one field. The idea of fresh fruit and vegetables made his stomach growl. An apple would taste like heaven. Were apples winter fruit?

The radio was playing softly, so Terry turned up the volume.

"*—the connections between us all run deep. When I created*

29

Threads in 1984, I drove up to the top of the San Fernando Valley, ate a 'shroom, and just looked out, lying across the hood of my Beamer."

After yahanna, it might be a while before anyone ate mushrooms for fun. Or anything else, Terry guessed. Anyone who'd taken the diet mushroom and then followed it with a flu shot had had one hell of a surprise.

"I looked out at the lights, and instead of seeing a thousand points of light, I saw the connections between them. All the connections . . . then I looked up at the stars, that I'd always seen as points of light, a billion points of light, and seemed to see the same thing. All of those stars were connected by threads of light, of gravity, of love, and I realized that there were only two types of people: those who cut the threads, and those who wove them together—"

"Turn that crap off," Ursalina said.

"Threadies aren't so bad," Sonia muttered. "More like Trekkies than Scientologists."

Piranha interrupted. "Sorry, baby, but if staying here means we have to listen to that noise all day, we need to bounce as soon as the Beauty's fixed."

If the Beauty could be fixed, Terry thought. He turned off the radio. As if the radio had been keeping the bus on life support, the engine finally seized and sputtered out. Ahead, the pickup's brake lights went on. Darius and Dean buzzed around the bus like flies.

"Come on, sweetheart," Terry whispered to the steering wheel. "Just a little more, darlin'."

Piranha laughed. "I already told you—get a room."

"Promise her the world," Ursalina said.

The engine started again, but barely. Every few yards the bus shuddered again. Terry was relieved when the pickup truck's turn signal came on and the driver motioned for them to follow them left. More houses dotted the roadway now, hinting that they were closer to town.

Dean and Darius sped ahead, veering into the driveway of the mechanic's shop. The shop looked like a regular ranch house, except for the repair bays in the two-car garage. Rows of junk cars were parked to the side, hoods up, many of them stripped. Terry hoped the Blue Beauty wasn't arriving at her graveyard. A Christmas wreath hung on the front door.

The pickup honked twice, although no one could miss the Beauty's racket. She finally hissed and shook, the engine dying again.

Jackie hopped out of the truck. "Myles!" she called. "Customer!"

"You made it," Terry whispered to the Beauty, stroking the dashboard. Damned if she didn't seem like a living being. He felt as happy as he would have if he'd taken a loved one to the ER. "Thank you for getting us here, old girl. We owe you everything."

Four

A **black** man with a narrow face walked out of the house, wiping his hands with a red rag. The petite woman who followed him was also black; she looked a little like Queen Latifah, but three sizes smaller. Both were about her parents' age, in their late forties. A boy who might have been thirteen wandered out with them.

A sharp twinge of envy assailed Kendra—*Why couldn't this be MY family?*—but she was glad to see any family that might have been hers. Sudden hope flared so brightly that it took her breath away.

Jackie approached the couple, giving them both quick hugs. Another good sign. "These folks are headed to quarantine, but they wanted you to look at the bus."

"I'm lookin', all right," Myles said, frowning as he circled the Beauty. "Could smell it from the house."

As they climbed out of the bus, the mechanic's wife shook her head as she stared at them one by one. Her eyes glistened.

"Oh my goodness, you're just kids," she said, gazing at Sonia and Kendra in particular. "I can't imagine what you've been through!"

To Kendra's surprise, the woman leaned closer to give her a hug, resting her palm gently across the back of Kendra's head. "I'm so sorry, pumpkin . . ." she whispered, as if she were to blame. She hugged and soothed Sonia next. She made a move toward Ursalina, who backed away. Not the hugging type.

"Careful, Deirdre, they haven't been through quarantine," the man in the yellow shirt snapped. The woman gave him a sharp look but didn't argue, taking a step back.

No one messes with the guys in the yellow shirts, Kendra noted. She searched the woman's face for more information, but she turned her eyes away. Deirdre didn't like Yellow Shirts at all.

"Hope you gave as good as you got," Myles said, putting his finger in one of the bullet holes tattooing the bus. In some places, it was artwork.

"Yessir," Ursalina said.

"The Yreka Pirates, they're called," Terry said.

Myles nodded. "Oh, yeah. Heard of those bastards."

The boy made a sour face. Kendra remembered a time when the word *pirates* could light up a boy's face with a grin. Now pirates were back where they'd begun, murderers and thieves. The boy seemed to like standing near Kendra. Did she remind him of someone?

"What's the other news?" the woman said.

"Everybody's dead?" Darius muttered. Kendra hoped Deirdre hadn't heard him.

"A few less assholes at the Siskiyou Pass," Ursalina said. "But if you're headed north on the Five, bring firepower."

Myles pulled a tab in the bus's cab, then came around and fished under the hood.

"What about . . . towns?" Myles said. "Places where people go? Portland?"

He sounded so hopeful, Kendra hated to tell him that Portland had purged itself with fire. "Portland's gone," she said. "Longview's coming back, but not like this. Most people up there are hiding, keeping to themselves. No organization."

"Down here is as good as I've seen since Freak Day," Terry said.

Deirdre looked crestfallen. After sharing a glance with Myles, she lowered her face, wiping imaginary dirt from her hands on her jeans.

"No time for tea and cookies, folks," the man in the yellow shirt said. "Let's get the bus situated and move on."

"Forgive my brother," Jackie said. Again, she seemed to be speaking to the Twins alone, who flanked her on either side. "Sam's always been bossy."

"Quit it, Jackie," the man in the yellow shirt whined. "There's protocols."

"Well, we don't want to mess with the protocols," Myles said mildly, hiding his sarcasm so well that Kendra almost missed it. His voice was muffled beneath the bus's hood. "You're free to leave your supplies on the bus. You can lock it."

"What do you think so far?" Terry said.

"If you're voted in and you decide to stay," Myles said, "you won't need it. If you decide to go—or if they decide for you—I don't know . . . Maybe you can get thirty, fifty miles down the road. Maybe not. Miracle you got this far."

Terry looked as if he'd been punched in the stomach. Had the man just told them they were trapped?

"She's a fighter," Piranha said. "She can probably fly."

"Uh-huh," Myles said. He dropped the hood back down and slapped it. "Used to drive one of these. Drove a truck too, till I lost my night vision. Now I just fix 'em. I'd get this thing running just for the fun of taking it on a test drive. A bus on stick! They don't make 'em like this anymore."

"That's for sure," Darius said. "Probably for a good reason."

"Sir," Ursalina said, "is there any reason we wouldn't *want* to stay?"

Myles seemed surprised by the question, hesitated. His eyes flickered to his wife. Kendra's heart jumped. She wished they could take this family aside privately.

"Domino Falls has been a godsend to a whole lot of folks," Myles said evenly. "But staying's a decision you'll have to make for yourselves."

He hadn't answered the question. Kendra glanced at Ursalina; she'd noticed too. Good news: if they could decide to stay, they could decide to leave, too.

Since there was no paperwork, the man outstretched his hand. "Like you heard, my name's Myles. Myles Bennett. My wife's Deirdre. That's our son, Jason."

Deirdre smiled. "Call me Mom. Everyone does."

Kendra nodded. The river of energy flowing from this woman brought Kendra within a hair of saying "Okay, Mom" before the words choked her throat.

They all shook hands, one by one, even Jason, who had a firm, well-trained pump. But Deirdre was staring at Kendra the way Jackie had eyes only for the Twins.

Suddenly, Kendra recognized the look on the woman's face. A memory seized her with so much vividness that she felt transported back to Longview, having dinner with her parents at the burger shack they had only visited once, when they first moved to town and hadn't known any better.

They'd run into a man at the restaurant with a big belly and an unkempt black beard, a stereotypical biker or long-haul trucker type sitting alone with his cheeseburger. He'd stared at her family like they were a movie screen. Dad had started getting agitated, muttering under his breath, and Mom shushed him.

Then they'd all noticed that he wasn't staring at them all— only Kendra. He turned away when Kendra locked eyes with him, but she would peek back and find him looking again. It was the first time she'd thought her father might physically confront someone, a whole new side to Dad.

Then the biker had come to their table. Kendra had watched her father's hands tighten, seen him ready to rise to stand between his family and this mountainous stranger.

"Excuse me," the stranger had said in a sad, polite voice at odds with his biker demeanor. "*The Karate Kid?*"

Kendra blinked. Her dad blinked. "What?"

"The shirt," Mom said softly.

Kendra looked down. She'd forgotten that she was wearing her *Karate Kid* T-shirt, with the silhouette of little Jaden Smith throwing an impossibly high kick with perfect form and balance. She'd loved that movie. The shirt was faded now. It had once hung loose on her, and then it was almost too small.

"Love it," Kendra said.

The big man had smiled but blinked, as if his eyes stung him. "I . . . uh . . . my son loved that movie too. He got into Red Dragon Tae Kwon Do after that, did nothing but kick things all day long. Well, sorry. He used to have that shirt. Loved that shirt. That's all." He turned around and was gone before they'd had time to consider that he'd spoken of his son in the past tense.

That was what Deirdre's stare was like.

The woman who called herself Mom was staring at a ghost.

• • •

By the time Terry was stark naked and shivering, he wondered what he'd traded away for entrance into Domino Falls. He hadn't been strip-searched since his arrest, and he'd sworn he would never stand still for another man's prodding again.

But here he was lined up with Piranha and the Twins while a physician and a swarm of guards in yellow shirts studied them—everywhere—for bite marks and hidden injuries. Terry hadn't realized that Dean's wrist had been cut by flying glass during the shoot-out, just as Piranha seemed surprised by the deep cut on Terry's shoulder, which bled fresh when he moved the wrong way.

Somehow, despite his adventure helping Terry clear the stalled bus from the road, Piranha didn't have a scratch on him. Lucky SOB. And that wasn't Piranha's only luck. They'd never been fully undressed in front of one another, and Terry and the Twins could barely keep from gawking at Piranha. Too Much Information.

"You may get dressed again," the reedy man who'd identified himself as Dr. Meyer told Piranha.

The receiving room—a converted family room in the quarantine house—was too cold, and Dr. Meyer was examining Terry's cut shoulder as if he thought something would crawl out and bite him if he missed a single angle. Terry was shivering.

"You're infected," Dr. Meyer pronounced to Terry, and guards reached for their guns. Red-faced, the doctor went on quickly. "I mean the cut's infected. It's clearly a cut, not a bite. You could probably use some antibiotics. You're lucky it's not worse." Like all doctors, he spoke in chides.

"Yeah, well, the line at the free clinic was too long," Terry said, winding his arm to stretch his sore shoulder. The injury throbbed and might spring another leak, but he'd barely had time to notice it.

The doctor patched up his injury, and Dean's, and they were allowed to dress. Dean looked more pissed about the strip search than Terry. The guys in yellow shirts never left them alone, but they had an ounce of privacy and distance while they dressed behind a curtain. Terry still smarted from the thorough search. At least he'd been promised a chance to shower.

"Maybe the worst is over," Terry said.

"Better be," Dean said. "Or I'm outta here."

"Better not go without me," Piranha said.

The quarantine house was an L-shaped ranch model with four bedrooms, a basement, and an attached garage. They would each get a separate room, they were told at the orientation in the kitchen—since if anyone was infected, it would be risky to bunk them together. In addition to their group, there was one other thin, bleary-eyed white guy in his fifties Terry never heard mutter a word. He looked like he'd passed Weirdo Manor quite a ways back, accelerating straight on into Crazy Town.

"This is a voluntary quarantine," said the crew-cut guy in the yellow shirt who was in charge of the house. "Anyone who doesn't want to be here, you'll be escorted back to the perimeter. Those of us in these yellow shirts are part of Domino Falls's security details—we're called Gold Shirts, or just 'sir' or 'ma'am.' This is a community built on mutual respect. We work in partnership with D.F.'s Citizens Patrol. Some of us are assigned to monitor the quarantine houses—this is one of four. As you'll see, your windows are barred. That's for your protection. You can stay in the common areas like the kitchen and living room until dark. Watch a DVD, read a book. Once you're in the room for the night, your rooms will be locked until six a.m."

Dean sighed loudly. *This just gets better and better,* Terry thought.

"The locks are freakproof," Crew Cut continued. "Keys get lost, so we don't use 'em. Any human with a brain cell can open your door from the outside, but freaks can't figure 'em out. If you're not infected, you'll live through quarantine fine."

"You see freaks here?" Piranha said. "Past the fences?"

"There's freaks everywhere," he said. "Fences keep most of 'em out, but once in a blue moon, one gets in. This town smells like dinner to them."

"Is there a Lisa Whittaker here?" Terry blurted suddenly. The question had been in the back of his mind since the checkpoint. Lisa probably hadn't come so far north from Los Angeles, but he had come a long way too. "She's my sister."

"There's a lot of people here. I don't keep a roster," he said. "Make it past quarantine . . . and you'll get your questions answered." His tone was a thinly veiled *Shut up and let me do the talking.* He went on: "Chili's on the stove, so if you're hungry—"

Suddenly the quiet white guy pushed his way past Darius toward the front door, where a Gold Shirt was posted with his arms crossed. The stranger muttered under his breath.

"Help you, sir?" Crew Cut said. His voice rose. "Excuse me? Can I help you?"

The stranger was gaunt. He looked like he could use a meal, or two or three. His shoulders sagged inside too-big clothing he'd picked up who knew where, grimy enough to be his only clothes. "Take me back to my rig," he said. "I'm hittin' the road."

The Gold Shirts didn't look surprised. Crew Cut gestured, and the man at the door stepped aside to open the door and walk him out. Apparently people had walked out of orientation before. *But why walk now? Why not before the strip search?* Was he bitten or somehow infected? Could the doctor have missed it?

The stranger looked over his shoulder at the rest of them, as if in apology. "I spent six years in San Quentin. I ain't goin' back to prison," he said. "No thanks."

The locked rooms had been the final straw.

"He won't last out there," Sonia whispered, saying what they were all thinking.

He was ushered out quickly, without any attempts to change his mind. Kendra looked like she wanted to say something to him, but the door was closed in a heartbeat.

Crew Cut shrugged. "Prison tats gave him away," he said. "Probably never would've gotten past the Council, but he coulda had a couple days' harbor. Idiot. You got a record? Keep it to yourself."

Terry's heart raced, and he fought not to glance at Piranha and Darius. Good thing the town couldn't just go to a computer and check them out. He hoped.

Kendra slipped her hand into Terry's, squeezing gently, sign language for *Relax*. He felt an impulse to pull away for reasons he didn't understand, something to do with the eyes of so many men he didn't know. But he held on, if only because somebody might think twice about bothering Kendra if he did. Sonia was standing close to Piranha too, and Crew Cut noted the pairings with a gleam in his eye Terry couldn't place.

"I see you kids like to play a little mix 'n' match," Crew Cut said, and Terry suddenly realized what he'd seen in his eyes: mockery. None of them said anything, although Terry could practically feel the wave of irritation rolling through Kendra's hand.

Let's just get through the night, Terry thought.

The chili was fresh, with what tasted like real ground beef, although there wasn't much meat. Terry and Piranha had at least three helpings apiece. Within five minutes, Terry's stomach

41

hurt. Ursalina went to a recliner in the corner, covered her face with an old magazine, and was snoring softly in ninety seconds. Darius tried firing up the DVD player, but even *The Hangover* was too hard to watch: a time capsule to the world they'd come from. Piranha turned it off without a word.

"How about *Threadrunner Apocalypse*," Sonia said, waving a DVD over her head. "It's not bad. It's about—"

Piranha rolled his eyes. "Don't get her started," he muttered, glancing toward the Gold Shirt watching a small TV in the kitchen.

"Nothing with the word *Apocalypse* in the title, please," Kendra said, but Sonia had already inserted the disc, and the FBI was threatening them with fines or jail if they made copies or charged friends to watch. Sonia clicked ahead to the opening scene, which reminded Terry of *The Shining*. From above, a bright red sports car navigated a secluded mountain road. Seeing the road put a bad taste in Terry's mouth. The pass ahead of the car looked like the perfect hiding place for pirates.

Darius snatched the remote from Sonia, and the movie skipped ahead. A wild-eyed Joseph "Josey" Wales pushed a sheriff against the wall, holding him by the collar. *"What if it's your virgin daughter they take as their next offering?"* Wales growled on the screen, just before Darius clicked it off. Terry was glad for the quiet.

"Are you seriously a Threadie?" Dean whispered to Sonia.

"Man, she can quote whole speeches," Piranha said.

Sonia made a face. "People make fun of what they don't understand. The movies might seem cheesy on the surface . . ."

"Might?" Piranha said.

"On the *surface*?" Darius said.

". . . but they're really kind of deep. Don't you believe we all have a connection?"

"Do they have *Threadie versus Jason*?" Darius said.

Piranha snickered. "*The Hunt for Thread October*?"

Even Dean cracked a rare joke. "*Where Angels Fear to Thread*?"

Terry smothered a laugh, glanced nervously at the Gold Shirt in the kitchen. The more he tried to stop, the harder he laughed, until finally his ribs hurt. Terry and Piranha literally fell to the floor. Sonia threw the DVD case at Piranha, but that only made him howl harder.

Ursalina stirred, snapping her magazine to get their attention. She gestured toward the Gold Shirt in the kitchen, who was ignoring them . . . or seemed to be. "Use your brains. You think he's not listening to every word you say?"

"Yes, *mamacita*," Darius said, and made a kissing noise.

But that killed the laughter. Afterward, Terry could barely remember why it had seemed so funny.

But it had felt good to laugh.

Lights were out at eight o'clock, so Kendra went to her room, which looked like it might have been a sewing room before Freak Day, with lacy curtains and framed prints of kittens on the walls. The daybed with a gold-colored frame waited beneath her barred windows, and the mattress was firm. Even her bed at Grandpa Joe's had been old, musty, and lumpy—this was the first good bed she'd slept in since she left home. Was she dreaming?

She'd scrubbed her body raw in the tepid shower, crying the whole while. Any moments of rest let her sadness in. But she'd been thrilled to find clean underwear in a plastic bag on the bathroom counter; pink granny panties that were nearly too big, but handily beat the alternative. She hadn't had time to do laundry on the road and had barely realized how filthy she was. She had taken two pairs, leaving at least six behind for others who might need them. She'd also grabbed a handful of tampons and pads. Hallelujah!

Whatever else Threadville might be, it had hospitality down to a science.

Kendra no longer believed the quarantine was about waiting for the infection to show up; this was a time for observation and learning on both sides, judging how they might fit in. If you weren't willing to give yourself completely to the town and its rules, you wouldn't fit in. And maybe they caught a few freaks in the process.

Maybe that was all. If they were lucky.

Kendra tensed up when she heard footsteps in the hall, relieved when they passed. What if someone came in while she was alone in the dark? Were the others close enough to hear her screams? Faint tremors began in her bent knees. Kendra's imagination played such tricks on her in the dim lighting, especially near the shadowed window, that she finally closed her eyes, preferring visions of her imaginary demons.

Mom's worried face. Dad's shock and surprise. Grandpa Joe's irreparable bite mark. The suddenness of losing them was mild compared with the horror on their faces at the end—their worry for her.

"We'll be all right," she whispered to her family, or maybe just to herself. She breathed, yoga-style, deep in her belly the way Mom had taught her. Counting her exhalations.

The muted shaking in her limbs stopped. With the sole light from a battery-operated lamp she discovered after about twenty minutes, Kendra saw a stack of Thread literature piled neatly on a night table—a strong suggestion. She picked up *Thread War* and flipped through it, although she couldn't make out a word until she pressed the page to her nose and held it directly in the dim light.

It sounded like a science fiction story: "... *and the threads fell like clumps of luminous snowfall across the mountains and flatlands alike, knitting and binding, scouring the vast Oneness for the unifying ties that create universal transcendence...*" Did Sonia swallow this stuff without chewing? Kendra could hardly believe that a whole town had genuflected to Wales's ramblings.

Kendra stared out of her window at the pitch-dark night. She saw a few twinkles, campfires or flashlights, but otherwise the entire town was dark, still a mystery. She'd have to wait to see the rest of Threadville.

Kendra hated to admit it, but it was worth it. The locked door. The strip search. She might have done far more for a bed and a freakproof lock for the night. She didn't feel locked in— she felt *safe.* And Terry was safe too, just down the hall.

A smile flickered to Kendra's face, and her palm sizzled with the memory of sitting beside him on the sofa, holding his hand. She wished Terry were in her room, that she could settle against his chest. Maybe one day soon? The idea fascinated her. *And then what? You'll have to tell him you're a virgin, like Wales said in the movie. Or are you ready for a change?*

It seemed absurd: only hours ago, she'd been afraid of getting bitten or shot, and now she was fantasizing about a boy like she was back in high school in the normal world; as if she and Terry were on the beach again, listening to the song of the waves. Kendra planned to use the lamplight to write in her journal.

About Terry. About Threadville.

Instead, as soon as she lay on her stomach across her bed, still fully clothed, pen in hand, she rested her head on her clean, fluffy pillow ... just for a few minutes.

Almost before her eyes closed, Kendra tumbled into a deep tunnel of slumber.

She dreamed vividly of falling red threads. Distantly, she remembered that she'd had the dream before she knew anything about Josey Wales, his town, or his Threadies.

She'd had the same dream right before the end of the world.

Five

December 20

Terry was awake by five a.m., before daylight, and couldn't get back to sleep after the rooster began its throaty calls. His bed was fine, and the room was bigger than the one in his real house with his mother and sister, but it felt like a cell. He'd never slept well in lockdown.

An unfamiliar bark in the hall made Terry shiver. Sniff test time. He hadn't been bitten. Not that he remembered. But what if infection blurred the memory?

Two Gold Shirts, including Crew Cut, entered his room without knocking, bringing three leashed dogs—two burly German shepherds and Hipshot. Hipshot jumped up on Terry, licking his face, happily christening his human. When the other dogs only ignored him, Terry breathed with relief. He didn't want to sleep away from Hippy again.

Crew Cut shrugged. "Welcome to Domino Falls."

But his eyes said *We'll see what happens now.*

Kendra, Piranha, and the others all gathered groggily in the hallway. Crew Cut opened a satchel, and their handguns gleamed inside. "These are the ones you came with. Your rifles and shotguns are tagged at the arsenal—patrols only. But we encourage everyone to carry their sidearms. An armed society is a polite society."

"Great," Ursalina said, reaching for her Colt 9mm. She checked the clip, slid it back. That left only three handguns for six of them. Terry, Piranha, and Dean all grabbed Smith and Wessons.

Crew Cut nodded toward Ursalina. "Army?"

"Corporal, National Guard Hundred and Fourth. Vancouver. You?"

"Captain. Coast Guard Air Station, San Francisco," he said. "What happened up there?"

"Freakstorm we couldn't handle."

He nodded with sympathy. "Lot of that going around. Good to have a soldier." He extended a hand.

She slapped it. "This soldier'll be glad to have a bunk."

The ranch house was at the edge of town, near a cluster of fenced-in homes and the two-lane road leading to a more densely built area barely visible through the mist about two miles down the hill, probably a main street. A closer neighbor housed a stack of chicken coops, and another land parcel was home to grazing cattle. Cows. Cheeseburgers, on the hoof.

In the driveway, a surprise: Darius and Dean found their motorcycles waiting, still damp from an early-morning washing. Terry hadn't realized how grimy the Kawasaki and Honda were until he saw the clean cherry-red metal sparkling. Terry was happy for them, but he wished the bus were there too.

The Twins circled the bikes, whistling approval.

"Looking good!" Darius said.

"Who did this?" Dean sounded suspicious.

"I did," Jackie said, behind them, just turning the hose off. Terry had thought he'd picked up a vibe from Jackie toward the Twins, but now he was sure of it.

In tight jeans and clinging sweatshirt, Jackie wasn't a bad picture either. Kendra glanced at him while he was appreciating the redhead, so Terry turned his studied gaze to the bikes instead.

Dean grinned. "Welcome wagon?"

"Nice wheels deserve a nice bath," Jackie said.

"That's awfully . . . nice," Darius said. "So, what do you deserve?"

Jackie winked. "Between the two of you, I'm sure you'll think of something." Behind Terry, Piranha sucked in his breath and whispered *Dang*.

"Home sweet home," Dean muttered, and grinned for the first time since Freak Day.

Jackie took over to escort them into town in her huge white pickup, and they left the Gold Shirts behind. Terry wasn't sorry to be free of them. Darius and Dean guided the truck with their bikes, happy with the stares they triggered.

Downtown Domino Falls seemed to be about two dozen stores along a couple of blocks, and then a network of narrow roads leading off toward farmland and orchards. Three saddled horses tied to bicycle posts made the street look like a set from a Western. Except for that, Domino Falls might have been an ordinary town.

Terry had barely noticed that Kendra was holding his hand

again, as if their palms belonged together. That was just fine. The closer she stayed the better.

"Look at these," Kendra said, tugging him toward a closed storefront. A store crammed with what looked like junk— antiques, maybe—had three paintings displayed in the window. The largest, in the center, was so realistic that it looked like a photo: a snapshot of the exact spot where they were standing on the street. But while the buildings were sharply focused, hundreds of blurry, identical people crowded the street from end to end, their faces turned upward to look at a single red ribbon hovering above them like a long, curled snake.

"Weird," Terry said. He had never had much of a taste for art.

Kendra didn't answer, staring. After a moment, he moved her along to follow the others, who were already halfway down the block.

An elegantly painted wooden sign designated a two-story brick colonial building in the middle of Main Street, the town hall. After a quick heads-up from Jackie's walkie-talkie, they were met by a short, balding man in faded jeans and a checkered shirt. He spoke in an enthusiastic whine.

"Heard we had a group of young people!" he said. "Welcome, welcome. This is Domino Falls—or, as some of us like to call it, Threadville. We're so excited you made it. Been quite a while since we had seven in one day, much less in one group."

"Hope you have room," Piranha said.

The man laughed, but it changed tenor midway, more like a moan. "Oh, we've got room—a Travelodge and empty houses from folks who didn't make it. Fewer than a third of the people here are original townies. I'm Van Peebles, pretty much acting mayor, except we really never had a full-time mayor, just a town council. But since things changed, we're a little more formal around here . . ."

Terry forgot Van Peebles's rambling as he stared at the waking town. With sunlight, more people were streaming to the main street: most on foot, many riding bicycles, a couple of Gold Shirts on horseback. Some had vendor carts and baskets they were setting up in front of empty storefronts or inside shops that were otherwise mostly barren. The people were clean and warmly dressed, gazing at them with only mild curiosity.

And there were dogs everywhere, about a dozen roaming without leashes. Hippy was having private sniffing exchanges with the town canines who ruled the streets. In a world where dogs could smell impending death, they were man's best friend indeed.

A few people smiled as they greeted one another. Terry overheard two stout men wondering if it would rain soon. A woman and a young girl were *laughing* over a shared secret in the woman's palm. Even the stray dogs looked well-fed. Domino Falls was more than Terry had hoped for. What *wouldn't* he give to stay in a place like this?

"We can't let everyone in," the mayor said suddenly, stealing his thoughts. "That's the bottom line. Trade here is healthy, so we'll let you visit if you have reasonable barter, which means products or services our people want. Sometimes we can use good field hands."

"What crops?"

"Good survival crops," Van Peebles said. "Beans, peas, broccoli. Potatoes, cabbage, carrots, melons, peppers, sweet potatoes. High-yield, high-nutrition crops. Then we have specialty fields like craftsmen, physicians, nurses . . . that's always good. If you want sanctuary, you need the ability to work the jobs we assign. Children are exempted, and their parents are given special consideration.

We'll treat the infirm as best we can before we send them on, but . . ." He paused, watching them, perhaps projecting his own discomfort. "We're not monsters. We're just trying to survive."

"You and the rest of the world," Terry said.

"What happens to the people waiting outside?" Kendra said, the same question simmering in Terry's own mind.

Van Peebles sighed. "We've got our hands full with our own. They can stay outside the fence a few days, but then we send them on. Like I said, we can't take everyone."

Terry thought of the old man by the fire and his crutch. Where would he go?

There was an awkward pause and Kendra leaped into it. "We'll be perfect citizens. If we stay, you'll never regret giving us a home."

"And if we decide to leave, we'll leave as friends," Terry said.

They all looked at one another, to make sure they were in agreement.

Van Peebles nodded but didn't smile. "Any relatives who can vouch for you?" he said. "Helps you get past probation much quicker."

"No, sir," Kendra said. "We just followed the radio."

"That's too bad," Van Peebles said. "Like most of the surviving townships, there are strong sanctuary rules for relations. If you petition to stay here . . ."

Kendra suddenly squeezed Terry's hand. Was it unconscious? He guessed she wanted to know more about other townships like Devil's Wake. But she kept silent.

"We're definitely petitioning," Sonia said. "As of yesterday."

"Probation first. The tax for joining the community is half of what you brought, however much or little that might be. Wealth is of no interest to us. Sincerity is."

Terry felt the others staring holes into the back of his neck.

They had fought hard for every scrap they owned, and now they had to give up *half*?

"Sounds fair," Terry said. "A trade's a trade."

"While you're on probation, hope you came to work," Van Peebles said. "What we need most are people willing to go into the city to scavenge. I won't lie: it's our most dangerous job. We've always got openings."

Ugh. Going into San Francisco would be a hard way to make a living, but they would probably fly through probation if some of their party took on the toughest work. Terry expected Ursalina to volunteer, but she didn't say a word.

"Also pays well," Van Peebles went on. "You keep half of what you find. Top choice in housing. Extra rations. Short rotations. We send you out two days max, and you're back here three days for every day you spend outside." He leaned toward Piranha, a conspiratorial glimmer in his eyes. "And scavs tend to be very popular with the ladies."

Piranha nodded. "Sold. I need to get to San Francisco. I'm out of contact lenses, so I'm a scavenger."

In the sunlight, Terry suddenly noticed how red Piranha's eyes were. Just how blurry was his vision these days? Piranha looked like he needed the backup, and the loot wouldn't be bad. Who knew what they might find? *Besides hordes of freaks?*

"I've got your back out there," Terry said, bumping his fist. "But what's up with your eyes, man?"

"Nothing some fresh contacts and saline solution won't cure," Piranha said, weary. "Don't suppose you've got an optometrist here?"

"Not yet," Van Peebles said. "Contacts are scarce, so I doubt you'd find any you can use. But one of our vendors, McPherson, has a huge box of eyeglasses. You might not want to ask him where they came from, though." He pointed toward a corner.

Piranha nodded. "McPherson. Cool. I'll check him out."

"But nothing here is free except dinner. Expect to trade for everything."

"As long as we still have our stuff on the bus, trade is no problem," Terry said.

"What other jobs are there?" Kendra said.

The mayor explained that the radio station needed staff to keep up their goal to produce twenty-four-hour programming. "For some folks out there, we're the only voice of civilization," he said. "There's lots of fencing to be done. Good shooters sail through probation. We've also got a growing day care that's short of help. There's lots of kids."

"I want the day care," Ursalina said quietly.

They all shared a surprised look.

"You're kidding," Terry said.

"I like kids," Ursalina said, avoiding eye contact with them.

"The radio thing sounds good," Sonia said. "I always wanted to do that."

When Van Peebles gazed at Sonia, his eyes seemed to melt. "You'd be a lovely addition to the station, my dear."

"Yeah, I like radio too," Dean said.

Van Peebles gave Dean a skeptical look. "Maybe, but I rather saw you and your brother as fence crew types. Let's all go take a look at the fence factory, shall we?" he said. "Whether or not you stay, I want you to see how our town has survived."

As he said it, he rested one hand on Kendra's shoulder and the other on Sonia's. A harmless enough gesture, maybe even paternal, but to an alert part of Terry's hindbrain, the mayor almost seemed to be claiming the girls as his own.

• . •

The mayor had said it himself: the town didn't take in the infirm, the sick, the blind. In this terrible world, who would? If you couldn't take care of yourself, there was no one to take care of you. The freaks had seen to that.

The fence factory was a huge rectangular mass to Piranha, probably a solid block long at the edge of town. When he got close enough, he saw that it was sturdy white brick. An ashy silhouette on the wall suggested some kind of fire, but the rest looked reasonably well kept. All of the windows on the lower floor were barred with iron or wood, and some on the second floor. One corner was leaping distance from the rooftop of a warehouse across the street. That was all Piranha could see. Piranha fought not to blink too much, not to rub his eyes. Rubbing made the pain worse.

This was beyond bad, worse even than the endless wondering about his family, knowing he probably would never see them again, each day feeling more and more certain that even if they were alive, he had no way to find them.

Day by day, he was going blind.

He had been in seventh grade when an eye doctor first used the term *extremely myopic,* like it was athlete's foot, explaining that he needed to protect his eyes and would wear corrective lenses his whole life. His mother had told him not to worry, that in modern society people with bad eyes lived just like everyone else, but Piranha had stayed awake that night imagining utter darkness. Years later, his stepfather had taken him to a Lasik clinic, but he'd been told his eyes were too far gone for laser surgery.

With the comfort of contact lenses—one of them in each eye at all times—Piranha had avoided really knowing how little he could see. He'd lived in a bubble of denial.

No more. Piranha's eyes were an agony of constant stinging,

and his vision was so foggy that he'd given up on seeing faces since right after the Siskiyous. It was as if his eyes had said, *We got you past the pirates, bro; you're on your own from here.*

Piranha recognized large objects and knew his friends from their height and voices, enough to get by on the bus, but he'd been terrified he would have to take an eye test at quarantine. He'd rifled through the box of eyeglasses the Irish vendor had on his table in town. None were close to his prescription.

He was down to his last pair of lenses now. He'd made the mistake of trying to rinse one with precious drops from a bottle of purified water a few days ago, and he'd been lucky to get the lens back in. It hurt so much, constant slow grit in his eye, he'd nearly screamed. Had he torn it minutely? He still didn't know, but he kept it in.

Light hurt. Blinking hurt. Closing his eyes hurt. Opening his eyes hurt. He was probably giving himself an eye infection, but what could he do? He couldn't be blind now. He remembered the cloudy eyes of Sharon Lampher, the woman they'd met on the beach, and wondered how long she would last if her husband got killed or bitten, or if he died of a heart attack. How long would any of them last out there?

The factory smelled of cleanser and rust. The wiry blur at the factory door had introduced himself as Tom. Piranha also knew that the woman named Jackie was there hanging close to the Twins. All Piranha could see of Jackie was her chest. The Twins were trying to sidle up to her, nudging each other out of the way. Not playing it cool at all.

Piranha stuck close to Sonia, but she seemed irritated by it. She inched away from him again as soon as Tom came into the room. She would deny it, but today she moved away from him whenever a new man came into sight. Keeping her options open.

Piranha was pissed off, but his eyes were a bigger problem.

Sonia had asked why his eyes were so red, but he hadn't told her everything. He hadn't wanted to scare her . . . and he didn't know how it might change things for them.

After all, he and Sonia were just alike. They were survivors.

"You guys seeing lots of freaks?" Piranha said to Tom's blur.

"Always, and right behind you," Tom said. "Past three months, we've killed about a thousand, maybe more. They keep coming. They're attracted to clusters of humans. But only a dozen or so had ever made it into town, and we handled 'em quick. Lost a couple of dogs, though."

Piranha, Dean, and Darius whistled at the numbers.

"But this here's our secret weapon," Tom said.

Piranha could barely make out the huge rolls and rolls of fencing piled inside, but the gray mass Tom gestured toward was tall enough to stir his heart. Hell, yeah!

"My family's been running this factory since World War II," Tom said. "We had four orders ready to go out when the freaks hit. We just kept the fence for ourselves. Scavenged from the surrounding land. Got a hold of all the raw stock we could. We can always put it to good use." He lowered his voice. "Town's biggest industry was my daddy's fence plant. That's what really saved Domino Falls—not Wales."

No mistaking he wanted to make that point good and clear.

If Piranha's eyes had been working right, filled with distraction, he might have missed the tremor in the man's voice, something that sounded more like anger than pride.

Six

The woman who met Kendra and Ursalina at the main intersection in town was slightly plump and ruddy-faced, with pinned white hair. She called herself Granny Daisy. Kendra felt better about her first separation from Terry since quarantine.

"I thought that was the schoolhouse at the edge of town, out by the fence factory," Kendra said. The quaint building had reminded her of *Little House on the Prairie.*

"Too hard to patrol out on the fringes," Granny Daisy said. "Besides, that old elementary wasn't near big enough. That's why we keep the kids at the theater. Dead center of town. I have any problems, I ring a bell and the whole town is here. A town's not worth a snot if it can't protect its children."

The Olde Domino Theatre was a redbrick building in the middle of Main Street. The red lettering in the marquee read All Children We come, missing a letter in *welcome,* although the message still got across. The theater was fenced off from its neighbors. Except for the barred windows and razor wire above the fence, it looked like a regular theater. If the outer town defenses failed, the freaks would have to start over again if they wanted to get to the kids.

Traditional classroom desks crammed the lobby, and twelve students between the ages fourteen and nineteen were getting a wicked geometry lesson on a rolling chalkboard from a pockmarked woman with bright red hair. Life had taken everything but math out of the teacher. Her voice was strong as she tapped the board.

The students were rapt on the teacher, barely noticing Ursalina and Kendra. People must come and go often.

"The high schoolers have to hit the classroom at four-thirty," Granny Daisy said.

"In the morning?" Kendra said.

"Yeah, class is by lamplight so they can finish their schooling and get to work. Everybody works. Kids grow up fast. Most of these kids have been through something that could turn your hair white," Granny Daisy said, patting self-consciously at the snowy ponytail that made her face youthful. She leveled a look at Kendra. "We don't force 'em, so these here really want it. Like we tell the kids, the world's going to sort all this out sooner or later, so might as well go out there knowing something. You're the new leaders of the world."

"Hear that, Madame President?" Ursalina teased Kendra. "Hit those books."

Kendra had expected to be working at a day care, not going to school. She hadn't survived this long just to bisect triangles again.

Ursalina snickered. "I'll be your alarm clock," she said.

"As if," Kendra whispered.

Double doors from the lobby led to the theater space. Kendra hadn't walked two steps into the room before her eyes filled with tears.

Children filled every space in the room. The theater had seating for at least a hundred people, and there were children in almost every seat. There were kids working in circles on the stage ahead of her. On the floor. If not for the bruises and bandages, their laughter would have lifted her spirits.

One boy about six sat in an aisle seat, busily drawing on a pad in his lap. He had only one arm. His other elbow was a stump in a grimy bandage. The boy's face was knit with concentration as he drew. Kendra had heard stories that it might be possible to stop the infection if a limb was chopped off within seconds after a bite. Was that what had happened?

Kendra heard Ursalina suck in her breath. For a moment, they both just stared.

"Why so many?" Kendra asked.

"Some came with their parents. Some were rescued from their parents, or strangers dropped 'em off. There's a do-gooder a few miles up who drives an old ice-cream truck and rescues kids, brings 'em here. Parents died outside, or on one of the crews. We do all we can, but it's barely enough." Granny Daisy's words died into a sigh. "I've heard some towns won't even take children. Too much of a burden. Not useful enough, or some such doodley. How can anyone turn a child away?" She smiled a sad, wise smile. "When we stop making room for children, we're lost."

Kendra remembered the sad look on Reverend Meeks's face as he had stared at her. He'd probably been thinking the same thing.

"What you got there, huh?" a woman's gentle voice said nearby. The voice flowed like a waterfall of loving patience, but that was impossible. It was Ursalina!

Ursalina had wandered to the one-armed boy to see what he was drawing.

The boy glanced toward Granny Daisy, uncertain. He didn't trust strangers.

"It's all right, Skylar," she said. "This is Kendra and Ursalina. You'll be seeing them here for a while."

Skylar seemed to relax, but he didn't smile. He went on drawing. "Hey, Skylar, this is some picture you drew!" Ursalina said, voice bursting with amazement.

Skylar bit his lip, trying hard not to let out a smile.

"Look at all that red!" Ursalina said. "That house looks so real."

"It *is* real," Skylar said, almost angry.

"Yeah, Skylar, I know," Ursalina said. "It's as real as it gets, buddy."

Kendra peeked over Ursalina's shoulder to see the picture. It was a two-story house engulfed in bright red flames. Stick figures big and small were running, their mouths exaggerated black Os as they screamed. A tall figure in a dress was bleeding from her head. Or maybe just her mouth.

Kendra tried to tell Skylar what a great job he'd done, but her throat was frozen.

". . . so we rotate them around the room in shifts. The seats. The stage. The floor. We use it all. There's a fenced-off area out back where they can run off their energy . . ." Granny Daisy's ongoing orientation helped Kendra forget the burning house.

Other drawings by the children were showcased on the walls, shrieking histories. Smaller people running from larger people. Larger people running from smaller people. One older child had drawn a huge pair of eyes, nearly the size of the entire page, with pencil sketches of anime-inspired mayhem in the background. Art therapy.

Mom and Dad would have liked this place, she thought.

Was that the first time she had thought of her parents in past tense? Mom and Dad had receded into a foggy space behind her, a part of a life she knew she would barely remember one day. They didn't hurt so much in the fog. *Stand still, Kendra. Listen to yourself,* Dad used to say. But Kendra didn't want to listen. Not today. She had no right to cry in front of these kids.

The day got easier. The children were just like any others, as far as she could see. At least, their hearts were the same. One little pale redheaded kid named Jaxon had lost part of his left arm to a freak bite. Someone had grabbed a machete damned fast. The kid was fine, his stump was bandaged and slung, and he seemed to have decided not to notice as long as no one else did.

The kids teased, laughed, cried, and chased one another the way they might have in happier times. Kendra had always heard people talk about how resilient children were, but she'd never witnessed the miracle.

They would probably make out better than anyone, she thought. She hoped so.

Ursalina darted around the room to tie shoelaces, wipe noses, and even change diapers, which was where Kendra drew the line. Ursalina unearthed something in a two-year-old boy's Pampers that looked like a scientific experiment. The smell alone was worthy of study, but Ursalina didn't complain. She tugged, taped, and snipped like a pro.

"Do you have kids?" Kendra asked Ursalina before she could stop herself.

It wasn't a question you could blurt out lightly. Kids weren't a phase people outgrew, or old belongings left in storage lockers. If she did have kids, where were they?

Ursalina hung her head so low that her chin touched her

breastbone. Her body language said *Back the hell off.* Or she was closing up like a turtle. "Not me," Ursalina said, finally looking up at her. She picked up the two-year-old like a bag of flour and set him running off on scurrying legs. "Granny Daisy," she called. "Taking a break."

"All right, dear," Daisy said. "We'll survive."

Ursalina motioned Kendra outside. She leaned up against the redbrick wall and shook a cigarette out of a wrinkled pack. She halfheartedly offered one to Kendra, smiled when she refused. The soldier lit her cigarette, inhaled deeply, exhaled, and finally spoke. "My partner, Mickey. She had a daughter, Sharlene."

"Wait, never mind," Kendra said. "I'm sorry to . . ."

Ursalina shrugged. "I don't mind remembering. Hate works for me."

"Love can work pretty well too."

Ursalina gave Kendra a sour look. *Don't push it,* chica.

"We were together four years, through my deployment," Ursalina went on. "She was in Chehalis, Washington, so it was my turn to move." Ursalina's face went stormy. She sighed long and hard before she went on. "Sharlene. Man, that little angel was a real beauty, inside and out. The coolest human I've ever met. So damn smart. Funny. A good little heart. That kid was our whole world."

Ursalina shook her head, working through her memories. "We were trying to get gas so we could make it to the Vancouver base, so we stopped at this station. There was still gas then, the first few days. It looked safe."

Her eyes burned with her betrayal at how badly she'd been fooled. "Sharlene is standing right next to Mickey at the tank. I'm on guard, but . . . he was just on the other side of the pump. Right where we couldn't see him. Not even hiding, one of the slow ones. Like he fell asleep on his feet and we woke him up.

Two steps, he grabs Sharlene's arm, and . . . she's bit." She shook her head, still trying to wrap her mind around it.

"One minute it's like a family trip. You know, 'Are we there yet?' Then . . . she's infected. We were sure her shirt stopped the bite. We rolled it up, looked for the mark. We thought we were okay, all of us crying and thanking God, all that. But we'd missed it. Sharlene was sleepy as soon as we got back in the car.

"Suddenly we were the people they'd been talking about on TV. We had a sleeper. We'd seen it a million times, people trying to keep 'em awake. Coffee. NoDoz. Cold showers. While I drove, Mickey did everything she could to wake that kid up. Shook her. Yelled at her. Slapped her. Back then, we still thought there was a cure around the corner, so I'm thinking if I floor it to the Barracks, a medic can patch her up. Maybe I knew better, but I had to have a plan.

"You can guess the rest. All they gave Mickey was a locked room where she could sit with her and be there. Rocking to her. Singing to her. She wouldn't even let me in. I sat outside listening to Mickey singing . . . then I heard the gunshot."

Kendra heard a gunshot too. She flinched at the shared memory, her teeth gritted.

"After that, Mickey didn't really want to be here anymore. In this world. This life. She hung around for me, to have my back. As soon as you guys showed up at the Barracks, she pushed me out of those doors . . . she checked out."

"I'm sure she wanted to come with you," Kendra said, even if she wasn't sure it was true or even the right thing to say.

Ursalina shook her head. "Nah," she said, exhaling a pale stream of smoke. "She looked like she was alive, but Mickey was already gone. And you know the hardest thing about this place? I'd started telling myself maybe it happened the way it was supposed to. Maybe it was a blessing. If Sharlene had been with us at the Barracks, if she'd seen what we saw . . . it would have been worse. Maybe she's better off dead." Glassy-eyed, Ursalina stared at the sea of children in the theater. "Now I know we would've had somewhere to bring her. Other kids to be with. Even if it was just for one day."

A sob tried to sneak into her last words, and Ursalina turned away.

Kendra wanted to hug her companion, but instinct told her she would get shoved away, maybe hard. Ursalina was saving her hugs for the children.

The soldier stubbed her cigarette out on the ground and went back in.

"You got a little boo-boo," Ursalina told a girl who was howling because she'd tripped and scraped her knee. "Bet that hurts, doesn't it? It's gonna be okay, princess . . ."

Ursalina's voice was full of light, but her eyes were broken.

Kendra didn't want to hear her using the syrup-sweet voice she'd used with Sharlene, the voice from the gas station when she'd told the infected girl it was okay, she and Mommy would get help for her boo-boo from the bad man's bite.

Instead, Kendra drifted toward the stage. There, alone on the shadowed steps, a girl was working on a project with poster board, glue, and red glitter. Glitter twinkled in her face and hair.

The girl was dark-haired, about thirteen, with a moon-shaped face. Soon, this girl would be old enough to work instead of playing. The price of adulthood was steep here.

"I saw it in a dream," the girl said, before Kendra could ask.

She'd drawn a convincing landscape of farmland draped in fences.

Glitter sparkled from bright red ribbons floating down from the clouds.

Seven

Darius couldn't believe that he and his cousin had landed their dream job—mobile support for fence crews. They had a wheelie contest up and down an empty stretch of road, celebrating their luck. They were two miles from Main Street, and the only sure way to avoid the fences was to take the east-west path through town. As long as they had their bikes, they were still free.

Overnight, the road had changed faces. The dangers had been washed away, replaced by a fantasy. Even Dean felt it; Dean was in the best mood he'd been in since he'd come back from his folks' place. Done what he'd done. Dean had never flinched when they'd fired at the Siskiyou pirates; none of it was real to him anyway. Not since the trailer park. *Everybody had it,* he'd said. Three words. Dean had never said so outright, but Darius thought he might have hunted down his family one by one so he wouldn't leave them that way.

One of the trucks in the convoy honked, and a window came

down. Blond hair whipped in the breeze, almost close enough to smell. It was Jackie! Darius had no statistics to back it up, but she might be the finest woman left in the world.

If I'm dreaming, please don't let me wake up. Ever.

"Thought you were on guard duty!" Darius called to her. She was definitely following them; he hadn't been sure, until now.

"That was yesterday!" she called back. "Every day's brand-new."

She was flirting. The truck drove on and seemed to pull Darius with a tug of heat. Laughing, he dropped back to Dean. They pounded fists across the roadway.

"Dibs," Darius said. "She wants me."

"No way. This is war."

Yep, the old Dean was coming back. Darius might let Dean have Jackie if she could repair whatever was broken in him. He'd like to think he would, anyway.

When the convoy stopped, the crew leader parked beside her white pickup and waved Darius and Dean off the road. The freeway was bisected by dirt paths on either side, and one of them was Claremont Road. A cloud of dust brought them to the perimeter of a sun-faded farmhouse set back about fifty yards. Fields on three sides, woods on the other. There was already some fencing up near the cow pastures, but the path to the woods gaped open.

The crew leader, a thirtyish, sun-broiled Gold Shirt, looked as if he lived in the weight room. He wasn't particularly friendly, but Darius didn't need him to be. The freakfest had burned off people's manners. The crew leader tugged what looked like a pile of leaves out of the bed of his truck.

"Homemade ghillie suits," the crew leader said. "Sniper's paradise. While we put up the fences, you watch our backs. Get yourself downwind, and the freaks won't smell you or see you. First, we need to see if you can shoot."

"Cool beans," Dean said.

"Hell to the yeah," said Darius.

Dean's uncle Bucky, a deepwater fisherman and hunter, had taken Dean out every other weekend during hunting season, teaching him everything he knew about tracking, trapping, and shooting. Dean had never said if Uncle Bucky had been bitten too, but his silence said it all.

Dean had taught Darius everything he could. Dean had the practice, but Darius had the eye.

Darius eased the loose-fitting bodysuit over his shoulder. Dean mirrored him, and they grinned at each other. The suits were painted standard green, but the twigs and leaves looked real enough to fool his own eye, although some of it was fake plants and AstroTurf. Someone had spent serious time on the ghillie suits.

The fence was being built for a farmhouse that looked like it belonged to several families, with bystanders spilling from the porch. The farmhouse already had fencing, but the crew had come to fortify it like the fences along the roadway toward town.

If you lived in Domino Falls, the government protected you. Darius wondered what the protection cost, or if everybody got treated the same.

"First we gotta make sure neither of you knuckleheads will shoot us in the back," Jackie said. Beyond the farmhouse, in the open field that had already been burned away, Jackie sashayed over to a shooting range with aluminum cans on rows of wooden poles.

Darius took extra time to appreciate her easy walk as she led them. Her faded blue jeans were about a size too tight. Dean was staring too. They grinned steel at each other. *Back off, she's mine.* Darius hadn't thought about the possibility of a girl in so long that he'd forgotten how nice smooth skin and scented hair could be.

Sonia and Kendra were spoken for. Ursalina was unavailable. But Domino Falls was a world of possibilities. Jackie probably liked shooters, so he was about to shoot the hell out of those cans.

A crowd was gathering to watch the new guys. The sole Gold Shirt was Jackie's red-haired·brother. Two others were teenagers about their age, and three were in their thirties and forties.

"Wanna borrow my bow and arrow, chief?" one of the boys said.

"We burn our freaks, we don't scalp 'em," another kid said.

The crowd chuckled.

"Tell me something, Dean," Darius said when the boys were done.

"What's that, Darius?" His cousin fell right in, like a comedy routine.

"Why do people mess with the guys holding the big guns?"

Dean cycled his rounds with a loud *clack.* "Just dumb, I guess," he said.

Synchronized, they flipped on their sunglasses and stared lasers at the boys. Without looking and with unnerving precision, they checked the action on their rifles. The laughter died, but the older guys were still smiling.

"We only shoot freaks," Jackie said, warning them. "Just so you know."

Darius grinned at Jackie and tipped an imaginary hat. "Yes, ma'am," he said.

"But first you're gonna knock down some cans," Tom said.

The cans were about thirty feet away. Wind gusts from the southwest tickled his ears. "Ladies first," Darius told Dean.

70

Dean gave him the finger, and the watching boys laughed. The day felt amazingly good-natured, considering what a bad mood the rest of the world was in. Even the boys they'd considered shooting were smiling again, ready for entertainment.

"Watch this, Kimosabe," Dean said, and aimed.

He took three of the five cans, enough for Jackie to clap and cheer. Dean cursed to himself, his eye flinching with annoyance. Without the wind, he might have hit four.

Dean took it all too seriously, was too tight with it; to Darius, shooting was like feeling energy flow to the trigger. Only a small part of him was thinking about it. Instead of fighting the wind, he rode it.

Gunfire pummeled his ear. Six in a row went down.

The crowd hooted.

"Definitely seen worse," Jackie said, eyeing him up and down.

"You boys can shoot," Tom said, impressed. "You want work, you've got it. Shooters are the eyes and ears. If you're good at it, you're sure to get in. The hours can be rough, but the pay is good—at least what counts for pay here. Nice house. Plenty of food. You'd have your pick of the Threadie chicks."

Jackie made a face. "Wait'll you see them. That's a punishment."

The crowd laughed.

"Thought you were all Threadies out here," Darius said.

"No way," one of the boys said. "My family's lived here since before Wales."

"Never call a townie a Threadie," Jackie said. "By local custom, someone might give you a black eye."

"Try to, anyway," Dean said.

There were always layers to learn. Threadville looked like

paradise from the outside, but up close it was easier to see the blemishes. Domino Falls's nickname saluted the Threadies, but it wasn't just a company town. That felt better to Darius—less like they'd be joining a cult, pledging to believe in something, or anything, if they stayed.

The tallest and oldest of the teenagers stepped forward to bump Darius's fist. "I'm Eric. Call me E.J." His cousins Sean and Warren introduced themselves next. If someone had fired some franks on the grill, they could have been at a barbecue.

"We've got twenty miles of fence, all told," Tom said. He grunted, carefully unspooling a roll of fence with nasty barbed-wire accents alongside the poles they had all pounded in. "If these things could climb, we'd all be shambling and moaning."

"They can't climb?" Dean said.

"It's smartest not to put anything past 'em," Tom said. "Sometimes one'll do something different from the others. Six might run right past you when you're in a tree—and the seventh stops and looks straight up."

Darius wondered if one of Tom's men had learned that from experience.

Jackie shook her head. "They can't climb. The fast ones, maybe a little. Up a few steps. But the slowpokes? Come on."

Tom met Dean's eyes. "Like I said, don't put anything past 'em. That way, you're never surprised." He took his pliers and brought up a section of metal fence, demonstrating how to join two pieces of wire. "See how you have to twist?"

Darius fought to keep from wondering about Trinidad, the town they'd heard about from the reverend at the checkpoint. What had made a town fall? Had it been as big as Threadville?

"We heard some freaks got in," Darius said.

"Bad day," Tom said, his face iron. He didn't want to talk about it.

"Then what do you guys do around here for fun?" Darius said. When he asked, he was staring straight at Jackie, and she smiled. Dean didn't have a chance.

Suddenly, playfulness sparked across E.J.'s face. He ran up to Jackie to ask her something privately, and she shook her head. "Count me out," she said.

"What is it?" Darius said.

E.J. and his cousins grinned. "You guys ever heard of . . . freak tipping?"

A quick word to the crew leader, and Tom led them toward the side of the property closest to the woods. Dean and Darius never took off their ghillie suits, and once in a while one or the other flopped to the ground, testing his camouflage.

The rest of the fence crew was drawing farther and farther away, except for Tom, who had his Remington a few yards back, watching for movement. Tom had told them to pay attention to his cover to see how shooters worked.

Jackie watched them from the hood of her pickup with binoculars, which looked like a sensible place, and Darius wished he'd stayed behind with her.

The woods were awash in mid-afternoon shade, full of hiding places. The closer they drew to the outer stand of sycamore trees, the more Darius wanted to be somewhere else. Freak tipping? Was it some kind of town rite of initiation? An intelligence test?

Darius edged close to E.J., who was bounding ahead. "They're not that easy to sneak up on," he whispered. "They smell us."

"*Shhh,*" E.J. said, stopping to drop to the ground. "Here."

Darius and Dean dropped too. Act first, ask questions later.

73

They were virtually invisible in their canopy of green. They stank of hard work and adrenaline.

E.J. pointed toward his two o'clock. "We spotted these two day ago. We let 'em alone to get a *little* bit riper." He spoke in a singsong, delighted with himself.

Terry followed Tom's pointing finger. Two withered freaks stood only ten yards from them, eyes facing forward. Their eyes were sunken so deep in their sockets, they stared out from shadows. Their faces were crusted by something red that grew like moss. The smell of rotten oranges was stronger, sickening. The closer one was wearing a Las Vegas T-shirt dirtied nearly beyond legibility; the second one, maybe a female, had lost her clothes and all recognizable body shaping. In her former life, she must have weighed three hundred pounds. A mountain of loose skin sagged from her. Or . . . *him.*

The two freaks swayed in the gusts, arms dangling limply at their sides. They were staring straight toward them with dry, unseeing eyes.

Darius's heart knocked in his chest in a way it hadn't since Vern woke him from sleep at camp to show him the world had ended.

E.J. chortled. "Look at 'em. Can't move. Don't even know we're here."

Says who? Darius thought.

"Make a wish," E.J. said, and charged the freaks with a yell. Darius ignored his knocking heart and a *nononono* roaring in his head, giving a scream as he chased E.J. He heard Dean screaming beside him, an unspoken agreement between them that made Darius wonder if they were both crazy together. E.J. went for his freak at full speed, like a football tackle. Darius took the huge one, pushing with all his might.

Darius was careful to avoid the freak's mouth, but the lips

seemed sewn shut. The freak felt like a soft ball of cooling skin, crumpling beneath them.

"Don't get that crap all over you!" Tom called to them.

The freaks fell over without attacking or struggling. They hardly moved, except to flop like scarecrows. E.J. and his cousins were laughing like maniacs. Even Tom was laughing. The laughter was contagious. Dean gave him a wide-eyed I-can't-believe-we-did-that look, as if he'd been liberated, and his face made Darius laugh until his ribs stabbed him.

"You idiots are sick!" Jackie's voice yelled from the distance, and Darius laughed harder because she was so right.

Dean wasn't laughing; he was studying the freaks, brushing red dust from his jacket. The freaks had fallen, but their ankles had literally snapped, exposing bone and blood the texture of corn syrup. The soles of their ragged shoes were sprouting with something that resembled vines. Dean squatted to stare at the odd, viscous red puddle ensnaring the freak's feet with a bed of tightly woven pink vines, rooting them. Something was growing into them, or out of them. When freaks planted themselves, they planted for real.

What the hell were they supposed to be growing into? And were there enough scientists left to figure it all out?

Darius's heart started hammering again. He suddenly felt like he might throw up. The freaks weren't getting up, but Darius backed away. Two gunshots made Darius jump. Smoke curled from the muzzle of Dean's rifle. He'd shot the freaks in the head.

"They used to be somebody," Dean said. And he walked away, head down.

The whole walk back to the farmhouse, Tom, Darius, and E.J. were laughing until their faces were bright red, streaked with half-crazed tears.

Eight

They all agreed to meet in front of the town hall before dinner was served at five-thirty, and no one minded waiting an extra half hour for Darius and Dean. The weather was turning cold, with a misty drizzle. Terry looked forward to the group's reunion so they could compare notes on their training day.

The local citizens gave them long looks as they climbed the steps to the dining hall, not overly friendly, but not unfriendly either.

"... shot six cans in a row ..." a farmer muttered as he passed.

"Seen 'em on those bikes?" another said.

Everyone in town had heard of the Twins already. It didn't take much to pass for news in this place.

"The Legend of Darius and Dean," Piranha said, and they laughed.

"Maybe it'll help us get in here," Terry said.

"Yeah, if the Twins remember us tomorrow," Sonia said, only halfway kidding.

Finally, the bikes roared up, accompanied by everything short of a light show. Darius and Dean ran wide, lazy circles in the street before parking neatly side by side. Kids and girls flocked up to them as if they were rock stars.

"Someone please explain this to me," Terry said.

"Motorcycles," Ursalina said. "Simple."

Kendra and Terry were holding hands again, and he wasn't sure who had reached for the other first. Their hands fit together. "They're a spectacle," she said. "Entertainment. Look at them: matching good looks, long hair, and style for miles. They're a whiff of fresh new air."

Kendra was a poet whose words seemed to flow across Terry. She saw details that he missed, giving him new eyes. Sharper eyes.

Speaking of eyes . . .

Terry tried to glance at Piranha's eyes while they climbed the town hall's steps, but Piranha turned his face away. Last time Terry had caught a glimpse, Piranha's eyes looked as if he'd just walked out of a smoke-filled room. Something was wrong, worse than he'd let on. At least twice during that day's training, Terry had been sure Piranha couldn't see where the crew leader was pointing. Guessing at things. And scav crew would be intense, like a combat mission in the old army, except with less time for training.

Their first patrol left at four-thirty in the morning. If they couldn't go, they had to tell somebody. Every crew needed six men. The training was specific.

"What's up with your eyes?" he whispered to Piranha as they walked to the doors.

"Hurt like hell." Piranha walked ahead, and the din swallowed them.

"You the Washington group?" said a burly, bearded man at the door. The man smiled. "I'm Miller. Welcome to Threadville."

Miller led them toward rows of rectangular folding tables, brightly covered with red-and-white-checkered tablecloths. A banner over the front stage read WELCOME. A huge Christmas tree on the stage, sparkling with lights and garlands, looked like an exhibit in a museum, so beautiful that Terry forgot to breathe.

About eighty people were bustling in the hall, maybe about half of them townies. Clusters of girls wore tights or were draped in black. Threadies, Terry guessed. He recognized them from the high school hallways, although these women were all ages. He could tell the Threadies by their smiles; the townies looked more tired, less giddy. The large room's walls were lined with paintings like the ones he and Kendra had seen.

"Take a seat anywhere," Miller said. "We have group dinner every night. Helps the newbies meet folks, frees up people from cooking after a long day. Helps us be good neighbors. It's fried chicken night, so you got lucky."

Terry's stomach growled as he was assailed by the scent of frying meat. Had anything ever smelled so good? His mouth flooded as if he were starving.

Miller was huge, with a lumberjack's massive forearms, so Terry tried not to notice the way his eyes were enjoying Sonia . . . and Kendra. Miller's eyes seemed lost somewhere in them even while he was talking. For the first time, he was glad Piranha couldn't see. He might say something that would get them thrown out.

"Let me know if any questions or concerns come up," Miller said. He walked on, towering above the room. He made one last look over his shoulder, toward the girls.

"Ewwwwww," Kendra murmured, pretending to smile.

"As long as they only look and don't touch," Ursalina said to the girls, shrugging. "Young and cute has worked since Adam and Eve. If you got it, use it."

"It is good to be a god," Darius agreed.

They'd all had a good day. Even Kendra, so eager to contact Devil's Wake, admitted she'd had a memorable day at the school. Terry saw the glow in her face. Ursalina's too—her cheeks had color, maybe from laughing, maybe from crying.

The kitchen doors opened and the food train began. It was plentiful, simple food for hardworking people, but it was clean, and hot, and there was plenty of it. A pile of golden fried chicken. Mashed potatoes. String beans. The hall howled with pleasure at the chicken, with calls for the chef.

"I wasn't sure I'd ever say this again," Piranha said reverently, "but pass the chicken and biscuits!"

The dinner felt good enough to be worthy of a last meal. No one talked at first, concentrating on their plates, cramming their stomachs. Terry sat next to Piranha so he could talk to him. "You can't go out like that, P," Terry said finally.

Piranha glanced up at him, wiped a fleck of food from his chin. His eyes looked like a baptism of fire. He needed a doctor. Piranha leaned closer, whispered in his ear. "I'm going. Drop it."

His whisper drew stares from the Twins. Piranha squirmed when the others' eyes were on him. "Mind your own business," he told the table.

"You're a lot of fun when you're like this," Sonia said sarcastically. Piranha concentrated on his food, ignoring her. Sonia's ears turned pink with irritation.

Terry wanted to say *His eyes are hurting,* but if Piranha hadn't told the others, even Sonia, he thought he had a good reason. The mayor had told them point-blank that Threadville didn't welcome the halt and the lame. Terry was sure that was why Piranha wanted to go scavenging.

But if Piranha couldn't see, he might get someone killed. Like . . . Terry, for instance.

"I won't go," Terry said quietly.

"Then don't," Piranha said.

Van Peebles vaulted onstage, breathing hard from the display's exertion. He reminded Terry of his high school principal before the pep rallies, trying to rouse them into a cheer. "We've had another day of life, folks!" he said.

"Still here!" the crowd hooted in unison, a practiced custom. The room thundered with applause. No one took a day of life for granted. There were a few scattered *amens*.

"We'll have announcements and open mic in a few," Van Peebles said, "but right now we have a few words from the Man himself. Author, director, actor, and savior of Domino Falls, California . . . Joseph 'Josey' Wales!"

Sonia's eyes widened. "He's here?" she whispered. She sat ramrod straight, searching for him.

The room applauded, although not as loudly. The Threadies rose to their feet, but everyone else stayed seated. As Terry had thought, about half were townies. A group of girls in the corner chanted, *"Threads, threads, threads!"* in quick unison, and then fell silent. Josey Wales might be the most famous person left in California, Terry thought. But in the old world, he might have been bumped off *Celebrity Rehab* by Zeppo Baldwin.

"He looks so much better in person," Sonia said, mostly to herself.

He did look like a movie star, Terry had to admit. The man who walked to the stage was in his late fifties, maybe sixties, a little chunky, but he had a deep tan and a thick head of salt-and-pepper hair he kept gelled in place—the kind of grooming that took time. Or a good rug. His gut sagged, but he had a movie star's klieg-light smile.

Three Gold Shirts flanked the stage near Terry. Were the Gold Shirts the town's security force, or Wales's? Or both?

"Folks," Wales said, hands up, bringing the crowd to silence, "you're not here for speeches, but we have twenty-two newcomers since I talked to you last—a crop of seven young people popped in just yesterday. I understand a couple of 'em can really shoot."

He nodded toward their table, and Terry felt the eyes of the room on them like a warm spotlight, and people applauded. Darius and Dean waved, and three boys cheered. Even Ursalina smiled. Wales's spotlight was a bright one. Terry had never heard a room clap for *him*.

"We are *so* in," Ursalina murmured.

"I love this place," Sonia whispered.

Kendra looked like she was still making up her mind about Wales. She leaned closer to study his every word and gesture.

"Old friends." Wales raised an imaginary glass. "We've had another week, and grow stronger every day. For my new friends, welcome to Domino Falls, California. We're one of fifteen surviving townships we know of in the western United States, and there are probably more out there, just lyin' low. You could take your chances on the road or some of you will stay with us. Let's get to know each other and see if we can make a home together. The world gets rebuilt one family at a time."

The crowd hooted. Terry noticed he'd called the town Domino Falls, not Threadville. And he wasn't pushing his Threads philosophies at dinner.

"Did you hear that?" Kendra said. "Fifteen townships." But what if Threadville was as good as it got?

Terry watched the families that were barely listening,

completely at ease while they ate and spoke in low tones. The longtimers were simply living their lives of hot food, running water, and soft beds. The novelty had worn off.

"One thing: if you're new, please come on out to the ranch. I built it to share—anyone who knows me knows that. Take a look around the grounds. Pick up some of our literature . . ."

The hard sell, right on schedule.

Wales gave a parting grin. "Take a look at us. And let us take a look at you. Oh! And folks, don't forget next week's Christmas parade—" He had raised his arm midway for his good-bye wave when a man's voice boomed from the dining hall's doorway.

"I want to see my daughter," he said. "Please let me see her."

His voice was loud, but his tone was gentle. Pleading.

Van Peebles looked embarrassed, jumping to the stage and standing in front of Wales as if the man had pulled a gun. "No one's keeping you from Sissy," he said, looking pained. "We've been through this, Brian. I'm a father too—I know how you feel—but Sissy wants something different. You know this isn't the time—"

The dinner crowd stirred, restless. "Leave it alone, Brownie!" a woman called.

The patient smile never left Wales's face as he watched it all unfold.

Kendra was disappointed. She'd just started to think maybe . . . just maybe.

Now real life was creeping inside the dream, pulling up the pretty rugs. This problem with Brownie was giving her a stomachache, as if she'd just feasted on stolen food. The man was standing erect, a SF Giants baseball cap politely held across his chest. A grown man was near tears, begging to see his daughter.

Brownie spoke slowly, like a tourist who hoped the locals would magically comprehend English if he slowed his speech. "I just want to talk to my little girl."

"That's no little girl!" a man called from the back, and a few men laughed. Brownie stood stoically, ignoring it all, trying to catch Wales's eyes. Van Peebles bobbed his head between them.

"My office, Brian," Van Peebles said. "Not here."

"I just want five minutes."

"Brownie?" Van Peebles said gently. He gestured with his eyebrows, and Kendra noticed the Gold Shirts sidling up to him on either side of the hall.

The air crackled. In that instant, something terrible was poised to reveal itself. Then Brownie nodded and turned away, leaving the hall with loud, solitary footsteps in the room's silence. The skin on the back of Kendra's neck itched.

Kendra whispered to Terry. "That was . . ."

"Don't worry about it," he said, cutting her off. She was annoyed, but his pointed gaze told her he merely didn't want to be overheard.

Wales went back to the mic, waving. "Enjoy Nettie's chicken! Good night!"

Like nothing had happened. Or like it happened all the time.

A spattering of applause, although Brownie had changed the mood.

Kendra kept studying Wales and his smile, looking for signs of anger as he walked down the stage steps, came close to their table almost as if he meant to greet them . . . and walked past, unruffled.

Sonia leaped up, blocking Wales's path. A Gold Shirt walking behind Wales moved as if to touch Sonia, but Wales winked at him and gave a subtle shake of his head. Sonia looked oblivious to everything except Wales's face.

Sonia awkwardly held up her hand to shake Wales's, but he raised it and gave the back of her hand a polite peck. Clark Gable style. Sonia blushed.

"I've seen all your movies," Sonia said. "You have no idea. I still have my *Better Thread Than Dead* button in my locker." Her eyes defocused with sudden remembrance. "I mean . . . I used to."

Sonia had transformed into someone unrecognizable. Wales eyed her carefully.

"Your name, young lady?"

"Sonia," she said. "Sonia Petansu."

Wales looked at the closest Gold Shirt. "Did you get that?" he said.

"Yessir," the Gold Shirt said. "Sonia P. with the Washington crew."

Wales still held her hand, lingering. "Be sure you come to the ranch, Sonia."

"I wouldn't miss it."

When Wales woke from a kind of momentary daze, he gestured to the table. "Bring your friends. We love new people. You're all welcome."

This time he stared squarely at Kendra, and his charisma jolted her like static electricity. The power of his eyes startled her. His eyes were like a laser light portal that made his features exotic. Warmth rushed to her face. *What the—*

Wales went past them to the next admirer on the way to the door.

"I may never wash this hand again," Sonia said.

"That was pathetic," Piranha said. "You were drooling."

"What do *you* care?" Sonia said.

Kendra felt Terry watching her, but she avoided looking at him. She didn't want Terry to see any sign of Wales's appeal in her face. She was already embarrassed enough.

"He's got a dozen just like you back at the ranch," Piranha said.

"You don't know a damned thing about him," Sonia snapped. Piranha and Sonia usually hid their arguments. Maybe it would be harder for them to stay together now that they had other choices. Would that be true with her and Terry too?

"And one last thing, 'fore I forget," the mayor's voice rang from speakers. "Let's give a warm welcome to our visiting traders from Santa Cruz Island, off Santa Barbara. They've hauled us building supplies and lots of other goodies you'll want to take a look at. Next three days, they've set up camp out by the old thrift shop on Washburn."

A man in rumpled clothes at a table near theirs waved his hand. Santa Barbara was in Southern California, Kendra remembered. That must be close to Devil's Wake! Grandpa Joe used to say that when God closes one door, he opens another.

Kendra jumped up. She'd had her eye on another drumstick, but food could wait.

"Where are you going?" Terry said.

"I have to hear about Devil's Wake," she said.

She went to the islander's table. He was thin-faced and professional, like a college music teacher. His upper lip had been smashed sometime in the recent past, and he was missing fragments of his front teeth. Other than that, he looked fine after his trip.

She introduced herself.

"David Crisp," he said. "Nice to shake hands and use manners again."

"What have you heard about Devil's Wake?" she said. "It's an island."

He nodded. "Sure. Hard to get in—they're at capacity, or near it. We're not built up like they are."

Kendra's heart bounded. "It's not just . . . a myth?"

Crisp shook his head. "It's as real as Domino Falls, although I'd never get a dinner invitation there. Wish I could. On an island, you don't need the fences. It's a fortress."

Kendra felt as if a stone had rolled off her heart. She suddenly imagined herself back in the truck with Grandpa Joe, seeing his frightened eyes as he told her to go to Devil's Wake. Grandpa Joe seemed to be standing beside her again.

"I have an aunt there," Kendra said. A great-aunt, actually, but the details were none of his business. "My grandfather said she can get us sanctuary."

Again, he nodded. "They take care of their own," Crisp said. "To a fault, some of us say. Hell, put in a good word for Donald Crisp. C-R-I-S-P."

"And . . . my friends?"

He shrugged. "Depends. Some they let in, some they don't. Their reasons don't always make sense." He thought of an idea. "But they broadcast on 3950 kilohertz. Try to talk to them. Can't hurt. Be sure you know your kin's name."

Kendra had forgotten that her heart could race with joy and excitement, not just fear. She didn't remember meeting her great-aunt, but she was a piece of her family left behind. She had memories Kendra wanted to learn, or no one would be left to put the pieces of her family's story together.

Devil's Wake was real! The possibilities left Kendra speechless.

"Thanks, sir," Terry said, steering Kendra away from the table while the man repeated his campsite's location. "I don't know what that look on your face means," Terry told her, "but it's not that easy, Kendra. We don't know if we have a bus yet. And even if we did . . . that's a long way down."

"I have to talk to them," Kendra said. "Right now."

Terry looked flustered, but he trailed after her as she searched the crowd.

"Who are you looking for?" he said.

Kendra almost didn't know. Her plan was formulating by itself. "The mayor," she said. "I need a shortwave. He said to ask him any questions."

Van Peebles was standing over the dessert table, picking over the last crumbs in a pie tin. Kendra wasn't as brazen as Sonia, but she put on a bright smile when she reached him. He looked delighted to see her.

"Having a good time?" Van Peebles said.

"Very much," Kendra said, remembering Sonia's charm. Smiling a bit longer.

"Is there anything I can do for you?"

"I need a shortwave," she said. When he asked why, she told him. Would he try to keep her from communicating with the outside?

Van Peebles didn't hesitate or blink. "Few of those in town," he said. "Closest one's the gas station. They might let you use it, might not."

Nine

The mom-and-pop Arco station was a block's walk south. It was after dark, but a man was lighting the lamps and a few people were still outside, men and women. Citizens Patrol teams strolled the streets, recognizable from their powerful flashlights. A sole Gold Shirt astride a horse passed at a steady clip, another guardian. Despite the incident at dinner, Threadville seemed a safe place to walk after dark.

"You might not find what you're looking for," Terry said. "It might always feel this way for a while, Kendra. No matter where you are."

Kendra was surprised by Terry's insight, and a bit nervous. She stared at her grubby sneakers walking on the street's smooth cobblestones. "I don't know what I'm looking for," Kendra said. "I just know I have to talk to her. At least this one time." She paused. "That man was begging to see his *daughter*." She couldn't forget it, even now.

"I know," Terry said. "It creeped me out too. But let's keep a low profile."

They stopped talking when two men approached from the opposite direction. Kendra was glad to feel Terry's gun pressed to her side as they kept close. The men strode past them without slowing, leaving plenty of space among them, all of them pretending they weren't trying so hard to keep out of one another's way.

A dim light was on inside the gas station, although the first gas pump wore a sign that said NO GAS TILL FRIDAY.

The gas station's convenience store was small, its shelves modestly stocked. Each item for sale had a detailed label instead of a price: *Will trade for batteries,* said the label beneath a precious-looking bottle of motor oil. A box of Almond Joy candy bars was marked *Make an offer.* Tempting.

The young woman behind the counter was buried in a copy of *Mademoiselle* dated the year before, and Kendra wondered how many times she'd flipped through the wrinkled pages. "No gas till Friday," she said. "Probably Saturday, truth be told."

Kendra spotted the small ham radio under the counter. The black box–like device looked like a bulky CD player covered with knobs and windows.

"Do you let people use your radio?"

"Depends," the woman said. "Why do you want it?"

"To call Devil's Wake? I might have family there. It's—"

The woman glanced at the wall clock, an old glittering image of the Bay Bridge, something from a tourist shop. It was after seven-thirty. "Might be a little late for Max to be there," she said, "but let's give him a try."

The drumming began in Kendra's chest again. Terry gave her a warning look—*Don't get your hopes up,* he seemed to say. What was wrong with hoping?

90

The attendant operated the radio for her, calling out with a cigarette-roughened voice. "This is CrazyLady, Domino Falls, California. Looking for Devil's Wake," she said. She waited a few seconds, and then repeated her call. "Devil's Wake—do you copy?"

Kendra's chest felt tight. What if no one answered?

The radio sputtered to life. "CrazyLady?" There was static. "You're dropping out."

"Newbie asked me to give you a holler," the woman said, and gave Kendra the handheld transmitter. "Quick, I might lose the signal."

For a moment, Kendra didn't know where to begin. "My name is Kendra Brookings. Is there a . . . Stella Carver on the island?" She was so surprised to reach Devil's Wake, she'd almost forgotten her great-aunt's name.

She expected a long wait while he flipped through records, but he answered right away. "Stella? Sure! The librarian."

Kendra froze, wondering if she was dreaming. Maybe that was it. She'd been dreaming since they first drove into Threadville. The attendant smiled, happy for her.

"She's my great-aunt," Kendra said. "Can you get her on the line?"

The guy on the other end, Max, laughed. "Hey now, I'm not a phone operator. Doesn't quite work like that. I'll have her here at noon tomorrow, though."

The woman behind the counter shook her head, taking the mic from Kendra. "You know I'm dead air without the power," she said. "I've got juice for another twenty minutes. Can't you go run and get her?"

Half of what Max said next was lost to static. "—your own personal valet service out here, Gloria, I shoulda been home an hour ago—" When his voice cut out again, Gloria's mischievous smile gave her away. She was interfering with his transmission.

"What's that?" Gloria said into the mic. "I didn't copy that. So you'll go run and fetch Stella Carver so she can talk to her surviving family? Her name's Kendra."

This time, the radio buzzed with silence, and Kendra was afraid he was gone. Finally, Max sighed. "If Wales ever sends you out here on a goodwill mission or whatever, you better duck if you see me coming, lady. I'll get her, but you owe me."

"Hurry, Max—seriously, blackout in twenty minutes."

Max cursed, and the radio went quiet.

For the first few seconds, Kendra held her breath as if she expected Aunt Stella to simply materialize. "Thanks so much," she told the girl. "Will he really go get her?"

"He's gonna try." She stared at the clock warily. "Don't know if he'll make it."

Kendra's heartbeat pulsed in her fingertips, so she squeezed Terry's hand.

"Thanks so much for helping us," Terry said to Gloria, the first to remember his manners. "Just the way you're trying like this . . ." He didn't finish. "Just . . . thanks."

Gloria shrugged, winking at him. "You kidding? With everything going on out there, I get a chance to bring a family together? You just made my week! Braiding the Threads, like Mr. Wales says."

They shared a moment of giddiness, which veered to anxiousness as the bright red second hand ticked around the clock. Terry and Gloria made small talk about Threadville, but Kendra didn't hear a word of it. Ten minutes passed like an hour, but the next five sped by. *We don't have enough time,* she thought.

Gloria glanced at the clock. "Sorry, my radio's about to die," she said. "Max is gonna kill me, but come back in the morning. Or go to the main radio station—"

92

The radio hissed with feedback.

"Threadville?" Max's voice said. "You copy? I've got Stella Carver here."

Gloria shrieked, overjoyed. At first, Kendra could only stare at the radio. The dreamlike sensation came back, stronger than before. Just as she'd felt at Portland General, and then with her parents, she couldn't believe it was true.

"Hello?" a garbled woman's voice said. Kendra had expected her father's aunt to sound like an old lady, but the woman sounded vibrant if breathless. "Who's this?"

"Aunt Stella?" Kendra said. She forgot to press the Talk button at first, so Gloria patiently reminded her. "Aunt Stella? It's me: Kendra."

"Kendra!" the woman shouted, and this time her voice was loud and clear. "*Devon*'s Kendra? He said it was a Karen." Her voice was muffled as she said something off to the side. "This is my grand-niece Kendra! From Washington!"

Gloria pointed at the clock, made a move-it-along motion.

Kendra pressed Talk again. "My grandpa Joe said to call you—"

"—all right, baby?" Aunt Stella said. "Are you with your dad and mom?"

Kendra breathed through the bubble of grief. Stella Carver might be the only person left who had known her parents. "No," she said. "Mom and Dad didn't make it."

A painful pause, then, "I understand," Aunt Stella said, clipped. "I'm sorry for what happened, sugar, but you survived. Are you all right? You hurt?"

Kendra laughed through her tears. "I'm fine!" she said, fighting a wave of hysterical mingled joy and grief. "I have friends with me. We're in Threadville."

"Well, thank the Lord!" Aunt Stella said. "Safe and sound. Praise Jesus!"

Less than a minute left on the clock, Kendra realized, alarmed.

"Aunt Stella, is there sanctuary in Devil's Wake?" she said. "If I come to you?"

"Come to me?" Stella said, as if the idea shocked her. "All that way? Sweetheart, from the stories I hear, I don't know how in the world you got as far as Threadville. You better stay put a while—"

Kendra's next words were a pleading whisper. "But if we can get there . . . could I get sanctuary?" Kendra said. "For me and my friends who've kept me safe?"

"I . . ." Aunt Stella paused, sounding flustered. "Well . . . It's getting tight here, but I know people who've brought family in. If you can make it as far as Long Beach airport, then they could send a plane over . . ."

"They have planes?" Terry said behind her. Kendra had forgotten about Terry.

Aunt Stella went on, fretful. "But stay safe in Threadville until things get closer to normal. I couldn't bear it if something happened—"

"Out of time," Gloria announced. She leaned closer to the mic. "When you need to talk again, I can put you through."

"Kendra?" Aunt Stella said. "You're family, child, and I'll do what I can for you. You take care out there, you hear?"

"I will," Kendra said, her voice soft and hopeful.

The radio died, the lighted LCD fading to black. Kendra realized only later that all of the lights in the gas station were suddenly gone too. Even the moonlight seemed to have winked away. The room was pitch darkness, silent.

Terry's voice broke the quiet.

"They have planes?" he said again.

Ten

No Gold Shirts hovered about the probation dorms, an old Motel 6 bordering farmland close to Myles's garage. Terry and the rest of his crew might not be full Threadville residents yet, but they had earned a measure of trust.

Terry and Kendra had missed the last shuttle to the dorms after dinner because of their visit to the gas station, so they were still walking on the roadside past acres of farmland at nearly nine. There weren't enough residents to tend all of the farms, so some of them were dead, awaiting new crops, alongside others bursting with green stalks. How would this place look in a year?

Terry was eager to know the status of the Blue Beauty, but he didn't have another mile's walk in him. He would check on the bus once the scav mission was over.

Besides, he needed his rest. The scavs were leaving for San Francisco before daylight, and he and Piranha still hadn't worked out a survival plan. What if they found a nest of freaks like the one at the Barracks?

Kendra had been talking about Devil's Wake nonstop, trying to soften him up to the idea of maybe taking her, but Terry couldn't think about that now.

"Nervous?" Kendra said.

"Yeah." He itched to tell her about Piranha, but girls talked to each other.

"Then don't go," Kendra said. "You don't have to get killed, or bitten, to prove you deserve to live here. You already deserve it, Terry."

If his stomach hadn't felt like lead, he might have kissed her.

"I know," he said. "I'm going to look out for Piranha. He'd do the same for me."

"Terry, I think there's something wrong with his eyes."

Was it that obvious? Or was Kendra just more perceptive than Sonia? The whole story sat on Terry's tongue again, ready to spill. But he kept silent.

Kendra gave a knowing, dark chuckle. "Don't think it's not true just because nobody wants to say it. If he can't see, he's a danger to you and the whole team. With me and my grandpa Joe, there was just one freak in the store—*one* guy—and he almost got both of us. Grandpa Joe was hurt and couldn't get up. It happened"—she snapped her fingers—"just like that."

The sound of her snapping fingers evoked the image of a snarling face. And teeth.

"I know," Terry said again, weary.

"You say that now," Kendra said. "But when I wake up tomorrow, you and Piranha will both be gone. I know that already. So good luck." She sounded angry, but then she sighed. "Please be careful, Terry. Some of them can talk. They'll seem like regular people." He heard her hidden tears.

He slid his arm around Kendra's waist, pulling her close. She was as warm as a fever. "We'll be careful," he said. He wished he weren't giving her a reason to be worried tonight. They'd all had enough worry for a while.

Terry could smell the Motel 6 before they saw it. The motel might have looked like a relic from normal times, except that residents had built carefully tended fires in the empty parking spaces in front of their rooms; some of the bigger ones in sawed-off barrels, where they were cooking and selling strips of grilled meat. Other fires were just big enough for heat and light as people sat outside on lawn chairs before they went to bed, avoiding their dark rooms. There was laughter from one boisterous group on the end, where Terry suspected alcohol was flowing, but most people were quiet, trying not to draw attention to themselves.

Signs were posted clearly on the wall to tell newbies the hours: the town had electricity between six a.m. and ten a.m., and again from four to eight p.m. They followed the sign to the manager's office. The man waiting was barely five feet tall, nearly as wide as he was tall, with large ears and a face splotched with razor stubble.

"We were about to send a search party," he scolded. "I'm Marv, the housemaster. Nobody gets past probation without the housemaster, so if you're wondering which ass you kiss, it's right here. And I like to be back in the room with my wife by seven-thirty."

They nodded, apologizing. Marv spoke quickly, without leaving spaces for explanations. He'd only waited to tell them the rules.

"No fires in the rooms—not even candles. If I see a fire, expect the wrath of God. If your room's too dark, get a battery lamp. You can buy one on credit in town, or trade some food. Need to cook? Cook in your parking space. Never leave a fire unattended. Clean up your mess. The toilets all work, so leave the woods alone. If your toilet stops working, come tell me. You're back in the civilized world, so act like it."

"Yessir," Terry said, feeling giddy. He'd hoped he would have a toilet. Last night's bathroom in quarantine had felt like a luxury vacation.

"If I catch you stealing, if *anyone* catches you stealing, you're bounced. Theft is the number one reason folks hit the road, so bear that in mind when you're coveting thy neighbor's stash. Is it really worth it?" He sounded baffled by the stupidity of the thieves he had known. "One lady was a mother with a baby—stealing food. Didn't matter. She was gone. We let her leave her kid, but she is not welcome back."

He waited a moment to let his story sink in, hoping it would make an impact. It was hard to imagine a mother walking away from her own child, but it was harder to imagine a mother taking her kid back outside.

"That said, sometimes people steal. So lock your doors. Keep your keys. If I have to come open your door for you, it won't be service with a smile. If you make me replace this key, you'll be on my bad side. And it'll cost you. Big. These aren't the old days, when we could run out to Home Depot."

He handed Terry a motel key dangling with a number 5. Terry had expected to be locked up another night. Instead, they had their own key!

Marv wagged a stubby finger at Kendra. "Sorry, you'll have to knock. Only two keys per room, and there's three of you staying there—"

Kendra blinked, confused. "Three of us?"

"The three young ladies," Marv said. "You're in room eight. I know newbies like to stick close at first."

Quickly, Terry did the math. Sonia must not have shared a room with Piranha. He wondered whose idea that had been.

"Where's Piranha?" he said.

"Room five, if you mean the black boy," Marv said. "You're

bunking together. Seemed like he was having some troubles with his eyes . . ." He wasn't hiding the questions in his face. *The selection committee at work,* Terry thought. He also wondered, vaguely, if there was something significant about the way he'd called Piranha "the black boy," more than a convenient description. Terry might not have wondered, except for the way Kendra tensed beside him.

"His eyes are fine," Terry said, probably too quickly. Too defensively. "He's one of our best shots."

"Better be, if he's a scav."

Apparently, word traveled fast in Threadville.

"Excuse me . . . sir?" Kendra said. "Do you know anything about a man named Brownie who wants to see his daughter?"

Inwardly, Terry groaned. He'd planned to ask other residents, not the housemaster! Marv's face flattened to utter blankness.

"Everyone knows Brownie," Marv said. "But I don't pry in his family business."

He said it like a pastor dedicating a sermon to the evils of gossip. Terry squeezed Kendra's hand: *Let it go.* Not the way he'd hoped to make a first impression.

"He just had a fuss at dinner with Mr. Wales," Kendra said.

"I eat here," he said coolly. "I wouldn't know about that."

"I'm sure it's all worked out," Terry said.

Terry glanced at Kendra, and her eyes apologized.

"Oh, I'm sure it has," Kendra said. "I just wondered."

Marv went on with his orientation as if the exchange had been forgotten, but Terry seriously doubted it. Kendra was a hazard.

Terry stared down at his key. He and Kendra hadn't talked about sharing a room, but when the housemaster had handed him the key, he'd imagined them in a room together. Maybe in a bed together. Had she thought about it too?

"It's ladies' night," Kendra said, rubbing his hand. Her touch told him how much she wanted to stay with him too. "You and Piranha have a lot to talk about."

Eleven

Terry opened the door with his key, closed it again. Utter darkness. Piranha was a vague shadowy mass sitting on the far bed. There were two double beds, a desk, and a dresser. This place felt like the Taj Mahal.

Terry flipped the light switch, right before he remembered the electricity rations. No more electricity until six in the morning. He flipped it again to be sure.

"Dang. It *is* dark in here," Terry said.

"We start burning candles at ten," Piranha said. "There's some in my pack." Piranha had everything mapped out already. "Where were you?"

"We found a radio at the gas station. Kendra wanted to call Devil's Wake."

"What for?"

"She's got a great-aunt or something there." Kendra hadn't sworn him to secrecy, but it felt disloyal to reveal so much. What was a great-aunt, anyway? Like second and third cousins, the distinctions confused him. Was it your grandparents' sister?

"And?" Piranha said. More like *so what.*

"She lost her whole family right in front of her," Terry said.

Piranha didn't say anything, but he didn't have to. They had all lost everyone. At least Kendra knew if they were dead or alive.

"She just . . . wants to feel like something's left," Terry said.

"Yeah, me too," Piranha said sarcastically. "So let's drive back up to Seattle so I can pop in on my stepdad and say hey."

Terry never wanted to see a road again. "Maybe one day," he said.

"The Siskiyou guys almost got us at the pass."

Terry sighed. Piranha was right, but he had forgotten one thing: there was no one left to look out for Lisa. No one except him.

"It's an island," Terry said. He hadn't realized how much he'd thought it through. "It's not that far from L.A., and there's refugees applying from everywhere. She might be there. Or she might go there. She wouldn't come this far north."

For the first time, he stared at the truth: he hadn't found Lisa in Threadville. It hadn't really been reasonable even to hope, but there you were.

"I'm not leaving here till I have a real good reason to," Piranha said.

"Nobody's said anything about leaving."

"Yet," Piranha said, knowing.

"Anyone leaves, we'll divide up our stuff—everyone gets a share."

"I didn't ask about the shares," Piranha said. "Just don't want you to wonder one day, 'Why didn't anybody try to stop me?' "

Terry was tired of talking about it. "How bad are your eyes?"

Piranha breathed harder, not answering at first. "Pretty bad. This is my last pair of contacts. I'm screwed."

"What about the guy with the box of glasses?" Terry said.

Piranha shook his head. "My prescription's too strong. I've got two choices: I find some contacts soon, or I'm about to be blind."

Marv had already noticed Piranha's eyes. Marv was watching them. Piranha might have to leave Threadville whether he wanted to or not.

"What do we do tomorrow?" Terry said.

"We stick together," Piranha said. "I can still see enough to shoot freaks."

"Make sure it's only freaks you shoot," Terry said.

If Piranha was too quick to fire, he might hit someone in their crew; if he hesitated, he might get someone killed. Tomorrow sounded like a train wreck.

"Remember that cop up in Seattle?" Terry said.

"I'm blind, numbnuts. Not retarded. Of course I do."

"Right," Terry said. "He kept grabbing and biting people. Remember? And some of them can talk. They might seem like regular people . . ."

Ursalina had claimed the bed closest to the bathroom, lying in it dead center, so Kendra was left to share the bed with Sonia. The soldier had brought a thigh-leg chicken combo to perfume their room with fried grease, gnawing under her covers.

Sometime during the day Sonia had acquired a battery-operated compact. She rested the mirror on the bare desk, staring at her ghostly glow. She looked like she was primping to go out for the night, although she was only wearing a long T-shirt, legs bare.

"Terry and Piranha shouldn't go to the city," Kendra said.

"The freaks need to worry, not you," Ursalina said. "Piranha told me their plan; it sounds tight. These guys are pros, like I said. They're in, they're out."

Sonia only flipped her hair in the mirror, testing a new style, pushing strands behind her ears. Kendra wanted to ask why Sonia and Piranha weren't in a room together, but that wasn't a matter of life or death.

"What's wrong with Piranha's eyes?" Kendra asked Sonia instead.

"There's nothing wrong with his eyes," Sonia said. "He needs some saline solution. Every drugstore had it."

Emphasis on past tense, Kendra thought.

Ursalina spoke up. "Could he see well enough to spot a freak behind him?"

"Can we not be scared for one night?" Sonia said in a high, thin voice, glancing at them before she went back to the mirror. "Is that too much to ask? Last I checked, Terry didn't need a babysitter either."

"They'll be fine," Ursalina said. "The scavs have a good plan."

A sound of laughter came through the wall. Men's laughter. And a woman.

Kendra recognized Darius's laugh. The Twins. Of course. Jackie was probably in their room with them.

"The locals are friendly," Ursalina said.

"Treating them like Wild Bill Hickok and Wyatt Earp," Sonia said. "Little kids asking for their autograph! Hell, I could've shot those cans down."

"I don't know about that," Ursalina murmured. "They

104

shot more than cans today. Besides, you were getting the star treatment yourself, *chica* . . ."

Sonia giggled—the first time Kendra had heard such a girlish sound from her—and Kendra suddenly understood that Sonia was preening in the mirror because she was still starstruck by Josey Wales. Now that Kendra wasn't in a room with him, she didn't see the appeal. He seemed like an aging TV star trolling for groupies.

"You're going to his house?" Kendra said.

"First chance I get," she said. "You should come too. Both of you."

"Wouldn't miss it," Ursalina said, like they were planning for prom night.

Kendra realized she probably would go too, if she had the chance. And she would try to dress up and look nice. She didn't like knowing that, but she had no doubt.

"Did you hear anything else about that guy's missing daughter?" Kendra said.

"His daughter isn't missing," Sonia corrected her. "She's an adult who doesn't want to talk to him. There's a big difference."

"How do we know if she doesn't *want* to talk to him . . . or they won't *let* her?" Kendra said.

Ursalina flipped her chicken bones into the trash can beside her bed. "I heard family drama, kid. Why are you looking for reasons not to like it here? You've got hot meals, running water, electricity, and nobody's grabbed you in an alley. Take it from me: when you've got a bunker, you hunker."

"No candles," Sonia said, in schoolmarm mode. "Rules are rules. Agreed?"

"Yeah," Ursalina agreed. "We'll grab some flashlights off the bus tomorrow. Maybe I better work the fences instead of day care. They like shooters. Makes sense . . ."

Kendra was surprised that Ursalina wasn't more cynical, but then again, the soldier knew more about what was waiting outside. Their only mission was to get on the fast track to Threadville citizenship.

Kendra wanted to tell them about her conversation with Aunt Stella in Devil's Wake and how they might be able to get in, but then they would spend the rest of the night trying to tell her to forget Devil's Wake. Even Terry wouldn't understand, if not for his sister in L.A.

But the more Kendra saw of Threadville, the less she wanted to stay.

Despite a sinfully comfortable mattress, Kendra could hardly sleep. When she dozed, she snapped awake with a sensation that felt like falling off the edge of the world.

Kendra woke, looking quickly around the dark room to see what might have wrested her from slumber. She heard something from the other bed and sat up. Ursalina was tossing and turning. She thought about waking her in case her new friend was reliving her visit to the gas station with Mickey and Sharlene.

Then the door rattled.

Kendra gave a start, hoping she'd imagined it. The door rattled again, more urgently. Not a rattle from the wind—a persistent shaking, someone trying to get in.

"Terry?" she said. A wild hope. He was coming in the middle of the night to tell her he'd changed his mind about scavenging.

But it wasn't Terry.

The door burst in with a crash, wood cracking like toothpicks. The windows broke next, *bam bam bam*. Three in a row.

At first she'd thought it might be Marv, or Gold Shirts,

checking on them. But a sudden din of low growling and snuffing and a rotten fruit smell told her it was worse than bad manners. Something had gone badly wrong. Freaks! No time to wonder how, or who, had failed. All that mattered was what would happen next.

They were penned in, and the door and windows hadn't held. The door fell into the room as if it were riding a powerful wind. Hot, putrid air washed Kendra's face. Slivers of red threads floated everywhere.

Kendra imagined herself vaulting out of bed, rolling to the floor . . . but she was shocked to discover she was still in bed clutching her bedsheet. She was tired of running, and she'd run out of places to go.

Hands grasped through the broken windows. Endless shadows played in the darkness. Where was Ursalina's gun?

"Ursalina—wake up," she said, and tried to climb out of bed. Vines strangled her arms and legs, rooting her to the bed.

The first freak to reach the beds looked like Wales. He moved with impossible speed. A runner!

Wales ripped at her sheet, yanking the fabric from her frozen hands.

Kendra sat up in bed, shrouded in darkness. She was sopping with sweat as she gasped for air. A thin oily sheen pasted her hair to her forehead. Ursalina and Sonia snored softly. A dog barked outside, then hushed when someone whistled. The sound of her breathing filled the room.

Just a dream. Just a dream.

Shadows played in the darkness, tricking her eyes with ghostly faces and grasping arms. But the door was closed. The dream had seemed real because the darkness made everything look like a dream. But she was awake now.

Kendra stared at the door a long time so her eyes could see it and believe.

Yes, the door was still closed. With freakproof locks.

Kendra's hand reached for the nightstand, where Ursalina had left her 9mm—*Better be close enough for any of us to grab it,* she'd said. Kendra chambered a round and slid it beneath her pillow. Her heartbeat slowed, but she stared toward the door.

She would keep watch tonight.

Terry and Piranha were going into town. They would be waking in only a couple of hours, in the dead of night, and the trucks outside would rumble.

If she stayed awake, she might be able to open her door and wave good-bye.

Twelve

December 21

Terry was so caught up with shaking hands and learning names that he didn't notice Kendra waving in the open door at the motel until they were near the corner.

Terry leaned out of the pickup's bed to wave back. To make sure she could see him in the near darkness, he waved a long time.

Piranha chuckled. "How are you gonna act when she gives it up?" he said, biting open the foil wrapper of his protein bar. The other guys laughed, and Terry didn't mind the joke. He doubted Piranha had seen Kendra, so he was guessing to fool the other guys. Terry wouldn't have seen her if she hadn't been bathed in moonlight.

"Stay focused, man," one of the other guys said, giving Terry a playful slap.

There were two trucks filled with the scav crew, six in each truck. Terry was relieved when he and Piranha were teamed together. Terry had never taken part in an operation with so many other armed men. They were a war party.

The driver put on old-school Ice Cube, "It Was a Good Day," and turned it up loud, with his windows open. Terry had never heard a truck's stereo go so loud, booming across the farmland. There was no one to wake up. They all yelled the lyrics to the wind.

Even the Gold Shirt bobbed his head to the beat until the other young guy, a kid named Bobbie, said he'd jump out of the truck if he didn't hear Metallica. For the next few miles, rock once again hailed supreme. All the stalled cars had been cleared to the side and stripped, so they had nothing to do but play air guitar and sing "Enter Sandman" at the top of their lungs.

They got ten minutes of music, about ten miles' worth of freedom.

Then they hit the 101, and the music died.

"Playtime's over," the Gold Shirt said.

Fifteen minutes later, they peeled off in what was left of Sausalito, and the trucks went in opposite directions at Martin Luther King Park. Alpha truck was going north, Beta truck, their truck, south through deserted, windblown streets.

Terry hoped their truck would land near contact lenses. They twisted and turned, heading toward the bay and then inland again to a business district. Piranha had told him the kinds of places that would have them: Optometrists' offices. A 7-Eleven. Kmart. Drugstores had saline solution and a moderate range of contact lenses. His were too strong to be common . . . but that also meant less likely to have already been scavenged. When in doubt, Piranha had said, just grab what he could.

• • •

But these were no ordered city streets. The area seemed desolate, more like a warehouse district. Where would they find contacts here?

"Downtown's been thoroughly picked over," the Gold Shirt said. "So we're sticking to outlying areas. Put on your scav sacks. We'll hit a few cars on the way that haven't been cleared. Hopefully the owners are gone too—but grab a hankie out of this bag to keep down the smell." The bag smelled of Vicks VapoRub.

Terry had forgotten about the corpses.

During their road trip from Seattle, they'd never left gas behind unless they had no choice, but they hadn't picked over corpses since Vern and Molly. When they found cars, they'd taken what they wanted, but they left the bodies alone. They didn't have use for wallets and wedding rings. Now, picking over bodies was part of his job description.

"I'm not gonna forget this," Piranha said quietly, knowing.

"No—you won't," Terry said.

A dark-haired man in his forties raised his hand. He wore glasses, and his black jogging suit looked new. "I'm Riley. If we see freaks . . ."

"We *will* see freaks," the Gold Shirt said. "Get used to it. *If* is just you in denial. What's your question?"

For a moment, Riley forgot his question. No one said anything. Terry felt a bizarre mixture of terror and exhilaration.

"How many?" Terry said in Riley's silence.

"Sometimes a few, sometimes a lot," the Gold Shirt said. He was round, jolly, rubber-faced, like the love child of Jim Carrey and Jack Black. "Be ready for anything. Be on the lookout for explosive triggers from pirates. Chances are, by the time you've taken three runs, you've seen somebody bitten or shot. Not everyone who drives out always makes it home. If the crew is

111

compromised, you'll be left behind. There's a reason this is the toughest job."

"But we get to keep half?" Bobbie said. The kid in back.

"Bobbie, how old are you?" Gold Shirt said.

"Eighteen, sir."

"You're a liar. You're sixteen. Your father ought to know better."

"Wasn't up to him," Bobbie said.

The Gold Shirt tossed a glove at Bobbie, and he caught it before it bounced into the road. "Yeah, you get to keep half—so make it something worth keeping. Scrap metal. Batteries. Medicines. But don't line your pockets. Holding back is pinching, and that's the same as stealing. You'll get your half, but bag it and tag it. Thieves won't just get banned from the scavs, you're bounced from town. Any of you."

But probably not the locals, Terry guessed. Any town went easier on its own.

As Terry glanced at the other scavs, he wished he'd worn more layers. He had on good jeans and a sturdy jacket, unlike people he'd seen dressed in rags, but the more seasoned scavs were wearing two pairs of jeans—harder to bite through—and had their gloves taped to their sleeves. Terry cursed himself. If he hadn't spent so much time thinking about Kendra and Piranha, he might have remembered what was waiting.

Piranha's face was grim. If these guys found out how little Piranha could see, they might leave Piranha outside for endangering the crew. Which meant leaving him too, because Terry would stay with him. He hoped getting stranded was the worst thing that could happen today.

The sky was growing gray and light pink by the time they reached South Sausalito, just in sight of the Golden Gate Bridge. The severed cables and shattered concrete dangled into the bay.

"What happened to it?" Piranha asked.

Horatio shrugged. "No one really knows. Just one day the Sausalito side was fighting off freaks on the bridge, and the next, someone had parked a fertilizer bomb in the middle and blew it the hell up."

"Terrorism."

"One man's terrorist is another man's freak fighter," he said. "If you fill up your scav bag, you come get another one. The idea is to fill up as many bags as you can. Everybody partners up. No one goes out alone. Ever. It's the quickest way to get left in the cold. If we get swarmed, I guarantee we won't stick around because we're feeling sentimental."

Only the seasoned scavs laughed. Riley and Bobbie looked gray in the face, and Terry thought he might look the same way. The truck's swaying made his stomach hurt.

A vehicle appeared in the road ahead, but it was off to the side. There was movement in a window. Their truck swung to the lane farthest away but didn't slow.

Terry stared as they sped past. At least three women were huddled around a Ford SUV with the hood up, hissing steam. The movement he'd seen in the window was from two small girls. The children waved frantically as the truck drove past.

"We're also not a rescue service," the Gold Shirt said. "Out here, no good deed goes unpunished. The best way to get hurt is to divert from the plan. So if you feel sorry for those ladies and they're still here when we come back, toss 'em a bag of your loot. Food or bottled water. Other than that, you can't help them. And if they don't have guns, only God can help them anyway."

"But . . ." Terry started.

The Gold Shirt raised his voice to be sure he was heard. "They will offer you the world! They will scream and cry! They will look just like friends and loved ones you haven't seen since Freak Day! But repeat after me: *I will not bring home strays!*"

The experienced scavs sounded robust as they repeated their mantra, stomping their feet in unison on the last word. Piranha said it loudest of all. Terry was still trying to forget the sight of the waving women and children. His sister could have been in a car like that.

"Young man?" The Gold Shirt was looking at him.

"Sir?"

"I want to hear you say it."

Terry's tongue felt flat in his mouth. "I will not bring home strays," he said.

The Gold Shirt stared at Piranha. Then his eyes went back to Terry.

"See that you don't," he said. "There's no room for strays on this truck."

Much of the morning fog had burned off by the time they reached the knots of cars, lanes tied up in both directions. At first, their truck's driver was able to steer around the stalled traffic by driving on the shoulder, but then he stopped behind a multicar tangle. Terry remembered the Siskiyou ambush.

"One crew clears the left lane, two crews cover," the Gold Shirt said. "Who's clearing?"

"We will," Piranha said, raising his hand. They knew how to clear cars—it would be easier for Piranha to steer or push than it would be to see an attacker in the distance. As an afterthought, he looked at Terry: "Right?"

"Yeah," Terry said. His voice wasn't nearly as reluctant as he felt.

"Don't forget your bags," the Gold Shirt said.

"The cars are empty, right?" Piranha whispered to Terry as they hopped out of the truck. Terry looked at the shadowed forms

114

behind the tinted windows of the PT Cruiser stalled closest to them. At least two people. With any luck, they were dead.

When Terry didn't answer, Piranha cursed. They tied kerchiefs around their faces. "Sorry, man," Piranha said.

"Sorry doesn't even begin to cover it," Terry said.

"Make sure they're dead!" the Gold Shirt called.

Guns chambered as the crew covered them. Terry almost vomited when they opened the PT Cruiser's door. A family of four. By the looks of it, the father had shot his wife and two young daughters in the head with a .38 and then shot himself—the gun still dangling from his hand. They were huddled in the backseat as if they were sleeping. Terry couldn't stand to look at them. The smell in the car was unholy.

"Strip it," the Gold Shirt called.

"I got it," Piranha said, slipping on his gloves, and Terry didn't argue.

"When we're done, I'm steering," Terry said. "You push." He didn't want to spend one second longer with the corpses, but at least he could see the road to steer.

The next car was empty, and they only had to clear two to make the path. The other scavs patted them on the back when they climbed back into the truck's bed, making jokes about popping their cherries and the aromatic smell on their clothes.

A digital wristwatch. A wedding ring with a fingernail-sized diamond. An iPod with a quarter of its battery power remaining. A GPS navigator. An unopened box of Froot Loops. A wallet, a purse stuffed with cash (useless, of course), and two cell phones. A toy called a Leapster.

That was all that was left of the PT Cruiser's family of four. No contact lenses.

Terry wished he could warp himself ahead in time: day over. It was barely light outside. The day hadn't even started.

Thirteen

The route to the docks and warehouses was familiar to the crew—many of the lanes had been cleared on their last trip and hadn't been tampered with. Threadville's scav crews were like ants burrowing into a tunnel, taking pieces at a time. The Gold Shirt, whose name was Cliff, told them to keep talking to a minimum. It was hard to hear each other in the bed of the truck anyway, but they had to keep watch for pirates and freaks.

They didn't have to wait long to see freaks.

In Sausalito's lost neighborhoods, the infected walked streets that gleamed with broken glass. They weren't the collected horde at the Barracks, but there was movement almost everywhere Terry looked. Crossing the streets. Hovering near mailboxes. Pawing at storefronts. Tangled in downed power lines.

And they had enough ammo on the truck to light up the city. Dean and Darius weren't the only ones who could gain fame as shooters in Threadville.

"Let's clear this area out," Terry said. "Right?"

"What did I tell you yesterday?" Cliff said, annoyed.

"A gunshot is a dinner bell," Piranha said quickly. "Freaks who hear gunshots gather, and a gathering of freaks will attract others. If more than ten come, it crosses some kind of a threshold, and you're likely to get a swarm."

"Glad one of you was paying attention," Cliff said.

Yeah, and only one of us can see your face, Terry thought.

Cliff went on. "Getting swarmed in the city is a problem that can get very big, *very* fast. A wall of shamblers can stop this truck and jam every street in sight. When are the only times we pop off in the city?"

"To create a diversion, or to save our asses!" the veteran scavs said in unison.

"In the event of gunfire, be ready to clear out in five minutes. Within five minutes, enough freaks will respond to repeated gunshots to send a swarm signal."

"You mean . . . they talk to each other?" Bobbie said.

"Kid, I wouldn't call it talking," Cliff said. "But whether they use smoke signals, Morse code, or body odor—you have five minutes to grab your bags and get back to the truck, or you're hitchhiking home."

Five minutes wasn't much time if they were inside a building. Cliff had given them the same talk during orientation, but it was more vivid when so many shabbily dressed freaks strolled the streets, stopping their mindless shuffling when the truck passed, staring after them with longing, sniffing at the air. Men, women, children. They looked ridiculous and sad in the costumes from their old lives—bloodstained ties askew, bright baseball caps, wrinkled dresses and skirts.

Piranha was stoic behind his sunglasses, nothing bothering him. Terry wondered how many of the freaks Piranha could see, and if seeing was worse than not seeing.

"Runner!" Riley said, alarmed.

The woman was wearing a Berkeley sweatshirt and pajama pants, so fresh that most of her face was still human. She rounded the corner like a cheetah in full pursuit, barefoot, her hair flying behind her. For the first few strides, she was nearly close enough to reach out and touch Terry as she clawed toward the bed of the moving truck.

She was pretty, in her early twenties. Square-jawed, smooth skin, an athletic body. Except for the red eyes and gnashing teeth, she would have been a hottie.

And she must have been on the track team, because she could *run*. After his first moment of surprise, Terry joined the laughter of the other scavs as they watched her struggle to keep up with them. When the truck picked up speed, she ran harder. Her face was bright red from exertion, spittle flying, cords on her neck protruding.

"Faster, baby!" one of the scavs called to her. "You want it, come get it!"

The other scavs taunted with kissing noises and obscene gestures. Terry's nervous laughter left him queasy. When the girl fell behind, the driver slowed slightly, making it a game to see how close she could get.

Cliff surveyed them like wayward schoolchildren, his eyes landing on Piranha. "You," he said. "Pick up your rifle. Take her out."

Piranha sat straight up, surprised. "But you said . . ."

"Diversion," Cliff said. "We're not where we're going yet. Take her out."

Terry's laughter died. The runner was closer now that the truck was taking its time, but she was fifteen yards back. Could Piranha make her?

Dutifully, Piranha lifted his gun, bracing the stock, taking aim. Or seemed to be.

"Middle of the road," Terry said quietly. "Dead center."

"Who are you, his mama?" Cliff said. "We don't have spotters. Let him shoot."

Piranha hesitated. The truck slowed more, and the runner was gaining. Terry readied his own gun, nervous. If she reached the truck's bed . . .

"What the hell are you waiting for?" Cliff said. "Take her out!"

Bam. Piranha fired, but the runner kept coming. The shot had gone wild. Perspiration gleamed across Piranha's forehead. Ten yards. Eight. Six good strides, and the runner would be on them.

Bam.

Piranha's second shot chipped her shoulder, making her stumble, but she ran on, reaching out as if to leap—

Bam. By the third shot, she was close enough even for Piranha to see. The runner crumpled to the street, shot in the crown of her head. He'd almost missed her again, but it was good enough to take her down. She was still twitching as they drove.

"You tryin' to shoot her or kiss her?" Cliff said, angry. "My four-year-old coulda hit her faster'n that!"

The other scavs joined in the ribbing. "Annie Oakley here sure ain't coverin' me," one said.

Terry's heart raced. Would they stop the truck and throw them out?

Piranha shook his head, still hidden behind his shades. "Man, I'm sorry," he said, his voice thick with emotion. "She just . . . she . . . she looked like . . ."

Piranha was pouring it on, pretending he'd been overcome instead of blind.

"*That* is what I'm talking about!" Cliff said. "You newbies are too soft! I don't care if it looks like Angelina Jolie. *If you hesitate, you or someone on your team dies!*" He was practically nose to nose with Piranha, yelling in his face. If Cliff told Piranha to take off his shades, he would know.

"Yessir," Piranha said. "It won't happen again, sir."

"Kindergarten is over," Cliff said. "Rule number one: do not fire unless necessary. Rule number two: if you fire, dammit, make it count."

Their truck finally parked at the edge of a warehouse district looming gray and brown, streets glistening from either water or glass— Piranha couldn't tell which. As it got later in the afternoon, he could see less and less. He needed to take off his shades for more light, but he couldn't show his irritated eyes while the other guys were around.

Thanks to his piss-poor showing as a shooter, nobody wanted him to keep watch or cover other scav crews. No problem; he hadn't missed that girl on purpose, but it had worked out for the best. He and Terry had been sent inside time and again. It was the best job for picking the choice loot—although, technically, the crew shared it, custom was dictated by the old "finders keepers" rule.

So far, in the burned-out shells of an office supply store, a boating showroom, and a hardware store, he'd loaded at least eight bags to cram in the truck. They'd found rubber bands, glue, motor oil, fishing supplies, hammers and nails (highly valued), batteries of all sizes (*very* highly valued), lightbulbs, and building materials—everything except contact lenses.

He and Terry had autonomy, disappearing behind shelves, so Piranha had been able to keep the other guys from noticing that he could barely count his fingers in front of his face. He couldn't read labels, so he pressed his face close to the shelves to try to see what he could before he shoveled it into his bag. Sometimes he didn't see first, and he ended up lectured for wasting space with junk.

But they were getting through it, and they hadn't found many corpses. So far, no freaks had surprised him, hiding in corners. A casual succession of miracles had kept the two of them alive.

"We're done here—one more to go!" Bobbie called into the hardware store. "You guys come on out!"

Piranha cursed. He didn't have a wristwatch, but the waning light told him it was getting late. This was a day run, so they would drive back out to Threadville before nightfall. His last chance was vanishing with the sun.

"Hear that?" Terry said, suddenly beside him. "Grab your bag. Whatcha got?"

"Hell if I know," Piranha said.

"We're coming up on the last stop, P," Terry said, hushed. "I haven't seen anything like what you want. No eye doctor. No pharmacy. We better just say what—"

"No," Piranha said. "If they figure it out now, we're screwed."

Piranha had never had a friend like Terry, who was willing to back him so far, against his better judgment. Threadville's scavengers had spent months leaving survivors behind, and a few comments made Piranha wonder if Cliff had put a few persistent "strays" out of their misery. *I'm about to get T killed,* Piranha thought.

They lugged their bags back out to the truck, where Cliff and the watchers hoisted them into the bed and the passenger cabin that was bigger than it looked. Piranha trailed Terry's bright red down jacket, staying close to him, avoiding obstructions, trying not to trip or give himself away. He felt like they'd been out a week.

"We'll drive down thirty yards and park outside that side door," Cliff said, pointing, and Piranha tried to follow his shadowy pointing arm. A mammoth beige blur waited down the street. Another warehouse?

"Last half hour," Cliff said. "You're going back in, Brokeback."

"Brokeback? What?"

Cliff chuckled. "Everybody gets a nickname around here. And ya'll are *really* tight."

The other guys laughed, and Piranha's face burned. *I'm only allowed to shoot freaks,* he reminded himself.

Cliff and his most experienced scav, a thick guy nicknamed Meat (Piranha didn't ask), stayed behind to guard the loot with the driver. It was a newbie run: the kid, Bobbie, and the other newbie, Riley, walked with them toward the blur at the end of the block. The truck sped past them.

"Don't get lost!" Cliff called. "Or you'll miss your ride!"

"Jerk," Riley muttered, practically speaking Piranha's thoughts.

"He's not so bad," Bobbie said.

"This place was picked over months ago," Riley said. "He's gotta be kidding."

The blur was only bigger, no more distinct. He saw large loading doors; they were approaching a huge building from the rear. Definitely not a doctor's office. Piranha tugged Terry's jacket: *What is it?*

"Sorry, man," Terry whispered. "It's just Walmart."

Piranha's heart leaped, and he grinned.

Until the smell hit him.

• • •

In Terry's experience, a dose of good luck meant the other kind was on its way. They'd finally found somewhere that *might* have contact lenses, according to Piranha, so Walmart, of course, was where something would go wrong.

The last bay door had been yawning wide open and the store's front windows were smashed, so there were sure to be freaks inside. The store smelled of rotten citrus and human waste. Makeshift camps lay throughout the store; tents and blankets draped across the aisles. The mini camps were mostly empty. In others, lumps under the blankets were no doubt corpses. Unless the bundles moved, Terry didn't bother them. It would be a great place for pirates to hide, but they didn't have time for a sweep. They had to find the pharmacy.

Terry had convinced Riley and Bobbie to take the rear of the store, since Piranha said the pharmacy and other specialty departments were more likely to be at the front. So far, nothing moved except dirty sheets flapping in the store's breeze. Piranha stumbled into a shelf, tumbling a pyramid of empty tins cans to the floor. He cursed, fluently.

"*Shhhhh,*" Terry said from behind his handkerchief. "Don't call the freaks over."

Sure enough, was that movement from a couple of aisles away? Someone scurrying? Maybe a pirate or a refugee? The sound was gone. Nothing stirred.

Riley was right; the store had been picked over like a chicken bone. A few torn pieces of clothing were scattered on the floor, but the clothes racks were empty except for hangers, shelves had been pulled down, refrigerated cases stripped of everything except old food wrappers and rotten perishables. The aisles were so unrecognizable, it was hard to orient himself until he remembered to look up at the signs.

Checkout, one said far across the store.

Vision Center, said one beside it.

Terry grabbed Piranha's arm, pulling him. "You were right!" he said. "There's an eye doctor!"

"If there's anything left," Piranha said.

Cliff probably wouldn't be happy if they came back with only bags full of eye supplies, but Terry didn't care. He was going to grab everything in sight.

The optometrist's nook had fared better than most parts of the store. The wood paneling was intact, there were still two chairs to indicate where patients had sat, and a few shelves still hung on the walls where the eyeglass displays had been. Only a few cracked pairs of empty frames were left on the ground.

Piranha fumbled around like a madman, flinging drawers and cabinets open, crawling on the floor to fling papers aside. Cursing as he worked. Panicking.

Terry noticed a gray curtain in the rear of the enclave, pulled askew.

"In the back?" Terry said.

Piranha leaped to his feet. "Yeah, let's check it out—"

"Slow down," Terry said, yanking his arm to stop him. "Don't charge in."

They crept toward the doorway, one on either side. Terry forgot that Piranha couldn't see, expecting him to move ahead. The storeroom was small and dark, a third the size of the outer office. High cabinets to his left, above a sink, remained closed.

"Hey, P, I think—"

The low moan sounded beside Terry's right ear. He smelled the freak behind him before he turned around. He smelled rotten oranges, the breeze a blessing.

"Watch it!" Piranha screamed.

Terry whirled around and backed far enough into the storeroom to raise his rifle. The freak moaned, took a tortured step toward him. A shambler! If he'd been a runner . . .

"Don't shoot!" Piranha hissed.

The freak was wearing a doctor's smock with the name Raul on his identification badge. He wore round-frame glasses, but his face was a bed of red moss. Terry's finger throbbed from desire to shoot; he fought every self-protective instinct he had. The shambler was close, and he didn't know if another one was behind him. They might have walked into a nest!

Piranha swung his rifle butt like an ax, clubbing the freak in the back of the head.

The freak turned away from Terry, toward Piranha, startled. Piranha's second blow caught the freak across the temple. This time, Raul fell.

Terry realized he was gasping for breath. A foot closer, and the freak would have had him! He ran through the rest of the storeroom, dizzy with adrenaline, looking for any other signs of life. The room was empty.

"We're in—" Terry said.

Then, gunshots.

Not one shot, or two. The far-off crackling sound was like a string of fireworks. The shots were coming from outside the store, not inside. If Cliff was firing, the truck must be under siege. Six shots. Seven shots. Eight.

The dinner bell was ringing.

Cliff's voice suddenly blared from Terry's radio: *"We got company—and lots of it. Get back NOW."*

Terry fumbled with the radio. His hand was shaking slightly. "Copy," he said.

"Go!" Piranha said. "Get out! I'll be okay from here."

"Bite me," Terry said.

Breathing hard, they both flung open the cabinets. Eye supplies rained on them. Cleansers. Wipes. Eye drops.

"Saline solution!" Terry said, excited. He shoved at least twenty small clear bottles into his bag.

"Contacts . . . contacts . . . contacts . . ." Piranha was whispering. "Come on . . ."

There were so many gunshots outside, Terry wondered if Cliff was facing off against pirates instead of freaks. Or both. Another snapping round of gunfire came from another direction—*inside* the store. Riley and Bobby had found trouble too.

Terry eyed the narrow doorway. There was no other way out of the storeroom. If they got penned in . . .

Two large wall-mounted cabinets in a far corner were locked. While gunfire raged outside, Piranha pounded at them with his rifle stock, and one of the doors finally fell open. They pried open the second door.

Rows and rows of neatly stacked tiny boxes.

"Yes!" Piranha said. "Thank God for Bausch and Lomb! I need a fourteen minus-twelve, man. Anything close."

Terry tumbled every box he saw into his bag, but most of the numbers were nowhere near twelve. Lots of fives, sixes, sevens, eights. A few nines . . .

"I can't believe this," Terry whispered. "They're not high enough."

"You better be at the door, Brokeback, or you're out of luck!" the radio warned.

Piranha reached up high for the last few boxes, bringing them close to his face to try to read. When he took off his sunglasses, his eyes were as red as a freak's.

"Got it!" he said. "Elevens and twelves. This is as high as they go here!"

Piranha jammed fistfuls of boxes into his bag.

"We're coming!" Terry told Cliff over the radio.

They ran.

Five dead freaks lying just inside the bay doors told them what to expect outside.

The truck had changed directions, facing the other way, all on board. Everyone except the driver was firing at the shamblers and runners converging on the truck from every alley and street in sight, dozens. At least twenty stilled freaks littered the alley like twisted marionettes.

As soon as Terry and Piranha stepped outside, the truck started driving away, picking up speed.

"Get over here!" Cliff bellowed, waving.

There wasn't much in Terry's bag, but it was slowing him down. The truck was moving too fast for a jog or a sprint. Terry was running full out, his legs pumping. He felt Piranha behind him, but if Piranha stumbled over something, then what?

No time to look over his shoulder, but Terry heard runners behind them, tireless feet pounding against the asphalt, matching them step for step. Gaining.

And the truck was farther away. Bullets whizzed hot in the air as the scavs fired at the freaks giving chase. Cliff and Riley held out their hands over the edge of the bed door, in impossible distance. Terry saw their mouths moving, saw the guns smoke and spark, but he heard only his heartbeat and the stampeding feet of the freaks.

He touched the truck's chrome. Felt an iron hand wrap around his, tugging.

Terry was flung face-first into the truck, bumping his head

against something hard in a burlap bag. He heard Piranha's heavy panting, and then Piranha tumbled on top of him, knocking his head again. But they had made it!

Terry peered back for his first good look at what they had left behind. The street was filled with runners, like a marathon. There had been a nest nearby—maybe as many as there had been at the Barracks. If they'd gotten close enough, the freaks could have pulled them all out of the truck. The team had waited until it was almost too late.

"Holy . . ." Terry whispered.

Cliff, Meat, and the others were patting them on the back.

"Can't shoot worth a damn, but you can run!" Meat said. "You see that, Cliff?"

"Yeah, they can move," Cliff said. "Let's see what they almost got us killed for."

Here it comes, Terry thought.

Cliff reached into Piranha's bag. "What's this? Contact lenses?" The Gold Shirt grinned at both of them. "Jackpot, newbie! Do you know how much these are worth?"

Terry and Piranha bumped fists.

Terry never, *ever* wanted to go scavenging again.

Fourteen

8:30 p.m.

Hey!" A man's voice, sharp in the empty moonlit street.

Kendra jumped, her heart racing, and Hipshot barked beside her. The steady *clip-clopping* of horse hooves closed in on her from behind, and her body went rigid. A Gold Shirt in a suede cowboy hat rode up, shotgun ready, and Kendra thought of posses and lynch mobs.

"Yessir?" she tried to say, but her voice caught in her throat as a squeak. She wondered what law she'd broken, feeling tiny beneath the man on the horse.

But the Gold Shirt wasn't looking at her. He shined an impossibly bright flashlight a few yards behind her. Another man stood nearly hidden in the shadow from a closed fruit stand's awning. He had his own dog on a leash—a much bigger dog. His dog looked half wolf, half Sasquatch.

"What's your business?" the Gold Shirt demanded.

"I'm just . . . taking a walk," the man's gravelly voice said, an obvious lie.

"Then take it somewhere else. You over at Marv's camp?"

Suddenly, the man sounded concerned. "No reason to bother Marv with it—"

"In Threadville, we don't walk the streets drunk. We don't follow girls in the dark. I'm writing you up. Move on before I get creative."

Follow girls in the dark? Kendra's heart jumped. Was that true?

The man walked on, hurrying past Kendra with his dog and a sack over his shoulder. He reeked of alcohol. His dirty skin smelled like a pirate's.

Suddenly, the bright light was on Kendra. She shielded her eyes. Hipshot growled, and Kendra pulled his frayed rope leash close.

"What's your business?" the Gold Shirt said, his voice no more gentle.

Kendra pointed toward the corner. Two blocks hadn't sounded far in the crowded dining hall fifteen minutes ago, but now it was after eight. Lights out. The streets suddenly seemed ominous. "I'm just looking for my friend. They said he'd be—"

"Then hurry up and get where you're going. Don't walk alone after dark."

"Was he following me?"

Instead of answering, he said, "Where's your sidearm?"

"I . . . don't have my own yet."

"Get one. Keep moving."

Kendra didn't like his bossy manner, but she didn't argue. She made a kissing sound for Hipshot, and they kept a steady pace toward the building on the corner. The Gold Shirt didn't say anything else, but his horse walked a slow pace just behind her. Once she had made it to the front door, the Gold Shirt rode away. Kendra had been happy for his protection, but she was glad when he was gone.

The Hungry Dog was on the far end of Main Street, a corner bar left over from old times. Aside from the wood planks nailed up where picture windows had been, the bar probably looked the same, an old-fashioned English pub with a faded crest over the door. Well-fed stray dogs loitered in the doorway and just outside. Hipshot had learned to keep his curiosity to himself, so he stood stoically while four other dogs sniffed him. When he got annoyed and nipped at a German shepherd mix, the other pooches left him alone.

Thank goodness. Kendra had enough trouble with human politics.

Even with Hipshot trotting at her side, Kendra knew she shouldn't be out alone at night. But the returning scavs at the dining hall had reported that Terry and Piranha were probably at the bar, a rite of initiation.

The Twins and Jackie were off having their own adventure, and all Sonia and Ursalina wanted to do was plot about how to ingratiate themselves to Wales and Threadville. Sonia had been eager to sift through the clothes she'd acquired that day, trying to find a way to look cute. Did she care that Piranha was half blind?

Without Terry, Kendra felt alone again. The intensity of the loneliness surprised her, a heavy cloak that had robbed the taste of food from her mouth. She didn't know how to tell if it was love or just mourning, but she needed to be with Terry, even if it meant walking at night to a bar full of rowdy strangers.

No Credit was spray-painted on the wood outside the door. *No Cash, Either. 2 Drink Limit.*

The bar was loud enough to be heard for blocks, spewing

off-key, off-beat music. With one guy playing the upright piano, a woman strumming an acoustic guitar, a teenage boy on fiddle, and a long-haired person of ambiguous gender pounding the drum kit, Kendra almost recognized the music. Between songs, the crowd clapped and cheered like they were at a U2 concert. The intro to "The Devil Went Down to Georgia" was so bad that Kendra was afraid to hear the rest.

A burly dude in a fleece-lined denim jacket waited just inside the doorway. Bouncer. It was hard to see his face; the only light inside was from candles and lanterns, so all she saw was a bushy beard. He looked like a pirate, except he didn't stink.

"Uhm . . . Can I come in?" Kendra said. "I'm looking for . . ."

He waved her inside. "You're older'n fourteen," he said. "Old enough to work, old enough to drink. Hell, you might not live to twenty-one." His voice and face were way too jovial, but he wasn't joking.

"Ain't all she's old enough for!" a nearby man called, and his table laughed. Kendra refused to look in his direction. She was glad she'd worn her heavy jacket to dinner, and tried to shrink inside it.

"Keep Lassie leashed," the bouncer said.

Keep your customers leashed, Kendra thought, clinging tightly to Hipshot. There were more dogs inside, sniffing at tables or sleeping across the walkways. Only a few of the dogs were leashed close to their masters; the others seemed like regular customers.

In Domino Falls, dogs were truly man's best friend.

She'd almost given up on finding Terry when she heard a familiar laugh from a group of men huddled at a small round table near the dartboard.

"So I said, 'You gonna shoot her or kiss her?'" one of the men finished, and the table of men laughed in unison, nearly falling over in their hysterics. Terry and Piranha were laughing harder than the rest. Someone patted Piranha on the back.

There was no room at the table for her, so Kendra hesitated. Terry and Piranha were bonding with the guys they worked with. Would Terry want to see her now?

The answer came when Hipshot barked. Terry looked over at her, and his face broke into a grin. He climbed over Piranha and the man at the end of the table as he came to her. He leaned down to peck her lips, like they were an old married couple.

"What are you doing here?" he said, still grinning, breathless. His face was ruddy. "This place is kinda rough."

"Tell me about it. But I wanted to see how your scavenging went."

"She just grazed me," Terry said, turning over his shoulder to share a private joke. Scav humor. The table laughed again. Terry steered Kendra toward the bar counter, tugging at his pocket. "Oh! Let me get you a drink."

For a moment, Kendra expected Terry to pull out his wallet, maybe an ATM card. Instead, he pulled out a two-pack of AA batteries. He winked at her. "These are like gold bars. You'll need to get stamped. Two-drink limit. Some kind of town law. If you want a buzz, there's vendors with warm beer and weed out back."

Kendra didn't need any buzz other than seeing Terry in one piece, still here, but Terry had reached the shiny bar. Kendra saw eyes hanging on the pack of batteries, which he was holding high enough for everyone to see. Was Terry limping slightly?

"Gimme one for the young lady, Louie!" Terry called. "Keep the change!"

Patrons in the crowded bar grinned, but Kendra noticed steel in some of the smiles. Showing off wasn't a good idea in front of people who had lost everything.

A foaming mug slid to him across the bar right away. Terry grabbed it for her. An unsmiling bartender absently stamped her palm with a red smiley face.

"Cold beer!" Terry said, still amazed by the sight. "Whooo-hooooo!"

"You can have it," she said, but he might not have heard her. She'd never seen Terry so wired, and she didn't think it was from the alcohol, even if he'd had more than one drink. She held the mug but didn't sip from it.

"Was it scary?" Kendra said.

Terry nodded and puffed his cheeks full of air.

"What about Piranha?"

"He got new contacts. Wearing 'em now."

"You going back out?"

"Not if I can help it," Terry said. He moved closer to her ear, and in the glow of a candle on the bar counter, she saw his troubled eyes. "No respect for the dead," he said.

Ugh. Terry and Piranha had been scavenging corpses, not just dodging freaks. He must have showered a long time, or she would have smelled the day on him.

"I'm sorry," she said, and nuzzled his cheek.

"I'd love a cold beer," said a woman who sidled up to Terry. She was maybe in her late twenties and model thin, as tall as Terry. Her face and hair seemed plain, but she'd chosen her jeans and tight-fitting turtleneck with care. Her blond hair floated on a cloud of perfume. Kendra's stomach soured at the way she pinched Terry's bicep.

At least a dozen other women were at the bar too, and several were gazing at Terry. Kendra hadn't wondered how Terry looked to other women, but suddenly his wavy brown hair and broad shoulders made him a target. Not to mention his double-As.

"Aren't you at your limit?" Terry said to the blonde.

She held up clean palms. "Thought I'd save myself for the right man."

On another night, Kendra might have been more amused than annoyed. Instead, she imagined herself ordering Hipshot to attack Blondie: *Freak, Hippy! Freak!* Kendra thrust herself between them, a boldness she'd never had in her old life.

"You can have this one," Kendra said, handing the woman her mug. "Bye."

Kendra hadn't planned to narrow her eyes to homicidal slits, but the blond woman got the message. She took the mug and raised it in a toast to Terry. "Welcome to Threadville," she said. "Let me know when you graduate from kindergarten."

Then she walked away like a woman who expected men to watch her walk.

"Why'd you give that to her?" Terry said. "Do you know how much beer costs?"

"I should have thrown it at her."

"Easy," Terry said. "No competition here, Kendra." Terry was gazing at her the way he had at the beach, then leaned forward and kissed her lightly. "Come with me while I hang out with the guys. Where's Sonia?"

Sonia better keep an eye on Piranha. Apparently, the Hungry Dog was more like the Horny Bitch. "In our room," Kendra said. She didn't want to say that Sonia was choosing clothes for her visit to Wales's mansion. "She said she'd see him later."

They both left it at that. Talking about Piranha and Sonia might be bad luck.

When they got back to the table, Terry pulled up a chair for her, and everyone scooted around to make room. Piranha leaned over to kiss her cheek. He didn't ask about Sonia.

"When I was growing up here, Domino Falls was just a wide

space in the road," said the jokester, spiraling off into a history lesson. A Gold Shirt, Kendra realized when she saw his shirt hanging across his chair back. She'd heard the others call him Cliff. "Most of it owned by a Spanish mining family, made a little gold strike back about 1890. They bought some land, named it after a local waterfall that dried up in 1910, when they put in new irrigation. Just a few farms, then the fence manufacturer. Then twenty years ago Wales came in. No one knew who he was, except he had money. Lots of it. And Hollywood flash. He bought up most of the town after his movie came out."

"How'd that sit with the town?" Piranha said. He was still wearing his shades; despite the new contacts, his eyes still bothered him.

"Didn't have much to say about it," Cliff said. "He owned most of it by then. We thought he was strange and that his Threadies were wacko. But harmless, overall."

"What about Freak Day?" Kendra said. "How'd it happen here?"

A hush fell over the table. Cliff's voice grew sober. "We'd heard the news bulletins. San Francisco, Oakland . . . rioting. Lot of traffic on the Five, but how could we believe those stories? It was like something out of a movie." He sighed. "Then came Manny Cobb. Older guy. Retired dentist. Rotary Club president. Drove his car into a ditch, ran into town biting everyone he found. Another one came through an hour later, and then we were just flat crawling with them. Never thought I'd see anything like it."

He picked up his mug for a swig, but it was empty. He barely seemed to notice. The mug was just a comfortable habit from before, like the bar.

"How'd you keep clear?" Terry said.

"I locked myself in the basement. Pissed in a bucket for a

week. The freak attack must have wiped out every town for fifty miles."

"How'd you survive *after* the basement?" Piranha said.

"Not how," Cliff said. "Who."

Two other men at the table raised their empty mugs to clank them together.

"Wales," Cliff and the men said in unison, and Cliff went on: "His estate. They'd been using it for parties . . . role-playing Threadie games. He had high, safe walls. Professional guards. Gates. And he had a school bus—like yours," he said, nodding at Terry. "Mounted loudspeakers, took it out into the town. Gave cover to the survivors, got them out to the ranch. Took in half the town, maybe two hundred people—the half that survived. And then we took the town back, freak by freak."

"What's the deal with you guys?" Piranha said. "The Gold Shirts?"

"Gold Shits," one of the men murmured, and the other chuckled.

"I didn't hear that," Cliff said. "Shirt's off."

"Who do you work for?" Kendra said. "Wales or the town?"

"Depends on who you ask," Cliff said. "But Wales pays me, not the so-called mayor. Wales runs the show here. That's the first thing you better figger out."

Way ahead of you, Kendra thought.

"Wales had these idiots he called the Threadie Irregulars. Got all amped up playing war games from his books. So when the world ended, they had contingency plans. They were ready. The ones that weren't total loonbags became the first Gold Shirts. The rest of us earned our way in. Most of the Threadies couldn't fight their way out of a bag of popcorn."

The table laughed again.

The bar stirred with excitement, heads turning, and Kendra

glanced up to see the Twins saunter through the doorway, arm in arm in arm with Jackie, who walked between them, rolling her hips with every step. The Twins were a memorable sight in their matching bomber jackets. Darius spotted them right away, so they came to the table with Jackie in tow. Cynically, Kendra remembered that Jackie had latched onto the Twins as soon as they walked through the front gate. The blond skank could have learned a thing or two from Jackie. Kendra bet the Twins were learning quite a bit.

"They live and breathe!" Darius said, grinning. Piranha and Terry stood up to greet them with full hugs, like brothers after a long separation. Maybe they were.

But instead of listening to a humorous story Piranha was telling the Twins about a female runner chasing their truck, Kendra watched Jackie lean over Cliff on the other side of the table. Jackie's eyes glinted.

"Well?" she said.

Cliff shrugged. "Well what?"

They sounded like exes having a spat. Jackie pursed her lips and glared. Kendra had to read lips to understand them over the bar chatter.

"What do you expect me to do, Jax?" Cliff said.

"You said you'd ask around."

"I did ask around, and nobody's heard anything. Just relax. Let Sam ask."

Jackie made a hissing sound, her face getting red. "You know Sam's just glad to have his shirt. He's not gonna ask questions that'll—"

Cliff leaned closer to her. ". . . makes two of us. Don't do this now. You barely know that girl. Let me buy you a drink."

"Beer won't fix a broken promise," Jackie said. "I'm real disappointed, Cliff."

140

"Well, you've got plenty of company to cheer you up."

That pretty much killed conversation, and Kendra knew they were exes for sure. They stared each other down a moment longer before Jackie pulled away and pasted on a bright smile to return to the Twins. Whatever was bothering her, she'd yet to share it with Darius and Dean. With them, she was fun and games.

Kendra felt the same unease she'd felt watching Brownie at the dining hall. She *had* to find out what Jackie and the Gold Shirt had been arguing about.

Kendra followed Jackie into the bar's wood-paneled ladies' room. The two-stall bathroom was surprisingly clean even if the dark was forbidding. The candles near the sink didn't cast light into the stalls, but they had real toilet paper and, more important, actual working toilets.

Kendra forced herself to pee while Jackie stood in the mirror applying makeup. When Kendra washed her hands, Jackie was packing her eyeliner away, ready to go. "Aren't the Twins awesome?" Kendra said, reaching for conversation.

Jackie stared at her with an arched eyebrow, suspicious. "Yeah," she said finally.

Jackie made a move toward the door, so Kendra blurted, "Do people go missing here a lot? Like Brownie's daughter?"

Jackie froze. Slowly, she turned around to look at Kendra, examining her. "What have you heard?" she said.

"Just . . . what you said at the table. You're looking for someone."

"A newbie grew on me," Jackie said. "Rianne. I haven't seen her in weeks." It was too dark to interpret the look she saw across Jackie's face. "Wales calls them his ambassadors."

"What kind of ambassadors?"

"Setting up agricultural trades. Weapon and equipment

trades. Spreading Threadie gospel. Wales has small planes, helicopters. He's recruiting people, some of them your age or a little older. Rianne decided to go for training, moved onto Wales's ranch. I haven't talked to her since."

"What happened to Brownie's daughter?"

"Sissy? Same deal," Jackie said. "She moved to the ranch to be an ambassador. Rianne kept saying she was gonna be a part of something special the last Friday of the month. Well, that's in a couple of days. I just wanted to talk to her and make sure she doesn't do anything stupid. Girls on the road? It's a bad idea."

"My friend was invited to the ranch," Kendra said. "We might go tomorrow."

Jackie silenced a dripping faucet with a hard twist of her wrist. "Don't get lost there," Jackie said. "And don't mention my name." Her voice was ice.

No one wanted to piss off Wales.

"I won't," Kendra said. "But if you want . . . I can try to ask about Rianne."

"Wouldn't be smart," Jackie said. "Asking the wrong questions will get you bounced back to the road. Maybe worse. My brother Sam's a Gold Shirt, but he's a good guy and he's told me stories. Be careful out there. Wales is running his own world."

Kendra felt a shiver. She should convince Ursalina and Sonia to forget about going to the ranch. No way was *she* going to Threadville's ranch now.

No. Way.

"But if you can," Jackie went on, her voice pained, "try to find out what's happening around here, maybe for your own good. Then get the hell out of there as fast as you can. And stay out."

Fifteen

December 22
6:45 a.m.

Terry didn't expect good news, but he wasn't ready to give up. He was up early despite his aching arms from lugging scav bags. He'd pulled a thigh muscle during the mad dash from Walmart, so he walked at a slow pace with the others toward the garage. Hipshot trotted ahead, tongue lolling happily.

Despite the early hour, everyone had agreed to go, especially Kendra. She was ready to start up the Blue Beauty and ease on down the road.

Yeah, right.

The others wanted only to retrieve the food, flashlights, and blankets they'd left back in their unheated rooms. Sonia was walking beside Piranha, but they barely looked at each other. Terry had roomed with Piranha again last night. The Twins walked in the rear, and Kendra was interrogating them.

". . . but she hasn't said *anything*?" Kendra said. "You've been hanging with her nonstop since we got here."

"Maybe it's girl talk," Darius said. "If she thought Threadville was such a bummer, she would have told us."

"Maybe she's keeping her options open," Kendra said.

Dean whistled a warning. "Play nice."

"She wants allies," Kendra said. "The more the merrier."

Ursalina chuckled and lit a cigarette with a match that popped like a sparkler. "Kid's got it all figured out."

Damn, Kendra was a pit bull. Terry scooped up an apple he spotted by the side of the road, only brown on a part of one side. He nibbled around the soft parts. It didn't feel like stealing since the fruit was rotting, but Terry kept an eye open for Gold Shirts. The apple was so good that Terry grabbed another one, and the others followed his lead. Fallen apples dotted the roadway, a reminder of how lucky they were. Food to spare!

Kendra sighed. "There are two girls missing—that we *know* of. They're *our* age. And Wales's movies are about weird stuff. Virgin sacrifice—"

"Oh, stop it," Sonia snapped. "It's not as if a Threadhead OD'd on movies. That's *fantasy*. Come to Wales's ranch and check it out for yourself."

Piranha threw an apple core at a tree trunk, smashing it. "Yeah, Kendra, and if you're worried about being sacrificed, Terry can give you some antivirginity insurance."

Everyone except Sonia and Kendra laughed, and Terry's face burned. Kendra was probably embarrassed, so she walked ahead with Hipshot, arms crossed.

"She needs to lighten up," Dean said. That was pretty funny, coming from him.

"I'll talk to her," Terry said. At the same time he wondered:

And say what? Kendra had probably expected him to jump to her defense, so she might be pissed at him too.

Terry caught Piranha's eye and gestured toward Sonia: *What's up?* Piranha shrugged, slowing his pace slightly, allowing Sonia to walk on with Ursalina.

"Whatever," Piranha said. His eyes still looked irritated, but not nearly as bad. After a hard fight, Terry had convinced him to take out both contacts and let his eyes rest overnight. Piranha said the new contacts were heaven.

"Sonia and her new girlfriend want to hang out and play dress-up for Wales," Piranha said. "Guess she's trading up. What about you and sister girl?"

Terry shrugged. He'd kissed Kendra good night at her door, but he'd kept it quick because of the staring eyes of other campers. "Time never seems right."

"Won't hurt my feelings if you get a new roommate."

Terry warmed himself with the idea of sharing a room with Kendra. Why not?

Trucks rumbled from behind them. Two scav crews were on their way to the city, crammed with six men each. Terry didn't see Cliff today or recognize the crews, but he and Piranha waved and called out good luck. The scavs waved back. The trucks blared music as they whizzed past. One of the newbies on the end looked scared to death.

"Don't do it, man," Terry said, resuming last night's argument. "We'll be shooters like Darius and Dean. We shoot tin cans and freaks, fix fences. It's nothing."

"Sounds great for you," Piranha said. "Not me. I'm gonna stay with the scavs."

The memory of runners stampeding after the truck made Terry's hands tremor, so he shoved them in his pockets. He'd loved having batteries to wave like thousand-dollar bills, but he'd never find Lisa if he died outside. He couldn't look out for Kendra.

"I don't get it, P," Terry said. "You weren't scared?"

"Yeah, I was," Piranha said. "I couldn't see, remember? That's why I couldn't drive the damned bus. And I'll still be scared. But I learned a lesson out there, man: there's no substitute for getting it yourself."

"What else do you need so bad?"

"I'll know it when I see it."

"No batteries are worth dying over."

"Unless they are," Piranha said, and how could Terry argue? In the wrong time and place, light could mean survival. Terry hoped Piranha wasn't trying to impress Sonia somehow; his efforts were being sorely wasted.

"Don't say nobody tried to stop you," Terry said, repeating his words to him.

Piranha sighed. "Scavs are free, man. They go get what they want."

They didn't say anything for the rest of the walk.

At the mechanic's house, a dog tied in the backyard barked as they came up the walkway, but Hipshot didn't answer. Hippy chose his conversations carefully in Threadville. No one was in sight. The windows were boarded, so Terry couldn't see light inside to tell if the mechanic was up yet.

It was early, but they knocked. Terry noticed a scuffed skateboard, and a red BMX racer that reminded him of his first childhood training bike. The sharp sting of his lost childhood assailed him; for once, the feeling didn't seem to have anything to do with the freaks.

After checking her peephole, the woman opened the door. Terry was glad she was already dressed and looked wide-awake, as if she'd been up for hours, but he didn't like the frozen phoniness in her face. *Bad news,* he thought.

She gave him the Beauty's key. "Nothing's been touched," she said. "You can unload what you want. I'll send Myles right out. We're just finishing breakfast."

At the bus, the others celebrated like it was Christmas Day, rediscovering supplies they'd forgotten. Kendra and Ursalina would get half shares when it was time to divide up the supplies—they'd earned that much in firefights—but that didn't matter yet. For now, it was a free-for-all.

"Thank you, God—*shampoo!*" Sonia shrieked. They'd always had shampoo and soap from camp, but rarely anywhere to stop to wash.

The others were gathering supplies by the armloads, loading up on flashlights that hadn't worked in weeks and lamps from the camp they hadn't been able to use at all. Access to batteries changed everything. Piranha had a point.

"Don't bring too much," Terry said. "Nobody's watching the rooms all day."

Ursalina held up a pocketknife. "And don't forget small items for trade."

Kendra waited outside the bus, hugging herself, staring toward the house. Terry rubbed her shoulder before he climbed into the Beauty, his thigh complaining. Touching her made him remember Piranha's offer to vanish that night.

Broken glass littered the Beauty's floor like tiles. The cracked green leather driver's seat waited, still flat from the journey. It was already hard to believe they'd slept on these seats, but dammit, the bus felt like his only home.

Terry sat and slipped the key into the ignition. "Come on, girl," he whispered.

He turned the key. Not even a click. The Beauty was so ghost silent that no one noticed the key's turn except for Kendra, who watched sadly from the open doorway.

Terry's mind did acrobatics, sparked by Kendra's paranoia. What if the Beauty had been sabotaged? What if Threadville didn't *want* them to leave? He tried the key again.

"Mechanic's coming," Kendra said in a dull voice.

Behind her, the family was approaching, even the kid. They looked as grim as a medical team notifying the next of kin. Terry climbed out of the bus to meet Myles. The others leaned through the windows to hear his report.

"Well," Myles said, "the transmission is pretty much fried, and the suspension's shot." Terry had never taken auto shop, but that didn't sound good.

"English?" Terry said.

"Means you're stuck here. At least for a while. I don't know how this vehicle got you over the state line."

"There's no way to fix it?" Kendra said. She sounded as heartbroken as Terry felt.

Myles shook his head. "Even if I could cannibalize every truck I have—and that's stealing—I'm not sure I could get her moving."

"Would anyone sell us parts?" Terry said.

Myles shook his head with a sour chuckle. "Parts she could use don't come along every day. You'd be better off paying a scav to bring you some wheels. You have enough gas to grab one of the junkers along the road. Sometimes traders bring vehicles to sell, but it's cheaper to train your own scavs."

Terry felt a sharp sadness, realizing that the pirates at the pass had cut the Beauty down. She'd gotten them to Domino Falls with her last gasps.

Kendra had slipped her hand into his. "We can't be stuck here. We *can't.*"

148

The earnestness in her voice made the mechanic's wife cock her head to the side, studying Kendra. She even took a step toward her, as if to protect her. "You don't like it here, sweetheart?" she said.

"She's not speaking for me!" Darius called. Sonia, Ursalina, and Dean agreed.

The mechanic's wife caught Kendra's eye, a silent language between them. Terry squeezed Kendra's hand to keep her quiet, but he was too late.

"Do you know that guy, Brownie, who can't find his daughter?" Kendra said.

Myles's face turned to stone. Their kid, Jason, moved closer to his mother, staring up at her with wide eyes, as if to ask: *Well? What are you going to say?*

"We do some business with Brownie," Myles said, his voice clipped. "Haven't heard anything about his daughter."

The mechanic was lying! Alarm bells sounded in Terry's head.

"Kendra's just excitable," Terry said, trying not to show his concern.

"More like psycho," Darius muttered.

Kendra stepped closer to the mechanic's wife, speaking only to her. "I also heard there's another girl missing . . ." she said. "A . . . Rianne?"

Jason let out a small gasp. The mechanic's wife seemed to go pale.

Myles cursed. He glanced quickly toward the road, perhaps to see if they were being watched. "Come in the house," he said. "We can't talk out here."

• • •

The first thing Kendra noticed in the living room was a family photo on the mantel, perhaps five years old. Jason was shorter and younger, posing opposite a teenage girl who looked eerily like her. No wonder Deirdre had such a strong reaction to her!

"Where's your daughter?" Kendra said as soon as the front door was closed.

Deirdre picked up the photo, hugging its face to her stomach. "Imani was in school. Cornell, upstate New York. We haven't heard a peep in months."

The others had stayed outside to loot the bus, but Terry had accompanied Kendra into the mechanic's house. He was the only one who believed in her instincts—or he tried to, anyway. Mostly, Terry didn't like letting her out of his sight, a kind of protectiveness she thought she had lost with her family.

Deirdre pointed out a sofa, so they sat. The living room was surprisingly well decorated, Mexican and Southwestern art, and Kendra wondered how many of the furnishings had already been in the house when they arrived. One family out, another in.

"You ask a lot of questions," Myles said.

"She gets excited," Terry said. "She doesn't mean anything by it."

"I'm just trying to figure out what we've gotten ourselves into," Kendra said. "I'm grateful to be here, but . . . are you from this town?"

Myles glanced at his wife. "Past five years, but it's changed . . . a lot. Most people are gone. After the worst was over and I thought Deirdre and Jason were safe, I fixed up some cars, formed a crew. All of us had folks east. We made it as far as Phoenix. But . . ." The cloud that passed across his face probably meant that some of his crew had died. Kendra couldn't imagine crossing the country now.

"He was gone a month," Deirdre said, the memory bitter in her mouth. Jason stood close to his father, one arm hooked around him. Jason was tall enough to be thirteen, but he acted younger, just like she had with Grandpa Joe. The sudden memory of Grandpa Joe seemed to kick Kendra in the stomach.

"I had to try," Myles said. "Not knowing only makes it harder."

Terry made a sympathetic sound. *At least I know what happened to my family,* Kendra thought, although her knowledge felt more like a wound than a comfort. She would rather fantasize that they had survived.

"What do you know about the missing girls?" Kendra said.

"Rianne fell in with the Threadies, like Brownie's Sissy," Deirdre said. "About a month ago, she came and told us how excited she was because she'd been chosen for 'special duties' by Wales. But she wouldn't say what. She was going to the ranch every day, staying long hours. One day, she never came home. When we ask, all they'll say is that she's in training, whatever that means. But we can't talk to her."

"She lived here?" Terry said.

Deirdre nodded sadly. "Ja . . ." She stopped herself. "One of the townspeople brought her from camp, thought she'd fit in with us. She was new, practically alone. Seventeen, but so sheltered."

Had she been about to name Jackie when she stopped herself? *Innocent,* Jackie had called Rianne. Jackie had felt fondness for Rianne, found her a safe place to live. Myles sighed. "It was almost like . . ."

". . . Imani was home," Jason finished. "Rianne reminded us of her. A lot."

No one in the family had dry eyes, suddenly. Myles looked away.

"Have you talked to the mayor?" Kendra said.

"Van Peebles?" Myles said. "Just a figurehead. He can't do nothing."

"So, wait," Terry said. "This girl vanished at the ranch? And nobody will let you talk to her?" He looked at Kendra, the situation dawning on him.

"Just like Brownie's daughter," Kendra said.

"Brownie stood up in the dining hall and made a fuss," Deirdre said.

"Made accusations right to Wales's face, so we hear," Myles said, nodding. "Brownie's got guts. When it comes to family, you do what you have to."

Their tones were casual, but there was nothing casual in their words. Kendra could almost feel the floor moving beneath her feet, like the time she'd felt the tremors of a six-point earthquake in L.A.

Kendra had planned to do her best to talk Sonia and Ursalina out of their planned excursion to the ranch later. She had vowed not to set foot on the grounds. Never.

Now, nothing could keep her away.

Threadrunner Ranch

The tyrant is only the slave turned inside out.
—Egyptian proverb

Sixteen

4:30 p.m.

A white van drew a crowd up at the Motel 6. Its side was painted with a glittering gold TR insignia: Threadrunner Ranch.

The driver was a Gold Shirt . . . but more than a Gold Shirt. In addition to the customary garb, he wore glittery gold brushes on his shoulders and had a row of medals pinned across his breast like a four-star general. His black gold-rimmed Captain Hook hat was the crowning absurdity. Kendra expected him to break into song like an Oompa-Loompa. If she hadn't been worried about the consequences, she might have burst out laughing as soon as he hopped out to open the van door.

"Can you believe this?" Sonia whispered, charmed.

"No, not really," Ursalina murmured to Kendra, and giggled. Actually giggled. Kendra hadn't been entirely certain Ursalina could even make sounds like that.

Kendra hadn't spent her night obsessing over what to wear,

so she'd been stuck with the dowdy castoffs left on the beds. Better than jeans, anyway. She wore a black pleated skirt that almost reached her ankles and a lacy black blouse that was too big for her, so she had a tank top underneath. She hadn't found any pumps or sandals, much less heels like Sonia's, so she was still wearing her dirty sneakers. But the gathering crowd made her feel like a celebrity being picked up by a stretch Hummer. Someone whistled, probably at Sonia's short dress or Ursalina's firm calves.

"Good afternoon, ladies," the Gold Shirt said with a bow. "It will be my honor to drive you to the ranch." Did he have an English accent? She was almost sure.

No Dogs, said a sign in the van's window, in bright red ink. *That* was a first.

The van was spotless, with plush leather seats as soft as a baby's cheek. As she boarded, Kendra thought about Rianne, wondering if the van had looked like a prince's carriage when it came to fetch her at the mechanic's boarded-up house.

A DVD played a little too loudly from overhead: a collection of clips from Threadrunner movies, tanks and soldiers battling insects the size of Transformers. But she knew the DVD was a distraction. Kendra reminded herself to mentally map where they went, and how far.

On the screen, Wales appeared in a fatherly turtleneck, sitting in front of a fireplace. He raised a steaming coffee mug and smiled. "Welcome to Threadrunner Ranch," he said.

"Where are we going—Universal Studios?" Ursalina whispered.

"Where's the shark?" Kendra said, but disguised her giggle as a cough, so convincingly that Sonia didn't even notice, mesmerized by the TV screen above them.

"Located just two miles outside of the gold rush town

of Domino Falls, California, Threadrunner Ranch is my lifetime's pride and joy after a film and television career spanning more than thirty years." He blinked, expression somber. "But as we all know, those days are past. What we once knew as Hollywood is a burned-out freak zone. Gone are the frontier fantasies about gold twinkling in the hills. Our world has changed in the blink of an eye, and every one of us has suffered personal losses we never imagined our hearts could survive. Now, we only have each other—and the threads that bind us."

Despite the cheese factor, a tear came to Kendra's eye. Tears were never far.

"My home is now your home," Wales went on, and Kendra's guard was back up. *Yeah. That also means your home is* his *home.*

"Our destiny hasn't brought us together by accident. Soon you'll understand, as I do now, that coincidences are only a myth. How do I know? I saw it in a dream."

His image dissolved, and suddenly the screen was filled with tiny red tendrils spiraling down from a black, blood-streaked sky.

Kendra's mouth dropped open.

On the screen was Kendra's dreams.

A dream. For Sonia Petansu, that was the only word that fit. For the first time since Christmas morning when she was four, waking to a wonderland of gifts in her living room, she pinched her arm to make sure she was awake.

It was as if Freak Day had never happened. Erased.

She'd found shampoo, so her hair smelled like hers again.

157

She was wearing a black cocktail dress she would have bought—or at least swiped—from Macy's. It fit her so well that she'd barely recognized herself in the Motel 6 mirror. And after being stripped of every aspiration, suddenly she was about to fulfill the fantasy she'd talked about with her friends at every ThreadieCon: their pilgrimage to the ranch. *The* ranch.

And now they were here.

Threadville Ranch was nestled in the hills east of Domino Falls, guarded by a twelve-foot gate that stretched like the Great Wall of China. The Threadrunner complex, which looked like about a hundred acres of vineyards and quaint colonial outbuildings, was surrounded by hundreds of acres of undeveloped land. Dozens of Gold Shirts patrolled the fenced perimeter, holding German shepherds by their leashes. Freaks lurched across the distant hillside like lost, hungry cattle, too many to count. They seemed a world away. The ranch was well guarded.

They were hustled through a whirlwind of checkpoints where it seemed every uniform was fancier and more elaborate than the last—culminating with the Gold *Coat* who met them inside the house's gleaming marble foyer. His coat hung past his knees in a princely fashion.

"Like a fairy tale," Sonia whispered to Kendra, who hadn't said a word since the van ride, when she couldn't stop staring at the DVD playing on the screen.

The sprawling foyer was a museum, the walls covered with lighted display cases, movie posters, and enlarged book covers. A tattered gray raincoat in the nearest display case leaped out to Sonia on sight: Wales's coat from *Threadrunner Apocalypse,* the one that had whipped around in slow-mo when he'd been attacked by the giant grasshopper with the human head. Sonia had skipped school to see the Threadrunner double feature with her friends, returning home to find she'd been ratted out by her little brother. Tears pooled in her eyes, pricked by deep nostalgia. The past seemed close enough to touch.

"That's from the shoot," their guide said in a basso whisper. "He wore it."

"Cool." Even Ursalina agreed.

When Wales was suddenly in the room, Sonia's weight seemed to vanish, as if she could float away on her dream.

"There you are!" Wales was walking straight to her with a grin as if they had known each other for years. "I hoped you'd come today, Sonia. You and your friends. This is a good time to visit. We're all very excited."

Yes, Sonia tried to say, *we're all excited too.* The floating sensation came so strongly that Sonia's ears failed her, so she missed some of Wales's welcome.

". . . reason for our existence here, after all," he finished with a good-natured laugh, patting her shoulder. She knew he'd said something vitally important, even life-altering, but she'd missed it because she couldn't keep her thoughts in order when he was in the room.

"Let me show you ladies around."

From the outside, Threadrunner Ranch looked like a prison dressed up as a mansion, which Kendra did not consider a good sign. Still, that wasn't what bothered her most and made it hard for her to keep her thoughts in a single line.

She couldn't stop thinking about the DVD.

How did he know my dreams?

The DVD could have been a bizarre coincidence, or maybe

the dreams were only a false memory, but her mind wouldn't let it go. The déjà vu feeling sharpened once they were in the mansion's foyer, as if she had been here many times before.

No, that wasn't it—she felt like she'd been meant to come, as if it was the sole reason she'd been spared when Grandpa Joe was bitten.

"Kendra, is it?" Wales was standing directly in front of her, and he seemed like a tall oak above her. Kendra didn't remember telling him her name.

"Yes."

He squeezed her hand with his soft palm, free of work calluses.

"I'm especially glad *you* came," Wales said. She'd never seen such earnestness in any man's lingering gaze, even Terry's. Wales stared as if they shared a great, wonderful secret. She felt herself leaning toward him, waiting for him to reveal what they both already knew.

Was he hypnotizing her? She'd been to other mansions and met other celebrities when her parents worked in Los Angeles, so she shouldn't be starstruck. But there was *something* about Wales . . .

Something about her . . .

Something about . . .

What?

I've been having Thread dreams since before Freak Day, she realized.

The thought startled her so much that she nearly blurted it aloud, but she could swear that Wales seemed to know already. He kept glancing at Kendra the way he might a daughter who was expecting her first child, watchful and gentle while he guided them through his museum and library. A large number of bookshelves were dedicated to international editions of

Threadie books, but the library was also stocked with enough classics and DVDs to make her wish she could spend a day exploring.

Kendra fought to pull herself out of her daydreams. She had to listen to try to learn something about Rianne and Brownie's daughter, Sissy. Terry was right: she couldn't just barge in and ask questions, not with an army outside. How could she find out without courting disaster?

"You'll have to come back and spend some time in our Special Collections," Wales said to her. Secrets played happily behind his eyes, teasing her.

"I thought I might like to be an ambassador," Kendra said, her voice soft.

"A what?" Ursalina said.

Wales's face changed, his cheeks sloughing off their too-bright smile.

Kendra was sure she'd jumped in too fast, just like Terry kept warning her. But the light in Wales's eyes put her at ease. The smile returned, full of delight after the surprise had passed. "Would you?" he said. "Then you're familiar with our program?"

"Ambassadors to the others," Kendra heard herself say, full of confidence. "Wherever they are."

Wales waved toward his attendant suddenly, and the Gold Coat held up a small notebook. "Is that K-E-N-D-R-A?"

Kendra spelled her first and last names, feeling breathless. She might be digging herself deeper into trouble. What if she wasn't allowed to leave with the others? If he said she should start her training right away?

Sonia's face was pinched with irritation. "You don't know anything about Threadie culture," she said pointedly.

Kendra's face flared. She felt like she was back in high school, sparring with the head cheerleader to catch the attention of the star quarterback.

"I'm here to learn," Kendra said, trying to sound lighthearted. "And the ambassadors program sounds like a great way to travel and see what's left."

"No," Wales corrected her gently. "To see what's beginning."

Kendra nodded. "Exactly. I want to see what's next."

Then she purposely took two steps away from Wales, toward Ursalina, just to show Sonia she wasn't trying to jump in her way. Sonia gave her a grateful smile before she darted to take her place.

"That *does* sound like a great program," Sonia said, snatching the baton. Wales's face soured just long enough for Kendra to notice. Then he flashed his smile again and seemed to disappear into Sonia.

"There are a host of other jobs here, not just ambassadors," he told her. "We'll find a place for you, darlin'."

Sonia's face glowed. Wales was flirting with Sonia, different from the way he had been with her.

"A real *pendejo*," Ursalina muttered to Kendra. "But what's he selling?"

Kendra hoped they were out of earshot of the Gold Coat who was walking slightly ahead of them. But maybe not.

"He's selling hope," Kendra said. It wasn't a lie, but it wasn't the whole truth.

"Don't jump into the fire to get warm, *chica*."

Kendra nodded, but she had already jumped.

". . . in the kitchen . . ." Wales's voice prattled. "You wouldn't be interested in housekeeping or groundskeeping, but we have decorators . . . radio operators . . ."

"Yes, I've been to the radio station!" Sonia said, as if they were soul mates.

Kendra was admiring Sonia's poise when she felt a steady burr, a pulsing thrum that seemed to shake the floor. The feeling grew stronger as she trailed Wales, Sonia, and the Gold Coat through the vast hall.

Was it an earthquake?

Kendra grabbed the wall for balance, but the others walked steadily on, unaware. Sonia never stopped asking questions about the ranch, and Ursalina never gave her a glance to say *Did you feel that?*

Her nervous breakdown must have arrived. What had taken so long?

Wales threw a gaze at her over his shoulder. His lips were moving, talking to Sonia, but his eyes were talking to her again. *We're the only ones who feel it, Kendra,* Wales's eyes seemed to say. *Don't be afraid.*

Then Wales smiled at her. It was the closest Kendra had come to believing she knew what was in someone else's mind.

"If you have special skills, of course, I'd love to know what they are," Wales said to Sonia, not missing a beat.

Kendra felt dizzy. Had someone drugged her? But when? What was going on?

Her legs stopped walking. The pulsing tremors stole the strength from her knees, forcing her to rest her palm against the wall.

And her palm met another's. Kendra was certain that someone else stood on the other side of the wall, palm pressed to hers. She could almost feel the heat of the fingers splayed open on the other side of the block of marble, a perfect mirror.

Someone was there—a massive presence, like a lodestone concealed behind a sheet of paper.

Was this where the pulsing was coming from?

There are no dogs in here, Kendra realized, such a random

thought that she was *sure* she'd been drugged. A sign in the van had banned dogs, she remembered. Scores of dogs patrolled outside, but she hadn't seen one inside.

But Threadville Ranch needed more dogs. Any dogs in the library or this vast hall would have been barking themselves hoarse. There was no actual *smell* in the air, but every fiber of her being said that the hall, the foyer, maybe Wales's entire mansion . . . reeked of freaks.

Seventeen

Kendra's shaking didn't stop until she was back at the Motel 6, knocking on Terry's door. A glance inside, and she saw Piranha lounging on his bed. She didn't want to hear jokes about virgin sacrifice, so she kept her mouth shut.

"What?" Terry said, concerned.

Kendra shot her eyes toward Piranha, and they both understood.

"Give us a minute?" Terry said to Piranha.

"Thought we were heading over to dinner," Piranha said. "I'm hollow."

Terry gave him a look that could melt iron, so Piranha shrugged. "Ya'll have five minutes. Sonia back in your room?" Piranha asked Kendra on his way out.

Kendra nodded, but it felt like a lie. Sonia was back in the room physically, but she was nowhere Piranha would find her. At the ranch, Sonia had said that she would stay behind, since Wales had offered guest bungalows for the night. They had practically dragged Sonia back to the waiting white van. Sooner or later Sonia would go back to Wales's mansion; she was probably already laying plans.

The memory of the ranch danced across the hairs on Kendra's arms. Her hand still seemed to vibrate from touching the wall—from *something* on the other side. She had thought the feeling would go away once Threadville Ranch was in the van's rearview mirror, but she had brought it with her.

And it would never go away. She didn't know how, but she knew that too.

"Good luck," Terry said to Piranha.

"Gonna take more than luck," Piranha said. The depth of his sadness surprised her.

And he was gone.

"What happened?" Terry said. "What's got you so worked up?"

Now that she was free to talk, Kendra didn't know what to say.

Terry came closer. "Hey, are you shaking? Here, Kendra." He pulled a thin brown blanket from the bed and draped it over her shoulders. The blanket smelled like it hadn't been washed since Freak Day, but it felt perfect because he had given it to her.

"What happened?" Terry prodded.

Kendra held up her palm as if Terry might *see* the feeling she'd brought back with her from touching the wall. She felt marked now. Terry only peered at her, confused, so Kendra hid her palm inside the blanket.

"Nothing I can describe," she said. "It's just . . . I got a very funny feeling there. The way Wales kept looking at me . . . Something's not right, Terry. I know it. The DVD player was showing my dream—exactly."

Terry looked concerned. She must sound crazy to him. "Did you see those missing girls?" he said, trolling for useful information.

Kendra shook her head. Terry was so much taller that she had to upturn her face to see his eyes. They were standing nearly close enough to touch, but Terry had never seemed farther away. What could she say to reach him?

"It felt like freaks inside," she said.

Terry's eyes narrowed. "Where?"

"Everywhere," she said. "It felt like freaks all over his damned ranch."

"Did you smell anything? Rotten oranges?"

She thought for a moment. "No. Nothing."

"See?"

Kendra shook her head. "No. I didn't say I smelled flowers but not freaks. I said I smelled *nothing,* as if there was some kind of odor-eater working overtime. Maybe one of those ozone generators or something."

Terry struggled to make sense of her, sighing when he failed. His eyes looked pitying instead of intrigued. He thought she'd had a nervous breakdown too, and she hadn't even told him about the loud noise, or how the floor had seemed to shake.

How often did crazy people realize they were crazy?

Terry slipped his hands inside the blanket to rub her shoulders above her jacket. When his warm lips touched hers, she knew she would stop trying to explain. For those seconds, Wales's ranch didn't exist.

"I'm not going to let anyone hurt you, Kendra," Terry said when the kiss ended. "Don't worry so much. We're safe. Let's go get some chow."

And kissed her again.

Her eyes fell closed, as if she were asleep on her feet.

His kiss carried her away.

Sonia left her room in such a hurry that she almost ran into Piranha on the way out. Her face drooped into a guilty frown.

Piranha hadn't seen Sonia with eye makeup on since the early days of camp, before the freaks, when she'd routinely sashayed past him to make sure he noticed her. He'd forgotten how dark mascara framed her eyes and made them leap to bright life.

But she hadn't dressed up her eyes for him.

"How was it?" he said, trying to sound neutral.

"Good."

A long silence wrapped around them. The doorknob was still in Sonia's hand, the door cracked open an inch, but she slowly pulled it closed. He'd seen in a glance that the room was empty, but Sonia wasn't inviting him in.

"Thought we'd talk," Piranha said.

Sonia snorted, as if to hide a laugh. He knew what she was thinking: after they started hanging out at camp, she'd cornered him from time to time saying, *Can't we talk? What do we call this?* He'd told her to play it cool, not to push so hard. He'd punished her by ignoring her for a day or two afterward, and she'd always come back as if she had to apologize. After Freak Day, she'd stopped asking to talk.

"Since when, Chuck?"

"You're right." Piranha's head screamed at him to keep his dignity and walk away. But he couldn't. "Where you headed so fast?"

"Trying to get to town before dinner shuts down."

"They didn't feed you at the Big House?"

Sonia's eyes flashed. "Oh, there was plenty! Fruit. Little bitty sandwiches. Egg rolls, even. But I was so busy taking it all in, I didn't eat much. So now I'm hungry." Her voice dared him to say another word about the ranch.

"Then I'll walk with you," Piranha said. "It's getting dark."

Sonia sighed, impatient. He followed her eyes to the motel's driveway, where two Gold Shirts were waiting at the edge of the road, smoking cigarettes. They were young, close to her age. "I met a couple of guys who said they'd walk with me."

The alarm panel in Piranha's hindbrain blared loud and bright red. He didn't know how he'd come to this crossroads so fast, but he had lost her. His anger was like a cloud of gasoline vapor: one wrong word might ignite it.

"Let me walk you instead?" He was careful to phrase it as a question.

Sonia sighed. "Piranha, look, I don't think—"

Not here, he thought. Not on the second-level balcony of a Motel 6 in the plain view of every camper in the parking lot and bored spies through the windows. Not when he didn't have anywhere else to go.

"I thought I was going blind," he said. "That's why I was a jerk. I was scared."

"All you had to do was trust me," she said. "You know it's not just that."

But Piranha didn't know, so he sighed with frustration. He and Sonia had weathered the worst time of their lives together, back when neither of them had anyone else. Now she was breaking away, an ice cap melting. She could barely look him in the eye.

When she began walking toward the stairs to the first level, Piranha didn't follow until she beckoned him. He walked behind her in silence. The road was flat, but the walk felt steep. He couldn't see a star in the sky beyond the fog.

"Let me talk to my friends," she said.

Downstairs, he hung back to give her the space with the Gold Shirts. One of them turned to give Piranha a glare. Piranha fought the urge to flip him the bird.

In the parking space nearest Piranha, a man was cooking a foul-smelling stew from God knew what scraps. Piranha wasn't sure why, but many of the newbies avoided group dinner, especially if they didn't have children, maybe for fear of imposing too much. Maybe for fear of something else. The old man's bundled belongings were piled in a cart, quickly replaced if he moved them. He was always ready for a quick escape.

"She's good as gone," the man said, nearly under his breath.

"Excuse me?" Piranha said.

The old man met his eyes, but only for a blink. "If she's got an eye on the Golden Boys. Nothing you can do about it except keep out of their way."

"Mind your business," Piranha said, even when he knew he should be thanking him.

The man grinned and chuckled, exposing a jagged hole where his front tooth was missing. His face was sun-broiled to shoe leather. "Fine by me. When you're back out on the road— or worse—don't consider it a mystery."

Piranha watched while the Gold Shirts turned to make their way toward town, without Sonia. He remembered the guy trying to see his daughter at dinner that first night, and the mechanic's family worried about a missing girl. Now a warning about the Gold Shirts. Coincidences? Realities of a harsher life? Or was it a pattern he needed to warn Sonia about until he was hoarse?

Sonia waved to him, beckoning.

"You know how it is." Piranha shrugged to the old man. "People have to learn for themselves." He was almost sure he could hear the old guy laughing behind him.

While he half-jogged to keep up with Sonia's rapid pace, Piranha had an epiphany: He loved Sonia. *Loved* her like no one he'd known who wasn't his blood. The revelation nearly shocked him, but the burning in his gut was all the evidence he needed. If he'd thought it would do any good, he would get down on his knees and beg.

But that would be the exact wrong move. And any warnings about Wales or the Gold Shirts were sure to sound like jealousy. He didn't want to piss her off. If he had to give up Sonia as his lover, he'd live with that, but he didn't want to lose his friend. Even walking in silence was better than avoiding each other.

"I get it," Piranha said finally, when they were close enough to downtown to see the glow from the lighted windows—a constellation of shimmering golden stars.

"You get what?"

"Wales," Piranha said. "It's not just about Threadville for you; you've always known about the Thread thing, and now, *bam.* Here you are. You want to be part of it. New history in the making, I guess."

Sonia looked at him suspiciously. "Right," she said, waiting for an attack.

"I'm not mad. I'm not gonna try to tell you what to do. But this is a big place, that's all. There's gonna be nice people, and people who can't spell 'nice.' So if somebody does anything you don't like, don't forget you're not here alone." His throat felt like sandpaper, but he forced the words out.

Bingo. Sonia's face softened into a girlish smile, her armor gone. "Thanks, P. I couldn't stand thinking you'd be mad. I want us to always be friends."

Friends. The word kicked him. She slowed her pace to give Piranha a quick peck on the lips, and she slipped her hand into his. Her fingertips were freezing cold, so he squeezed as they

171

walked, trying to keep her warm. Remembering the shape of her thin fingers. Pressing the pad of his thumb against her firm fingernails, one by one.

Most people were leaving the dining hall when they arrived, not going in. Families. Couples. Groups of traders. People walked close and kept their eyes alert, but everybody gave cordial nods or smiled. *Good to see you* had taken on a new meaning: *Thank you for not trying to bite me.*

The Twins were walking out of the dining hall with Jackie as they walked in. Darius gave him a thumbs-up sign when he saw him holding Sonia's hand, and Piranha's face went hot. He didn't feel like explaining that he was only Sonia's buddy now, so he winked a lie. When Sonia slipped her hand free to get her food tray, Piranha was glad. The bread was long gone, but the room still smelled like garlic butter.

Ursalina sat by herself smoking at a table in a far corner. Apparently, clean air recommendations had relaxed since Freak Day. She guessed nobody expected to live long enough to worry about secondhand smoke. They joined her there.

Within five minutes, Terry and Kendra had found them too, breathless from rushing as they set their plates of spaghetti on the table. They hadn't been alone long, but the brightness in Kendra's eyes was evidence that it had been long enough to do more than talk.

"You feeling better?" Ursalina said to Kendra, patting her hand. Kendra nodded.

"She's fine," Terry said. Piranha thought that if he'd hovered over Sonia the way Terry did over Kendra, she might still be his, Wales or no Wales.

"She felt a little sick at the mansion," Ursalina said.

Sonia gave Kendra a scornful look, as if she'd insulted Wales.

Piranha hoped Wales would be good for Sonia, or he and Wales would have an ugly future together.

"She's got a hell of an imagination, all right," Sonia said. "Or she's just crazy."

"All right," Terry said. Always the mediator.

Kendra stared at her food as she ate, ignoring Sonia. They might all need new sleeping arrangements soon.

"What did you think of Wales's place?" Terry asked Ursalina.

"Seemed all right," Ursalina said. "A little creepy culty, but nothing to wet your pants over." She sounded like she was scolding both Kendra and Sonia.

"And you couldn't feel it?" Kendra said suddenly. "It felt like that freakfield we drove past in the bus. How could you miss it?"

"I didn't smell any freaks," Ursalina said, probably for the dozenth time.

Kendra's voice dipped low. "That's why the sign on the van said no dogs! He doesn't want us to know."

You are out of your mind, Sonia said. "What do you think, he's got a secret freak factory? Maybe he's the one who started it all, right?" Her voice cracked.

The people at the table stopped eating to stare. Sonia, Terry, and the rest fell silent on cue. Two women in black dresses at the table were Threadies for sure. Two Gold Shirts joined the neighboring table, and Piranha recognized them as the guys who had been waiting for Sonia by the road. They never glanced toward Piranha, but they sat close to him. They knew he was there. *Jerks.*

But so what? Everyone said being a scav was the fastest way to get approved, if he didn't blow the politics. Ursalina was figuring out the politics in her way, Sonia in hers, and he would figure out the politics too. He was good at games.

173

Piranha moved to sit next to Terry, although it was hard to watch the way Terry leaned forward to lap up Kendra's every word, or the way she kept flicking strands of hair from his shoulders. He tried to feel happy for them, but he couldn't find anything except a pain like he'd swallowed a hot stone.

"Anybody else want some water?" Piranha said.

He wasn't that thirsty, but it was hard to resist the coolers and tin cups in the back of the room, free to anyone. Water was nothing to take for granted. Piranha gulped down two cups of the cold water just because he could.

He took his time getting back to the table, studying Wales's strange paintings on the wall. Webs and nets and constellations connecting all the stars in the sky into alien geometries. When a group of women he remembered from the Hungry Dog beckoned him to their table, he flirted politely even though all of them looked too old, or too everything, to keep his attention.

Piranha didn't glance at Sonia the rest of the night.

Eighteen

On the street, Kendra noted a few strings of Christmas bulbs strung here and there and was shocked to remember that the twenty-fifth was only days away. Apparently, despite the end of the world, 'twas the season.

Only one sign was lighted in bright white neon: THREADIE THEATER. The entrance to the alley beside the sign was crammed with a gathering crowd. *When people congregate, we warm ourselves in each other like firelight,* Kendra thought. She planned to write in her journal later.

"Awesome!" Sonia said. "I heard they show movies once a week. Like a drive-in, except nobody drives. And free popcorn!"

"Think I'll pass," Piranha said. He bumped shoulders with Terry, ready to go.

"Headed to the room?" Terry said. Piranha only shrugged, walking on.

"Hey, P? Wait up," Terry said, and ran to speak to Piranha privately.

Kendra tried to overhear them, but she could only watch as they rounded the corner. She thought she knew what was on Terry's mind, and it made her heart race. Suddenly her palms were sticky.

Ursalina glanced back at Piranha, as if to follow. Then she looked in the direction of the Hungry Dog a block away, weighing her options. Kendra could hear the piano's sour version of Bob Seger's "Old Time Rock and Roll."

"So tired, but so wired," Ursalina said.

"Should Piranha walk alone?" Kendra said, trying to prod Ursalina home. If she could coax Sonia to go home too, she might be alone with Terry. Besides, the Gold Shirt at the table next to theirs had been staring daggers at Piranha.

"That kid needs no bodyguard," Ursalina said.

"Let's give him some space," Terry said.

"Can we all stay and watch the movie?" Sonia said.

The word *we* grated in Kendra's ear, but the more time she spent around Threadies, the more she would learn. She felt safer on an open street in Threadville than she had in the seclusion of the ranch.

Besides, Kendra heard corn popping. The sound and smell reminded her of the last movie she'd seen with her parents. She couldn't name which movie, but she remembered sitting between them, nestled in their warmth. The popcorn's smell was a tunnel through time.

Kendra looked up at Terry. "Could be good times," she said.

Terry rubbed her shoulders. "Finally! Let's have some fun."

The only thing Kendra really wanted, she realized, was for Terry to rub her shoulders . . . and maybe work downward from there.

Many people had brought blankets to the surprisingly lush grassy field between two old brick buildings that were boarded

176

up like mummies. A blinding light from a third-floor window projected a giant white box on a sheet draped from the building across the alley. In Threadville's darkness, the box looked as crisp as a TV screen.

The light from the screen was bright enough to show that the grass was crowded with residents, many of them with their children chasing one another and squealing. Although the grass still had room, the back wall was crowded with scavs and other men and women talking, laughing, drinking, and enjoying the screen's light. There were a lot of Threadies, shiny-faced young women and Gold Shirts sharing blankets with their families in the grass, mostly in the front. But there were townies too, and several newbies.

Newbies were easy to spot. They were the ones staring up at the white movie screen with gaping jaws, or tears in their eyes, remembering their last time at a movie. The ones with fresh bruises. *It's easy to dazzle people who are already in shock,* Kendra thought, another line for her journal. And she would know, wouldn't she?

"Here," Terry said to Kendra, spreading his jacket out on the grass.

"What about you, Terry?" she said. "It's getting cold."

But Sonia joined in when Terry insisted, so Kendra sat on his warm jacket and enjoyed the smell of him. They all huddled close as Threadville's masses crowded around them.

"I'll get us popcorn," Terry said. The line to the old-fashioned popcorn carts in the back was twenty deep, maybe more.

"Grab me a Coke Slurpee and some Twizzlers!" Ursalina called, and strangers around them laughed.

"Butter on mine!" Sonia called.

Kendra was glad to giggle with her. The day at the ranch had erected a wall of mistrust between Kendra and Sonia, as if she and Sonia were breaking up too. Kendra didn't feel the uncomfortable knot anymore. She hoped it wouldn't come back.

"Can we stay friends . . . no matter what?" Kendra said.

Sonia wrapped her arm around Kendra. "When that psycho pirate on the snowmobile was firing at me, you held on tight and pulled me into that bus, Kendra. You saved my life. We're not friends—we're family."

"Back at you," Kendra said. "So don't just vanish on us."

"I'm not vanishing anywhere," Sonia said. "You know Terry, P, Darius, and Dean are brothers to me." Her voice cracked.

"I know," Kendra said quietly.

"But I have to follow my bliss," Sonia said. "You and Terry have to follow yours. Life starts right here, right now."

Ursalina chuckled. "No such thing as no regrets," she said. "But good luck."

Before Terry got back with the popcorn, the Gold Shirt who had been glaring at Piranha showed up with a friendly smile. He looked about nineteen, and Kendra remembered him as one of the guys outside of the ranch fence, maybe a newbie like them. Maybe his glares at Piranha were only childish jealousy.

And now he had no reason to be jealous. After all, he had won.

"Everybody, this is Chris," Sonia said, as if he'd been her date all along.

Chris nodded politely, shaking their hands one by one.

"Me and the guys have a blanket closer to the front," Chris said to Sonia.

"Ooh . . . sounds great! Thanks." Sonia grabbed Kendra's hand. "Want to come?"

Kendra's heart surged as she realized part of her *did* want to go. She wanted answers just like Sonia, even if she was asking different questions. She wanted to dive into Threadville and find the truth.

"No, I'll stay with Terry," Kendra said.

Sonia giggled. "Oh, right—*duh*. You guys be good." She wagged a finger at Kendra, drunk on her excitement. She knew Kendra was watching her walk away, so she turned to give her another reassuring wave before she vanished into the sea of strangers.

"Yeah, good luck with that," Ursalina said after Sonia was gone.

When the movie studio's logo appeared on the screen, the crowd hooted and cheered. The searchlights and trumpet fanfare were tokens of a civilization's man-made wonders. Kendra cheered with the rest, feeling the world shift into place.

Then the movie started: a bird's-eye view of a bright red sports car racing along a winding mountain road. Instantly, the movie's spell was broken.

Threadrunner Apocalypse! She hadn't been to the movies since the freaks, and they were showing the same one she'd just tried to watch on DVD? Was that a coincidence? Or was that the only movie that got any play in Threadville?

Kendra smelled the fresh popcorn before she saw Terry. He nestled close behind her. "Sorry it took so long. I kept staring at people. Everybody looks like Lisa tonight."

"You'll find her."

"One day." His warm breath skipped across her neck. "Where's Sonia?"

"Making friends," Ursalina said. She nodded toward the front rows.

"Guess that's no surprise," Terry said. "Same as Darius and Dean."

Kendra vaguely remembered a gatekeeper or one of the Gold

Shirts saying that groups liked to stay together in Threadville—
at first. The night felt sad, suddenly.

"'Scuse me?" a woman's voice whispered. She was in her
forties, and heavy for a survivor. People who couldn't run fast
enough had died first. "Are you Ursalina?"

Ursalina nodded, wary. The woman had come in close, too
fast for comfort.

The woman beckoned someone. "My nephew's been talking
about you all day."

Jaxon, the redhead from day care, came bounding to them,
his left arm's stump hidden in his jacket. Day care was a safe
space, but no one would advertise a child's disability.

"That's her!" Jaxon said, not quite a whisper.

"Quiet," the woman said. Then to Ursalina: "Would you like
to join us? We can't hold them all at once, and they like to sit
in somebody's lap. We can't trust just anyone. But if we get too
noisy, they'll make us go."

She pointed to a group about fifteen yards parallel to theirs,
four women trying to control a group of at least twelve children,
all of them under the age of seven. The children were arguing
over popcorn, eliciting soft hisses of *Shhhhh* behind them.
Kendra didn't recognize all the faces, so some of them weren't
in the day care. Half the children were mesmerized by the movie
screen, but the other half weren't.

"Sure, of course," Ursalina said, quickly on her feet.

"I'll come too," Kendra said.

"No way," Ursalina said. "Stay here. Let him help you work
it all out."

Just like that, impossibly, Kendra and Terry were alone. At
a movie.

Kendra felt a floating sensation, but it filled her with wonder,
not fear. Suddenly she was leaning back against Terry, a sturdy

tree trunk, and she was rising and falling with his breaths. Her fingertips and toes tingled.

And the popcorn! It rang with flavor, not bland like the food in the dining hall seemed in comparison. Salt must be like gold again, but someone had spared no expense.

This might be the most perfect moment in my life, Kendra thought with a distant, faraway voice that wasn't quite hers. Tears came to her eyes in a wave of guilt. How could she feel that way? And even if it were true, what would the next tragedy be?

A tragedy could come tonight.

Could come tomorrow.

Terry squeezed her hand, as if he could feel her anxieties pulling her away. She hid from her thoughts by staring at the movie screen.

The movie had already progressed beyond the brief viewing she'd had at the quarantine house. Wales had appeared—barrel chest and square jaw, unsoftened by too many years and too many beers. He *looked* like a hero, even if his acting might have embarrassed David Hasselhoff. He gestured a lot, reminding Kendra of a silent film star, as he made desperate attempts to convince a small-town sheriff that aliens had contaminated the cornfields with eggs like spider sacs. *"They'll take us from the inside out,"* said the giant Wales on the movie screen. *"Make us forget who we were."* A few in the audience gasped, seeing how prescient the movie had been.

Terry grinned. "I'm just glad we're finally on a real date."

He was right: they had a movie screen, a tub of tasty popcorn, and body heat to keep them warm.

"So . . . is this a date?"

He winced. "Oh, wait. Never mind. You're one of those proper girls. I'd have to put on a suit, meet your parents . . ."

He realized what he was saying. "Oh, damn, I'm sorry." He sounded so aghast that Kendra felt sorry for him.

Kendra tried to smile. "That's all right. Dad would have liked you. But I'm a little out of practice. This is my first date in a while."

Her first and only "boyfriend" in junior high had been in name only most of the time, except for necking sessions in his Toyota. Her disastrous eighth-grade dance with Taylor Pinkney probably shouldn't count as a date, but it was better than saying she'd never had one. When Kendra remembered the Pinkneys, she couldn't help wondering how they had died. Who had gotten infected first? Who had bitten whom?

She stared at Ursalina and the other women playing with the children, wondering again how people could bring babies into this world clotted with pirates and freaks.

When Terry leaned close to kiss her, the movie screen and the world disappeared. Kendra floated above time and memory, somewhere new. They might have only kissed for thirty seconds, but to Kendra it lasted all night.

"By the way," Terry said, more breath than voice. "Piranha's working it out so he's gonna get his own room."

Kendra didn't know what to say at first. She felt frozen. "Too bad about him and Sonia," she finally said, heart racing.

Terry squeezed her hand. His skin broiled her. "Yeah. Too bad."

Nineteen

When Terry opened the door and peeked into his room, he expected to find Piranha on the bed with an excuse about how Marv wouldn't give him his own space on such short notice. But Piranha's stuff was gone. He'd left the tiny battery lamp on the nightstand on, and his blanket was pulled up and tucked beneath his mattress like an army cot. He'd tried to leave the room looking nice for Terry.

I owe you, man, Terry thought. *Again.*

Hipshot waited by the door, tail wagging. The world's best dog. Terry rubbed the mutt's chin and smiled. He and Kendra were sharing custody of Hippy, who lived between their rooms.

"Is it safe?" Kendra asked behind Terry, teasing.

Gazing at the drab room, Terry had a sudden inspiration. "Yeah. One second."

He closed the door behind him and rushed to fling open the nightstand drawer. Perfect! Piranha had left his stash of candles. Candles were against regs, but girls thought they were romantic.

While Hippy trotted behind him, he lit one on the nightstand, one on the dresser, and one on the bathroom counter. He hoped Marv wouldn't make a late-night room check or see the glowing contraband, since there was no mistaking candlelight.

Terry was nervous, despite having had steady girlfriends since he was fifteen—until juvie, anyway. His first girlfriend, Loretta, had only been a novelty, a senior when he was a sophomore. He thought he'd loved Gwen for real, until she banged half the basketball team and turned love to loathing. Then he'd practiced all of Gwen's evil on his last girlfriend, Paige, who had finally gotten the hint after he stopped answering her calls and texts. After a month.

Not the greatest track record, maybe, but he was no stranger to girls.

So why did Kendra make him feel like he'd never kissed a girl before? Or like her brown eyes could see everything he'd ever thought or done? Why did her cheekbones remind him of a wood carving? How did such a compact body hold curves that filled her jeans in a way Loretta, Gwen, and Paige could only have dreamed about?

Kendra was like no other girl he'd known, and so smart she was almost scary. Knowing that she'd been on the bus seat behind him all that time, relying on him to stay awake and keep them safe, might have been the single most important reason the Blue Beauty had made it to Threadville.

Now if only he could make Kendra happy here, so she wouldn't get kicked out with her wild stories. Or get *him* kicked out, because he couldn't let her go back on the road without him. Kendra seriously needed to get . . . distracted. That was what Dean had been trying to tell him on the way to the mechanic's house.

"Okay," he said, opening the door.

"It's safe now?"

"You tell me," he said.

Damn, why was his heart whirring so loudly? He watched her face as she walked into the candle-bright room, waiting for her reaction.

The smiling curve of her lips was a jolt of pure lightning.

Kendra had never looked so beautiful.

"You did this . . . for me?" Kendra said. The most any other boy had ever done for her was Taylor's wilting carnation corsage. And he'd stuck her with the pin.

But Terry had already done so much more.

Terry closed the door and stood behind her, wrapping his arms around her. They swayed together like they were rocking at sea, sharing silent music. She stared at their reflection in the bureau's cracked mirror, so many contrasts; he was tall and broad-shouldered, she was short and narrow. Suntan against naturally dark skin. What a curious, fascinating sight they were. Hipshot settled down on the floor, bored.

"Remember that night on the beach? Our first kiss?" Terry whispered, nudging closer to her.

Kendra's heart seemed to stop. He was aroused, and he didn't care if she knew. His fever infected her. "I've thought about that night a lot. When I said . . . I mean, I hope you didn't think . . ." He fumbled for words.

Kendra's cheeks flared hot. "No, it's my fault. I hope I wasn't . . ."

When neither of them could form a sentence, they laughed at how ridiculous they were. Some of her nervousness evaporated as she remembered the moonlight across the ocean.

She turned around to drape her arms across his shoulders, keeping a few inches between them. "That night on the beach, I thought it was the end of the world," she said. "It would never get better."

"And now Domino Falls has changed your mind?"

"It's amazing," she admitted. "It's proof that we *are* still here. But I'm worried about my friends. I think Devil's Wake would be safer, and I'm not sure you'd go with me. But it's not the end of the world. Not tonight."

"Devil's Wake? Never say never, Kendra," Terry said, resting his chin atop her head. Few people ever touched her hair, and Kendra nearly flinched from him. She felt self-conscious in a dozen ways. At the same time, she couldn't pull herself an inch away from him, as if he might vanish if she did. "I'm not going to forget about Lisa—ever." Terry's words vibrated through her scalp. "Just not right now. You know what it's like on the road. We need to rest. Make plans."

"What would make you go?" she said.

"Like, right now?" he said. "Something big. Our lives at risk—because that's what we'd be facing out there."

Kendra drew in a deep breath. "What if I told you . . . I feel something like that? That whatever's going on here beneath the surface puts us all in danger?"

Terry stared at her as if he wanted to read her mind, trying to see through her eyes. "I'd say you need to make your case. Starting with me."

"And you'll listen?"

"Sure. What do I have to lose? I might learn something I need to know."

Kendra grinned at him. Terry's ability to make her feel better surprised her again. Then her grin withered. She would have to find language for what she'd felt at the ranch. She hadn't smelled or seen or heard anything. How could you explain the presence of . . . a *void*?

She would have to spend more time with the Threadies to collect information for Terry. "What if we find out something awful . . . but the others won't believe us? Or they don't care?" she said.

Kendra didn't like seeing Ursalina's point, but unless someone was taking potshots at them, why was it any of their business? On the outside, nobody held a meeting if you got shot. Nobody noticed. Outside, death wasn't remarkable.

"Then we'd go," Terry said. "Just you and me."

"And Hipshot," Kendra said. Hearing his name, Hipshot jumped up and came to her side with a bright doggie grin, tail wagging. He basked in them while they stroked Hippy's coat. When their fingers touched, Kendra felt jolts of static electricity.

"Hipshot for sure," Terry said. For half a second, Kendra enjoyed an image of setting off with Terry on the road in a well-armored SUV, with Hippy panting through the backseat window. She froze the image, before anything ugly could reach it.

"I have something for you," he said, and fished in his pocket, bringing out a plastic bag with a Seiko lady's digital watch in it. Couldn't have cost more than fifty bucks in the old world, but as he buckled it onto her wrist she felt like a princess.

Their lips met, his mouth salty from popcorn. Their kiss started just inside the doorway and ended on the closest bed, where they lay wrapped around each other. Kendra had never been on a bed with a boy.

"I'm a virgin," Kendra said. She hadn't planned to drop it so plainly, but it fell out, the barest whisper.

Terry's eyes dimmed. He tried to catch himself, but she saw it. He was silent far too long, and Kendra wished she hadn't told him. Just when they had time together, she'd said the one thing that might push Terry away. Suddenly, her skin felt uncomfortable and itchy.

Then he kissed her again, deeper this time. He smiled, their lips still brushing. "Then this is my lucky night."

She sighed, melting. Terry eased her back onto the bed, and his hands touched her in ways she had never let a boy touch her. Not in the front seat of the Toyota, not beneath the bleachers. She was losing control of thought. If someone had asked her to multiply single digits for millions, she couldn't have gotten a dime.

Now it was a single hand that teased and tormented her. He was doing something else with the other hand.

She studied the ceiling of the room. So, this was where it would happen, and how, and with whom. One of life's urgent, simple questions answered at last.

"A moment," he whispered, and turned away from her. Foil or plastic crinkled. Suddenly, he was still. He cursed under his breath.

"What is it?" she asked.

"I . . . it's . . ." His voice sounded absurd, almost like that of child who has dropped an ice-cream cone on the floor. "It's busted."

"What?"

"The . . ." His voice dropped. "The condom. I only had the one. Traded my triple-As for it. The pack was a little old and crinkled, but I thought . . . ah, *shit!*"

He looked back at her, so woebegone that she suddenly burped laughter. After a moment, he broke out guffawing as well, and they were holding each other, and kissing gently, and then laughing like fools again.

"It's not the last one in the world," she said.

"No," he said. "It's not."

"You're disappointed?" she asked.

"Of course."

"But not trying to talk me into anything."

"This isn't the time or place to have any kids. I want it to be right."

She kissed him again, smiling with infinite mischief. "It will be."

He held her to his chest. There were so many things he could have said. Requested. Done. But holding her right now, just the two of them still in their clothes with the ruined foil packet crumpled on the floor, somehow seemed the best, most romantic, and most appropriate thing of all.

She listened to his heartbeat through his shirt.

Is this love? she asked. If not, how much better could love possibly be?

Twenty

Sonia let Chris lead her by hand to the rocky ledge, his gold shirt folded ceremoniously across his arm, and she saw his grim face replaced by an easy smile. He'd told her he'd been a newbie until he won a spot on the Gold Shirts two months before, after passing a quiz on Wales and "The Unification Philosophy of Threadism."

We're woven of threads joined by threads. To sense this is to tap the true power within—

Threadwise, Chris was in another league.

The moonlight was bright enough to show the craggy hillside to the east and fields north and south, all of it draped in fences. Occasionally, in the distance, the fence sparked with a faint, sudden glow. Chris gave her his binoculars. Shadowy figures congregated beyond the fences in the hills. Sparks popped like fireworks. It was too dark to see how many, but the foothills teemed with freaks. Maybe hundreds!

We feel safe, but they're right out there waiting, she reminded herself.

Sonia drew closer to Chris and couldn't help contrasting his thin, hairless arms to Piranha's thicker ones. "Are you sure they can't get in?"

"Between the fences, patrols, and barricade?" Chris said. "Not in this life. But there's no such thing as shooting them all. I've tried."

"What barricade? Where?"

"Protecting the tunnels," he said. He kept his voice low. "In and out of the ranch. Wales has a whole system of tunnels, built on the old mine system. Had it for years. He was always ready."

"It's like he knew."

"He did know," Chris said, certain.

They were on a perch behind the Threadies' permanent camp, a ranch house within view of the mansion's front gates, a quarter mile back from the main house, ringed by small tents. Wales had made it easy for his fans to be near him, and they had enjoyed his apparently endless hospitality even before the world had ended. The Threadie camp was more like a commune, a miniature village. No one had separate fires like they did at the Motel 6; the fires and food were shared by everyone. Most people were smiling.

"I expected more survivors to be nuts," Sonia said as they walked the camp. "Completely babbling-out-of-their-minds crazy. Barking and howling at the moon."

Chris laughed. "Plenty of those, but they don't get past the checkpoint."

"I wonder what happens to them outside."

"Same thing that happens to everybody," Chris said.

But there were other settlements, so Threadville wasn't the only safe place. Sonia wondered if her family had made it to a settlement like Threadville, or if they were still living in their basement. Had they survived? Those thoughts cramped her stomach.

Just when Sonia was about to ask, Chris told her his story.

He'd lived with his parents and two younger brothers in San Jose. Their family had escaped infection when the neighborhood shelter at the high school was overrun. His father found them a car, and they had been on the road a full day before pirates blew out their tires. Chris had only survived by pretending to be dead, silent through the worst. He remembered the broadcasts and headed for Threadville, his only chance.

Chris's eyes ran with tears, but his voice remained a monotone.

They'd just met earlier that day, but she felt as if she could tell him anything. Everything. So she told him about the stealing, the judge, and the camp. About Terry, Piranha, and the Twins. And Kendra and Ursalina. She told him how, together, they had survived the pirates.

"You're lucky," he said. "You could fight back. We couldn't do a damn thing."

"I'm really sorry," she said.

He shrugged as if his family's terror was a bad day that could escape his mind. "Guess now we've learned what's underneath people."

"It's not underneath all of us," she said. "Not like those pirates."

"But too many. Way too many." He shook his head, his eyes suddenly fierce. "I'm not the same anymore. That's for sure."

He walked her to a bonfire that had drawn at least a dozen Threadies, and a round of backslapping began as they made room for Sonia and Chris at the fire. "They're proud I got my

Gold Shirt," he told her privately. "I used to be one of them, ya know?"

The pride in his voice made Sonia smile to herself.

"Yeah, he used to be a mortal, and now he's just a god in Gold," a chubby boy laughed. He introduced himself as Moe, and his haircut reminded Sonia of his namesake from the Three Stooges. His BETTER THREAD THAN DEAD T-shirt was faded nearly beyond recognition, pulled tightly over his stomach. His face was a riot of acne.

One by one, they introduced themselves. They were like everyone she'd ever met at a ThreadieCon or Norwescon science fiction convention: bookish, gently weird, welcoming. Maybe some of them would have been considered geeks at their schools—okay, *most* of them—but the schools were gone. Survival of the geekiest.

They were passing around a small piece of wrinkled tinfoil, and each person grabbed a small brown item between their fingers, popping one into their mouths. When the foil came to Sonia, she stared at a wrinkled ball of something unappetizing.

"What's this?"

"Yahanna," Moe said. "Mushrooms. One's plenty."

Ice water flooded Sonia's veins, and she nearly dropped the foil. "What? The mushroom that caused the Freak Day?"

The circle erupted into protests. "No way!" said Manny, a wiry Latino man in his twenties. "It's propaganda. That damn flu shot caused the outbreak. Either that, or the poisons big pharma added to the diet pill. We grow these from spores. The *real* deal. Wales says it's good for the mind."

Don't do it. Kendra's voice was suddenly so vivid that Sonia thought she must be standing over her. Sonia considered passing the foil along, but the eyes of the others were watching her, waiting. Was this a rite of initiation?

"But what . . . happens?" Sonia said.

"Clears your thoughts," Moe said. "Lays everything out simple. Oh, and you won't be hungry all day tomorrow."

"Or the next day," someone muttered.

They laughed—a few of them too hard, sounding stoned. *No thanks,* Sonia thought she heard herself say, but instead she placed a small strip of a mushroom on her tongue. Slightly smoky taste, but not unpleasant. She swallowed it without chewing.

The circle applauded her. "Welcome to a whole new world!" Moe said.

Sonia passed the foil to Chris, but he shook his head and passed it along. "Gotta work in the morning. Can't spend the next eight hours daydreaming."

"*Eight* hours?" If Chris wouldn't take the mushroom, why had she?

"It's not like that," Manny said. "For me, it's more like six. Won't kick in for a half hour, so relax. It's a real smooth ride."

Chris tried to hold Sonia's hand, but she politely found ways to pull away and busy her hand whenever she could. She liked Chris, but she wasn't ready to stake out a new guy when she could still feel Piranha's hand in hers. Besides, she had to choose carefully. Sonia remembered the twinkle in Wales's eyes. She might never be Wales's official girlfriend, but she could be one of his ambassadors. The next time she went to the mansion, who knew what might happen?

The group was playing a strange role-playing game with twenty-sided dice ("It's an interpretation of a game from fifteenth-century Japan," Moe explained), just like they were at a never-ending party at a ThreadieCon.

"You all live here?" Sonia said, surveying the tents outside of the house.

Moe rolled the dice and made his move. "Yeah, everyone who

works at the ranch is either a Threadie or a Gold Shirt. Most of us stay here. Convenience, protection . . . plus, it's way more fun than town."

The group groaned. "That's for sure," said a half-pretty girl who'd introduced herself as Cindy Lou. With orange pigtails despite being at least sixteen, she reminded Sonia of Pippi Longstocking. "You've seen town. Gloom and doom. Backstabbing and gossip. Everybody spying on everybody else." Cindy Lou looked sideways at Sonia. "We might have room for another Threadie."

Moe snorted softly. "Wales would like her. He likes 'em skinny."

Sonia tried to hide the surge of excitement she felt. "And he pretty much gets anything he wants?"

Cindy Lou laughed. "What do *you* think? The whole town is alive because of him. What he did. What he built. He's a great man."

"Yes, he is," Sonia said, hoping she had proper enthusiasm in her voice. "A hero."

Chris's voice dropped a confidential octave, and he reached for her hand again. "You don't get it. There's so much more. I'll tell you for a kiss."

"Go fish," Sonia said, playing coy. "Just tell me."

Chris sighed, although he didn't look mad. "He sees things. He saw all this coming, and wrote about it. Didn't realize even what he was writing. I think maybe we all saw a little of it, and that's why the movies were so popular."

"But without the spaceships," Sonia reminded him.

"Instead of a space invasion, it's a freak invasion," he said. "Same difference. And there's something else . . ."

The night assumed a deeper silence between their words.

"What?"

"A miracle," said chubby Moe, and Sonia almost rolled her eyes. The only miracle, she thought, would be if this guy ever got a girlfriend.

"You've seen a miracle?" Sonia said.

"No," he admitted. "But . . . some of the Gold Shirts did. Right, Chris? And one day, we'll all see it."

"That's the rumor," Chris said, noncommittal. His mood had changed.

"Come on," Sonia whispered to Chris playfully. She kissed his cheek. "Tell me."

Chris's face turned bright red even in the firelight. "Not one day," he said. "Soon. Everybody at the mansion's excited about something. Then the townies will have to shut up and take Wales seriously."

Cindy Lou suddenly pointed. "Hey, see that? Maybe it's starting now."

A large dark pickup truck was headed toward the mansion from town, driving so fast that it kicked up a cloud of dust. Red brake lights flared.

"Nah," Chris said. "I'd have heard." He kept watchful eyes on the mansion while the others played on. "That's weird."

"What's so weird about it?" Sonia said. "People don't drive onto the ranch?"

"I know that truck," Chris said. "He doesn't exactly have an invitation." He propped up his binoculars to get a better look, a pose that reminded her of Piranha. Or Terry. She sidled a bit closer to him, but he had forgotten her.

"Whose truck is that?"

"I can't discuss work stuff, Sonia," he lectured her, and her face turned red. He was the one who'd brought up the truck, trying to impress them. But she didn't argue.

Moe was in the midst of trying to give Sonia instructions on

197

the dice game when Chris stood up and put on his Gold Shirt, carefully buttoning it to his collar.

"You said you're off tonight!" Cindy Lou complained.

"Just curious," Chris said. "I'm gonna ride the scooter over."

He cast an apologetic glance at Sonia, almost an afterthought. He had promised to ride her back to the Motel 6 on his scooter. Now what?

Chris held his hand out to her. "Come with me," he said.

"I'm just a civilian. You sure that's okay?" She didn't hide her sarcasm.

He winced and smiled apologetically. "I'm sure. We won't get too close."

Could she feel the mushroom already? The night seemed to dance before Sonia's eyes as Chris pulled her to her feet.

During the quick ride to Wales's gates, cool air caressed Sonia's face as she wrapped her arms around Chris's narrow waist. She wished she could enjoy the ride, but she could tell right away that something was wrong.

The large black Chevy truck was parked outside the gate.

"Wales!" a man's voice boomed. "Send her out here *right now*!"

Chris sounded shocked as he coasted to a stop. "What the . . . ?"

"I'm guessing this is weird too?" Sonia said.

"Townies aren't this bold."

Sonia recognized the man at the gate as Brownie, who had stood up at dinner that first night to ask about his daughter. Apparently, he'd come to ask again. More forcefully. He shook a crowbar in the air. "So help me, I'll break in!"

198

"Stay here," Chris said to Sonia. "Don't get any closer."

The scooter was parked fifteen yards back from the gate, near an old oak, and Sonia was happy to keep her distance. It had been a long time since she'd been alone in the dark. She cursed herself for leaving her gun in the room.

An army of Gold Shirts clustered behind the gate. Maybe . . . twelve? And like Chris, more were on the way; she heard running footsteps from the mansion, getting closer. A stampede of bad news.

And the mushroom was definitely kicking in, because the night had a surreal feel: colors brighter, sounds sharper. A megaphone erupted so loudly that Sonia was sure the Threadies could hear it back at their fire, or maybe all the way to town: *"Step away from the gate, or you will lose electricity privileges!"*

"If she doesn't want to go, let her come out and tell me herself!" Brownie shouted.

The megaphone went on: *"Breaking and entering will get you expelled from Threadville."*

"You gonna throw me out of my own town?" Brownie said. "My town is called Domino Falls! You can stick Threadville up your ass!"

Maybe it was only the mushroom, but Sonia felt attuned to every motion, every nuance of the scene before her, as if she were standing inside of it. Noticed Brownie shifting nervously from leg to leg, as if he wanted to run. Heard a slight tremor in the man's voice on the megaphone. Adrenaline crackled like lightning.

Slowly, the double gates began to open, folding inward. Sonia gasped. Three rows of Gold Shirts stood in formation, the first row kneeling, all of them pointing rifles like an image from the Civil War. Sonia's heart withered when she realized the men looked like a firing squad.

Sonia was afraid Brownie would charge in or the Gold Shirts would charge out, but both sides held their ground.

"Go back home, Brownie! Bring up your grievances through proper channels!"

"Proper?" Brownie spat. "What the hell does that mean? Is that a joke? Let me hear her say it in her own words. Just send her out!" Brownie's shout might have been heard even through the mansion walls, but his voice was angrier now. He slammed the crowbar against the fence, and it clanged like a bell.

"Counting to three, Brownie," the man on the megaphone said.

He didn't have to say what would happen when he reached three, at least not to Sonia. She already knew. Her racing heartbeat made her dizzy.

"You don't have any right to keep her from me!" Brownie said, surging toward a scream. "Where's my little—" He raised the crowbar again and started to bring it down.

No one counted to three. The crack of a single rifle shot silenced Brownie, and he crumpled mid-sentence. On the ground, Brownie groaned loudly.

Sonia's scream came out as a loud gasp. She felt herself running toward the gate, as if a Super Nurse version of her could treat Brownie, unharmed by bullets. She might have made it to the gate if someone hadn't grabbed her around the waist, lifting her from her feet. "No!" a man said, and it took her a few seconds to realize it was Chris. He pulled her toward the Chevy, off to the side, his heart hammering through his gold shirt.

Sonia pushed past him to crane her head around and see what was happening.

Brownie's face was contorted in pain, turning red, and a host of personnel were running out of the mansion toward the gate. Everyone moved with a strange fluidity, almost slow motion, and Sonia remembered the mushroom. Could it all be a bad dream?

A tall, blond-haired young woman ran ahead of the others. She looked ethereal dressed in a semi-sheer white dress, angelic, her hair whipping behind her. "Daddy?"

"Sissy!" Brownie wheezed when she leaned over him. He lay on his side, a giant bloodstain was growing fast across the back of his shirt, an ugly exit wound.

Tears ran down the woman's face as she stared at her father with shocked disbelief. She gaped at the blood on her fingertips when she touched him.

"Baby . . . I just wanted to know . . . you were all right." Brownie's voice was faint.

Sissy trembled, unsteady. She looked at her father and then around at the onlookers, seeming confused about where she was. Who she was.

"Daddy, you're ruining everything!" the young woman said. Her face and voice were flat with contempt. "Why didn't you listen to me?" Blood bubbled from the wound in his chest.

She didn't notice. "You shouldn't have come," she said. Then turned and walked away.

Twenty-one

Threadville is wrapped in darkness. A fog bank obscures the town hall, with hazy tendrils floating across storefronts like questing fingers. Kendra can't remember how she got back to town. Where is Terry? How will she walk back alone in the dark?

Half a block ahead, a lone figure stands in a reddish haze in the center of the road.

"Terry?" she tries to call out, but her voice is a mosquito's whine.

And the figure doesn't look like Terry. He—if indeed it is a he—is taller than Terry, and so thin he seems a scarecrow.

Kendra stops walking.

A drizzle begins, playing across her face. But when she wipes her cheek, she realizes it isn't rain—confetti? A wisp of thin red thread nestles along her fingertip. Gently twirling threads tickle her cheeks. When she looks up, she sees threads falling as if she's the sole marcher in a street parade.

But she's not the sole marcher, she remembers. It is waiting for her.

The reddish haze haloing the figure brightens and fades, a heartbeat gaining strength. Come to me, Kendra, *a voice says, filling the street, the air, even the ground beneath her feet.* You're ready now. Do not be afraid.

Although Kendra has never been more afraid, she takes one step closer to the figure, sees its bald scalp glowing in its odd light.

No, she realizes. She can't go to this creature. If she does, everything will change. Something worse is waiting for all of them. Not just Freak Day, but something beyond Freak Day. Unimaginable.

"*Leave us alone!*" *Kendra tries to scream.* "*We don't want you here!*"

Her pitiful voice barely carries into the air.

The creature chuckles, impossibly loud.

We're already here, *the voice hisses.*

Kendra woke, sitting up straight in bed with a gasp so strangled she expected to wake up underwater, drowning. But she was only in her bed.

A dream, she assured herself. In her half-waking state, she remembered an earlier dream about freaks tearing down her walls, but this latest nightmare felt worse. All she remembered was a shadowy voice raking across her spine, so real she could almost feel her eardrums vibrating from the sound. Couldn't she?

A whine came from beside her bed, and Hipshot's muzzle appeared. Kendra wrapped her arm around his neck.

"I'm okay, boy," she said. "I'm okay." After she'd said it a half-dozen times, she finally believed it.

She was at the motel. Safe.

A figure was curled beside her on the bed, and she almost reached out to touch Terry when she remembered that she wasn't in Terry's room. She had decided to go bunk with the girls, to make sure Sonia found her way back. Ursalina was snoring in the next bed, so it was Sonia in bed beside her. The Con Goddess had made it home after all.

Kendra gazed at the digital watch Terry had given her: four a.m. At least Sonia had made it safely back from her adventures with the Gold Shirts. She hadn't disappeared into Wales's mansion like the other missing girls. Yet.

Kendra was about to rest her head on her pillow when she heard soft crying beside her. "Sonia?" Kendra said, touching her shoulder. "What happened?"

Sonia's only answer was a sob.

December 23

At dawn, they had their first Council since the quarantine house. Ursalina had hunted down Dean and Darius and brought them too, all of them crowded into the girls' room. The sun wasn't quite up, so they looked ghostly in the light from two fluorescent battery lamps.

Terry felt nauseous from Sonia's story. He'd asked her to keep her voice down a dozen times while she told them what she'd seen at the ranch. "Remember," Terry reminded them again. "The walls are thin."

"You're sure the guy's dead?" Piranha said.

"I know what dead looks like," Sonia said.

They looked at each other, trying to see what the others were thinking. Terry combed his hair away from his face slowly, his habit since he was a kid when he needed to think. His mind raced with possibilities, none of them good. He could feel Kendra staring at him, but he didn't look at her.

"Makes you wonder how often people get shot around here," Terry said.

Sonia sighed, wiping tears from her face. "Chris swore he'd never heard about anybody shot at the mansion," she said.

"Chris?" Piranha said pointedly.

Silence chilled the room until Sonia went on, ignoring Piranha's question. "He said there are shootings in town, but it's the usual stuff—domestic disturbances, arguments. They have a Citizens Patrol and people get expelled. Never anything involving Wales."

"It involves Wales now," Kendra said.

Darius looked at Kendra. "We asked Jackie about Rianne, and yeah, she's not happy about it. But she didn't want to come to this meeting. Her advice: Don't make waves."

"Did we invite her?" Sonia said. "Did we ask for her advice?"

"A man is dead," Kendra said.

"Who isn't dead these days?" Darius said.

Ursalina moved to the front of the room. "I was just thinking the same thing as Darius." She angled for lead position, so Terry stepped aside to make room for her. "So what if a couple of grown women are in there with Wales, or a drunk guy shows up at Wales's gate? That's our business? Why?"

"They *shot* him, Ursalina," Kendra said, angry.

"I listened to Sonia's story like my life depended on it," Ursalina said. "She said a weapon-wielding man got shot when he tried to break through the gate. Are you kidding me? That's way more courtesy than we got in my neighborhood. Don't make him a martyr. Get the whole story."

Terry hated to admit it, but he wished he'd said it first. Were his feelings for Kendra muddling his thinking? Kendra's eyes begged Terry to back her up, but Terry looked away. "Ursalina's right," he said. "Sonia saw a guy shot in front of her—that's hard. But we don't know enough to say what's going on." Kendra's look was scathing, a look that said she would deal with him later. Or not.

"I know you won't believe me," Kendra said, looking away from him. "But we need to find a way to leave here. This affects all of us. It's not just about Brownie."

Terry sighed. He didn't want to challenge Kendra, but what were his choices? "Kendra, I respect your instincts, you're smart as hell, but all you've said is you have a feeling. That's not enough to start talking about leaving the best place left in the whole world. And going back out there, where the world has gone to shit." His voice shook at the end. Terry heard an imaginary gunshot, this one at close range. He nearly flinched.

"I'm not going anywhere," Ursalina said. *"Punto."*

"Me neither," Piranha said. "I'll push my luck getting rich as a scav. I'm through with running, hunted down by pirates and biters."

"And the Beauty's gone," Terry said. "I'd feel naked out there without her. Worst-case scenario, say one of *us* had been shot last night. What would we do now? Steal cars? Go on foot and leave most of the supplies? We're stuck here—for now. So why don't we concentrate on figuring out what happened?"

"I'll tell you what happened," Sonia said. "I saw a man shot to death because he wanted to talk to his daughter. I thought I'd painted a clear picture."

Piranha turned to Sonia. "You said his own daughter said it was his fault."

The look Sonia gave Piranha made Kendra's earlier glare seem tame. "Chuck, think about it: He's her father. Her family.

She's not affected by that? The guy's bleeding to death right there, and she practically cussed him out."

"Some of them have it coming, Sonia," Terry said. He couldn't help the poison in his voice. He hadn't thought about his stepfather in a long time, but the rage was still fresh. "We don't know that family. My neighbors never knew what was going on in my house. Once that door closes . . ." He shrugged.

"She wasn't acting normal," Sonia said. "It was like she was brainwashed."

Ursalina laughed. "Now it's brainwashing? Are you kidding?"

"Use your imagination," Kendra said. "Everybody's in shock after the freaks, and this guy acts like he's a god. You've never heard of Stockholm syndrome? Deprogramming? Wales was a crowd-pleaser before Freak Day. Now he's got his own kingdom."

"Easy, Dr. Freud," Ursalina said. "I'm still waiting for the reason I'm even having this conversation."

"Knock knock," Dean said. It sounded like the setup of a joke, but he wasn't smiling. They all went silent, waiting.

"Who's there?" Darius said.

"I'm So Glad."

"I'm So Glad who?"

"I'm So Glad nobody's taken a bite out of me today." Dean's deadpan delivery couldn't be called a punch line. He stared straight at Kendra with blank eyes.

Ursalina sniggered, pounding Dean's fist.

"Anyway," Darius said, "the general feeling over here? Ignorance is bliss."

"But you're not ignorant," Sonia said. "Did I tell you the way his daughter acted? She didn't care at all. He was just roadkill. That's just wrong."

"Spare me the morality lecture," Darius said. "Maybe there's more to the story?"

"There always is," Piranha said.

"Could be some stupid politics that are none of our business," Ursalina said. "Half of them want to worship the sun, the rest want to worship the moon. I don't care. My only politics are food, a bed, and my rifle."

They thought they had it all figured out. Kendra looked as if she was about to hit someone or she might cry. The shooting sounded like a bad situation, but Kendra and Sonia wouldn't win the others with emotion or moral outrage. What was worth giving up their belongings and risking everything to go back on the road?

"If Terry had been the one who'd seen it, you'd take his word," Sonia said.

Terry groaned. This argument felt like a slowly breaking bone. When it was over, something would have changed between them all. "That's not true," Terry said.

"Sure it's true," Sonia said. "All of you would. We'd be halfway to gone."

"You sound halfway to gone," Piranha said. "What are you on, Sonia?"

Sonia's face snapped away from Piranha when he asked her; he'd struck a nerve. Terry had thought maybe he'd imagined it, but Sonia seemed a step behind her usual self, like part of her was sleepwalking. If she'd been out doing some kind of drugs with the Threadies, how could they trust her judgment?

"What, Sonia?" Kendra said quietly.

"They gave me a mushroom, that's all," Sonia said. "That doesn't change anything. I know what I saw."

"What kind of mushroom?" Ursalina said, although she already knew. She stepped away from Sonia, as if making a mental note not to let her out of her sight. "Better not be that yahanna all these Threadies are into."

"Hope to hell you haven't had a flu shot," Darius said. The room had grown a little colder.

"I haven't!" she said, embarrassed and just a little scared, as if just then understanding the implications.

"Hell, girl," Piranha said. "You know the routine. Mushroom plus flu shot equals freak. Have you ever had a flu shot?"

"Five years ago!" she said, voice breaking.

"You'd better hope that's long enough," Terry said.

"Different strain too," Piranha said. "Every flu shot is different. Avian flu would be different antibodies, different proteins."

Sonia seemed to relax a little. A little.

"Did anyone see you there?" Kendra said.

"I was with a friend," Sonia said, and faltered, glancing at Piranha. "Chris is a Gold Shirt. He's the only one who knew I was there. I played it cool with him. I asked him some questions, but I'm not stupid."

"You sure you can trust this . . . friend?" Piranha said.

"I trust him," she said. "He likes me. He seemed really shocked—"

When someone knocked on the door, they all jumped and stepped away from each other as if to hide what they'd been talking about.

Marv was at the door. He glanced at them one by one.

"Take it you've heard what happened at the ranch," he said.

Sonia gave them a triumphant look: *See?*

"We heard," Kendra said, staring too hard. Sonia avoided Marv's gaze, wiping her face, glancing at the floor. Terry hoped Marv wouldn't notice how upset she was.

"Yeah, a longtimer here got shot and killed," Marv said. "Real sad business. Town meeting in two hours."

"What's going on?" Terry said, voice low. "Anything we should know about?"

Marv shrugged. "I wasn't there, but I'd say it's about a man who drank too much since he had to put down his son and his wife when they turned."

Then Marv excused himself, dewy-eyed, and was gone.

Ursalina grinned, her point made. "That never happened in my neighborhood either. They're coming to us to explain?"

"He could be spying on us," Kendra said.

"I don't know if he's spying, but he just lied," Sonia said. "Brownie wasn't drunk. That's not how it happened."

"He said he wasn't there," Darius said. "Get the mushroom out of your ears."

"Anyway," Terry said, "they're having a meeting to air it out."

"And we're not going to miss it," Kendra said.

The dining hall was packed shoulder to shoulder. People must have gathered early, Kendra guessed. Sorrow hung across their anxious faces; even the children seemed to know not to stir or make too much noise, recognizing how fragile their world was. Anything that threatened the peace was a threat to them all.

The meeting began as a memorial service to Brownie, and Kendra felt like a spy at his funeral, an uninvited guest. A man dressed in farming clothes climbed to the stage to take the microphone. Formal dress seemed to have died on Freak Day. Jeans, sweatshirts, and sneakers ruled. The man was nervous before the crowd, barely raising his eyes to the audience as he spoke.

"Nobody here didn't know Brian 'Brownie' Browne. A lot

of us have stood with him at the fences, and a few of us knew him back before we needed the fences. A lot of us knew what happened that night at Brownie's place, and what he had to do. We know Sissy was all he had left to hold on to. And the last thing we know is this: Brownie was a good man."

Townspeople murmured and hummed with recognition.

"It's gonna be hard to swallow whatever happened at the ranch last night. So in the end, it's only what we believe. But a good man was forced to do something back at his house, to his own blood, that nobody in this room wants to even think about."

A sudden movement caught Kendra's eye: Dean was flicking away a tear. She had never heard him talk about his family, but Dean might know exactly what Brownie had been through. Suddenly, the memories of her father's loveless eyes and her mother's screams gouged Kendra's chest.

"What that does to a man," the speaker finished, "none of us can judge."

The room was stone silent as they remembered Brownie's horrors and their own. In the back, a woman sobbed as if she'd been holding her breath.

"So I'm here to celebrate the life of a good man. A generous man. A good husband. A good father. No matter what you hear about what happened last night, nothing can take that away." His voice choked off at the end. As he climbed down the steps from the stage, most people clapped loudly. But a few hissed. Were they hissing at Brian Browne? At the story to come?

Instinct made Kendra reach for Terry's hand, and she was glad she was beside him. She was watching her future unfold.

The mayor took the stage next. He stared down at the microphone a moment, transforming himself from the bumbling, solicitous mayor to a man standing as tall as the power and poise of his office. The proceeding veered from memorial to trial.

"Last night, Brownie went to Wales's home with his hunting rifle and tried to shoot his way in," Van Peebles said. "That's the cold, hard truth of it."

Sonia's mouth dropped open. Kendra opened her notebook and started recording every word.

Van Peebles went on. "Brownie pulled a gun, threatened the Gold Guard, and crashed through the gate. Brian Browne is dead, yeah. But we all know who killed him . . ." A pause, and his jaw trembled. "Brownie did. The bottle did. And we, each of us, have a Brownie inside, and if we don't learn to control that fear, we're all going out like Brownie. One way or the other."

"Lying sack of shit," Sonia whispered to Kendra, so she wrote that down too.

In the back, a few people applauded enthusiastically. The applause sounded out of place, strangely synchronized, but Kendra couldn't make out who was clapping. While she scanned the room, she spotted the mechanic and his family. His wife, Deirdre, caught Kendra's eyes, and they shared a sad smile: an orphan and a grieving mother.

"Where's Wales?" a hard-faced older man called from across the room.

Van Peebles pursed his lips as if the question disappointed him. "He was too upset to come out here, Ned. Mr. Wales is not to blame for the irrational actions of others, but yet, that man is back there blaming himself. It's not right. And it's not right for any of you to blame him. This whole terrible incident was a family matter that got too big. But you don't have to believe me. Sissy can tell you herself."

Sissy! Kendra stared with fascination as Van Peebles guided Brownie's daughter to the microphone with a hand on her back. She looked like a long-legged bird stumbling through a haze. *Maybe she's in shock,* Kendra thought.

"Thank you for all the well-wishes and prayers," Sissy said. She named several townspeople who had given her words of support, names Kendra didn't recognize. "I keep thinking Daddy's still waiting for me at home like he always did, eyes glued to his clock. You can imagine what he said when I said I wanted to be an ambassador and go out into the world."

The audience murmured its empathy.

"After what happened . . ." She paused, taking a deep breath. Sissy's face seemed to divide itself down the middle, one side mourning, one side . . . smiling? Kendra blinked to make sure she wasn't imagining it. Sissy went on. "That wasn't easy for me and Dad. Now I just wish I could stay his little girl forever. I'll never forget the sight of my father . . . killing himself like that. Because that's what it was—a kind of suicide. I'm just so grateful that right before he died, I had the chance to cradle him in my arms and tell him I would be all right."

Then she sobbed so long that Van Peebles had to hold her upright. Kendra felt a crack in her resolve; Sissy didn't sound anything like Sonia had described. But what about that strange expression that had crossed Sissy's face?

No way, Sonia mouthed, stunned and angry. She moved as if to raise her hand and object, but Kendra, Terry, and Piranha surrounded her and held her still.

"Not here, Sonia," Kendra said.

"Don't be crazy," Piranha said.

Kendra glanced at the two Gold Shirts near the stage, but no one was paying attention to their group. Kendra watched the people of Domino Falls, California, population 931. They didn't seem to quite believe the story of how Brownie died or how Sissy had comforted him. Maybe they'd heard conflicting accounts too.

But they wanted to believe. They wanted to—badly.
And finally, they did.

"That's not what happened," Sonia said once they were outside the
meeting hall.

"Shhh," Terry said. "Just wait."

On the street, the crowd broke into small huddles of people in
passionate conversation. The true townies, the longtimers, were
eyeing their neighbors with suspicion. Gold Shirts lined the
streets on horseback, outnumbering the plainclothes Citizens
Patrol two to one.

Jackie's white pickup pulled up just as the Twins came down
the steps behind Sonia. *Does Jackie have a GPS tracker on them?*
Sonia thought. She'd never liked the way Jackie carried Darius
and Dean around like a hot new designer purse, but now she
wondered if Jackie was under Threadie control too. Keeping the
Twins happy for Wales.

"Give you a lift to the fences?" Jackie said to the Twins. "I've
got your guns."

Dean and Darius glanced at Terry and Piranha, and Sonia
was happy that the meeting seemed to have cracked their
resolve. They were trying to decide what to do.

Terry nodded. "Yeah, go shoot one for me," he said. "I'm not
on till tomorrow."

Apparently, just another jolly day in Threadville. As the
Twins climbed into the bed of the truck, Kendra went to the
driver's side window, so Sonia followed. Jackie smiled a greeting,
but then she turned her eyes to the windshield.

"Heard anything from Rianne?" Kendra said.

Jackie sighed, shaking her head. "Not yet."

"Sissy seemed kind of spaced out," Sonia said, double-teaming Jackie.

"What does Wales want with them?" Kendra said.

"I'm not the droid you're looking for," Jackie said, dismissing them with a wave of her hand. "I don't live other people's lives for them."

"Then why'd you tell me about Rianne?" Kendra said, keeping her voice low.

Jackie gave her a sidelong glance. "Fair warning, that's all. So you could make up your own mind without all the razzle-dazzle. Now if you'll excuse me, we've got to go protect the community of Domino Falls. There are good people here, and they need us. I don't win every battle, but I'll settle for a few."

For the first time, Sonia noticed Jackie's red eyes, as if she'd been crying. Darius and Dean were already perched in the truck's bed, guns in hand. Darius looked as grim as Dean usually did, and Dean looked grimmer than ever.

After the truck drove off, Sonia led Piranha, Terry, and Kendra to a less crowded street, near a vendor selling tamales from a cart. Bidders were too busy haggling to pay any attention to them.

"Suicide?" Sonia said. "Sissy was lying. They told her what to say."

Ursalina nodded. "Gotta agree with you on that one," she said. "She wasn't acting right. That story didn't even make sense."

Sonia glanced right and left, checking for spies. "The mayor was lying too. Brownie never had a gun. He had a crowbar, and he put it down. That man was on one knee, and Sissy saw the whole thing, which means she's signing off on her own father's murder. Am I the only one worried here?"

Piranha sighed. Maybe he was remembering his promise to always have her back. "So Domino Falls is a wholly owned subsidiary of Josey Wales," Piranha said. "Maybe it's time for us to decide if we can live with that."

Sonia wanted to kiss him, but when she moved closer, he narrowed his eyes and leaned back. In time, she hoped, he might forgive her.

A young teenage boy surprised them by rounding the corner and slipping beside them, and it took Sonia a moment to realize that it was the mechanic's son, Jason. The kid looked distressed all the time, his brow furrowed with constant worry like his father's.

"Are you okay?" Kendra asked him.

"Just read this," Jason said, and he gave Kendra a neatly folded slip of paper. Before she could unfold it, Jason scooted off on a skateboard. He raced down the sidewalk with surprising speed, full of purpose, as if he were running late or being chased. Or a combination of both.

They walked halfway down the block before Terry opened the note, and they all craned to read it. The note was in blocklike, masculine handwriting:

> We should talk—you and all of your friends. Barn beside the fence factory: NOON today.
>
> —Myles

"This isn't our fight, guys," Ursalina said.

But intrigue burned in her soldier's eyes.

Kendra and Ursalina arranged to take a lunch break from the day care, and Sonia, Piranha, and Terry had the day off, so everyone except the Twins made the fifteen-minute-long walk to the abandoned barn. The farmhouse beyond it was burned beyond recognition, a reminder of a day gone wrong. The empty barn waited.

"Hello?" Kendra said, calling inside after Terry and Piranha pushed the barn door open. Myles appeared from behind a column, waving with his red rag, which he then turned nervously in his hands.

Myles motioned for them to close the barn door. "You alone?" he whispered.

When they confirmed they were, Myles's wife and son emerged from behind a red John Deere tractor. Had Myles and his family been chased from their home? Piranha stayed close to the door, instinctively scouting through the cracks in the aged wood.

"Why are you in here?" Terry said.

"Small town," Myles said. "You never know who's watching."

"Shhhhh," Piranha cautioned, and they heard a truck engine roll slowly past. Through the wall's cracks, Kendra saw flashes of a white Ford turning around in the dirt, crunching pebbles before it drove back the other way.

"Gold Shirt?" Myles said.

"He's gone," Piranha said.

"Just a patrol, then," Myles said. He exhaled with relief. "Not a tail."

"Excuse me," Ursalina said. "No offense, mister, but are we cattle rustlers? Did we just rob the stagecoach?"

Kendra was so angry, she felt her eardrums pop. She was glad the Twins weren't there to chime in. "Why'd you bother to come if you don't want to listen?"

Ursalina pursed her lips, biting back whatever she wanted to say. All eyes went back to Myles and his family, who glanced at one another before Myles went on. "We were at the town meeting," Myles said. "And Sissy—"

"Sissy's not the same girl we knew!" Deirdre blurted. "We could see it."

Sonia sneered. "Told you guys."

Before Terry could shush her, Sonia told her story of what had happened at the gates. Myles and his wife grew more wide-eyed and distraught as they listened.

"I knew it," Deirdre whispered, horrified. "I knew he wouldn't have done what they said. We have to talk to Rianne . . . get her away from Wales."

Kendra's heart surged. "Yes, you should," she said. "We were inside the ranch, and . . ." Again, words failed her. The family stared, waiting for news. Should she tell them about the DVD and the dream image? About the strange sensation of touching the wall and feeling . . . *something* . . . on the other side? Instead, she blinked tears. "What can we do?" she said.

"Could you get in again?" Myles said.

Kendra and Sonia looked at each other. They hadn't talked about it, but one look at Sonia's wide eyes told Kendra neither of them had any interest in going back to Wales's ranch. But what if they could rescue Rianne?

Poor Terry was yanking so hard on his hair that Kendra was afraid he'd pull a hank of it out of his scalp. He looked scared. He had promised to help her make her case for leaving Threadville, and now Myles and his family were making the case for her.

"Why should they go back?" Terry said.

"Yeah, for what?" Piranha said.

Kendra couldn't tell if Terry and Piranha were trying to protect them or merely negotiating terms.

"You asked about your bus before," Myles said.

An expectant silence. Terry stepped toward Myles. "Yeah," Terry said. "What about her?"

"I can get her running," Myles said. "Give you enough gas to get to Southern California. What's that place? Devil's Wake?"

"You said she couldn't be fixed," Terry said.

"No," Myles said. "I said she couldn't be fixed without stealing."

Terry's eyes stayed riveted on Myles's. "Oh, I get it. So she stays dead unless we do something for you?" he said. "Like helping you get Rianne?"

"It's not like that, son," Myles said.

"It sounds exactly like that," Terry said. "Doesn't it, P?"

"That's what I heard," Piranha said.

Deirdre stepped forward, begging. "Please, just listen to him. Go on, Myles."

Myles held up his hands. "Nobody's saying 'Do it or else.' Could you buy the parts you need for your bus over time? 'Course you could. Brave, skilled kids like you will do well here. You could scavenge a better vehicle and take your sweet time deciding if you like it here or not, but I suspect in the end you'll want to move on. Rianne can't wait that long. Wales is shipping Sissy and Rianne out in the morning."

"We've heard things," Deirdre said. "From inside the ranch." Her voice fell to a whisper as she protected her source.

"Go on," Kendra said.

"People have disappeared," Myles said. "Outsiders. People nobody would miss, from the survivors' camp outside Threadville."

Kendra remembered the encampment beyond Threadville's checkpoint, where she had thought they might have to wait too.

"Wales's radio broadcast reaches a thousand-mile radius," Myles said. "People come here from north, east, and south. A lot get turned away."

"No one over sixty gets in, I've heard," said Deirdre. In a flash, Kendra remembered seeing white-haired men and women sitting around a fire watching the bus drive past. "Or anyone who's too hurt. Or too sick. So they wait at the camp, hoping to get in if they heal or fatten up. Hoping the policies will change."

"They have to be healthy," Myles said. "Fit to work. Like you."

Kendra's stomach tightened as she realized how lucky they had been. What would have happened if one of them had been badly injured when they arrived? She glanced at Piranha, and she saw the close call on his face. The family she'd met at the beach would have had to leave Sharon behind, she realized. What had happened to them? Kendra had been so happy to find refuge, she'd forgotten about everyone else.

"The camp is terrible," Deirdre said.

"You can see squatters on the way to the checkpoint, but they send the rest farther out, where you can't see," Miles said. "People stay a month or two, with a permit. Hard to imagine anyone would want to live there, but at least there's help against the freaks. They all work together. Gold Shirts might shoot you, though."

"If they just suspect you," Deirdre said. "If a dog barks at you. So we hear."

"We don't see that part on the inside," Myles said. "While we're at dinner and the movie. Those gunshots we hear all day and night aren't just shooters killing freaks. Don't think that for a minute."

Horror tickled Kendra's throat like chilled acid. Just as she'd thought, Brownie's death was only the beginning of what was wrong with Threadville.

"But at least they take children in," Deirdre said reluctantly. "Or, that's how we lived with it, for Jason's sake."

221

"Or kids get snatched and brought here," Jason said. His voice was hollow. "Kids have told me."

Ursalina's face stormed silently. The children at the day care didn't often talk about where they had come from, except the younger ones. Kendra had assumed it was mass trauma, but what if they weren't *supposed* to talk?

"Other folks just get snatched and . . . disappear," Myles said.

"How many?" Kendra said.

"At least five," Deirdre said. "Mostly young women. A couple of older men."

"How do you know?" Ursalina asked. Her first serious question.

The vibration Kendra felt reminded her of the visit to the ranch, but it was different this time. Something familiar and electrifying was growing in the barn between them; they were waking the part of them that had slaughtered the Yreka pirates, that had crushed everything between them and a place called Threadville.

We're just a little bit scary, aren't we? Kendra thought.

"We have a network at the camp, and we hear stories," Deirdre said. "We send food, blankets. When we can." She sounded like it wasn't nearly enough.

"But it was outside, so we put up with it," Myles said. "That's the truth. Well, now it's coming inside. Sissy and Rianne wander into Wales's mansion, enchanted by his Threadie talk. One comes back out a stranger, and Rianne never comes back out."

Deirdre held her dress sleeve to her nose, muffling her voice. "Now Brownie."

"We weren't the best of friends," Myles said, "but he traded fair and he aimed straight. That's how I measure folks now. And you're those kind of folks. I know what you've survived. I hate to say it, but you young ladies might just save Rianne's life."

Now that the whole business lay naked in the sunlight streaming through the barn's rafters, Kendra felt paralyzed. What had she been trying to draw her friends into? Maybe it was crazy to expect Devil's Wake to be any better than Threadville.

Sonia glanced at Kendra: *Well?*

"What are you asking?" Kendra said.

"Find Rianne in there," Myles said. "Tell her what's happened to Sissy and Brownie. Try to snap her back. If she'll come with you, bring her home. If not . . ."

Myles reached for his back pocket, and something metal gleamed. All of them tensed, expecting him to pull out a gun. Ursalina's hand parked on her holster, and she didn't relax until she saw a video camera in Myles's hand.

"This is digital, and it's fully charged," Myles said, giving Kendra the camera. "If Rianne won't listen and go with you, just press the red button to record. Let her tell us in her own words. If she'll do that, tell her we'll leave her alone."

"Wales won't like that," Piranha said. "We'd be burned here."

"That's where the Beauty comes in," Terry said. "We're back where we started."

"If Rianne comes, we'll all go," Myles said. "You've got your bus, and it's big enough for all of us. My last crew wasn't good enough, not enough experience. But you survived the Yreka pirates, so I'd take my orders from you." He looked between them, unsure about which of them was in charge.

He gravitated toward Terry and Piranha, but Ursalina and Kendra also caught his eye.

"Where would our little road trip be headed?" Ursalina said.

Terry looked at Kendra, eyes full of sad understanding and apology. "Devil's Wake," he said. "Just like Kendra's been saying."

"We hear good things," Myles said, encouraged. "Worth a try."

"What if Rianne won't go?" Kendra asked.

"Then you all still have your bus," Deirdre said.

"I guarantee you can get as far south as Long Beach, and she'll take you much faster than she was," Myles said. "Conditions notwithstanding, of course."

But conditions were everything. Of course.

"What'll happen to you?" Terry said.

"If we get stuck here, we'll say we were robbed," Myles said. "I know cars, so I'm well liked here. They'll leave me alone. Just drive like hell, so they don't catch you."

Deirdre heaved her shoulders as if she were unburdening herself of a great secret. "When Jason turns fourteen, they're sending him to the fences," she said.

"Better than a scav crew, Mom," Jason said.

"Don't be a scav," Piranha said. "Wait a while on that one, little man."

"But he needs to go to the fences," Myles said. "He needs to know how to shoot a moving target."

You may have to kill to survive, Kendra. Grandpa Joe's voice came into her head, as if Myles had brought him back to life.

"We've heard your proposal." Terry glanced around, checking their faces, lingering on Kendra's. "We've got to talk to our other friends. All of us . . . alone."

Ursalina sighed, hanging her head. To Kendra, it looked like *Let's do it.*

"I didn't expect a decision now," Myles said. "But decide soon. You could take off before first light. But you need to go to the ranch tonight."

Ursalina didn't raise her head. "How long did Rianne live with you?" she said, as if she were speaking to the ground.

The family paused. No one wanted to say.

"Two months," Deirdre said finally.

Ursalina raised her head, staring at Deirdre with laser eyes. "I had a daughter," she said. "But Rianne's not your daughter. You barely know her."

Deirdre rocked back on her heels as if Ursalina had struck her. Her jaw trembled. "You're right, we barely know her," Deirdre said. "And wherever that child I gave birth to is, I pray to God somebody's giving her a chance."

How could any of them argue? Kendra had known them far less than two months, but time went deep these days. Survivors aged years in days.

Ursalina sighed and walked toward the barn door. Deirdre watched her, alarmed, wondering what her departure meant. To Kendra, the frantic hope in Deirdre's eyes felt like body blows. What could a handful of people do? Kendra wanted to confess that they had no idea if anything good was waiting for them outside of Threadville, and that she couldn't talk to her great-aunt in Devil's Wake before four, when the power went on. Or that they didn't have enough time.

"Please." Jason's voice shivered. "We need help."

Twenty-two

Bang—you're dead."

Terry's knees almost buckled when the voice floated from the brush directly below him, someone invisible targeting him. When he reached for his gun, his fingers were so unsteady that he missed the butt on his first swipe.

"You ain't funny, man," Piranha said beside Terry. He picked up a small rock and tossed it behind the brush.

"Ouch," said a bush that sounded like Darius. "Hey, that hurt!"

The grass rose as Darius sat up, draped in his ghillie suit. Another mound of grass ten yards from them shifted as Dean sat up too. They were both perspiring. Jackie had directed Terry and Piranha to an old tire swing as a landmark, but Terry hadn't seen the Twins with their camo. A dozen men were building a fence around a field in the valley below, and Jackie had told them that the Twins were covering the wooded area just adjacent from a hilltop fifty yards away.

No freaks in sight now, but Jackie said they made an occasional appearance—smarter ones who wound their way around from other barricades. When Terry stared below, he saw at least two downed freaks who had wandered from the shaded woods and been shot almost as soon as they reached the light. A third, smaller form was nearly hidden in the tall grass. A child? Terry looked away, not wanting to see.

Piranha smiled. "I gotta admit, this looks better than getting chased all over the street," he said.

"Best job I ever had," Dean said, keeping his eyes on the tree line.

"But you won't get those scars the ladies like so much," Darius said. "By the way, you scratch my bike, I'll shoot you for real."

"Ditto," Dean said.

Since the Twins were stationed at the north end of Threadville, Terry and Piranha had borrowed their motorcycles, burning precious drops of gas. Nobody was allowed to touch their bikes, so Terry had figured they would complain. But this was an emergency. Instead of arguing about what to do about the mechanic's proposal, Terry and Piranha had agreed to see what the Twins thought. They couldn't consider leaving Threadville without their best shooters, especially if Ursalina decided to stay.

"We met with the mechanic," Terry said.

Darius snickered. "Did he give you a lube job?"

"Something like that," Piranha said.

Terry was sure he was wasting his time, but he told them about the Blue Beauty and the dangerous rescue that was Myles's condition for fixing her. As he laid out the story of Rianne, he realized he could be talking about Lisa.

The Twins listened silently, watching the woods.

"That's it?" Darius said.

"There's one other thing," Terry said.

"Let's hear it," Dean said. He sounded impatient.

"The camp?" Piranha said. "That what you mean, T?"

"Yup." Terry shoved his hands in his pocket, trying to draw the Twins out.

"What kind of camp?" Darius said.

Terry and Piranha glanced at each other, both realizing that they didn't have to say more. They could say *Never mind* and leave the Twins to their work, reporting back to Kendra and Sonia that the group had voted to stay.

Piranha went on first. "If you're not good enough to get in, they leave you in a camp outside," he said. "You know, like they told us. If you're too sick. Too hurt. Too old. You get a permit, stay awhile."

"Better than outside," Terry said. "More people."

"Unless you get shot 'cause a Gold Shirt thinks you're a freak," Piranha said. "Or says he *thought* you were a freak. Or the town snatches your kids from you. Or you just . . . vanish."

"Not that it matters," Terry said. "Nobody cares about the people in the camp."

Even swathed in camo-green face paint, Terry could see Dean's jaw go tight. An explosion seemed to shimmer the air. Smoke curled from Dean's rifle. A hundred yards downhill, a shadowed figure near the trees turned in a bizarre waltzing motion before it fell. Damn! Terry hadn't even seen the freak coming.

Down at the fences, people waved. Terry gazed at the fences and the people of Threadville as if he might not have another chance, already homesick for a home he'd barely known.

"Who says we don't end up in a camp," Dean said, "if we leave here?"

Terry reminded them about Kendra's great-aunt Stella and told them Kendra would be calling her later that day to find out if they could all get sanctuary. He told them about their first radio call.

"She said she might be able to send a plane to pick her up in Long Beach," Terry said.

"A plane?" Darius said, left eyebrow arched.

"But if it's gonna happen, tonight's the night," Piranha said.

The Twins didn't look at each other or at them. They settled back down flat on the ground, disappearing into the underbrush.

"Not our problem, right?" Terry said, sensing a way out.

Again, a nearly unbearable silence.

Darius spat a bug out of his mouth. "Don't know yet," he said. "Tell us what happens when our girl calls Devil's Wake."

Kendra checked back with Gloria at the Arco station once at two, then again at three, just to make sure she was welcome and the radio was still working. She kept expecting Gloria to cool off, suspecting her plans somehow, but Gloria seemed as excited as she was about her plans to talk to Aunt Stella.

Now Kendra was sorry that Gloria had heard as much as she had already, since Kendra had already hinted at leaving one day. The only alternative she knew was the main broadcast station where Sonia worked, and Sonia had warned her it was all Threadie. That would be like broadcasting to Wales himself.

By ten minutes to four, Kendra was pacing the Arco lot with Terry, dodging the dozen cars and trucks waiting to fill up with gas when the power came on. Gloria and her boss, a middle-aged Asian man named Ichiro, were busy bartering. The customers who brought livestock were turned away; other items like clothes and weapons were haggled over until Ichiro decided how much gas each item was worth. Few people seemed happy about the deals they struck, complaining loudly. *The price of gas must be going up,* Kendra thought. How long would it be before all the gas was gone?

Kendra watched Gloria in the gas station lot. "We have to make sure she stays out here when I get on the radio. She seems nice, but she could say the wrong thing. She might want to be an ambassador too."

Terry nodded. "I was just thinking about that. A goodwill trip. But you know it doesn't matter, right?"

"What doesn't matter?"

"If Gloria hears you or not," Terry said. "That Max guy will be on the other end too. Don't say anything you shouldn't."

Kendra nodded. She'd forgotten about the radio operator in Devil's Wake.

"Terry, can we do this?" she whispered. "Is this crazy?"

Terry looked at his watch and showed her the time: five minutes to four o'clock. "We're about to find out," he said.

Kendra went to Gloria, who was nodding compassionately while a wild-eyed woman told her she didn't have anything to trade except jerky and kerosene.

Kendra caught Gloria's eye, and Gloria nodded toward the gas station door.

"Radio's already set to the frequency," Gloria said. "Running on batteries now. It's okay if you don't know the radio lingo. Ham operators aren't supposed to use their names, but we're making this up as we go."

Even better than she'd hoped! But as Kendra walked into the gas station and tinkled the bell, she caught herself thinking about how much easier it would be if Aunt Stella weren't there, or if Aunt Stella said she couldn't come. Maybe they could keep out of trouble in Threadville and make a difference instead of running away.

The radio was lighted and ready. Sighing with something like dread, Kendra picked up the mic and pressed Talk. "Uh . . ." she began. "This is Domino Falls, California. Or . . . Threadville. We're looking for Stella Carver. Is Stella Carver there?"

"Take fifteen minutes. Stand by."

Kendra heard a beep and a whisper that could have been a thousand miles away. She waited fifteen minutes and then another five and was beginning to get nervous when a strong, loud man's voice spoke. "Hold for Stella," the radio operator said. He didn't sound like Max.

"Kendra?" Aunt Stella's voice crackled over the radio. For an instant, Kendra forgot about Brownie, Rianne, and her plan; she was awash in the memory of her grandmother's cadences, so closely mirrored in Aunt Stella's voice—even her father's ghost, hidden in the Southern-tinged inflection. Even without seeing her face, she knew this woman was family.

"I'm here," Kendra said. "I still can't believe I'm talking to you after all this—"

"I don't know if you remember, Kendra, but Devon and Cassie brought you to the Brookings family reunion in Houston. You couldn't have been more than five."

Memories returned in a flash. Kendra remembered her father in a chef's apron. Corn on the cob bigger than barrels, ribs that would have choked Fred Flintstone. Happy faces smeared with barbecue sauce. "I remember," she said. "And Grandpa Joe said you gave him a Paul Laurence Dunbar book."

Terry gave her a frantic look: *What are you doing?*

Carefully, Kendra removed her finger from the Talk button. "Don't you think we have a better chance if we have some kind of connection? Watch the door."

Aunt Stella was saying how impressed she was that Kendra could name Paul Laurence Dunbar, and talked about what a wonderful poet he was. Then, voice tentative, she asked about Grandpa Joe.

Another memory, blooming with shocking clarity: Mom had always joked that the friendship between her father and Dad's aunt was "unwholesome." They had met at their wedding and kept in touch over the years, back before her aunt Stella was single. Her aunt wasn't just family in name; Stella was part of Kendra's obliterated past.

"He didn't make it, Aunt Stella," Kendra said, remembering to be gentle. "But he saved my life. He told me to call you."

"Your guardian angel," Aunt Stella said. "That dear man."

Since Freak Day, people avoided curiosity about how people had died. No one asked for details. The best thing to tell someone was "The freaks didn't get him," or "It was quick." But neither case was true about Grandpa Joe or her parents, so Kendra said nothing. Grief sat on her, new and dazzling in its scope.

But Kendra's sudden mistiness went away when she glanced through the window and saw Gloria making her way toward the office. Terry was right. There was no time for family reunions.

Quickly, Kendra went on. "The last thing Grandpa Joe said to me was to find Aunt Stella. It's like he's still watching over me right now. But I'm not alone—and if I bring my friends, I want to make sure they can get in too."

A pause. "How many friends, child?"

Kendra counted everyone in her head. The Blue Beauty group was only seven people, including her, but what about Myles and the others? "There are ten of us." Maybe eleven, but she couldn't make herself admit it.

Aunt Stella gasped. Then she sounded sad. "Oh, Kendra . . . Ten?"

"Maybe less. But that's the only way we've stayed alive—power in numbers," she said. "My friends can bring me there, but . . . I can't leave them outside."

Another pause, and a crackle of static. "Ten's a whole lot of folks, Kendra. I was thinking you could stay with me, but . . ." She sighed. "I just don't know . . ."

"Nobody's hurt," she said. "We're all fit to work. We know how to shoot."

She almost told her a mechanic would be with them, but decided against mentioning Myles. Six strides from the front door, Gloria was stopped outside by a man pleading his case, trying to persuade her to examine something inside a box he held. "We'll do anything to live there. I want to be with you. I promised Grandpa Joe."

Terry gave her a thumbs-up sign, smiling. Nice touch.

"Well, Kendra, my friend here's shrugging his shoulders more than he's shaking his head, so maybe there's a chance. I can't promise for everyone, honey, but I can get you in, probably a few more. Maybe all of you—if they have skills . . ." She sounded near tears. Kendra hoped she wouldn't be bringing trouble to Aunt Stella's door.

Kendra glanced at Gloria again to make sure she was out of earshot. "We can leave tomorrow morning," she said.

"Tomorrow?" Aunt Stella said, brightening. "Yes, sooner's better. They're expecting a big group from Atascadero by New Year's. First come, first served. Think you could make it down to Long Beach Airport on . . . Christmas Day? I think I could bend their arms if we did it then. Everybody wants a miracle on Christmas Day."

Today was December 23. Two days.

Kendra looked at Terry, and he nodded enthusiastically. He'd been researching the trip since the meeting with Myles, checking his maps. Nearly four hundred miles was a long drive, only two hundred miles fewer than the drive from Portland, but Terry looked confident. Myles had promised him the bus would run much better.

"Yes!" Kendra said. "We can be there in two days."

"Well, you be at that airport—make it noon. Don't be late. Let me tell you, pumpkin. If I get these folks to send out a plane, but you don't make it on time . . ." She didn't have to say the rest. Aunt Stella would be pulling every favor she was owed to send a plane to her, and she could do it only once.

"Don't worry, Aunt Stella," Kendra said. "We'll be there."

By the time Gloria came inside, bell tinkling, Kendra had already signed off.

Twenty-three

Where'd you get this map?" Terry said.

The neatly folded map they had been studying on Myles's coffee table was colorful and detailed: *Your Threadrunning Adventure*. It looked like promotional material from an amusement park, but it had been thoroughly marked up with a dark pen. The map identified rooms like the library and screening room with quote balloons from a cartoon Wales: *"This is where I watch all of my movies! The Ranch Theater seats 20!"* But to Kendra, the handwriting was much more intriguing.

"Never mind where I got it," Myles said. "Point is, I have it. Got to be some way it can help us see Rianne."

"Great," Piranha said. "All we have to do is find the room marked Top Secret Dungeon, and we're rolling."

"We might," Kendra said. She leaned over the table, eyes arrested by the hurried handwriting: *Storage Room. Rear Entry. Staff Kitchen.* An insider had added information to the basic map, places that weren't on the public tour.

Kendra and Terry were both reading the map so intently that they nearly bumped heads. Kendra ventured a guess that Jackie had given Myles the map, since her brother was a Gold Shirt. Jackie didn't want it to show, but she was helping them.

Terry had convinced Myles that it made sense for them to come to his house because the bus was still parked there, although the Blue Beauty had been marked with a bright blue tag that said it was public property. Myles said the mayor had asked him to tag the bus until the probation period was over, since Domino Falls would claim rights to half of their belongings if they stayed. Someone had reported seeing them take home supplies from the bus on their last visit, Myles had confided.

They decided that Myles's house was no more suspicious than meeting in a barn, so they were in the family's living room instead, behind the shuttered windows, every lamp on to make the room bright. While they looked at the map, Deirdre served them from a white wicker tray, a memory of a different world. "You want some lemonade, sweetheart?" Deirdre said, touching Ursalina's shoulder.

Ursalina flinched. "No, thanks," she said, and muttered to herself: "More like Kool-Aid."

Kendra ignored Ursalina's jibe, hoping Deirdre hadn't heard. They had Darius and Dean, so they didn't need Ursalina. But if Ursalina wasn't on board for a rescue, why had she come with them instead of going to dinner?

"Mom?" Kendra said, finally able to use Deirdre's nickname. "I'd like some, please." Deirdre smiled at her, grateful, and gave her a glass. Lemonade meant citrus. Vitamins. Health. Lemonade was a luxury she might miss one day, and she sure as hell missed her mother.

Everyone crowded around the map, their puzzle for the past three hours. Slowly, a plan was coming to life.

"Myles," Terry said. "You're sure we can trust whoever gave you this map?"

Myles nodded, grim. "If we can't, we've got bigger problems than this map."

"It's Jackie, isn't it?" Kendra said. Although Myles denied it, she saw the truth from the flare of surprise in his eyes because she'd guessed. She didn't have to glance at Deirdre or Jason to know.

"We can trust the map," Kendra said, satisfied. She trusted Jackie, anyway.

Kendra remembered the walk from the foyer to the library at the ranch, and the map showed a doorway nearest to where she'd had her strangest experience, feeling a presence on the other side. Maybe the person she'd felt was Rianne! Maybe it was the aura or intuition Sharon Lampher had talked about on the beach.

No room at the spot was marked on the official map, but someone had scrawled *Special Collections* with letters nearly too small to see.

Sonia paced. "If we're getting all dressed up to visit Wales, we better get ready."

It was almost eight o'clock, according to the old-fashioned grandfather clock by the front door. Soon they would lose the electricity, back to battery lamps and candles. "No way," Ursalina said. "If the plan's no good, don't go. The plan comes first. This is where you find out if you're setting yourselves up— the plan." Ursalina didn't sound like she meant to come with them, Kendra realized. But at least she was helping.

"She's right," Terry said. "None of this happens if the plan doesn't feel right."

"I don't like you going after Wales like that," Piranha said to Sonia. "If you're alone with him, we can't protect you."

"I'll be fine," Sonia said. "I can protect myself."

The plan called for Sonia to distract Wales, hopefully getting him alone. Beyond that, Kendra hated to think about it. The idea of being alone with Wales the way she'd been with Terry made her feel sick. But that was Sonia's job now.

Kendra's assignment was to ask to study the Special Collections in the library to learn more about Threadism and wait for an opportunity to get through the door where she'd felt the strange presence.

If she found Rianne there, she would try to convince the girl to come with her. But then what? They couldn't expect to be allowed to walk back through the front door.

"Biggest problem?" Dean said. "No exit strategy."

They were all thinking the same thing. They stared at the map, waiting for the answer to present itself. Kendra nearly bumped Terry's head again.

"What about the tunnel?" Jason said suddenly. He'd left the room for a while, wandering into the kitchen, but he stuck his head back in.

"What tunnel?" Ursalina said.

Jason walked to stand over the map, and they cleared space at the table for him to join them. He leaned close, tracing the exterior wall with his finger.

"It's not on the map," Jason said, "but there's a tunnel behind the ranch. It goes under the fence and right to a door."

Myles and Deirdre looked shocked. "How do you know?" they said in unison.

Jason bit his lip. "I didn't want to get in trouble, but . . . it started with the RPGs."

Ursalina's eyes bulged. "Rocket-propelled grenades? Where? Wales has them?"

Jason laughed. "No, role-playing games," he said.

"What are you talking about, Jason?" Myles said sternly. "You were out there?"

"Not just me," Jason said quickly. "On school field trips, remember? But it wasn't just inside the ranch—he played games with us."

Deirdre suddenly sat on the sofa as if her legs had given way, her eyes hanging on her son, expecting terrible news. "Who?" Deirdre said. "What kind of games?"

"Mr. Wales," Jason said. "Sometimes him, sometimes his Threadie Irregulars. They were pretending it was the end of the world already. Called each other by weird code names. It was fun! They'd let us run around outside like aliens or zombies were chasing us, and they had all these plans to escape. Once I was hiding, and . . . I wasn't supposed to, but I went into a tunnel. It was way out in back of the ranch, near . . . like, a mine or something. There used to be mines around here, silver or gold. The door was open, so I went in."

Myles and Deirdre stared empty-eyed at Jason, beyond emotion.

"Yes!" Sonia said. "I saw a rise and a door behind the ranch that could have been something like that. Chris and I were standing on the bluff, looking down."

"Show me on the map where you think the tunnel was," Terry said to Jason.

Jason paused, uncertain. Then he tapped his finger on a spot just beyond the ranch's rear fence, roughly centered on the map. "That looks right."

Sonia checked his spot and nodded. "Yeah."

"And the tunnel goes into the ranch?" Terry asked Jason. "You're sure?"

"Yeah, 'cuz a door from the house opened and I almost got caught. The light inside was so bright, like a huge storeroom or something."

Kendra's heart raced as she ran her finger along the blueprint. Sure enough, a large room against the rear wall was marked Basement. "Here!" she said. "Maybe this is where the door opened. But why isn't there a tunnel on the map?"

"Maybe whoever gave Myles the map didn't know about the tunnel," Terry said.

"Kid," Ursalina told Jason, "we need to know everything you know about the tunnel. Anything you can remember."

"Want me to draw a map?" Jason said, grinning. What kid didn't like to draw?

Jason's sketch of the tunnel was fascinating. With an X marking the entrance beyond Wales's back gate, the tunnel must have been at least seventy-five yards long, if he truly made it to Wales's basement door. Jason was a nervy kid.

But one thing confused Kendra as she stared at the drawing: on either side of the tunnel, he'd created mirroring rows of small enclaves, almost like rows of teeth. Eight of them, recessed. "What's this?" Kendra said, pointing to one of the enclaves.

Jason hesitated. "You know they were playing games, right? Inside the tunnel, there's like . . ." He paused, biting his lip.

"What, darling?" Deirdre said.

"I just remembered," Jason said, blinking. "They're cells. Jail cells or storage rooms. I thought it was for the games, but . . ."

"Cells?" Myles said, alarmed. "Was anyone in the cells?"

"No, they were empty," Jason said. "They weren't even locked. Some of them didn't have bars. It was just . . . for the game, I thought. To make it more real—"

Myles's face turned hard with anger. He grabbed Jason by both shoulders and swung him around to stare him in the eye. "Are you telling me you knew Wales had cells down in that tunnel and you never said anything? *Why?*" He roared the last word.

Jason's eyes filled with frightened tears. Maybe he had never seen his father lose his temper. "Dad, I was a kid. I thought . . . it was just for the game."

Myles didn't soften his eyes or his grip. "Well, you're not a kid now, Jason! How long have we been talking about Rianne? Why didn't you tell us she could be locked up in a tunnel?"

Jason shook his head, mortified. "I . . . don't know, Dad. I didn't think of it."

Deirdre gently squeezed Myles's elbow, and Myles let his son go. Jason was sobbing by then, but Kendra barely had the spare energy to notice. At least he had his mother to comfort him.

"One of us has to get to that tunnel," Kendra said. "If we don't see Rianne when we get inside, we check there. If we can't leave through the front, we'll leave through the back. Even if we can't get her out of the cell, at least we'll know."

They all fell away to their thoughts, and silence came to their war room.

"We need to scout that tunnel exit," Darius said. "Beyond the gate. Make sure it's still a way out."

"I can take the gate lock," Piranha said, certain, "as long as there're no guards."

"I didn't see any guards from the bluff," Sonia said. "But there are probably cameras. And you'd have to be careful—the best vantage point is close to a Threadie camp up there by a big house. Someone might see you."

"That's what camo and ghillie suits are for," Darius said. "Nobody will see us."

Terry nodded, his face bright for the first time in hours. "That tunnel might also be a way in, not just a way out."

"No," Kendra said. "We know our way around way better

from the front. Too many surprises the other way to start there."

Sonia agreed. "Only if we have to."

Ursalina was nodding. "We've got a long way to go," she said, glancing at the ticking clock. "But this is beginning to sound like a plan."

The bedroom reminded Kendra of her own, down to the Barack Obama poster on the wall, although Kendra's pictured Michelle and the girls too: the perfect family. She wondered if the people living in her house now had left her poster up or taken it down.

Deirdre opened the sliding closet door and began pulling out clothes.

"Imani is a fashion plate," Deirdre said, carefully avoiding saying *was*. "So there's plenty to choose from. You two are close enough to her size."

Kendra had never been interested in fashion but was excited to find a pair of black jeans that looked like new. Between new jeans and any of the frilly blouses decorating the closet, she would look much better than she had during her first visit.

Not that Wales would care. Kendra still couldn't figure it out, but she was certain Wales had wanted something from her that had nothing to do with her clothes. When it came to seduction, Sonia had the edge; she knew Thread culture, and she'd already coupled sex to survival. Even she assumed she'd be the one, and something told Kendra she relished the role.

Sonia was excited as she held clothes to her chest, posing in the mirror while Deirdre watched. She looked at a black minidress for a long time.

"Cute but comfortable," Kendra told Sonia. "No heels. You might need to run."

"Oh, we'll need to run, all right," Sonia said matter-of-factly.

The guys and Ursalina were still in the living room, debating scenarios and strategies, their voices rising with disagreements. Everyone was getting nervous, having second thoughts. But it was already nine-thirty, and they needed to go to the ranch.

Deirdre closed the door, shutting out some of the noise.

"Girls," Deirdre said, troubled. "I know we're the ones who came to you, but I couldn't live with myself if I didn't say you don't have to do this. We all love Rianne, but there's so many more of you now. If it goes bad . . ."

"Oh, it'll go bad," Sonia said in that same eerie, matter-of-fact tone. "Even if we make it out of here and back to the road, the bad stuff's waiting."

She sounded like Ursalina. "Thanks for the vote of confidence," Kendra said.

Sonia shrugged. "Things always go bad. That's when you find out who you are."

"Then don't do it," Deirdre said. "What you're planning with Wales . . ."

"Conscience kicking in, Mom?" Sonia said, and Deirdre's face froze. Sonia wrapped her hair in a scrunchie she found on the desk. Sonia could vanish into a mirror in a way Kendra never had. To Kendra, it was like watching Sonia transform into a character on a stage: the sassy, sarcastic, invulnerable Convention Goddess.

"How old are you?" Deirdre said.

"Legal," Sonia said. "Eighteen going on eighty."

"Take it from me, Sonia, when you're eighteen, you can't imagine how long a lifetime is," Deirdre said. "Don't do anything you can't live with."

Sonia pulled her eyes away from her reflection to stare at

Deirdre. "That's the problem, Mom," Sonia said quietly. "I've learned I can live with quite a lot."

"We can both stay in the library," Kendra said. "Leave Wales out of it."

"And if Rianne's not near the library, or in that tunnel, maybe Wales will tell me where she is," Sonia said. "Hell, if I ask him right, maybe he'll take me straight to her. It makes no sense to leave Wales out of it. This is his circus; he's the head clown."

Her eyes went back to the mirror, the leading lady preparing for her close-up. Watching Sonia, Kendra felt her dinner twist in her stomach.

We can't do this, Kendra thought, wondering why she hadn't realized it before.

A knock on the door, and Deirdre rushed to open it. "Jason?" Her son had cried for an hour after his disclosure about the cells.

But Ursalina stood in the doorway, her rifle slung over her shoulder. Her gun had been locked on the bus, so Ursalina stroked the stock like it had fur.

"Got any clothes in here for me, Mom?" Ursalina said.

Kendra was holding her breath. She might have heard wrong. Understood wrong. "You're coming with us?" Kendra said.

"Hell yeah," Ursalina said. "I wouldn't send civilians in alone to do an extraction. What kind of soldier do you think I am?"

Kendra shrieked and, despite weak protests, showered her with hugs.

And didn't see the object Deirdre handed Sonia. Black plastic box, about the size of a pack of cards. And with it came two things: sixty seconds of instruction and a hard, ugly smile.

Twenty-four

Ursalina Maria de Campos Cortez didn't know why she was going to Threadrunner Ranch, another of the great puzzles to add to the growing list.

She still couldn't explain how she'd dodged her bullet in the snow with the Yreka pirates, or how she'd escaped a horde of freaks at the Barracks. Why hadn't she been bitten at the gas station instead of Mickey? Why hadn't she stayed behind with Mickey and let it all go when she had the chance? She had enough puzzles to last her a lifetime.

Want to come work the fences, Ursalina? Want to come be a scav? Oh gee, tough choice. Should she tempt chance in the freak zones, or wipe noses in day care? Only practicality would keep her alive in the post-freak world. But this rescue attempt was Practical's evil twin, Foolish. At best, it was a quick trip back to the road. And there were no depths to how bad the other way could go.

So Ursalina understood less than anyone why she was dressed in club clothes, leaving her precious rifle behind. No, she wasn't a soldier. There was no flag to die for anymore. But she was still a warrior, with her own battles and her own reasons.

The henhouse fluttered with nervousness; even the chickens knew. The mechanic's backyard reminded Ursalina of her grandfather's house outside San Juan: dirt instead of grass, rows of rusting cars, chicken wire, and a vegetable garden. The mechanic's garden was better tended than Abuelo's had ever been, neatly organized in rows, laden with shiny, perfect tomatoes.

The others streamed out through the mechanic's back door in couples, heads bent close in conversation; Sonia with Piranha, Terry with Kendra, the Twins side by side, the mechanic and his wife. Only she had no one left to lose. Ursalina stewed in her aloneness, waiting for it to hurt. *Nada.* Or maybe pain had become meaningless, like saying a word over and over until it was only gibberish. The past, present, and future were only babbling nonsense to her.

Mom had done a good job with the girls. Wales would wet himself when he saw Sonia, and even Kendra had transformed from naïf to sex kitten, all push-up bra and pouty lips. Ursalina was wearing lipstick and mascara only because Mamí's ghost hounded her when she didn't. If you were going to do a job, Mamí always said, might as well do it right.

Women were the oldest bait in history, never mind that Ursalina had loathed this game since her breasts had blossomed in sixth grade. *Here we go again,* she thought. Ursalina wished she could take Sonia's job instead, but Wales would know her heart wasn't in it.

"Talk to you a sec?" Terry said, and nodded her toward a junked Mustang a few yards away. The guys surrounded Ursalina while Deirdre worked on the girls' faces in a bright kerosene lamp on the back porch. Terry kept his voice low.

"We've been talking," Terry said.

Darius took over. "We need another shooter. Stay out with us."

"Forget it," Ursalina said. "They need backup inside."

"Maybe I could go in with them," Terry said. "I could say I want to read the Threads stuff with Kendra." The idea was so terrible, he could barely meet her eyes.

"No guys inside," she said. "The first thing guys do when they see each other is size up the threat. We need to fly under the radar. Girls only."

Terry sighed, nodding. He'd known what she would say.

"We'll be fine," Ursalina said. "If I didn't think so, I would scrap the plan."

"You're a better shot than I am," Piranha said. "Or Terry. If something goes down, we want the best we've got covering them. The shots might be tight."

The shining eyes from Terry and Piranha were hard to take. Ursalina never thought she'd be one to begrudge anyone love, not after how hard she'd had to fight that battle, but their eyes made her miss Mickey. On a list of one to a hundred, Mickey was the last person she needed to be thinking about tonight.

Or, possibly, ever again.

That voice. The one that wanted to seal her heart away, leave her in a shell. No. Mickey had died before her heart's last beat. She'd given her life that Ursalina might live.

"I'm the best," Ursalina said. "That's why I'm going in. I don't need a gun to take care of business." She grinned. "Besides, I'm scared of those big bikes."

The Twins laughed. The plan called for them to ride their bikes to the bluff.

"You could ride with me," Dean said, maybe the most words she'd ever heard him speak at one time. He was smiling, but his smile was sad. "You know, snuggle up behind me, grab something big to hold on to."

They all laughed, such an unexpected sound that the others glanced at them before continuing their makeup session.

"Nah," Ursalina said. "But if I change my mind, I'll bring my tweezers."

"You're killin' me, lady," Dean said. The fondness in his voice surprised her. In an instant, she understood: once upon a different time, in a different life, she and Dean would have looked good together. Might have fit. She'd never noticed it before.

Ursalina practiced her smile for Wales, resting her hand across Dean's hairless cheek, soft as a woman's. He'd never told her what he'd seen and done when he went to the reservation to find out what happened to his family, but she knew. "I'd be too much for you, *muchacho*. I might kill you by accident."

Dean squeezed her hand, wishing her good luck. Maybe good-bye.

"You're beautiful," Dean said.

Ursalina smiled. "*Gracias.* Too bad you're not a chick. With that hair, sometimes you fool me, though."

Dean tossed his hair over his shoulder, vamping for her. "What's a little plumbing between friends?" They laughed. But she couldn't forget that Kendra and Sonia came first for these guys. Ursalina knew that, and she didn't feel envy.

"We don't have to do this," Ursalina told them. Again. She'd had the same conversation with the girls.

"Planes," Darius said. "We've always wanted to fly. Maybe now we can learn."

"What about you?" Ursalina asked Terry. "Is this for Kendra?"

Terry seemed to blush. "Sure, I want to help Kendra see

250

her great-aunt," he said. "And I don't like what happened to Brownie, or whatever's going on with those girls."

Ursalina nodded. "Yeah, okay, but what about the rest?"

Terry sighed. "The truth? Even with everything I know about this place . . . if I don't go now, I might never leave. It's comfortable, and maybe it could be better. But my sister's somewhere out there, and she needs me. Maybe she's in Devil's Wake. Lot closer to L.A. than Threadville."

And maybe the Wizard will give us brains, Ursalina thought.

"It's a big world, kid," Ursalina said. "What if you never find her?"

"I have to try," Terry said. "I have to go farther south."

"Your turn, Ursalina," Dean said to her. She had surprised everyone, even herself, when she decided to take part in the mission. "What changed your mind?"

The puzzle was gone, suddenly. She realized it had never been a puzzle.

"It's just like Crazy Horse used to say," Ursalina said. "Today is a good day to die."

They nodded silently, agreeing on the point. The moon overhead was bright. All around them, families with children who might grow up were settling in for a peaceful night's sleep. Their stomachs were full. They were with friends.

They huddled in the moonlight, listening to the clucked omens from the henhouse, feeling more alive than they had since Freak Day.

Terry was glad to be in the Beauty's driver's seat again. As Myles had promised, the engine purred like a kitten when he turned the key, better than it had run at Camp Round Meadow. The wheezing and choking sounds were gone. The ember of faith he'd felt burst into a flame. The Beauty might take him to Devil's Wake after all!

Hold on, Lisa, he thought. *I'm coming for you.* The thought forced him to wipe away an unexpected tear. He rarely let himself feel how much he needed to find her.

"I hoped you might be the ones," Myles said, finishing his walk-through of the bus's repairs in the privacy of the garage. In the strong flashlight beam, the shiny new parts were a mismatch. "I started mapping it out in my head as soon as you drove up," Myles said. "Part from here, a piece from there. Broke my heart to tell you I couldn't fix her, knowing damn well I could, if I was willing to take the risk. But I didn't know if I could trust you yet."

"Why do you trust us now?" Terry said.

"Still don't know," Myles said. "Just praying I can."

"And if it goes bad," Terry said, "you'll say it was all our idea, right? No responsibility."

"You don't know me very well, son," Myles said.

"Maybe that's what you should say. You've got a wife and kid."

"You're just kids yourselves."

"Not anymore," Terry said. He hadn't ever asked himself what he thought adulthood was, but now he knew. You had to go through something that stripped everything else away. "Be packed and ready to go. When you get the all-clear, start creeping toward the intersection. You drive the bus; Deirdre drives your car. If we make it, we'll be in a hurry. This doesn't work without the Beauty."

"She'll be waiting," Myles said.

They shook on the deal. Terry patted the bus's hood one last time before they went out back to meet the girls at the Toyota Corolla that Myles had lent him from his row of rescued cars.

"Saddle up, pardners!" Ursalina drawled. "We're goin' to the ranch."

Ursalina was in the driver's seat, engine already fired up. Kendra was in the passenger seat, and Piranha was in the backseat with his arm around Sonia. *Way to go, P.*

The plan was to escort the girls to the ranch's front gate, then leave them and double back to try to find a way into the tunnel while Darius and Dean provided cover. Once they were inside the tunnel, they would be on their own—but at least they'd be armed.

Terry climbed into the backseat. There was no room for him in the front seat beside Kendra, so he leaned behind her the way she had on the bus. Piranha was speaking so softly in Sonia's ear that Terry couldn't hear him. When Kendra turned around, they only stared at each other for a long time. Their eyes were a resting place.

Myles and his family waved with sober expressions as they drove off, almost as if they didn't expect to see any of them again. Deirdre turned her face away. Terry still wasn't sure he could trust Myles or the situation, but it was too late now.

Ursalina drove toward Wales's ranch on the darkened road. Their only light was the battered car's single dim headlight.

"Follow your instincts in there," Terry told them all, but especially Kendra.

"Yes, Dad," Kendra said, smiling. She wouldn't admit it, but she was scared.

"I'll get you to Aunt Stella no matter what, Kendra," Terry said. "Even if it was just you and me, like I told you. You don't have to do it this way."

Kendra nodded. "I know," she said. "I want to. Terry, my instincts say if I don't do this . . ." She stopped, staring at her lap.

"What?" Terry said, leaning closer.

Kendra whispered to him. "We could disappear. All of us. The whole world."

Dread thickened Terry's blood. He didn't know which was more frightening: the scenario Kendra described or how nuts she sounded. He didn't believe she was crazy, but . . . wasn't it crazy to believe anything else?

"Just try to find Rianne," Terry said. "Don't worry about the rest of the world." He leaned into her, and they kissed like it was the last night before Armageddon.

Twenty-five

Solar lamps bathed the ranch's front gates. A spotlight stabbed the sky, and Kendra was sure people could see the glow for miles. *Almost as if Wales knows we're coming,* Kendra thought.

"Tomorrow's ceremony," Sonia said, remembering.

"It's showtime," Terry said. "Ursalina, stop the car."

They were still at least twenty yards from the gate, but Ursalina slowed the Corolla to a stop. The plan called for the girls to get out of the car before approaching the guards, so no one would peg them as a threat. Kendra's heart fluttered. It was time. Kendra saw movement behind Wales's gate as they were spotted.

"If you aren't out of there by midnight, we're coming after you," Piranha said. "Even if it's just a progress report, somebody better make it back to the front gate . . . or out to the tunnel. Don't make us go in there all Rambo."

They laughed. Laughing felt better than Kendra would have expected.

"Let's go," Ursalina said. "If I were them, I'd be getting nervous."

Kendra followed Ursalina's lead as she climbed out of the car; long legs stretched first, hips swinging. They looked like they were headed to a fashion show.

Piranha jumped out to take the driver's seat. He and Sonia locked eyes but made no move toward each other. Tonight, at least, Sonia belonged to Wales.

They walked toward the waiting gate in single file as the car drove away. Kendra wanted to wave back at Terry but decided against it. In a way, she belonged to Wales too.

The guard gate was manned by only four Gold Shirts, but Sonia had said that up to thirty others had lined up when Brownie came, so they probably weren't alone. Kendra hoped the tunnel would offer an easier escape.

Was this the spot where Brownie had died? Kendra looked for blood on the dusty asphalt, but she didn't see any. But she felt the echo of the night's violence.

A Gold Shirt wearing a tassel on his shoulder met them outside the guard booth, gun ready. After the Brownie incident, they were on alert. "What's your business, ladies? It's late."

Before Ursalina could answer, Sonia stepped forward, hip canted in a Marilyn Monroe pose. "I'm on the list," she said, her tone efficient. "Sonia Petansu. Washington Crew. Mr. Wales said to come back whenever we wished." She batted her eyes. "We wish."

"Kendra Brookings," Kendra said, thrusting her own hip and feeling idiotic.

The other Gold Shirts wandered out to them, appraising them as they listened. Sonia glanced at them and waved, suddenly. "Chris!" she called. "It's me!"

The youngest Gold Shirt was the same one Sonia had been

hanging out with at the movies. He seemed surprised to see her, and not happy. His face was sour.

"You know her?" the ranking Gold Shirt said.

Chris nodded, staring at Sonia with questions. "You're here for Mr. Wales?" He sounded so glum that Kendra almost felt sorry for him.

Sonia's smile looked apologetic. "He promised me a special tour. I want to know more . . . just like you did."

The other Gold Shirt checked a handwritten list, and his face brightened with recognition. "Right at the top! Sonia Petansu. I've also got Kendra. But . . ."

He peered at Ursalina, who gave him an Oscar-caliber smile. "Call me Lina."

Sonia and Kendra glanced at each other: *Lina?*

Kendra was sweating beneath her carefully prepared clothes. Her scalp itched. The Gold Shirt wrote down Ursalina's name and spoke into a radio, using codes.

"Copy that," he said, and turned back to them. "Good news: he's on his way."

"Who?" Ursalina said.

The guard dipped his chin to dramatize his announcement: "Mr. Wales."

Sonia bounced up and down, practically squealing, and Kendra didn't bother to hide her surge of excitement. If they were groupies, why not be happy to see Wales?

"You mean he's coming here to us?" Sonia said, in full character. "Right now?"

The guard's wink to Sonia made Kendra's stomach turn. "You must have made an impression," the guard said. A few nearby Gold Shirts gathered as if the girls were a fashion show. "Gotta love the newbies!" one of them said, and another whistled softly.

In less than a minute, a large luxury golf cart sped up; a Gold Shirt was driving Wales, who was in the passenger seat in a denim jacket with a fleece collar, and plaid wool pajama pants underneath.

"I thought I was taking a quick ride before bed," Wales said. "But I must already be dreaming." He stared at Sonia, then Kendra, with a nearly manic churning in his eyes that would have been more frightening without his grin . . . but not by much. "What an unexpected and delightful surprise!"

Kendra's heart knocked so loudly in her chest that the vibration seemed to fill the car. They were doing it! *Is life really this easy for girls who know how to work it?*

At Wales's invitation, one by one they climbed into the plush empty rear row of the golf cart, taking their time, crossing their legs, tossing their heads back to laugh at Wales's trite remarks. When the cart drove, they passed a small, elevated stage. Workers had draped it in tarp, and massive, shiny red-and-gold ribbons peeked out.

"Is that for the ambassadors?" Kendra said.

Wales peered over his shoulder to look at her. "Yes!" he said. "I figured that's why you're here, Kendra. But you're not ready to go out yet. Your training hasn't begun. But it can begin tonight."

"I don't want to waste any time," Kendra said. "I'm dying to start researching your Special Collections."

"She doesn't believe in waiting," Ursalina said. "Likes to jump right in."

"I don't believe in waiting either," Sonia said, driving her eyes into Wales's. She moved closer to him.

Wales's smile sharpened as he stared. "Is that so?"

"That's very so," Sonia said, and smoothed Wales's jacket collar.

Kendra was glad again that she didn't have Sonia's job. Ursalina's lip almost dropped to a touch-her-and-I'll-kill-you sneer as she watched Wales's heavy gaze on Sonia. She caught herself, but if the Gold Shirt had noticed, someone might have tried to slap Ursalina in handcuffs.

"You're all here for my personal tour?" Wales said.

"Uhm . . . just me," Sonia said, sliding closer still to his seat. "If that's okay."

"Oh, we can manage." Wales's breathing was already heavy. "I think your friends should get to know my friends."

Kendra and Ursalina winked at each other, as if ready to make a Threadie sandwich together.

Wales chuckled. "Gonna be a good night. A damned good night. Well, Sonia, ready for your very special tour?"

The golf cart dropped Kendra and Ursalina off at the bunkhouse, and Wales moved to the cart's backseat to slide next to Sonia. Before the cart drove away, he was twirling Sonia's hair with his index finger. *Gross.*

Sonia giggled. "Be good, but not too good!" she called to them, and gave them a thumbs-up sign as the cart sped away. When Sonia rested her head on Wales's shoulder, her smile faded just long enough for Kendra to remember that her friend was only acting.

Kendra's escort had been the one with the walrus mustache and long golden coat who reminded Ursalina of a crazy neighbor she'd had once, always overdressed for the weather. But at least he looked about sixty and hadn't seemed interested in Kendra the same way Wales was in Sonia, pawing her.

The guy who came for Ursalina was much younger, in his late

259

twenties, stout, and pimple-faced. He could also use deodorant. It would be hard not to stare at his pimples, much less pretend she liked him. Judging from his plain gold shirt, he didn't have nearly the rank of Kendra's escort. Whatever. She wasn't trying to make friends. She just needed to stay close to Kendra and Sonia, and possibly find Rianne.

Ursalina tried to keep her eyes focused on Pimple Face while he walked her through the main house, but whenever she had a chance, she mentally mapped it, trying to figure out where the tunnel was. *Hey, dude, so I hear there's a tunnel here . . .*

"I bet lots of girls come through here," Ursalina said.

"A buttload," he said, nodding with a grin. *Charming,* she thought. Too late, he tried to be suave, extending his hand for a shake. "I'm Josh."

"Lina," she said, the nickname she'd hated since kindergarten. She tested a smile on him, and his eyes fogged over. Bull's-eye. Lipstick had its uses.

"Well, ask me anything, Lina," he said, deepening his voice. "I'm here for you."

"What's the ceremony about tomorrow morning?" she said.

Josh looked excited. "It's mind-blowing. Most people are still scrambling to outrun the biters or find a safe shelter, and we're already sending out ambassadors."

"For what?"

"Trade, recruiting, spreading the Threads that bind," he said. "What else?"

You don't have room for the people already coming, she thought, remembering the camp, but she didn't press it. Threadville seemed to have a strong labor pool. Why did an overcrowded settlement recruit more people?

"How do you get chosen to do that?" she said.

"Wales has to like you. You get an orientation, like your

friend. When you're ready, you get sent away with a Gold Shirt crew to protect you. Like the Secret Service."

"What happens in the orientation?"

Josh wagged a finger at her. "That's a secret," he stage-whispered. "Hell, even I don't know. But lemme tell you, those girls come out *believers.*"

"Do you know a chick named Rianne?" She'd be stupid not to ask.

"Sure, Rianne's going out tomorrow."

"Yeah, I heard," Ursalina said, nodding casually. If she could only get what she needed, she could pull out Sonia and Kendra before they got in too deep. "Where is she? Maybe I could talk to her about being an ambassador."

Josh laughed. "Nah," he said. "Those girls only talk to each other. In fact, I'm not supposed to talk about the ambassadors, so . . ."

He shrugged. End of subject. Ursalina decided to try to circle back around.

"Is it always girls?" she said.

"Mostly for Threadie stuff. Trade could be anyone who can cut a good deal for our produce and stuff," Josh said. "But more girls than guys. Guys usually want to be Gold Shirts."

"So . . . were you always a Threadie?" Ursalina said, walking closer to him, her hand brushing his.

"Huh?" Josh's eyes were stuck midway between Ursalina's small, firm breasts. "Uh . . . sort of. I grew up around here, so everybody knew Wales. Threadism was just in the air, I guess. My parents and brothers are still here. My grandparents."

Suddenly, Ursalina loathed Josh. The feeling startled her with its intensity. Why were some families destroyed and others untouched? Why were other old people huddled outside in camps while his grandparents were safe inside?

Ursalina stopped walking, her face only two inches from his. Slowly, she wriggled out of Deirdre's lacy black shawl, draping it across her bent arm. Her bare shoulder glistened with lotion. "What's the craziest thing you've ever seen?" she asked him. "Since the biters. The one thing you'll never forget?"

Ursalina heard Josh's breathing accelerate, could practically feel his pulse climb. He was searching for an answer to impress her, so he thought a long time.

"I can think of the stupidest thing," he said.

He might as well be talking about her. "That'll work."

Josh swallowed hard, trying to keep moisture in his mouth. Onions from his dinner wafted into Ursalina's face, but she didn't blink or lose her intrigued smile.

"I need to start at the beginning," Josh said. "Remember how Wales was all about gaming? The Sega Threadrunner game made him richer than the movies ever did. He built a modular gaming facility here on his property that was un-be-lievable. And I used to hang out with the hard-core gamers. By hard-core, I mean they never wanted to play as humans. Hell, sometimes they slept outside in character, moaning and staggering, eating raw steaks, the whole routine. Totally out there.

"Then, after it happened for real and monsters started showing up, this one guy cracked or something. He didn't bathe. He splashed himself with blood—I don't know what kind, and I never asked. If you got too close to him, he'd bite you. Crazy, right?"

"Pretty crazy so far," Ursalina said.

"So we get word there's a swarm coming—the bad one, when a few got inside the fences—but this guy is still outside shambling around. A biter chick gets through. Instead of running away from her, the crazy jerk runs *toward* her, arms stretched out like they're Romeo and Juliet. I guess he figured a biter would think he was one of the boys."

"What happened?" Ursalina said.

Josh winked. "He was wrong," he said. "Very, very wrong."

"So he got bit?" Ursalina said.

Josh nodded. "You play with the bull, you get the horns."

A long silence followed, and Ursalina realized it was easier to stare into Josh's eyes than she had believed it would be. "Not bad," she said. "But I've seen Suicide by Freak. That the best you've got?"

Josh's eyes were slits as he fought his awareness of how close he stood to her. His warm breath blew across the bridge of her nose.

"I wasn't done yet," Josh said. "I tried to help him, but he got bit five, six times. Hell, she took off his ear before I dropped her. I offered to put one in his brain, but he said no. He begged me to let him feel what it was like. Not that he didn't fight like anybody else," Josh said. "Hell, he fought better. He lived on coffee and didn't sleep for fifty hours, give or take. Some of us took bets. I thought he'd made it to sixty, but he didn't." He pursed his lips with annoyance at the memory of losing the bet.

"And?" Ursalina said.

"Everybody has to sleep sooner or later," Josh said. "One second, the guy's standing there drinking coffee . . . then he closes his eyes, and . . . *bam*. It happened so fast, I almost missed it. He was still talking, see? Mumbling. He wasn't making sense, but who makes sense when they've been awake that long? When his eyes turned bright as blood, I whispered, 'Was it everything you wanted, Ralphie?' Then I shot him in the face." Josh inched closer, brushing against her. Ursalina forced herself not to pull away from him. He was just getting warmed up.

"That's pretty good," she said. "Anything else?"

Josh grinned, smug. His lips nearly touched hers. "Want to see him?"

Twenty-six

Without a word, Josh led her by hand through the empty, sparkling chef's kitchen to a door at the far end with no fewer than three dead bolts. Josh unlocked them all with his key ring and opened the door.

The stairs headed down into a basement. She tensed with excitement. Now maybe she could find out if Rianne was locked in the tunnel, or map out a route for a quick escape. Could she find a way to make Josh forget to lock the door on the way back out? Probably.

Josh flicked a switch, and fluorescent lights buzzed on from one end of the ceiling to the other. The basement walls were covered in murals. Ursalina had visited her grandmother in Spain when she was twelve, and she'd seen the Prado museum. All Ursalina remembered were the paintings by an artist named Francisco Goya, whose images seemed demonic to her. There were no screaming faces like Goya's on the basement walls, but the clashing colors and misshapen features looked like the work of someone whose brain was inside-out. Were these Wales's paintings? Most of the colors were shades of red.

This place looks like the doorstep to hell, she thought.

"Do you get scared easy?" Josh asked her. "Are you prone to heart attacks?"

"Not so far."

"O-kay," Josh singsonged, his grin wider. "Follow me."

He led her to another door, which had only one deadbolt instead of two. Josh jingled his key ring like he was king of the custodians before he opened the door.

"Be vewy, vewy quiet," he said.

The next door opened, leading to a dimly lighted corridor and concrete block walls without murals. Ursalina nearly stopped in her tracks when the sweet-sour citrus smell hit her like napalm. Kendra had been right! The corridor stretched into looming darkness. Was this the route to the tunnel exit?

"What's—"

Ursalina never had a chance to finish her question. All of her senses fixed to the movement from beyond her left shoulder, and a stench that whisked her back to the gas station where her life had ended soon after Freak Day. She only thought *Oh, sh—* before the freak was upon her. An ambush!

The creature was a shambler, moving in slow motion, but Ursalina could only watch with horror as a blur of stringy blond hair told her she was already too late.

The freak was biting her shoulder. She felt its mouth clamp across her clavicle hard, and cold slime sprayed her skin.

Ursalina yelled out and kicked, losing her balance, and found herself flat on the floor staring up. Only then did she see its face: rotted red, recessed nostrils, a missing ear, a bullet-shattered cheek bone, and sunken eyes. Not remotely human.

A fighting instinct surged in Ursalina, drowning out all

sound. She was bitten, but she only had to survive long enough to chase Josh down and break his neck. Then she would take his gun and shoot herself in the head, because unlike good ol' Ralphie, she wasn't the least curious about what it would be like to turn into a living ghoul.

Then Ursalina blinked, and the world snapped back into focus.

First, she heard raucous laughter. The soon-to-be-very-dead Josh.

Next, she heard a loudly clanking chain, and only then did she realize that the freak hadn't pounced on her because it was chained around both ankles, its progress stopped. If she had been a yard closer to the door, he couldn't have reached her. But Josh had made sure she'd been surprised.

"You should see the look on your face!" Josh said, and collapsed against the wall in uncontrollable fits of laughter. The look on her face must have changed, because Josh swallowed his laughter and backed away from her. "Wait . . . check out your shoulder!"

Instinctively, Ursalina wiped the drool from her shoulder, peering to see how bad the bite was. She was in too much shock to feel pain yet, or . . .

With the help of Josh's flashlight beam, she got a better look. The freak hadn't broken her skin! He'd only drenched her with pink slobber. If Ursalina hadn't been so relieved, she would have puked in relief.

"Gimme that light!" she told Josh in a husky voice.

She shined the beam herself to be sure, checking every angle. There had to be at least a scratch! How could—

"He's been neutered," Josh said. "He just gummed you."

Ursalina shined the light on the freak, who was moaning his disappointment, still reaching for her. His mouth was a toothless cavern.

"I know that was a messed-up thing to do," Josh said. Dimly, it seemed to occur to him that she might hold a grudge. "But now you can say you survived a freak attack, see? Don't be mad."

The room stopped its spinning. Ursalina saw herself through Josh's eyes, splayed with her legs wide open in a cocktail dress on the floor. He offered his hand, but she ignored him and climbed to her feet.

"What if I'd had a cut, ass-wipe? An open sore? If it gets in my mouth, my eyes—"

"Don't worry," he said, an inexplicable smile still plastered across his pimple-ravaged face. He gave her a yellow handkerchief. "I've seen him do that a hundred times, and he's never infected anybody. Come on—funny, right?"

"Funny?" Ursalina said.

She remembered her previous plan, surveying Josh's neck for the best fracture point. Instead, she pivoted and smashed the heel of her hand under his jaw, a blow the guys in her unit like to call the Terminator. His toes actually left the ground as he slammed back against the wall. Josh's eyes crossed and he slumped to the floor like a sack of wet sand.

"Now *that's* funny," Ursalina said. "And *this* is hysterical." She kicked him once in the crotch so he'd have a little something to think about when he woke up. Then she patted down his pant leg and took the .38 in the ankle holster she'd noticed as soon as she saw him.

Ursalina faced the freak and its soulless, darting eyes. Although she knew he was chained and toothless, her hindbrain didn't want to let him out of her sight.

He was so thin he was skeletal, swaying in place as if his legs might fold. His only human remnants were his ratty Led Zeppelin T-shirt and stringy blond hair curled where his ear would be. Ralphie moaned hopefully to her, racked by endless hunger.

Ursalina gritted her teeth and leveled the .38 at the creature's head. As she did, memories crashed upon her again: the gas station, the Barracks, Mickey. Ursalina's breathing quickened until she was panting. She wanted to shoot the freak so badly that tears streamed down her face for the first time in memory.

He stared, head listing to one side, giving her deeper study. His moaning sounded plaintive, even sympathetic, as if he were saying *I know how you feel. Go ahead. Do it.*

Instead, Ursalina lowered the gun, stifling a sob. A gunshot was too much noise.

As the shock of the surprise faded, Ursalina counted her blessings instead. According to her watch, they'd been at the ranch for twenty-five minutes. Pimple Face had led her right to the tunnel. And now she had a gun. And keys.

All in all, the mission was on time and on target.

Twenty-seven

A half mile beyond Wales's ranch, a hundred yards outside the double fences protecting Threadville, Darius and Dean walked their motorcycles to rest on a slight hill overlooking a clump of bushes set against another hill. According to Jason, those bushes concealed the mine entrance. Once Terry and Piranha were in place, they would wave a flashlight twice to let them know they were watching the right spot.

Behind them, set back a bit higher, and a bit farther, Darius saw the house and Threadie camp Sonia had told them about. He saw firelight and heard laughter, but an overhang concealed him and his cousin from sight. The camp reminded him of Round Meadow, the summer camp that had been their bane, and salvation. Lost, wondrous days.

"Pretty good line of sight," Darius said.

Dean grunted. "Good as it'll get."

Darius raised the night-vision binoculars he'd scored from Myles. Ursalina'd said they weren't military grade, but a hell of a lot better than nothing. He thought he could almost make out the tunnel entrance, or where he hoped it was. Woods grew thick around them, and he knew the darkness hid freaks he couldn't see.

"Think we'll pull this off?" Darius said. During some moments, the idea of the rescue, so daring and selfless, felt ennobling in a way he thought would make their families proud. As long as he felt the call of his parents' expectations, they weren't quite gone yet.

"Some of us will make it," Dean said.

Darius glanced at his cousin askance. It was hard to tell when Dean was kidding, but Darius didn't sense any levity.

"If we lose anybody," Darius said, "it won't be on my watch."

"Not the way it works, man," Dean said. "Plans go wrong. Don't fool yourself."

"And you're okay with that?"

"It's all the same to me."

"So you don't care if you live or die? Or if our friends live or die?" Darius said, although he knew that wasn't what Dean meant. "Everybody lost their families, Dean. Not just you."

"That's right," Dean said. "Everybody 'lost' their families, like a dog that pulled off a leash and won't come when they whistle. Kendra and Ursalina didn't 'lose' their families—they watched them get hunted and bitten like animals. They saw them bleed and scream. Ursalina's kid was stolen from her arms. And if something happens to any of these guys tonight, pampered one, it's gonna rain pain on your soft little soul."

"You think 'cuz I wasn't at the rez I can't handle pain?"

"I don't know what you can handle," Dean said. "You've never tried it. Instead, it's jokes. Jokes ain't gonna protect you tonight, apple-boy."

Red on the outside, white on the inside, roughly equivalent

to "Oreo" among black folks. Darius wanted to bloody Dean's nose, but only because he knew he was telling the truth.

"Then we better get it right," Darius said. "You'll shoot straighter if you give a damn."

Dean laughed the mirthless laugh he had brought back with him from Snug Harbor, walking a tightrope between sanity and madness. Sliding down the razor blade of life. "Give a damn? Listen to you, Darius. We don't know jack about this infection. Or what these Cujos are, or where they came from. We don't know if any of us will be left to wonder about it a year from now. So, do I care? Sure. But I walk around with my eyes wide open. I see the lie. Nothing we do matters now."

So much for the pep talk, Darius thought. He remembered the cousin he'd been able to laugh and dream with at Camp Round Meadow and wondered if he would ever find him again.

Just like Terry was looking for his sister and Kendra was looking for her great-aunt, maybe he would find his lost cousin in Devil's Wake. Maybe one day the Indian Twins would ride again.

Wales's tour took Sonia through sections of the mansion he said outsiders rarely saw, corridors crammed with artwork and towering sculptures of misshapen creatures that, to her, looked like insects standing on two legs. The art gave Sonia the creeps, but she asked Wales polite questions to keep him out of groping distance.

"You do all of these yourself?"

"Yes, it's my passion now!" Wales said, momentarily forgetting to brush the nape of her neck. "I use ceramic. Pewter and bronze are too hard to come by these days. I've always enjoyed other people's art, but I never knew I had so much in me until a couple of months ago, to be honest. I'm up all hours of the day and night, and the pieces seem to"—he paused to search for words, finally waving his arms in the air—"*appear.*"

Wales swigged from the engraved silver flask he kept in his robe pocket. When he made a sudden movement, brushing his hand across Sonia's shoulder, she was so startled that she reflexively nudged him away. But she caught herself quickly and pretended to have stumbled, losing her balance. Wales steadied her with the crook of his arm across her back.

"Here, sweetheart," he said, offering her the flask as if whiskey would help her coordination. Sonia smiled and faked a swig, all the while keeping her lips shut. Wales was already blurry-eyed from the booze, but she wanted to stay sharp. Wales's grip cinched around her waist.

"Wow," Sonia said, staring at the creepy art again. "You have hidden talents."

"My dear, I have secrets you couldn't dream about," Wales said, in a convincing Clark Gable imitation à la *Gone With the Wind*. "A few of them, I must admit, are best displayed in a more discreet setting."

His hot breath flooded her ear. Vaguely, Sonia wondered if this toad was old enough to be her grandfather, or just her father. Her flesh crawled.

"Really?" she said with her best wide-eyed stare. "Like where?"

Good. Privacy. She hadn't seen a Gold Shirt pass in the hall in two or three minutes, but they weren't alone yet. She would have to commence the more daring part of her plan, and she only hoped Wales had nipped enough whiskey to make it as easy as she'd planned.

274

"I think you know where," Wales said. "You're not as innocent as you look."

"I look innocent?" Sonia said. "Been a long time since I heard that."

"Then let me show you my favorite room," Wales said.

Naturally, he led her to his bedroom, which was big enough for two or three rooms—so large and luxurious that Sonia remembered what she would have given to be in Wales's room, in Wales's arms, two days ago. While the world outside was cowering in fear, she had dreamed of moving into Wales's mansion and living like a queen. Wasn't that the secret in every groupie's heart? You would be the One. A tear stung the corner of Sonia's eye. Was she mourning her lost dream, or was she ashamed that she was still tempted even now? She'd let Piranha go for Wales, and Piranha would have died to protect her. He still would . . . wouldn't he? Worse, if things went wrong, he still might. The freaks hadn't bitten Sonia, but they had changed her all the same.

Murals covered the walls in the bedroom too: more shapeless, bleeding into one another. Shades of red. To Sonia, they looked like the color of blood.

There was no way to avoid kissing Wales. No way to avoid the bed. Sonia artfully managed to keep her clothes on while she tried to work up her nerve. She had everything she needed, even old-fashioned iron bed rails she hadn't dared to hope for. She grabbed a thick rail, checked its sturdiness with her free hand while she massaged Wales's silken hair with the other. He wasn't bad-looking for a paunchy old guy, and he smelled clean in a way most people didn't anymore. The bastard was tempting, even now.

But the bed rails made her job easier. So much easier.

Sonia's basic magic kit had survived Freak Day, and so had

her favorite semisheer scarves. When Sonia pulled the first scarf from her bosom and began tying one end around Wales's wrist, he only propped himself up on one elbow and grinned.

"My, my," he said. "The wind has blown in a very naughty girl." He only chuckled when she pulled his wrist toward the bedpost and secured him deftly, manipulating her scarf until it might as well be a leather strap.

"That's a bit tight, isn't it?" Wales said.

"Sorry," she whispered, climbing over the mountain of him to reach his other wrist. "I didn't want it too loose or too tight. It's my favorite scene, you know which one, that edgy one from the first *Threadrunner*—let's be honest, the only really pure movie, before the studios ruined it."

"Yes!" Wales said, forgetting his wrist. "The more money they made, the less they invested in the franchise! And they took out the message, the teeth. In the end, I wasn't allowed to kill anyone on-screen! Even if I threw him off a building, they had to have a shot of him writhing below. 'See . . . no one's dead here!' Can you imagine?"

The second wrist was tied before he could finish whining.

"Poor you," Sonia said. She almost let too much of herself leak out, and she hadn't tied his feet yet. "Still . . . *you must to be very punished.*"

Alien-butchered English directly from the movie. Wales's grin returned as his eyes glazed. "You're better than this," Wales said, taking his cue to help her sink into the fantasy. "You didn't come to hurt us. You don't want to hurt me." Sonia almost laughed, wondering how many times he'd watched his own flicks.

Wales's eyes rolled a bit, a sign he'd had too much to drink. Even better.

"So much more you don't know," he said, nearly giggling.

He pulled against his binds, testing them. "I see you've done this before."

"Once or twice," Sonia said, leaning over him, close to his face. "What else don't I know?"

"So much, my dear, so much." He shook his head, giggling again.

She kissed him lightly. "You know you're dying to tell."

The kiss stopped Wales's laughter cold. "That's not all I'm dying for."

"Just give me a hint," she said. "Were you always expecting Freak Day?"

"Oh, no," Wales said. "That was only a game. But the game became real. It wasn't the way I imagined it . . . but suddenly, they were here."

They were here. The room spun slightly, as if Sonia had been drinking too. Her heart pumped adrenaline through her.

"What are they?" Sonia said, because her proximity to Wales's eyes revealed the truth: he knew, or thought he did. "Where did they come from?"

"Somewhere that's not here," he said, almost dreamily. "Somewhere else." He blew out a puff of breath. "Like summer dandelions. Seeds scattering. I saw that much in my vision, the first one. I saw red threads when I first had the 'shroom."

Yes, the mushroom was all mixed up in it, and she'd had one just yesterday. If someone gave her a flu shot, would she freak out too?

"Everybody in Hollywood was takin' 'em. Had been for years. Nobody guessed any of this. All of this." He wriggled as if to sweep his arm, but remembered his binds.

"So the books were . . . what?" Sonia said.

"Oh, the books!" Wales sounded dismissive. "I meant to try to crack the code, I suppose, or make a kind of blueprint.

277

I was so ignorant! The books were nothing, a trifle. My feeble attempts to understand, to put words to it. So laughable now!"

"What's changed?"

"What's changed?" He looked at her with disbelief. "Everything's changed. Not just the infected. That's only . . . a glitch! It's gone way beyond that now." He laughed so long that it almost sounded like crying at the end. Wales's eyes were moist. "Do you really want to know?"

Sonia fought a primal urge to leap away from Wales, to run for the door, because the insanity in his eyes looked contagious. Whatever he knew had done that to his eyes, and she didn't want any part of it, now or ever. What would knowing do to her?

"Yes," she whispered, nearly close enough to kiss him. "Tell me."

"I wrote the books, I grew my own mushrooms here, all to try to . . . reach them," Wales said. "To . . . bring me closer to the vision. Not this . . . horrible accident with the infection. My vision was peaceful, about an evolution. *Our* evolution."

Sonia's heartbeat nearly overpowered her ears. "Evolving into what?"

"Something beautiful," Wales said. "I knew I wouldn't get it out of my head unless I saw one again, to help me believe something so beautiful could come from . . ."

His voice trailed off. More and more, Wales's words sounded like drunken rambling. "Until I captured one, I couldn't be sure. But we have it now. Proof. We are waiting. Changing." He bit his lip hard, suddenly. "So much death and fear. It shouldn't have happened this way. But we can't change the past, only the future."

"What did you capture?" she said.

"One of them," Wales said, eyes glinting with pride. "Not the . . . bastards, the hybrids, out terrorizing the world in their infancy. You've seen the others, haven't you? Growing like the Tree of Knowledge in the Garden of Eden. The new creation from our ribs and our planet's soil."

Wales laughed with his eerie combination of mirth and sorrow. "Not all of them," he said. "Most of them rot as fruit on the vine. They're still adapting—chemical reactions, so much to try to anticipate . . ."

"But some of them turn into something else?" Sonia said. "And you caught one?"

Wales nodded. "Oh, yes."

The icy block of fear in Sonia's chest thawed a degree or two. "Can we use them for a cure?"

"A . . ." Wales looked at her, confused, then barked his pathetic laugh again. "A cure! Yes, that's it, exactly! They are the cure, Sonia. They are the cure for *us.*"

Wales's blue eyes suddenly cleared, instantly sober. "I'm tired of this game, my dear," he said. "Untie me."

Sonia tried to flash a seductive smile, but she doubted the look on her face was anything except petrified. She counted the levels of freaks in her head. "So, you have a fifth-level freak. Where is it? Is it here?"

Wales yanked at his wrists, hard. Sonia was good with knots, but Wales was strong and persistent. "Let me go!" he shouted. "Do you know the penalty for disobedience?"

The true personality emerges, Sonia thought, wishing the sudden anger in Wales's voice hadn't sent fear shooting across the back of her neck. She could imagine what happened to anyone who got on Wales's bad side.

"Where's Rianne?" Sonia said. "What are you doing to those girls?"

With a loud grunt, Wales slipped one of his ankles free of its bind and swung it over hard enough to knock Sonia from the bed. Luckily, she missed the corner of the night table when she landed, splaying awkwardly to the floor. Wales thrashed on the bed, working to untie himself.

Panting, Sonia patted herself for the parting gift Deirdre had given her, the same kind she'd given her daughter when she sent her to college. When Wales turned his head to examine his bound wrist, Sonia lunged back up to the bed and jabbed her hidden Taser into his neck.

Wales let out a strangled yell, convulsing. Sonia watched his odd writhing, intrigued, until she remembered to pull the Taser away.

"Stop!" Wales said. Begging. How many people had begged this bastard? Had he listened to their pleas?

"Tell me the rest," Sonia said. Quickly, she tested her knots and felt satisfied that they would hold. While Wales caught his breath, she quickly tied his foot again. "Where are those girls? What do you want with them?"

"Ambassadors," Wales panted. "To spread—"

"I don't believe you," she said, and pressed the Taser into his crotch.

The reaction was fascinating. His entire body clenched like a fist, muscles roping up on his pudgy body at the same time that a huge wet spot appeared on his pants.

"Please, please." He was slobbering now. "Sonia. Please. I don't know what you want. You don't know what you're doing. This won't make any difference. It's too late—"

Sonia Tased him again. "Waste my time again, and I'll fry you."

Wales sputtered wordlessly, and Sonia gave him a not-so-gentle slap to bring alertness back to his eyes. "All right, I'll tell you!" he said, his words slurred, and Sonia realized it was too late to ask herself if she really wanted to know. "Some of them do go out! Do you want me to send Rianne away to safety? I will. I'll send Sissy too."

"What about the rest?"

"I'm trying to . . . ease the transition. Prepare them with training. Meditation."

"What does that mean? Prepare them for what?"

"To . . . help them cross over. Willing disciples won't need to feed. They can go . . . gently. And they simply . . . change."

Sonia couldn't speak the question in her mind: *Change into what?*

"They're nothing to fear!" Wales said, his words slurred. "They're us, through the looking glass! You can meet him yourself. He'll tell you how he used to be an artist."

The world fell still. "It . . . talked to you?"

"Yes, don't you see?" he said. "Not the poor, mindless creatures trapped in the transition! He's made it across, to the next stage. Others of us can do it too, if only we will embrace and believe without fear. Of course there are casualties! I keep my failures underground. But he said even if it's only one in a thousand, it's our best hope for the future."

He said. The words chilled Sonia's blood. An ugly notion planted itself in her mind, steeping Wales's words in horror. Was all of it about the words of a freak? Or something more insidious than mere words?

"When did you say you first started painting?" Sonia said.

Wales looked confused but relieved, as if he believed he was finally converting her. "It was . . . a little more than two months ago."

"And when did you capture this thing?"

Sonia knew the answer before Wales spoke, saw awareness flicker in his eyes. "About . . . nine weeks. Yes, about two months ago."

"And you started painting all of a sudden?" Sonia said. "What about the ambassadors? When did that start?"

Even in the bedroom's dim lighting, Sonia saw color draining from Wales's face.

"About then," he said. "The same time. The idea came in a dream."

"How did you capture this thing?" Sonia said. "Where was it?"

"In the woods, just outside the fences," Wales said, his face growing pasty. "I dreamed the place where they found it, and I sent my men. It was rooted, but . . . it was talking. None of the other rooters could talk. And this wasn't the memory of babble, like the fresh ones—it could reason."

Sonia backed away from the bed, wishing she could back away from Wales, the ranch, and all of Threadville with a single step. Hadn't he learned anything from his movies?

"You incredible idiot," Sonia said. "Who captured who, Wales? You brought that thing here after a dream? Is that when you started snatching people too?"

"No, you're wrong," he said, although his eyes were wide and empty. "I'm still me. I'm not—"

"What does it want? *What does it want?*"

"It wants to help us!" Wales said. "The change is coming! We can't fight, but it can eat our fear! You can be a part of it, Sonia. You can help change the world."

Sonia found out every horrifying detail she could from Joseph Wales, then she pressed the Taser to his flabby belly and kept it there until he could speak no more.

Twenty-eight

A neatly piled stack of Thread literature waited on the library table, but the officious Gold Coat who had led Kendra to the library walked right past the tables.

"I've been asked to take you to the Collections Room tonight," he said.

Kendra was excited, until she wondered why they'd agreed so easily to take her exactly where she wanted to go. The Collections Room was where she had felt the strange vibration during her first visit. When the Gold Coat opened the door to the dimly lighted chamber, she hesitated.

"You're a lucky girl," he said. "Tonight, all of your questions will be answered." Kendra wondered if he knew why she was really there.

When Kendra walked into the room, its soaring ceiling seemed to swallow her. The room was crammed with mixed-media paintings and sculpture, one stranger than the next; discarded household items contorted into faces and limbs, with a sameness to the flat features. The oddly lighted room was crisscrossed with shadows.

When the Gold Coat closed the door behind her, she was afraid to check the lock.

Kendra had walked only two steps inside when she felt the certainty that she wasn't alone. No movement or sound, but she knew. She searched the shadows for a human figure, but saw no one. She was about to call for Rianne when she heard a voice.

"Kendra."

The whispered voice bubbled as if it were underwater, and Kendra's body went to stone, except for her thrashing heart. She felt small and alone.

Kendra opened her mouth to ask who was there, but no sound emerged. Her hand was reaching back toward the door with a mind of its own.

"No need for fear, Kendra," the voice said, impossibly reasonable despite its cloak of strangeness. *"We should have grown beyond fear by now."*

Kendra froze, her eyes darting to her left. Something was moving in the shadows with great deliberation, making itself seen. The figure was nearly six feet tall, with an oversized head. Another careful motion, and Kendra realized that the head was the size of a man's, but it balanced on a too-thin neck and limbs.

She stood fewer than ten yards from a skeleton with shiny, sun-reddened skin—or skin reddened by *something.* He blinked before disappearing from the light. His eyes were like balls of blood. Infected! One of the talkers, which meant he was probably a runner. The Gold Coat had led her into a trap!

Kendra's mouth fell open as she sucked at the air to breathe. What now?

The door was closed behind her, so she would lose precious seconds of escape time if she tried to go out the way she'd come—but was there somewhere else she could run? Kendra remembered teeth sinking into Grandpa Joe's calf and wondered: Would she kill herself on the spot somehow, or try to tell Terry first? Remembering Terry filled her with grief.

Kendra was shocked her legs weren't in motion already, but her mind paralyzed her with a question: *How did it know your name?*

"I see you have infinite questions. So inquisitive. You are interesting to me."

It wasn't going to spring at her! The creature had moved no closer, still half hidden in shadows. It glanced at her, but kept its face turned away, as if in shyness.

This *was* a freak, wasn't it? But if it was a freak, that wasn't all it was. This freak was nothing like the others. Instead of rotting flesh, this one's skin was as slick as a baby eel's. Her eyes quickly searched the room again, and she realized that the odd figures looked very similar to the creature before her.

"Is this your art?" someone calm and reasonable asked. "Or Wales's?"

She was talking to it! And the creature still hadn't sprung, although it began a slow rocking from side to side.

"Wales?" the watery voice said. *"He paints like a child. And color-blind! I don't think he knows it himself. He's good for a purplish flourish now and again."*

"So the other artwork . . . isn't Wales's?" Her voice surprised her again. How was one part of her conducting a conversation while the rest of her was preparing to die?

"You are far too fast to be so slow, Kendra." The *sssssssss* sounds were more reptilian than human. Kendra backed toward the door. If she went slowly, she thought, it might not chase her.

"Who are you?" the other Kendra said, the one who remembered how to speak.

*"I was called Harry. Now? Call me Harry if you like, but I have
no name."*

Harry. The simple name was absurd.

"What happened to you, Harry?"

But she knew, she realized. She knew what had happened
to Harry as well as she knew what had happened to her
parents, and Grandpa Joe. Then her certainty went beyond
intuition to a blurry image that suddenly sharpened in her
mind: an art studio, breaking glass in a dark bedroom, a man's
cries against a woman's attack. His girlfriend. Locked in a
bathroom, accidentally freed by a newcomer. Blood. Kendra
saw all of it.

Her breath died in her throat. What had just happened?

"Now you know," he said. *"Just as I know your story."*

"You can talk to my head?" Kendra said, using the only
words that fit.

"Talking is easy," he said. *"Communication is harder."*

"I can't see you," Kendra said. "Come into the light."

"I don't care to. There." The remaining lights died, left her
groping in shadow. Kendra heard no sound, but she felt the
creature move toward her. Patient. By inches, the creature was
closing in on her.

Kendra took another step away, could feel the vibration of the
wooden door just beyond her, a beacon if only she had time. Her
hand groped toward the knob. "I don't like the dark," Kendra
said, hoping she didn't sound like she was begging. "Turn the
lights back on."

"It disturbs my senses," the voice said. *"I have . . . a different
aesthetic now. I prefer darkness to light."*

"What are you? Tell me!"

"You know me," he said. *"From your dreams."*

"No!" Kendra said, surprised to feel genuine irritation inside her terror. "My dreams are just . . . pictures. They don't tell me anything!"

Soft laughter floated from the shape in the darkness, its most human sound so far. *"Fear makes you raise your voice. There is nothing for you to fear, Kendra—not you, nor any of your people. We are the same, in the end. We are one."*

"We're not the same," Kendra said. "You got bitten. You're a freak."

The creature bristled, its voice sharper. *"That is the word used against us, to make us monsters,"* he said. *"You casually fling such verbal violence, and then question our motivations?"*

"That word isn't what makes you monsters," Kendra whispered. "Look at what you've done! You've killed millions of us! Billions!"

The creature sighed. *"The innocent, mindless thrashings of a newborn entering a strange world. It was not supposed to be this way."*

"How was it supposed to be?"

Finally, Kendra's hand brushed the doorknob. She tried to turn it, but as she'd feared, she was locked in the room with the creature.

None of it was an accident, she realized. If this creature was influencing Wales's art, how could she know she hadn't been influenced too? She'd seen Sissy's vacant face at the town meeting. Had this creature done that to her? What about Rianne?

"Where is she?" Kendra said. "Where's Rianne?"

"Prepare your mind, Kendra. Join us, gently. You are different from the others. You . . . perceive more. You could be one of us."

"How?"

"You are an artist," he said. *"Your mind has an artist's flexibility. Look how you've accepted me already. None of the*

287

others, even Wales, have presented themselves as openly. With such courage."

"What about Sissy and Rianne?"

"They do not have your gifts, Kendra," the creature said. *"We are rare, you and I. Fewer than one in ten of us have the ability to make the transition. And because of the . . . circumstances, less than one in a thousand survives in the wild."* His voice trembled with the memory. She knew how hard it was for humans outside, but she'd never considered what life was like for the freaks.

"There are more of you?" Kendra said.

"Join us, Kendra," he said. *"Step into a future without pain, without fear."*

The creature had stopped moving forward. It was waiting, for now.

"Do I have a choice?" Kendra said, to be sure.

"If you come willingly, you have a much better chance of making the leap. And I will teach you so much."

In the dark, Kendra had lost her bearings quickly. She saw shadows from canvases and shelves where she might hide for a time, but the creature was better acclimated to the dark. If she was trapped, at least she would know why.

"Tell me where you came from," she said.

The creature made a sharp intake of breath, another sign of impatience. *"Our origins are not so simple to pinpoint. We came here centuries ago. We had drifted . . . I don't know how long. We only began to awaken when conscious beings ingested us. Ate the mushrooms that grew from the spores."*

The mushrooms! "Those spores traveled," Kendra said, to be certain she understood. "And then we began to eat them."

"Yes. Our spores did not grow freely, but some took root on the continent of Africa. Tanzania, on Mount Meru."

"Meru? Is that near Kilimanjaro?" That was the only

mountain she knew in Africa. Her father had climbed Kilimanjaro when he was in college. Would the creature spare her if she found the right words, the right questions?

"Yes," it whispered. *"And if it had been Kilimanjaro, this all would have happened long ago. But outsiders didn't climb Meru. Only the Chagga tribe knew about the mushrooms, and used us for their vision quests, and to stave off hunger. Then Europeans found us, and carried us around the world. Mixed us with chemicals. The infection would have been slow, painless. We would have become symbiotes to humanity, as we had for the sentient life-forms of so many other worlds."*

"But what happened?" Kendra asked. "What went wrong?"

And it began to tell her.

Twenty-nine

You sure this is it?" Terry said as Piranha coasted the truck to a stop in the high weeds. Piranha clicked the engine off. Crickets burred around them in the dark.

In the backseat, Hipshot growled softly, and Terry shushed him. Bringing Hippy might have been a mistake. If Hippy started barking, they might be busted before they began. He didn't see any Gold Shirts or other guards yet, but he was sure they were close. Cameras might even be monitoring the tunnel entrance. If so, the mission had failed already.

"That's his freak growl," Piranha said.

Terry nodded, surveying the high grass and sheltering stands of trees near them. "There might be a nest not far from here. And Kendra thought she smelled freaks inside, so keep your eyes open."

Terry nuzzled Hipshot's chin and tried to stare the dog in his alert brown eyes. Hippy looked away, submitting to his master.

"Hippy?" Terry said, wishing he could access dog language.

"We need you to be really quiet, boy. *Shhhh*. No noise. No matter what."

Hippy whimpered, uncomfortable under Terry's long gaze. But in a strange way, Terry thought the little guy might have understood him.

"You think that dog whisperer crap's gonna work?" Piranha said.

"It better."

As they climbed out of the car, Terry pulled on the thin, frayed rope they'd improvised as a leash to control Hippy. The dog hesitated before jumping out of the car, casting wary glances into the dark. Then he reluctantly hopped out behind them, and they began the short hike to the spot where they thought the tunnel entrance was, relying on the moon rather than their flashlights for vision. The sky was practically cloudless. Cool beans.

"Check it out," Piranha said, pointing behind them.

About three hundred yards east, a faint glow flashed once, then again, to show them where Darius and Dean were staking out the tunnel.

"The Twins see us," Terry said. *We're going to do this,* Terry thought, as if realizing it for the first time. *Or die trying,* a voice whispered that didn't sound like his.

"I'm glad we've got backup." Piranha hoisted the aluminum baseball bat he'd brought across his shoulder.

Hippy growled again, and Terry gave his rope a displeased yank. With a resigned whimper, Hippy trudged on with them toward the heap of brush Jason had told them concealed the tunnel. They had briefly considered bringing Jason to help them navigate and leave him in the truck, but it would have been too dangerous. Hippy's rope was always taut as they walked; the dog didn't want to follow them. He knew something.

For an instant, fumbling in the darkness, Terry thought their plan was futile. The tunnel might not still be there, and they might be nowhere near it. But Piranha made a sudden clucking sound, bending over to examine something to the right, and he rolled a mound of tumbleweed away.

The tunnel entrance was unguarded, and there was no camera in sight. Wales must be certain that no one would try to get in or that no one remembered it. The archway-shaped iron door was as rusty as the chain that locked it. Wales might not have thought about the rear tunnel entrance since Freak Day.

"Bolt cutters, Dr. Cawthone," Terry said.

"Step aside, son."

For the first time, they brought out the flashlight. First, they signaled briefly behind them to show the Twins they had arrived, and saw a reassuring flash in response. Then Piranha trained the light on the chain to search for the weakest link, which was the padlock itself. One powerful *snap,* and the chain clinked away.

Hippy whimpered again, stepping backward.

"*Shhhh,*" Terry said. "Easy, boy."

Terry and Piranha exchanged a glance for courage, and then they pulled the door's latch. It took both of them to tug the door open wide enough to fit their bulk in.

"Who's there?" Terry called authoritatively, as if in challenge, just loudly enough for anyone posted near the door to hear. No response.

"We're in," Piranha said. "Let's go get the girls."

The door opened to steep, rough-hewn steps that threatened to crumble under their weight as they descended down six feet. Once they were inside, they both turned on their flashlights, illuminating walls of stone and packed dirt. Carefully, they pulled the door nearly closed behind them in case an alert passerby might notice. Patrols might check the tunnel.

Terry's heart drummed harder each time he felt Hipshot try to pull the other way, but he stopped shushing the dog's growls. As long as Hippy wasn't barking, the soft warnings were a reminder to be watchful.

"Old mine shaft," Piranha said, pointing to a rusted length of abandoned discarded track barely visible as a ridge in the packed dirt. The tunnels were narrow, but wide enough for trolley tracks, even if there was no mine car in sight. The walls had been widened, and Terry suspected that the widening had been within the last few years. Wales?

"Damn," Piranha said.

They reached a gate much newer than the door outside, sure to be locked. But when they tested it, they realized it was a freakproof lock, much like the ones at the quarantine house and the Motel 6. No bolt cutters were necessary to open it. Another gate waited fifty yards ahead, as easy to open. Then a third. The farther they walked, the wider the tunnel and the louder Hippy's growls. And something else . . .

"You smell that?" Terry said.

He'd hoped it was his imagination, but now he had confirmation that Kendra had been right: Wales's ranch was awash with the stink of freaks. Then he heard a distant *bang-bang-bang* with an imprecise rhythm that reminded him all too much of Vern in the freezer. The muffled sound was coming from two or three places ahead of them. Ghostly faces raced toward him in the shadows, vanishing when he blinked.

Suddenly, Terry didn't feel well enough armed for their task. He had a gun, but had they brought enough ammo? He only had two extra clips. A few freaks wouldn't generate an odor that strong; the tunnel must be teeming with them. That explained the freakproof locks. Should they bring the Twins in? Did they have time? They'd planned to let the Twins give them cover outside, but although the tunnel entrance was only about a hundred fifty yards behind them, it might as well be in Mexico. Terry's unsteady legs tensed, ready to bolt.

Piranha stood at the last gate and shined his flashlight into the yawning void. "Think I see them. Looks like . . . cages. Cells."

"Like Jason said," Terry remembered, relieved. That made sense, but his knee joints still trembled. "Freaks locked up, trying to get out?"

"Let's hope they're locked up," Piranha said, and opened the gate. The hinge screeched, and the banging ahead got louder in response. *Much* louder. The banging swelled into a macabre chorus.

For the first time, Hippy barked.

"Shhhh," Terry said, accidentally yanking his leash so hard that Hippy yelped in pain. Terry didn't soothe him. The tunnel was cool, but a slick of perspiration pasted his clothes to his skin. As much as he'd experienced since Vern's attack, Terry couldn't remember being more afraid. Their flashlights seemed useless against the dark, like shining penlights into a muddy ocean.

"Zip it, mutt," Piranha said.

After a half-dozen steps, the vague shadows behind the bars ahead took a more solid aspect, framing shapes that were still confusing to the eye. Grasping, mindless hands reached through the bars, as if to capture the air, but the reaching arms were low to the ground. The hands were bigger than children's, but the freaks seemed shorter than even a child should be. What the . . . ?

"Too lazy to stand up?" Piranha said.

Then, Terry got it: their legs might be broken! The freaks

couldn't stand or run, but he and Piranha might not be able to avoid their touch. Rows of arms undulated near the ground like tentacles on both sides, growing in pairs. Freaks crowded the cells by the dozens. There might have been a hundred or more in the tunnel. Terry's skin crawled.

"We're gonna have to walk straight down the middle," Terry said. "They're dumb, but they're strong. We get pulled in too close . . ."

"No kidding," Piranha said. "Thought I'd let you test that path first, bro."

"You owe me, remember?" Terry said. "Ladies first."

Somehow, joking helped.

Hippy made the first move, pulling ahead on his leash with a low, throaty growl that made him sound like a rottweiler, except bigger. Terry wrapped the rope tightly around his palm to make sure Hippy didn't dart loose or lunge at a freak. He'd never heard of an infected dog, but why chance it? Even a few steps forward made the stench strangle them like a wet tarp.

Freaks moaned and grasped out, but Terry and Piranha had a six-inch buffer on each side—far enough to avoid being touched, but close enough to see the rancid flesh on the freaks' fingers and the red moss carpeting their nails. Eyes glowed red in the light.

The gallery of horrors in the tunnel felt endless, and Terry fought to keep his eyes on the path ahead instead of the questing fingers. Several already pressed themselves against the bars, and others crawled on the ground, laboring to get closer, pulling themselves with their arms while their misshapen legs dragged behind them. Some of the freaks' legs had simply been sheared off. Others tried to crawl toward them but couldn't, held in place by strong roots growing from their torsos, anchoring them to the ground. More than half were women. Many had white hair and wrinkled skin like the luckless vagabonds in the camp outside.

"Where is it?" a man's voice barked from behind them in the dark, and Terry turned around, expecting to see a Gold Shirt behind him. "I wanted my bagel with a big hole! *Thursday!*"

Only a freak's gibberish. It was so easy to forget that some of them could talk.

He tasted vomit bubbling in his throat, but swallowed it back. He didn't have time to be sick, and he needed all of his concentration to keep on his feet. His legs threatened to take him down to freak level.

After the too-long walk, a closed door came in sight a few yards ahead.

But one freak stood ahead of them, near the door, its guardian. He was the only freak who wasn't in a cage, and the sight of him sent Hippy into a barking frenzy. A symphony of moans answered Hippy, nearly popping Terry's eardrums.

"Freak!" Terry and Piranha said in unison, ready to run the other way.

Time slowed down long enough for Terry to see the light glinting from the freak's chained ankles, and his finger froze just as he was about to fire his gun. "Wait . . . he can't get to us!" Terry said.

Piranha got the message, but Hippy yanked so hard on his leash that Terry nearly lost his grip. The dog's barking echoed in the tunnel.

"Shut up!" Piranha said, swinging his leg back to kick Hipshot, but Terry blocked the kick.

"No, man!" Terry said, shoving Piranha. "What are you doing?"

"He better shut the hell up, or we're—"

Keys jingled loudly from the other side of the door the freak was guarding.

Breathing hard, Terry and Piranha raised their guns. *It's over,* Terry thought.

It was too late to run. As bad as the freaks were, Gold Shirts were worse. A shoot-out in the tunnel meant they would never see Kendra or Sonia again. They huddled close, as if they could build a human fortress.

When the door opened, a bright light momentarily blinded Terry.

"In a sneak attack," a woman's calm voice said in a schoolteacher's cadence, "the operative word is *sneak.* I told you not to bring that mutt."

Ursalina! She looked like a supermodel in her sexy dress, standing boldly close to the freak.

"Watch it!" Terry said, his voice shaky. "He'll bite you!"

Ursalina laughed and shrugged. "Ralphie here?" she said. "No teeth. The only time he bites is in his freaky dreams."

Ursalina came to them, and they shared a hug. Even Hippy stood on two legs, trying to lick her face. Terry didn't think he'd ever been happier to see anyone.

"It's safe in there?" Piranha said.

"Safe as it's gonna get," Ursalina said, beckoning them toward the open door. "Come on in, before you can't wash the freak stink out of your hair. Steer clear of Ralphie—he can't bite, but he slobbers like a dog. No offense, Hippy."

Hippy licked her offered palm. No offense taken.

The doorway led to a bland basement room with industrial carpeting and walls covered in weird Threadie murals, but it felt like the gates of heaven. A single young Gold Shirt was hogtied in a corner, moaning against a gag. He sounded barely conscious. Poor guy.

"Making friends?" Terry said, glancing at the stranger.

"I probably should kill him, but"—she shrugged—"what can I say? I'm a softie."

"Where's—" Terry and Piranha started to ask about Kendra and Sonia.

"Kendra went to the library with some old guy," Ursalina said. "But Sonia's with Wales, maybe in his room."

Terry felt uneasy relief about Kendra, but Piranha's face transformed into such a mask of rage that Terry wondered if he would shoot the helpless Gold Shirt on principle.

"Then what are we doing down here?" Piranha said.

He tossed Ursalina her Nine.

Thirty

The flu shot is to blame," the creature said. *"Designed to trigger the immune system against a viral intruder. But it triggered something else . . . in us. What should have been a peaceful process became a nightmare for us all. Do you think it's easier for us? Put yourself, for a moment, in my place."*

Kendra had backed as far against the locked door as physics would allow, but her body still pressed as if she could find a way through the solid mass. The creature's slow circling had become a straightforward approach, and it stood only ten yards from her, still veiled in darkness.

Kendra didn't hide her fumbling with the doorknob, turning and yanking with all her strength. If the door wouldn't give her an escape, maybe the lock would. The knob was slippery from the terrified perspiration on her palm.

"Fighting," the creature scolded with a sigh. *"Fighting makes it so much harder."*

"What are you?" Kendra said. The creature seemed to slow

its approach when it spoke, and her only hope now was stalling tactics, even transparent ones.

"I am you," it said. *"One of you, on the other side of it all."*

Then the creature moved again, part slither, part feline glide. Kendra let out a quiet yelp.

"What do you want from us?" Kendra said.

"A home," it said.

"And you'll kill us to take it?"

A gleam of a smile came in the darkness, almost as if its teeth were radiant. *"Not death, Kendra—life. We can live together. This has all been . . . unfortunate. It doesn't have to be as it has been. As you see, I have no need to bite you. No instinctive compulsion."*

Kendra's voice would only emerge as a whisper. "But . . . the others . . ."

"Do I seem like the others?"

The creature emerged into a small bar of light, enough for her to finally see its full face, and Kendra drew in a long, stunned breath.

It was . . . beautiful. That was the only word that felt right. She had expected visceral ugliness, but the creature bore the beauty of a newborn baby, or a praying mantis. God help her, those two images first came to mind. The eyes were large, covered in a red semisheer veil, enough for her to see black or deep blue underneath. With such eyes, how did it create art?

The creature smiled, and she saw that it had no teeth, but there was a chitinous ridge of white bone along the gums, as if all the teeth had fused into a single mass. Even that smile, in its oddness, felt reassuring. Exotic. She realized that she wanted to be closer to the creature, to examine it. She felt . . .

Attracted. When the right word came to her, she felt nearly faint. But she couldn't escape the sensation. Her skin broiled in the creature's sight. This wasn't the electricity she felt with Terry, but something warm and fiercely inquisitive.

Was he doing that to her?

"What do you want from me?" Kendra said.

"Your potential," the creature said. *"I've seen so much in the dream. You are an ally to my kind. You are capable of . . . loving us. You could transition without fear."*

"You're wrong," Kendra said. "I could never love your kind." Her voice rose, forceful and angry. "After everything you've done? I'll never forgive you! Never!" She might as well have been lecturing herself.

"We're all victims of this accident, Kendra."

"You're monsters! You'll always be monsters!" Her last words were a sob. She was flooded by memories deeper and much more vivid than the snapshots the creature had shown her from its past. She saw her father's grin, smelled her mother's bosom, saw the helpless terror in Grandpa Joe's eyes when he realized that he had made a fatal mistake and Kendra would be alone.

Sobs emerged as wails, wracking Kendra's body until she doubled over. Now she could only lean against the door, drained by the depth of her losses. She felt herself falling into a hole so deep she might never see the sun again.

Devil's Wake had always been only a dream. She had no family. There was no one and nothing left. She would fight to stay away from the creature as long as she could—fight to say she was *Still Here*—but she suddenly realized what Ursalina had been trying to communicate since the first day she fled to the Beauty: survival was a bitter joke. Survival for what? The next worse thing?

The world belonged to monsters now.

Kendra had to hear the voice outside of the door once, twice, perhaps three times, before she realized it wasn't only her imagination.

"Kendra!"

Somewhere nearby, Terry was calling for her.

"I'm here!"

Kendra's voice was so clear that she might be standing next to him. Terry and Ursalina hadn't been in the library long when Terry was sure he'd heard Kendra crying in the distance. She wasn't at any of the empty library tables, and each passing second increased the likelihood that a Gold Shirt might discover them.

Then he examined the library wall and realized that the glossy wood wasn't only a wall—it was a door. Kendra was inside!

"Guys, she's here!"

"Terry, *help!*" Kendra called.

Kendra's plea, so helpless and terrified, hit Terry's stomach like a physical blow. He would have broken the door down if he'd had to, but he found the gold-plated doorknob and turned it. Locked. He turned the pin and tried to fling the door open, but Kendra's weight was against it. He hoped it was Kendra.

"Kendra, move back!" he said, and suddenly the door gave freely.

The door opened to darkness that reminded Terry of the tunnel. Ursalina raced in behind him, gun ready, and found a light switch. Spotlights came on from above, illuminating eerie artwork and sculptures like the murals in the basement.

But Terry's breath withered in his mouth when he realized that the largest piece, the one closest to him, wasn't a sculpture—it was . . . what? Something else. As kids, he and

Lisa had watched an old black-and-white sci-fi movie called *The Deadly Mantis,* and although this thing's eyes were more humanoid than insect, its posture made Terry feel as if he was facing the beast in life, with shinier skin. Then it was gone, a hallucination.

"Freak!" Ursalina said, trying to track it with her handgun, but it moved too fast. Only a teetering easel showed its hasty path away from them. Kendra shrieked in fear, grabbing Terry's arm to draw close to him.

"Don't shoot it!" Terry said, and realized that Kendra had said it too, a unified thought. "Too much noise," Terry went on. "Not till Piranha finds Sonia."

But it was a runner! Faster than a runner. Dear God, had Kendra been bitten? Kendra saw the question in his eyes and shook her head emphatically. "It didn't touch me," she said. "But you can't shoot it. It's a new kind of . . ."

"A new kind of dead." Ursalina cut her off, her eyes tracking the beast's shadows.

"Not with your gun," Terry said, talking to himself as much as Ursalina. If he pulled the trigger, he would empty his clip from sheer repulsion.

"He talks!" Kendra said. Was she pleading for its life? "We can learn from him. His name is—"

A fully grown man's weight suddenly landed on Terry's back, and then he was on the floor. Where had it jumped from? When Terry landed too hard on his knees, he could only watch as the baseball bat rolled from his hand. Frantically, Terry tried to fling the thing away from him, but it held on. Terry bit his lip to keep from screaming. He felt the thing's hot breath like orange heat against his ear and reverted to a toddler.

"Don't let it bite me—"

Ursalina leaped on the pile to try to pull the freak away, and when Terry turned he saw the freak's mouth wide open as it moved to try to bite her exposed forearm.

"Stop it, Harry!" Kendra shouted, and the beast whipped around to stare at her, as if her voice had hypnotized him.

Harry? Seriously? And was that fondness in his eyes? Hers?

When Kendra raised the bat high, ready to strike, the beast shook its glistening head. *"You love him,"* the beast said in a watery, not-quite-human voice Terry would never forget. *"Bring him with us. I have so much to show you."*

Instead of answering, Kendra swung at its temple. The creature barely moved to try to avoid her, but despite a *chunk* sound, Kendra's blow was too polite. The beast was still on its feet, moving away slowly as it gathered its senses to run. Ursalina snatched the bat from Kendra and chased the thing step for step through the maze of sculptures.

"Ursalina, keep it alive—" Kendra tried to say, but Ursalina swung as if she were trying to send a baseball to the moon, hitting it square in the mouth. This time, the blow sounded more like a watermelon being pulped, and its teeth shattered. The creature screamed before staggering and falling. Ursalina took a broad-legged stance over its prone form and hit it again. And again.

Ursalina hit the creature until she was shaking, and Terry had to look away.

"Don't kill it," Kendra whispered through tears, long after the beast was dead.

Thirty-one

Terry and Ursalina had warned Piranha to wait for them to find Kendra instead of looking for Sonia first, but Piranha didn't think Sonia would be able to wait. Every time Piranha blinked, a lurid image of Sonia and Wales haunted his mind's darkness. So he was alone as he followed the map toward the corner of the mansion that was Wales's true residence, expecting a confrontation at any moment.

He was almost alone, anyway.

He and Hipshot had never been best friends, but Piranha had traded the bat for the dog, hoping Hippy would be able to keep quiet in the mansion's freak-free zones. The gold shirt he'd swiped from the guy Ursalina had captured probably wouldn't do him much good—he had yet to see a brother in the ranks of the Gold Shirts, much less a Gold Shirt with a mutt like Hippy—but camouflage might keep him alive.

Yeah, I'm the new guy, he rehearsed in his mind. *Power to the Threads.*

"Where is she, Hippy?" Piranha said. "Come on, boy. Make me a believer."

Dutifully, Hipshot sniffed the floor in a convincing mimicry of tracking mode. Piranha didn't buy the Lassie act, but he hoped they were headed the right way. The wings closer to Wales's quarters had fewer lights on, and more paintings like the ones he'd seen on the basement walls.

The echo of two sets of footsteps twenty feet down the hall froze Piranha, and he darted around a corner to avoid being seen, trying to reel in Hipshot's rope like a fishing line. "Heel," he whispered, an afterthought, and the dog suddenly sat beside him, out of sight. Well, damn, Vern had actually trained the pooch! Who knew?

Two Gold Shirts breezed past, never noticing them. They walked so close, Piranha could smell their deodorant.

Piranha held his breath for almost a full minute after they were gone, his heart a jackhammer as he tried to remember how to breathe. His gun was in his pants, which meant he had the map in one hand and Hippy's leash in the other. Bringing a map and a dog to a gunfight sounded like the punch line to a bad joke. He knelt down to untie Hippy's rope, kicking it into a corner behind a potted plant. Hippy wagged his tail, happy to be free. Remembering Terry's technique, Piranha rubbed the dog's chin and tried to stare him in the eye.

"If you run off, you're on your own."

Hippy licked his face. *Blech.* Still, Piranha smiled. "Stay," he said firmly.

Hipshot understood that perfectly. His tail stopped wagging, and he whimpered.

"You heard me," Piranha said. "Until I come back or call you—*stay.*"

Hipshot's haunches nearly rose, but he fought his protective instincts and sat. The damn dog would obey! He could stash Hipshot in a hidden corner, out of sight, and call if he needed him, like one of the cool pet tricks he'd watched on *Letterman*. If he survived this night, he and Hipshot might become buddies after all.

"Good boy," Piranha said, and left to the sound of Hippy's thumping tail. Feeling worlds better armed with both the gun and the map, Piranha continued his painstaking journey down what he hoped was the right hallway. He walked fast, almost a jog, and the ceiling opened up. A large glass-domed atrium filled with trees and tall plants appeared right where it was supposed to be, and if he got to the southeast end . . .

The next footsteps, from behind him, were so swift and soft that Piranha barely heard them, and he knew he'd been spotted.

The footsteps froze. Maybe this would be like a gunfight in Tombstone, and the Gold Shirt would give him time to draw. Slowly, Piranha turned. If he had to, he decided, he would toss his gun down to the floor.

But no such order came. Sonia stood six feet behind him, wide-eyed and petrified. Then she saw him in a shaft of moonlight, and heartbreaking relief washed over her face. Her clothes were mussed, but she looked unharmed.

"Piranha?" she said, hesitating, afraid to believe her eyes.

"Sonia! You okay?"

He ran to her, and they embraced. Sonia was trembling head to toe. She wrapped her arms around his neck and held on as if they were being swept out to sea. "You scared the—I thought—" She fumbled for sentence. "That shirt?"

"Ursalina swiped it," he said. "We're all here, just like the plan. The others went for Kendra." Piranha let out a soft whistle, and canine toenails clicked across the floor as Hipshot came running. Sonia was as glad to see Hipshot as he was to see her.

"What about Wales?" Piranha whispered, remembering others might hear them.

Sonia grinned like her old self, holding up a Taser. "Taking a nap."

"Good girl," Piranha said. He bit back his questions about what had happened between them. She would tell him in her own time, or not. Maybe ignorance was bliss. "Any news on Rianne?" Piranha said.

Sonia nodded. "Maybe. I'm following a hunch. Let me see your map."

They huddled behind a towering royal palm unnaturally planted indoors, and Sonia studied the map with light from his flashlight. Sonia was wearing perfume she must have gotten from Deirdre, and she smelled so good that Piranha's mind almost went blank. She spoke softly to him while she lowered her face close to read the handwritten scrawls on the map. "Threadheads believe in something called routing—as in sending thoughts from one plane to the next. One of my old high school friends was into it. It's a kind of meditation, like praying. If I could find a room . . ."

Piranha grinned. "Like this?" he said, pointing. One of the rooms on their floor, practically around the corner from the Atrium, was marked RT Sanctuary.

Sonia looked up at Piranha, ecstatic. "I knew there was something I loved about you, Charles Cawthone," she said.

Their kiss was deep and private, wiping the memory of Wales away.

Rianne.

Sonia knew her on sight, despite having seen nothing more than a cell phone–sized digital picture until this moment.

310

The willowy girl was barefoot, sitting placidly in a thronelike chair with crimson upholstery, facing the door. Her forehead and lips did vaguely resemble Deirdre's true daughter's, but she looked much taller even seated, and her skin was more olive than brown. She didn't open her eyes, lost in unknowable thoughts even after Sonia and Piranha came in and Hipshot began sniffing her feet. No sign that she was infected.

"Rianne?"

Sonia spoke softly, but Rianne gave a start and stood so quickly that she nearly tripped over her feet. Her almond-shaped eyes regarded them with more wonder than fright. *Of course—Piranha looks like a Gold Shirt,* Sonia remembered.

"Who are you?" Rianne said with bland curiosity. She stared at Piranha, trying to remember if she had seen him before.

"My name is Sonia," she said, walking closer to her. "This is my friend P. Deirdre and Myles sent us to talk to you."

Rianne's face shed all openness. "You're outsiders," she said, suddenly nervous. "You don't belong here."

Piranha had hidden his gun, luckily. He raised his empty, harmless palms. "We're just here to help."

"I don't need anyone's help. You shouldn't be here. The ceremony is only a few hours away. Don't you understand that you're . . . contaminating me?"

Sonia almost sniggered. *Don't worry, Wales has already done that,* she thought, but she blocked the sneer playing on her lips. "This is our last chance to talk to you," she said. "After tomorrow, you'll be gone." *One way or the other,* she finished silently.

"They're worried about you, Rianne," Piranha said. "The whole family. You're like a daughter to them."

Rianne sighed, impatient. "They're really nice people, but they're not my family. My family is here now. They never understood." Rianne and Sissy definitely had been studying the same script. Sonia didn't know how long deprogramming took, but she was damned sure she and Piranha didn't have time. They were beyond lucky they hadn't been spotted sneaking around Wales's house up until now.

Rianne sighed, resting a gentle hand on Sonia's shoulder. "I know you can't help being ignorant," she said, "but tomorrow is more important than you can imagine."

"What if I told you it wasn't what you think it is?" Sonia said. "That it's something big, all right, but it's a lie. Wales has been lying."

"That isn't possible." Her face was all earnestness.

Piranha tapped Sonia from behind, nudging her. "We don't have time for this," he said. "Where's the video camera? This is what they asked to hear."

"Yes!" Rianne said, eavesdropping. "I'll say good-bye on video. I don't think Mr. Wales would approve, but I don't want to get anyone in trouble. They were good to me."

"No way," Sonia said, turning to Piranha. "You didn't hear everything Wales told me. She can't stay here. He's making people disappear. Changing them. You don't know what he wants to turn them into."

"Are you kidding?" Piranha said. "I came in through the tunnel, remember? I think I'm beginning to get the picture."

The tunnel! The entire room seemed to brighten as Sonia got an idea. She linked her arm with Rianne's. "Listen, you're right: maybe there's nothing I can say to change your mind," she said. "But how about something you can *see*?"

Rianne held firm. "I'm not supposed to leave the Routing Sanctuary."

"We'll bring you right back," Piranha said, "if that's what you want."

"It'll only take us five minutes," Sonia said.

Rianne considered, glancing back at her abandoned throne. "I really don't want to cause you trouble," she repeated. "But after five minutes, I start screaming."

In five minutes, we might all be screaming, Sonia thought.

But she offered Rianne her sweetest smile.

Thirty-two

All Kendra saw, at first, was a bright gold shirt as three people moved quickly toward them in the corridor. Then she saw Hipshot trotting at the group's heels and realized that the Gold Shirt was only Piranha . . . and Sonia and another girl were with him! Rianne? Kendra's joy at seeing her friends erased the inexplicable sense of grief she'd felt when she watched the fifth-level freak die. Why hadn't she killed it herself? The creature had wanted to bite her, yet she'd felt such an odd connection . . .

She and her friends bumped fists and slapped palms.

"We were just on the way to rescue you," Terry told the others.

"Why send children to do a man's job?" Piranha said.

The stranger with them squirmed with discomfort, her arms folded as if she were covering a bare chest. "None of you should be here," she said. "I'll be banned from the ranch—"

"Everyone, this is Rianne," Sonia said, hooking her arm

around the tall, beautiful girl's waist. "She thinks she wants to stay here, but there's a little something we want to show her in the tunnel."

"Perfecto," Ursalina said. "It's on the way out."

"What about Wales?" Kendra said.

"Not an issue—for now," Sonia said, apparently choosing her words carefully in Rianne's presence. "But let's not hang around."

While the group made its way toward the rear, where the basement had appeared on the map, Ursalina sidled up to Sonia and whispered a private question. Sonia only smiled and shook her head, and Ursalina squeezed her hand.

Maybe this will work, Kendra thought, entertaining a ray of optimism.

Then, as if the thought were a jinx, a broad-shouldered Gold Shirt with butch-cut dark hair turned a corner and stood a foot in front of them. For an instant, everyone froze. Kendra was sure that the surprise on the Gold Shirt's face mirrored theirs. The stranger's eyes went to Piranha, confused.

The man reached for his belt—maybe a gun, maybe a radio— but he'd barely moved before Piranha smashed a right cross against his jaw and the Gold Shirt crumpled. Ursalina clamped her hand over Rianne's mouth to stifle the girl's horrified scream.

"Don't worry, he's okay." Kendra tried to reassure Rianne, although the man on the floor looked as dead as the creature they had left behind. Alive, maybe. Not okay.

"Hustle time," Terry said.

While Ursalina held her mouth, Terry and Piranha had to drag her, and Rianne's energetic writhing made every few steps a labor. In the kitchen, Piranha hoisted Rianne over his shoulder in a fireman carry, and Ursalina's hand slipped from her mouth. Rianne screamed so loudly for help that no one on the lower floor could have missed it.

"So much for the easy way," Ursalina said as they broke into a run. She, Terry, and Piranha headed straight for a rear door that looked as though it must lead to the basement. The door was unlocked, an easy passage except for Rianne.

"Go, go, go," Piranha urged, breathless, as the others ran down the basement steps. Hipshot barked with excitement.

"Put her down," Ursalina said. "We've got her."

While Kendra closed the basement door to make sure Rianne couldn't escape back into the kitchen, the others pulled and coaxed to get her down the stairs. Rianne was sobbing, so frightened that Kendra felt sorry for her.

"We're not the ones you need to be afraid of," Kendra said.

"How many others were there, Rianne?" Sonia said. "People you've never seen again? You're about to see why."

"Leave me alone!" Rianne shrieked.

Hipshot barked, but Kendra didn't need Hipshot to know that freaks must be nearby. Their tart, rotting scent filled her nostrils.

Downstairs, they reached a large room where a prisoner was trying to free himself from a binding to a pipe. When he saw them, he tried to yell out over his gag, red-faced, but they all ran past him as if he weren't there. He was bare-chested—so *that* was where Piranha'd gotten a gold shirt. The prisoner's words were muffled, but Kendra understood his last shout clearly: "You're all dead!"

Probably a threat, but it might have been a simple prediction.

The door Ursalina opened on the other side of the room led to darkness. Suddenly Terry's hand was on Kendra's shoulder, pinning her still. Terry's eyes shined urgently. "Careful down here," he said to her, but loudly enough for everyone to hear.

"There's a freak in chains by the door. He's got no teeth, but stick to the right to get past him. Then stay down the middle. No matter what you see, keep going. Fast."

"You're about to meet Ralphie." Ursalina grinned.

My name was Harry. Kendra remembered the freak upstairs and felt a shiver.

"I won't go in there!" Rianne shrieked.

"Bad news, sister—we're here now," Ursalina said, and pushed her through the doorway. When Rianne tried to run back out, they blocked her path.

"Flashlight?" Sonia said, annoyed.

And then there was light. Darkness might have been preferable.

The freak Terry had warned her about lunged from the left, his face a red-pitted atrocity. Hungry fingers tugged at the sleeve of Kendra's dress, and she felt a sharp pull that took her balance. Hippy growled and lunged at the freak, sinking his teeth into its calf. Only Kendra's worry about the dog kept her from screaming.

"Hippy's biting him!" she said as Terry and Ursalina pulled her free. She felt as panicked as she might have if Hippy were a human.

"Dogs are immune to freak juice," Ursalina said. "Keep moving."

"*Down,* Hippy!" Piranha said, and Hippy backed away from the freak, baring his teeth. Kendra's racing heart slowed, but only a fraction.

"Please," Rianne was begging. "Please, please, please let me go."

"We're working on it," Sonia said.

Their voices echoed throughout the endless passage. They plowed ahead in a huddle, picking up speed. A clamor rose from both sides of them, blows against metal. As the flashlight strobed from right to left, hands reached through bars, close to the floor, as if they were sweeping for crumbs.

"Wait," Sonia said after they'd walked only a few yards. "Slow down. She has to see the faces. Where's a flashlight?"

When Terry gave her a flashlight, Sonia shined the light into the cell closest to them, from face to face, searching for someone.

"I know about the freaks!" Rianne said. "He captures them to find a cure."

"That's not all he does," Sonia said. "There—look."

A red-robed female freak pressed her hollowed cheeks between the bars, teeth gnashing. Blond hair cascaded from her shoulders. Kendra gasped, believing she might be Sissy. She wasn't—this girl had been a freak so long that thin roots anchored her to the dirt floor. But she could have been any of them.

"Ring any bells, Rianne?" Sonia said. "Take a good look. Was she here when you first went into training? Did you know her name?"

At first, Rianne tried to turn her face away, refusing to see, but Ursalina and Sonia held her head still. While Kendra's eyes adjusted to the dark, she watched Rianne's face make a remarkable transformation: it seemed to stretch, then crack. Rianne's mouth opened wide, her jaw trembling. When Sonia and Ursalina let her go, Rianne sank to her knees.

"No!" Rianne said. "No. No. No." As if she could chant away the sight before her.

"Is that what you want?" Sonia said quietly, tears dripping from the bridge of her nose. "To help Wales recruit more people to come here and end up like this?"

"That's what it's all about," Kendra said. "Wales was never trying to find a cure. He's trying to help them take all of us. To create something beyond an ordinary freak. I talked to one of them. He told me everything. They need us. We're their only hope for a future." Her nose stung as she talked about Harry, tears threatening. As terrible as he was, he'd been valuable too. A treasure lost forever.

But there would be others soon. Probably many more. Harry didn't need tears.

Rianne reached out toward the blond-haired freak, and the freak reached back with an eager moan. Their fingertips came within an inch of touching before Kendra, Sonia, and Ursalina wrestled Rianne away. The girl crumpled into sobs, clinging to them. Kendra knew that terrible cry well; it was always hidden inside her too.

"That's not your friend anymore," Kendra said. "She's not here, but you are. And you have a home. You have people who care about you so much, they were willing to risk everything to bring you back."

"Yeah, and other people who need to get the hell out of here," Piranha said. "Like us."

Thirty-three

Joseph Allen Wales was unconscious, dreaming he was wrestling the frayed strands of a web that fell apart beneath his weight. Then the web freed him suddenly, and he was pitched into a terrifying free fall, plummeting toward . . . what?

Knocking. At his door. Yes, his room. A Taser. The girl!

With a gasp, Wales opened his eyes. He was relieved to find that Sonia was gone. She could be anywhere telling her tale by now, if anyone would believe her.

"Mr. Wales?" His bodyguard's voice called through the door. Vladimir, who had been with Wales for twenty years. Thank God!

"Yes, I'm here—come in!" Wales said.

He cringed at the idea of being found tied to his bedposts in his robe. Before his coming-of-age after the Change, he'd forced his staff to sign nondisclosure agreements about anything they saw while on duty—and they had seen plenty. But much more than Wales's ego was at risk now that he'd been so damned stupid with that little tease.

Tonight, at least, it was the hulking Ukrainian, and not one of the new recruits who might rush to the Threadie camp bonfire to gossip about what he had seen. Vladimir had been with Wales in Lost Angeles, as he'd always called tinsel town, and the nickname was truer than ever now. L.A. was a wasteland nearly beyond description, he'd been told. Awaiting rebirth.

Grief and shame seized Wales. God have mercy on him. What had he done?

Vlad's jaw set hard when he saw Wales, and he rushed to untie his binds. He avoided Wales's eyes, sparing him the disapproving gaze he'd perfected in Hollywood.

"The bitch?" Vlad said. Thirty years stateside had softened his accent, but not the ring of judgment. "Are you safe?"

"Safe enough. Get me out of these." His throat was dry, his voice stripped to dust. His muscles still jittered from the Taser.

Why had he told her so much? Why hadn't he endured in silence?

"Bring me some water, Vlad. Please. Then we must have a long talk . . ."

As his senses sharpened, Wales realized he had changed while he slept. Or *something* had changed. He felt like a human husk. The burning resolve that had raced through his spirit was gone.

Had the girl been clever enough to kill the Other too? Had the future he'd sold his humanity for always been fragile enough to crumble at the hands of a mere child?

He was alone now—utterly and irreparably alone, with nowhere to hide from the unfathomable memory of what he had done.

Wales trembled, barely able to prop himself to a sitting position on unsteady elbows. Vlad glanced at him but kept his thoughts silent. Vlad believed Americans were weak, to have been overrun so quickly. Wales hadn't yet established communication inside Ukraine, but Vlad had assured him that any freaks who tried to penetrate his hometown of Borodianka would quickly learn their mistake. His grandmother, Vlad always said, could fight freaks off with her garden shears.

Wales hadn't told Vlad everything, saving the more distasteful truth for acolytes who would not question him. Vlad had always been loyal to Wales, carrying out his duties, but he had loathed the Change. He read the Thread literature but had never embraced it. Now, as daylight reached hidden corners of Wales's mind without interference from the Other, he wondered how he could have believed it himself. He hadn't merely betrayed a nation or world, he had betrayed all of human history.

Tremors shook Wales in waves again. He had been dreaming even while he'd believed he was awake. And what now? Was he left with only this waking nightmare?

While Vladimir poured Wales a glass of water from the decanter in the bedroom's bar, his radio suddenly beeped the emergency code.

"Someone's found her," Wales said, full of hope.

"Vlad," he identified himself to his radio, impatient.

The voice was Finn's, from the security room. "I've got footage of five unknowns in the tunnel. Looks like Rianne is with them. They overpowered Warren, took his shirt."

"When?" Vlad said.

A long pause. "I've got a visual in the east tunnel now, but don't know how long ago they penetrated."

The Other had been one miracle, and perhaps Wales had just been presented with another—it wasn't too late! Wales struggled to make his limbs work properly, climbing out of bed. He had to lean on his mattress for support, to catch his breath, but he was on his feet.

"Intercept them," Vlad began, but Wales cut him off, hobbling to snatch the radio from his hand.

"No," Wales said, breathless from exertion. "This is Wales. Wait."

He flung perspiration from his brow with his palm as his thoughts raced. What to do? Without guidance from the Other, where would he find it now?

Vlad waited and wondered, staring at him with icy blue eyes. They had faced this same moment only two nights ago, when Finn radioed to say that Brownie was at the gate, demanding to see Sissy. And when Wales had given the order to do what he must, he had seen the quiet shock in the large man's face, the same look Wales had seen from his guardian many times since the Change: *I don't know you anymore.*

Until now, in Vlad's mind, Wales's good acts far outweighed everything else. But, of course, Vlad had never met the Other.

"They did us all a favor, Vlad," Wales told him quietly, his radio button off. "They did what I should have done."

"You'll let them go?" Vlad said, intrigued. "What will they say to the town?"

"They will say . . ."

His evening with Sonia unfolded in his memory. What had possessed him to let the toxic truth spill from his lips? Only the whiskey, or the weight of the secret? No matter how outlandish her tales would sound to Van Peebles and the townies, she might have seen the Other. Maybe all of them had seen it, to have killed it. They had seen more than enough to destroy Wales's influence, to vilify him.

As long as he preserved his standing, the acts of kindness he performed in the future would one day erase everything else. He would welcome the camp refugees to the town, regardless of age or infirmity. He had years to redeem himself . . . and perhaps salvage his legacy. But not if the terrible secret escaped with the girl and the other intruders. Could he ask his men to bloody their hands one last time?

"Mr. Wales?" Finn's uncertain voice crackled. "Should we intercept?"

"No," Wales said, licking his parched lips. "Open the entrance and ring the dinner bell. Flood the tunnel."

Vlad's eyes widened with something beyond disgust, but Wales was undeterred. In quiet moments of clarity in previous days, when the Other slept, Wales had wondered if he was insane. Perhaps he saw the answer in Vlad's eyes.

"Sir?" Finn said, to be sure.

"You heard me, son," Wales said. "Let the freaks take care of them."

Darius cursed, adjusting his night-vision binoculars against the sudden burst of light. A patrol! A large white pickup truck was racing toward the tunnel entrance on a winding path, driving with an urgency that couldn't be a coincidence.

Something had gone wrong.

Darius realized how right his cousin had been. He hadn't pondered the idea of true losses, and now his stomach felt stuffed with bricks.

"We're gonna have to take them out," Dean said matter-of-factly.

"More will come," Darius said.

"We'll take out the first crew. Change our position. Take out the next ones."

Darius's heart pounded against the soil where he lay propped on his stomach in his ghillie suit, his binoculars pressed to his face so hard he was digging grooves in his skin. Was it only one truck, or was another behind it? Dean was talking about Gold Shirts like they were freaks or pirates, expendable without a thought.

Jackie's brother, Sam, might be on that truck. These were the men who scavenged with Terry and Piranha, who built fences and shared beer with them.

Dean knew his thoughts from his silence. "Only way, man," Dean said. "Even that probably won't be enough. We don't know what's going on inside. If you can't do it, let me know."

"I can do it," Darius said, gravel in his voice.

"You might have to. I don't know if I'm ready to go there."

Darius raised his rifle, tracking the truck's motion through the scope. High brush and the truck's speed would make it impossible to make a shot until the truck got closer to the tunnel. But by then, his accuracy window would be next to nothing.

Maybe Darius had just lied. Maybe he couldn't do it.

The truck lurched to a sudden stop and two men hopped out, moving like lightning. Damn! The tunnel entrance was on the far side, and the truck blocked his shot.

"Relax," Dean said. "Once they pull that tunnel door open, they'll be clear."

Darius sucked air through his mouth, his finger sweating on the trigger. He saw flashes of the yellow shirts as they tugged on the door, was ready to fire . . .

But instead of running inside the tunnel, the men were climbing back into the truck, doors quickly slamming. The white Reverse lights flared as the truck backed up.

"What?" Dean said, confused. "They're not going in."

"Are they trying to let our guys *out*?"

Maybe they were Jackie's brother and Sonia's friend, or

other rogue Gold Shirts enlisted into their mission somehow. Whatever they were up to, they were in a hurry.

While the truck turned around, Dean had a clear shot at the driver. "Take it?"

"No," Dean said. "No threat, as long as they keep driving."

The truck raced away on the path, its lights clouded by rising dust. Darius felt dizzy and sick. He might have almost killed those men for nothing—or he soon might regret sparing them.

A high-pitched, deafening horn sounded, so loud that it seemed to come from everywhere. An alarm! The tone was steady at first, then it came in bursts at intervals. That was followed by the clear sound of an old-fashioned bell. The sound was hard to pinpoint, but it might be coming from the tunnel.

"We should've shot them," Dean said.

But at least the door was open and unguarded, and the truck was gone. If Terry and the others were in the tunnel, they still had a chance to escape.

Premonition tickled the back of Darius's mind. Before a coherent thought could surface, he saw movement in the shadows beyond the tunnel entrance, from the woods.

"D?" Darius said.

"Yeah, D?"

"When does it make sense to raise a racket so close to nests of freaks?"

"Doesn't," Dean said, "unless you're calling them."

As soon as Dean spoke, a male runner flew out of the darkness, racing straight for the open tunnel door. Then another, a female. Also fast.

If Darius had blinked, he might have missed the shot that sent the lead freak flying face-first to the ground only ten yards from the tunnel entrance. Dean spun the female freak with his first shot and smashed her head with his second. Almost immediately, a half-dozen other runners followed.

As if they'd been waiting.

As if they'd been *trained.*

Dry leaves crackled and hissed, betraying motion far too close to them from another hidden nest. Ghillie suits would do only so much good if freaks overran them.

"We're gonna have to switch positions," Dean said. "Too much noise."

As he spoke, his shot went wild, and Darius had to take out the bare-chested runner leading the pack to the tunnel entrance. It took six rapid shots to take down three of them. Then he could answer. "Gotta take the runners first."

"Too many," Dean said.

Their conversation was punctuated by rifle shots in quick succession while the woods vomited freaks. Runners led the charge, but a mass of shamblers would follow.

"Too many for us is *way* too many if you're in that tunnel," Darius said.

Somewhere behind them, a low moan floated on the wind. "Told you before," Dean said. "We're not all gonna make it."

"Says you." Darius fired again, and an overweight freak teetered and fell. "Take the runners. Can't be much more fresh meat around here. Then we go." He'd taken out two more runners while he spoke, although the second needed two shots. Damn. He didn't have ammo to waste. No more distractions.

While seconds passed as hours, the cousins littered the ground with freaks of all shapes, sizes, and ages. Darius shut out his awareness of movement close to them, focusing only on making his shots. Any freak he missed might make it into the tunnel, and any freak who made it into the tunnel could kill his friends.

As he'd feared, the shamblers were coming next. He'd only seen three so far, approaching from different points, but they traveled in packs.

But none of them seemed to be running now.

Dean was already on his feet. "Let's move!" he said.

The moonlight and high grass came back into focus, and Darius realized that a half-dozen shadowed shamblers were approaching from a knoll twenty yards west of them. If the nearby freaks had blocked their way to the bikes, they might have had to waste precious ammo on them.

"We won't get them all," Dean panted as they raced for the bikes, running awkwardly in the heavy ghillie suits. "But we can cut the numbers."

"Drive fast, and we still might keep them out," Darius said, straddling his bike.

Dean fired his engine, casting Darius a pitying gaze. "Don't look back, cuz," he said. "They're already in."

Thirty-four

The rifle shots had stopped, but the sound of the ringing bell filled the tunnel, sending the caged freaks around them into a riot. Cell doors rattled, ready to fly from their hinges. Terry was jogging so quickly that he tripped over a freak's forearm. Only Ursalina's quick reflexes kept him from falling to the floor, where a freak might have scratched his face.

"Terry?" Kendra said, frightened, grabbing his other arm.

"I'm fine," Terry said. "Everybody keep moving."

"What if they get out?" Sonia said.

"Take a look," Piranha said. "Can't walk, see? Legs are broken. We just have to get to the door. The Twins should have our backs after that."

"How do we know the Twins were the ones shooting?" Kendra said.

"I know their rifles," Ursalina said. "It was them. They probably took off to draw Wales's men away."

Terry hadn't been able to hear every shot over the tunnel's

noise, but he was sure he had heard at least ten, probably far more. Maybe Ursalina was right, or maybe the Twins had changed their firing position, but that didn't mean the Twins had taken out every Gold Shirt who might be waiting at the other end.

But so far, no one had challenged them. Did that mean Wales's men were waiting to ambush them, or was the way clear? Forging ahead into the tunnel didn't feel smart, but they couldn't go back after the way Rianne had been screaming. *Stick to the plan.*

Terry had just worked up his nerve to run faster when the bright image in his flashlight's beam made them pile into one another and take a collective gasp. How?

At least three freaks, maybe more, stood tall and ominously uncaged in their path. Their bent posture and shuffling feet identified them as shamblers, but how the hell had they gotten out? And why weren't their legs broken?

Hippy barked valiantly, but he didn't charge. Somehow, he knew better, which Terry took as a very bad sign. Hippy yelped as if he were facing an army.

"Aw, damn," Piranha said. "We didn't lock the gates when we came in."

"You said their legs were broken!" Sonia said. Instinctively, they all drew closer together. Thank God the freaks were shamblers, but how many were there? How long would their ammo last?

Three guns chambered, ready to shoot. Terry held the light steady with one hand and aimed his Glock with the other.

"Nobody fire," Ursalina said. "Not till we see how many there are."

"Maybe we missed a few," Terry said. "Maybe a cell door broke . . ."

They could handle three or four shamblers, easy. They might not even have to backtrack to the last freakproof gate they'd passed, which would cost them progress and might trap them in the tunnel. The shamblers were moving forward, leaning over eagerly as they dragged their near-dead legs, but they were still twenty feet away, which might as well be a mile, in shambler distance. So far, the three shamblers were alone.

"Okay," Terry said, slowing his breathing. "I say we take them down and—"

Then the shambler on the far left was pushed aside, and a runner broke his way through at full speed. He'd been an old man before he was bitten, but freak juice had given him new legs. "Tax time!" the freak growled, leaping at them.

Three of them fired at him at once, an explosion, and the freaks jerked, spun, and fell against the walls, scrabbling at the air as they collapsed.

"Hold your fire!" Ursalina yelled, but at least eight rounds had been spent before Terry realized she'd spoken. The discipline they'd had at the Barracks, and then with the Yreka pirates, had dissolved in the darkness.

Please let that be the end of it, Terry prayed.

But even if he'd imagined the mass movement in his flashlight's beam, he recognized the sound of freaks' moans and countless feet shuffling toward them. It *couldn't* be, and yet . . .

Sonia cursed, the first to understand. "The bell! Wales did this! The bastard *called* them."

They should have retreated as soon as they heard the gunshots. The Twins had been shooting freaks, not Gold Shirts. Who knew how many biters lurked in the surrounding woods? Wales had done worse than let the freaks in—he had invited them to feast. That was a dinner bell.

Come and get it!

"Back!" Terry yelled.

Rianne had curled herself in a ball on the floor, shrieking, while Kendra tried to pull her back to her feet. Where had the last freakproof gate been? Maybe twenty-five yards back? They could make it if—

As soon as Terry turned to retreat, the thunder of approaching footsteps told him there were at least two more runners coming fast.

"Runners!" Kendra shouted, still tugging on Rianne, not giving up on her. The terror in her voice made Terry wish he weren't so scared himself or that he knew how to protect any of them.

One runner seemed to duck Ursalina's shot, angling its head to the side, but Sonia slammed its head with the bat. The freak didn't fall, but its momentary misstep gave Piranha time to shoot it in the temple before it reached them. The freak had gotten so close that they smelled the sour *whoof* as its last breath escaped. Ursalina stopped the second runner in mid-step, before he broke past the wall of shamblers.

Terry's heart was beating so hard that his vision blurred and the walls seemed to collapse on him. How many freaks were there?

Outside, gunshots again.

"The Twins!" Ursalina said. "They repositioned."

"I say we keep going!" Piranha said. "They're thinning the numbers."

The shamblers were only fifteen feet away, lurching in a tangle of limbs.

"We can't," Kendra said. She sounded like she was begging.

"No, he's right," Ursalina agreed. "If we go back to the basement, we'll never leave here alive. This way, we've got a chance. We keep going and take them down."

Terry nodded. The plan was terrifying, but it was the only one they had. "Everybody stay together. Nobody runs ahead or back."

"I don't have a gun!" Rianne wailed.

"You and Kendra stick close to us," Piranha said. "Gimme that bat, Sonia."

"What?" Sonia protested.

Piranha offered her his gun instead. "Twelve rounds left. Don't waste them."

Sonia traded weapons with Piranha. She wiped away a tear.

"Where's your extra clip?" Ursalina asked Piranha.

He tossed it to her. "We need a miracle, *chica.* Do what you do."

"Give me your flashlight," Kendra told Terry. "Rianne, take the other one. Let's make sure they can see."

"How far till the end?" Ursalina said, shoving the clip in her bosom.

"Almost a hundred yards. A long way. So let's stay in a circle," Terry said, trying to calculate his own ammo. Eight rounds in his clip, maybe, and another clip in his pocket. At an average of two shots apiece, that was ten or more dead freaks. "Keep the light where we need it. Ready, guys?"

None of them spoke. They weren't ready. If they'd had time, they might have hugged good-bye. But even the shamblers were too close now, and another runner was surely coming.

With a war cry, Piranha lunged ahead with his bat, smashing the skull of the stick-thin female freak closest to him. Without missing a beat, he charged the next one, a man dressed in a grimy Mickey Mouse shirt. For an instant, Piranha vanished in darkness, but Kendra followed him with her light and they all waded behind him.

A wiry teenage freak turned to grab Piranha, and the tunnel flashed white with Terry's gunshot. The kid's head snapped back, a cratered third eye just above his nose. Ursalina's gunfire followed, taking down two freaks in quick succession.

"You shine left, I'll shine right," Kendra told Rianne, and suddenly the path ahead looked clear and bright, crowded with approaching freaks. Terry was too busy shooting to try to count them.

"Watch where you step!" Terry said. "Even if they fall, they might not be dead."

It was working! Somehow, they were bringing down enough freaks to keep moving forward at a steady pace, and no one had been touched.

"Light!" Ursalina called when Rianne's beam faltered, and Rianne shined the light left just in time for them to see a burly runner muscling his way past his slower cousins, his bearded face a mask of rage. The sight of him was so startling that all three shooters fired at him at once.

When the oversized freak fell, he pinned two shamblers beneath him.

"Watch it!" Ursalina called over her shoulder. "Somebody almost clipped me."

"Sor-ry," Sonia singsonged, or Terry thought she did. His ears were numbed, overwhelmed by the ringing bell and the gunshots in close quarters. His entire world was muzzle flashes and blurred motion. Hippy barked and whined, intelligent enough to stay behind them.

Terry never heard Kendra scream, but he saw her light swinging wildly, so he looked toward her in time to realize that one of the caged freaks had caught her by the ankle. He saw her mouth wide open with anguished terror. Terry ran to Kendra, stomping on the freak's wrist with all his strength, and felt bones snap.

"Go!" he told Kendra, his own voice muddy to his ears.

If Terry's hearing hadn't been impaired—if the light had been in place, if he hadn't been so preoccupied with Kendra—he might have noticed the runner sooner.

The oncoming freak had a mane of curly red hair, and he must have lost his balance, because he was pitching ahead on all fours instead of standing upright. Terry saw him only when he rose to his full height after skirting the mass behind him, and by then they were already wrestling. Terry's gun was trapped in his palm on the floor.

He's too strong. Oh God, oh God, Terry thought, panic poisoning rational thought.

The freak was stronger, driven by something more than an individual's will to survive. Bucking didn't throw him, and the freak's rancid teeth gnashed near Terry's face, nearly touching the tip of his nose. Terry turned his head away and tried to roll far enough to free his gun.

Liquid pain swallowed Terry's left shoulder blade. The pain was liberating, infused him with strength. With a frantic yell, Terry wrenched his other shoulder free to bring out his Glock and shoot the beast in the side of the head. The freak shuddered against him and fell still.

"Got him!" Terry called to reassure the others, especially poor Kendra, whose scream was so loud that it penetrated the din. "I'm okay!"

Piranha helped pull Terry to his feet, and Terry scrambled away from his attacker as if the dead freak might spring back to his feet.

"You good?" Piranha said, close to Terry's face, searching his eyes for the truth. Terry saw him try to glance back toward his injured shoulder.

"I'm good!" With his adrenaline sizzling, Terry almost believed it. "Keep going!"

All three guns fired at the diminishing wave of freaks, and Piranha slammed heads with his bat until Terry was sure he would collapse from exhaustion. Every close call met a happy ending, and they stayed on their feet and fought their way forward.

By the time the last gun was empty, the moonlight on the other side of the tunnel was close enough to touch. Terry blinked away grateful tears, pulling Kendra close to him. He had just lived through a miracle worthy of its own unholy book.

Thank God, he thought. *Nobody got bitten . . . but me.*

Thirty-five

Myles and Deirdre looked as shaken as Kendra felt when their car met them at the tunnel exit and they drove their bumpy passage over a field of fallen freaks. Only a few stragglers were still making their way from the woods, too far to threaten them.

The journey to the rendezvous point was circuitous, since they had to avoid the main roads. During the drive, creeping through the high grass with headlights off—praying they wouldn't run into freaks, patrols, or anyone who would try to stop them—the only sounds in the car were Rianne's quiet crying and their chorus of tense breathing. The far-off sound of gunshots reminded them that the night wasn't over for Wales and his men, who had more to worry about than a few escaped intruders.

They spoke only in whispers, when they spoke at all. Hipshot whined and shuddered, lying on Kendra's feet, his eyes closed.

"Think some got into the ranch?" Sonia said.

"Maybe," Ursalina said.

"Serve them right if they did," Piranha said.

"But they won't get to the town," Sonia said.

"Naw," Piranha said. "Too many fences."

Kendra's mind and body rang so violently from the night that she couldn't think clearly, her thoughts besieged by horrible images from Threadrunner Ranch and the unspeakable tunnel. Her legs felt like they'd fallen asleep with no chance of waking up. She rested her head on Terry's shoulder and dozed—his right shoulder, not his left shoulder. He'd hurt his left shoulder in the fall when the freak tackled him, and he woke her whenever he shifted against the car seat to try to get comfortable. He'd always had the same answer—he was okay—so she stopped asking.

It was four a.m. when they reached the abandoned cottage at the edge of Threadville where Jason was waiting, wide-awake, posted at the window. Myles had warned that they could stay only an hour before they lost the dark, but the cottage offered running water and a place to rest before they went to the road. The road always had its own surprises. Kendra wished they could put off the start of the trip.

But they couldn't. Ursalina thought they shouldn't stop at all—they should load into the Beauty and escape under the darkest possible sky—but she'd been outvoted. They had to pick up Jason, after all.

And they wanted to steal one last moment of peace.

Jason wasn't waiting alone. Jackie was with him, dressed for travel, with hopeful eyes and a packed duffel bag at her feet. Aunt Stella wouldn't have room for everyone, but Kendra was too weary to object. Undoubtedly, Jackie had skills. Whether they were marketable to a family audience was another question.

"This wasn't the deal," Ursalina said.

Darius shrugged. "Tough."

"That's Suquamish for 'She's coming with us.'" Dean said.

And that was pretty much that.

Deirdre lit a lantern and cradled Rianne on the floor, because the girl was crying like a toddler. Kendra waited for her turn in Deirdre's lap, but Rianne would need a long time, probably longer than their stay, so Kendra hugged Hipshot instead. The dog was still shivering. His nose felt dry.

Sonia had hurt her hand in the rush to close a gate behind them, since it hadn't been possible to kill all of the shamblers they passed on the way out of the tunnel. In the lamplight, Kendra saw that her hand was swollen two sizes too big. Ursalina was the closest they had to a medic, and Kendra noticed how long the soldier spent examining the injury, clearly looking for bite marks. Kendra didn't relax until Ursalina shrugged and said it might be broken, wrapping it tight to set it. Sonia could see a doctor in Devil's Wake.

Ursalina offered to look at Terry's shoulder—the left shoulder he'd hurt in his fall, maybe crashing so hard against the floor—but Terry asked for a bathroom and said he'd be all right. "I'm okay," Terry kept saying.

Kendra stood in his path when he turned the corner for the bathroom. She studied his eyes. "It doesn't seem real," she said. "Did we really make it out?"

He nodded. "We made it." As if to prove it, he leaned over to kiss her lips lightly, and she held on when he tried to pull away, hoping for more. But he pressed her away, and so she let him go.

What had happened in the tunnel was some kind of victory, but she'd never won anything that felt so wrong.

But Terry was okay. She was okay. The Blue Beauty was waiting.

Soon, they would be back on the road. They would find a doctor.

They only had to make it to Devil's Wake.

Mirrors don't lie. That was something his mother used to say, and her words replayed in Terry's mind as he held his shoulder close to his reflection in the cracked bathroom mirror. In the battery lamp's light, the upper teeth indentations that had punctured his skin made it look like he'd been bitten by a wolf or a vampire.

I'm bit. The phrase rolled in his head, knocking away his mother's faint memory. He was bit, just like Vern. Just like the freaks in those cages and the superfreak he had found with Kendra in Wales's library. He was no different from any of those others now, because he was good and bit. Warm freak juice coursed beneath his skin like snake venom. He'd heard stories of people chopping off hands or arms to try to stop the infection, but he couldn't chop off his back.

But it was a runner, he reminded himself. The freak juice didn't work as fast from the runners, and besides, he only had to stay awake. People could stay awake for days at a time. At least he could stay awake long enough to help drive the bus, to get Kendra to her happily ever after. That was something to live for.

The bathroom door startled Terry so much when it opened that he knocked the lamp from the edge of the sink, but he caught it before it hit the rusted bathtub. His reflexes still worked, anyway.

He was afraid he would have to face Kendra, but it was Piranha. Almost as bad.

"That's supposed to be locked," Terry said.

"Wasn't," Piranha said. After Piranha closed the door behind him and checked the lock, Terry felt him staring at his shoulder. He hadn't had time to hide it.

For a long time, neither of them said anything. Then Piranha drew in a long breath, seemed to hold it forever, and let it out in ragged bursts.

"Shit," Piranha said.

"Yeah."

"I'd blow your brains out, but we both know you ain't got none," Piranha said, and they both laughed, cutting their laughter short before it turned hot and bitter.

Silence again. The water dripping in the faucet was sometimes silent, sometimes as loud as a gunshot. Terry's ears were still ringing from the tunnel, but the bite had made him forget the ringing for a while.

"What's it feel like?" Piranha said, so quietly that Terry could barely hear him.

"Nothing much yet. A . . . tingling, I guess. Mostly around the bite, but it's like . . . you can feel it swimming around. Just my back now. More later, I guess."

Much more, of course. But Terry didn't want to think about any part of later.

Piranha sighed again. "I thought I saw you get bit in there. Hoped like hell I was wrong."

The bathroom was barely big enough for the two of them, and Terry felt claustrophobic in the small space. He was almost close enough to Piranha to read his mind from the way he breathed. Piranha had been his friend when he walked into the bathroom, but Terry didn't know him now.

Piranha fished a small flashlight out of his pocket. "Turn around," he said. It wasn't a question.

He shined a glowing silver-white circle on Terry's wound.

What he saw made his breath hiss between his teeth. "Turn around," he said, so Terry did. Next, he shined the light in his eyes. "Hold still," he warned, so Terry tried not to blink.

"What are you looking for?" Terry asked.

"What the hell do you think?"

Piranha shined the light at Terry's eyes, then away, and repeated the ritual.

"Do I need glasses, Doc?" Terry said.

Piranha didn't look quite directly into his face, gazing sideways toward the ceiling as if he were invisible. "Ursalina told me that when freak juice works fast, the pupils are slow to dilate. You can see the eyes turning red right away."

Terry's heart pounded. He didn't think he could take any more bad news, but he had to know. "Well?"

Piranha shrugged. "So far, so good. You're still here."

Terry's heart bounded. "Then maybe—"

"Maybe nothing," Piranha said. "Tick tock. Don't lie to yourself, or to the others. You can't come with us."

"Says you?" Terry said.

Piranha met Terry's eyes. "Take a car and a gun. Go drive somewhere far away. Lock the doors and shut the windows. Shoot yourself before you turn, or just sit there if you can't. You might not be able to get out of a locked car. But some of you guys are smarter, so tie yourself in to be sure."

You guys. The phrase kicked Terry so hard that he gave Piranha a hard shove.

Piranha shoved back, so hard that Terry toppled into the tub. His elbow pulsed with new pain. He scrambled back to his feet, embarrassed and hurt. For the first time since the bite, his sadness felt like dying. But he didn't have time for tears.

"That's all?" Terry said. "I'm one of them now?"

Piranha's low voice shook. "What else are you? Are we supposed to sleep with one eye open? Wait for you to get your freak on?"

"I'll stay awake," Terry said. "I'll drive the bus. I can get us there."

Piranha laughed as if he meant it. "You think you're the only person who ever said that?"

"Man, I'll load up on caffeine, pills, whatever it takes. I just want to see Kendra make it to Devil's Wake. Don't tell me you don't get that."

"Yeah, I get it," Piranha said. "But I've seen what sentiment buys, and I don't feel like shopping. So when I put a bullet between your eyes, don't act surprised."

Terry calculated the trip: Long Beach was four hundred miles south. If the roads were clear, they could make it in eight hours. Even if the roads were a problem, they could find a way to make it in forty-eight hours. He'd stayed awake that long partying with friends in high school, and he could do it again.

That wouldn't be the hardest part.

"Let me be the one to tell Kendra, okay?" Terry said. His voice cracked.

Piranha nodded. "Don't wait too long."

Terry caught Piranha's reflection in the mirror, and the sorrow on his friend's face made him wonder if any of them was strong enough. His hands shook.

"I know I can do this," Terry said, "but if I'm wrong, I hope you meant what you said."

"Guess we'll both find out."

Piranha's façade cracked, and he gave Terry a one-armed hug—a short one—and he avoided Terry's eyes.

When Piranha left the bathroom, Terry heard Sonia ask if everything was okay. He held his breath during Piranha's long pause. "I'll take care of it," Piranha said finally. Terry thought Sonia or Kendra might knock on the door to check on them, but no one did.

Kendra looked like she was in shock already. How could he tell her this too? He cursed himself for kissing her. Didn't freaks carry the infection in their saliva?

Terry's heart pounded with something beyond fear.

He turned on the faucet and splashed his face with the frigid brown water.

One last time, he was ready to face the road.

Good-byes

Nothing lives long, only the earth and the mountains.
—Chief White Antelope, Southern Cheyenne, 1864 (death song shortly before being shot while bearing a white flag and an American flag)

Thirty-six

December 24

Nestled back inside the Blue Beauty, which was running without shuddering or coughing, Kendra slept as if she had found a mother's womb. For six solid hours, following side roads east and then south on the deserted I-5, they drove without incident.

No road blockages. No pirates. Freaks often lurched through the countryside, but they were too distant to trouble them, so nothing jostled Kendra from her peace. She slept curled on her familiar seat behind Terry on the bus, propping her head on a mound of clean blankets. She had felt herself sinking as soon as she closed her eyes, and she slept without dreams.

When the mid-morning sun blazed through a cloud break and forced her to open her eyes, she didn't recognize the row of huge steel grain storage bins the bus rolled past, or the sagging ranch fencing where ominously plump crows stared back at her along the road. She was free from Threadville.

Kendra's spirits lifted in a way she'd forgotten was possible, a giddy burst that made her sit upright. They'd made it! A motorcycle engine buzzed beside the bus, and Darius's shiny black helmet sped past her window. Jackie clung to Darius's waist, her hair tangling with his as it flew behind her. Had one of the Twins finally won her, or was she still deciding?

She couldn't see Terry's eyes in the rearview mirror because of his sunglasses, but sitting behind him in the driver's seat reminded her of her awed feeling of security after the last of her world collapsed. *Home isn't a place,* she thought. *Home is being close to the people who love you, even if you haven't known them long.*

Had she only dreamed that they all made it out of Wales's tunnel of horrors?

The bus was crowded to capacity, between their supplies and the newcomers, a scene of unlikely calm. Sonia was sleeping two rows behind Kendra, her mouth gaping open with quiet snores as her cheek pressed against her window. Deirdre and Jason hunched over a book while Deirdre quizzed him on spelling words in a schoolmarm's monotone, as if they conducted school on the run every day. In the seat across from his wife and son, Myles studied his maps while Rianne stared out her window, hugging herself, probably trying to forget. They had saved a family from a madman. Even Ursalina was sound asleep in her seat, no longer on guard.

Contentment and hope washed over Kendra in alternating waves.

The unease didn't snake its way through the back of Kendra's mind until she saw Piranha sitting in the seat across from her—wide-awake, his eyes intently on Terry with no sign of joy or liberation. The coldness in Piranha's eyes puzzled her.

"Where are we?" Kendra said, but no one answered her.

350

Terry didn't turn around or glance at her reflection. Had Kendra missed an argument while she slept?

Their silence felt worse than battle scars. Hipshot, who had rarely been far from her and Terry during the drive to California, was lying on the floor in the rear, closer to Rianne, Myles, and Myles's family. Hippy's eyes seemed sad as he stared up toward Kendra.

Kendra made a kissing noise. "Come here, Hippy," she called. Hipshot wagged his tail but didn't move until she called him a second time. Even then, he walked slowly, his muzzle low to the ground. He had a slight limp he'd brought with him from the tunnel, so when he reached her, she examined his coat to make sure she hadn't missed a more serious injury. He wasn't bleeding anywhere, but . . .

"Hippy's acting funny," she said to Terry. "Think he got hurt?" Or infected? She didn't want to say it. Hippy had bitten some of the freaks in the tunnel, but she'd never heard about animals reacting to freak juice the way humans did.

"Hippy's fine," Piranha said.

But Terry said nothing.

Kendra's imagination raced to piece together her uneasy feeling and the behavior that didn't make sense, even from Hippy. Her heartbeat quickened.

Then she saw Terry smile at her in the mirror. "We're all shook up from last night, even Hippy. Right, boy?" he said, and dangled his hand for the dog.

Hipshot's tail wagged weakly, and he trotted to Terry's side to lick his hand. But his tail's wagging slowed. Hippy licked Terry's hand only once. Then he whined and backed away, his tail diving between his legs. He sat beside Kendra instead.

"See what I mean?" Kendra said.

Terry didn't answer.

Kendra's fear solidified into absolute knowledge: Hipshot was infected, and Terry and Piranha knew it. They were waiting him out, and they were hiding it from her because they knew how much she loved the dog. *I didn't know dogs could get infected,* she thought, dismayed. She bit her lip to stave off tears she didn't want to explain to the strangers riding with them.

She coaxed Hippy to jump on the seat beside her and wrapped her arm around his neck, burying her face in his fur. Was it still safe to be so close to him? Yes, he was already changing—she could feel it in his stoicism, the way he wouldn't rest against her, his oddly racing heart. He whimpered, glancing again toward Terry, not behaving like himself at all. Would he try to bite her?

When Hippy tried to pull away, she let him go. Tail between his legs, he slunk to the rear of the bus and lay down with his sad-eyed stare again. Poor Hippy.

The human mind gives us so many corridors where we can hide from what we don't want to see, her parents used to say, trying to explain her nightmares.

Kendra would soon wonder how she could have been so blind.

Maybe it was the thermos of black coffee he'd been sipping from all day even though it tasted like motor oil. Maybe it was the responsibility of the steering wheel and a busload of passengers, including Kendra, who were relying on him. Maybe he was just damn stubborn, like his mother had always said—but Terry didn't feel sleepy all day. For minutes at a time, chatting over his shoulder with Kendra or trying to make Piranha smile with a joke, he forgot he was supposed to be afraid. His shoulder throbbed steadily, but Extra-Strength Tylenol mostly put a stop to that. Sometimes he sang along to the round of silly songs Deirdre had started with Jason in the back.

Memories came to Terry more vividly than usual—his mind wandered to long-ago conversations with Lisa and his mother, and he remembered his attack on his stepfather so vividly that he bit his bottom lip until it almost bled—but other than that, he didn't feel any different. He certainly didn't feel sick.

So maybe . . .

Terry tried not to think about the maybes, but he couldn't help himself. Maybe the run of good luck meant they would make it to Long Beach without having to clear the road or fire a shot. And despite Hipshot's obvious confusion around him, at least the dog wasn't barking or growling—so maybe he *wasn't* infected like the others. Maybe something about the way he'd been bitten, or the location of the bite, would slow the freak juice down . . . or stop its progress altogether. He was sure there must be *someone* out there who had survived a freak bite without turning . . . right? Why not him?

Terry's illusions died as soon as the sky began to dim with dusk. A cloud of steam rose from the hood of the Blue Beauty like an omen. The heating gauge was all the way on *H*, and he hadn't noticed! He never would have missed the temperature creeping up his last time behind the wheel; the infection was affecting his alertness.

"We have to stop the bus," he said, and Myles came bounding up from the rear to check the control panel.

"How long's she been running hot?" Myles sounded alarmed.

"I'm not sure," Terry said. Piranha and Ursalina were staring holes in him, but he didn't look their way. "Maybe a few minutes."

"Well, pull over before we kill the engine. We gotta pop that hood."

The singing stopped, and the group fell into an empty, resigned silence. They had all known something would go wrong on the trip, and now they knew when. Everyone reached for their guns. In the rear, Hipshot let out his first bark, pacing in an anxious circle.

"Hippy never barks unless there's freaks around," Sonia warned, gazing out of her window. The back of Terry's neck flared hot with Piranha's stare.

"Maybe," Kendra said in a dull voice. "Maybe not. He's been weird all day."

Kendra knew something was wrong, but she wasn't sure what. Terry hadn't lied to her—Hippy *was* acting weird, he'd agreed—but his secret made his stomach squirm.

Trees and open land stretched as far as they could see under the graying skies, without a cabin or farmhouse in sight where a nest of freaks or pirates might be hiding. Both freaks and pirates favored populated areas for hunting grounds. And the embankment would partially conceal the Beauty from passersby on the two-lane road that was as much dirt as asphalt. Passersby seemed unlikely. Their path was still a distance from well-traveled Interstate 5. Myles's intelligence had advised them that the road would be clear south of Bakersfield, but not before. The 101 and coastal areas farther east would have meant doubling back after they avoided San Francisco, and the coastal road was considered more unstable anyway.

The Beauty cast the final vote in the debate about whether to stop for the night. Although the sun still peeked faintly over the edge of the sky, Terry could tell that it would have been hazardous to try to keep driving on the rough road at night.

Damn. Would he last until dawn? And then again tomorrow?

The Twins and Jackie pulled up alongside the bus on their bikes when Terry popped the hood. As soon as the cool air outside hit his skin, Terry nearly rocked on his heels from sudden fatigue. He righted himself quickly, but not before Piranha noticed.

"I'm good," Terry said, forcing liveliness into his voice. Piranha's staring eyes weren't convinced.

While the others took sentry positions or crowded around the hood to watch Myles at work, Piranha and Terry drifted toward the woods as if they were on a patrol. Kendra watched them, clearly wanting to come along, but stayed behind with Hipshot.

"You look beat," Piranha said.

"Coffee's cold, but the caffeine still works," Terry said.

Piranha held out his palm, offering him two white pills. "You'll need more than caffeine tonight," he said. Terry swallowed the pills dry without asking what they were. Briefly, he wondered if he should accept any pills from Piranha, but he flushed his doubts away. "Hippy's figuring it out."

Terry sighed. "I know." Losing the dog's friendship hurt. Terry had taken a chance on coaxing Hippy to his side earlier that day, but he wouldn't dare try it now. He and Hipshot were keeping their distance from each other.

"Listen . . ." Piranha said. "You need to tell Kendra. Soon. Tonight. The sooner the better. They all deserve to know, with night coming."

"I'm awake," Terry said. In that moment, it felt like the truth. The sky was vivid and crisp. The woods smelled damp and alive. He might never have been more awake, savoring every moment.

"What happened with the bus?" Piranha said. "Were you watching the gauge?"

Terry stared at the dry soil at his feet. "I don't know. It took me by surprise. Myles did a decent job fixing the bus, but I'm still the best to handle that clutch."

"Bull," Piranha said. "I'm driving tomorrow."

"P, I need—"

"You think I care?" Piranha said between gritted teeth. "Listen to yourself. What *you* need? That day is gone, man. You blink too long, and we could all be dead."

Terry's spirit sank, as if he were waking in a bad dream. Terry wanted to tell Piranha that he needed to drive the bus to have a reason to stay awake, to stay *alive*. But Piranha was right: the delay made it too risky.

Why hadn't he watched that heat gauge? Was there something he could have done sooner to avoid stopping?

"Radiator's clogged!" Myles called, sounding thrilled. "Not sure why yet, but I was afraid it was the cooling fan. I'll get it cleared out, but rodding the radiator will take time. I have to clean it and rebuild it."

"But you can do it tonight?" Terry said. "With the parts you have?"

"Oh yeah. Take a while, but I can do it."

A mechanic was a miracle. But not enough.

"Guess we're camping here," Dean said from above. He'd already taken a post in a branch of one of the fir trees with binoculars, staring out over the forest.

"I cooked last time," Sonia said.

It was as if they'd never left the road. Or Camp Round Meadow. But the voices were far away, as if Terry was already floating above them.

"I'll cook," Kendra said.

"No fires," Ursalina said. "Just MREs. And no loud noises. We don't want company." Even without knowing, Ursalina was easing herself into the leadership role. Terry could imagine her whipping Piranha into line after . . .

Just . . . after.

By dark, they'd all eaten and Deirdre, Rianne, and Jason were sleeping on the bus. Myles worked under the Beauty's hood with a pen flashlight he held clamped in his teeth. The Twins were guarding the camp, and Piranha was guarding Terry, practically following him step for step. Waiting for Terry's lead.

"What's with him?" Kendra said, irritated, glancing at Piranha as he lurked nearby while Kendra and Terry dug holes for toilets and trash a few yards behind the bus. The holes were concealed behind a juniper bush, a nod to privacy.

Toilet detail wasn't what Terry had imagined when he thought about how and when he would tell Kendra what had happened to him. But then again, most of his life was beyond his imagination now. This was as close as they would ever get to alone.

A low growl floated from behind them. Hipshot. Hippy was under the bus, watching them as keenly as Piranha.

Tears came to Kendra's eyes. "He's infected, isn't he?" she whispered.

"No." Terry jammed his foot against the shovel to pitch away a mound of hard soil. "Dogs don't get it."

"Are you sure? All day, he's been—"

Terry tossed his shovel aside and sat on an exposed tree root big enough to share. "Come here a second," he said. "I have to talk to you."

For a moment, Kendra stared down at him, as still as a tree trunk herself. Terry had replayed his bite in the tunnel from a hundred angles, and he was sure Kendra must have seen what had happened, or at least suspected. Yet she had never asked.

"About what?" she said, her voice thin and angry.

"About the tunnel."

"I'm trying to forget that tunnel." But she sat behind him. Her tiny frame was shaking. Hipshot growled again, slowly crawling forward to protect her.

"It's okay, Hippy," she said, and the growling stopped.

Terry couldn't think of words to soften it, so he didn't. "He bit me, Kendra."

"Hipshot?"

Terry's tongue was a mound of sandpaper. "A tunnel freak bit me." He had to clear his throat to go on. "The runner. When I fell, he bit my shoulder. I couldn't get him off me in time."

"What?" Kendra leaned closer, as if she hadn't heard.

He had to repeat it twice more before anything like recognition dawned in her face. Even then, she said, "So why aren't you infected?"

Terry didn't answer. He only stared, waiting for her to allow the knowledge in.

Kendra's face went slack, nearly lifeless. "Why aren't you infected, Terry?"

"I am," he whispered. "I feel it. I just have to stay awake as long as I can."

Kendra jumped to her feet, emitting such a wounded wail that both Hipshot and Piranha ran to investigate. Hipshot lunged at Terry, but Piranha pulled him back by the collar before he was close enough to nip at him. Hipshot's bark was full of heartbreaking rage and fear. Ursalina joined Piranha to keep him from getting free.

"Put him on the bus!" Terry said. "Just give us a minute."

Kendra stared at Terry, moon-eyed, as if he were an inanimate object suddenly able to walk and speak. She was shaking so much that she looked unsteady on her feet.

Terry tried to put a comforting hand on her shoulder, but she pulled away. Her eyes said: *Why didn't you tell me?*

Terry swallowed hard. "This is the hardest thing I've ever had to do. Piranha figured it out. I wanted to tell you, but . . ."

Kendra pressed her palms to her ears like a small child. With another cry, she turned and ran toward the woods.

"Don't let her go far!" Piranha said, still struggling with Hipshot.

"I'll get her," Terry said.

The sleepers on the bus were awake now, peering out the window to understand the fuss. "What's going on?" Terry heard Sonia say, and Piranha explained it to her in a low, fatherly voice. Rounds of shock followed Terry as he ran for Kendra.

For a perverse moment, Kendra was running away from Terry as he chased her in the woods, exactly the way she might after he turned. *I won't let that happen,* he vowed.

"Kendra . . . stop!" he said, keeping his voice low. He followed the pale flash of her shirt, wishing he had a flashlight. She was running fast.

Then Kendra let out a surprised grunt, and dried pine needles rustled. She had tripped. "Are you okay?" Terry said, breathless. This time, she sank against him when he grabbed her, shivering with sobs.

"It can't be true," she said. "It's not. You're wrong."

"I felt the bite," Terry said. "I've seen it. Look at how Hipshot's acting. I'm not sleepy yet, but . . . it's true, Kendra. If I let my guard down . . ."

Kendra seemed to sob in his arms for hours, but it probably wasn't more than a minute, maybe two, before flashlight beams swept the woods and Piranha and Ursalina found them, trailed by the Twins. A horrifying realization swept Terry: he'd *smelled* them coming before he saw their faces. Each of them had a distinct scent, vivid. He could smell their fear, like acid in the air.

Ursalina's rifle was raised. Even Piranha had his hand close to his gun, ready to draw.

"Stop it!" Kendra said. "He's just Terry."

"Terry . . . you good?" Piranha said.

"Still here," Terry said.

Slowly, Ursalina lowered her rifle. "Let's get back to the bus," she said.

She walked several paces behind them, as if Terry were a prisoner. The walk felt twice as long as it was. Terry kept one arm wrapped around Kendra, helping to steady her as she walked. Every few steps, she seemed to lose her balance, leaning on him.

While Hipshot still barked from inside the bus, the others waited in a semicircle, huddled close as they watched the party approach. Their eyes on him made Terry tired. Sonia's face glistened with tears as she stared at him, arms folded angrily.

"Sorry I didn't tell you all before," Terry told the others, since they were waiting for him to speak. "You deserved to know. I just wanted to see you get to that plane, that's all. I know I can't go to Devil's Wake."

Patiently, he answered their questions about how he was feeling while they stared at one another, uncertain. Then a sad, brooding silence followed, except for the barking.

"What happens now?" Myles said soberly, sticking close to his family.

Ursalina spoke up for the first time. "What happens now? Tick tock. That's all he's got. We leave him."

The uncertain silence lasted too long. Kendra wrapped herself closer to him. "No way," she said. "That's not going to happen."

360

For the first time, Ursalina met Terry's eyes as if he were still human. "We'll give you a six-pack and a gun. Walk until you get somewhere you can sit and think things over."

"No," Dean said finally, making up his mind. "If he wants to come to the plane, why not? It won't be that far."

"I'll stay awake tonight," Terry said.

"That's only a few million people's last words," Ursalina said.

"I won't be sleeping, so I'll keep watch," Terry said. "Me and Piranha." Piranha nodded, agreeing. They bumped fists.

"And me," Kendra said quietly.

"Me too," Sonia said. "It's not like any of us could sleep now."

"Don't worry, I can sleep," Darius said. He might not have been joking, but everyone laughed like they needed laughter to breathe.

Everyone except Ursalina. "I know Terry's our friend, but it's Council time. We vote. Who thinks we should let him come?"

In the end, no one voted to leave Terry, not even Corporal Cortez.

Terry was so moved, he couldn't say another word.

Thirty-seven

Christmas Day

Ursalina had promised them a long night, but it wasn't nearly long enough. Their vigil to keep Terry awake and give Myles time to fix the Beauty seemed over as soon as Kendra blinked. After a few stories and thin laughter at nervous jokes, sunlight crept across the eastern mountains.

Myles helped Kendra update Devil's Wake with his battery-operated shortwave, and their window of arrival was clear. The operator identified an abandoned road near the airport where he could land and take off with ease. If they didn't make any more stops, he said, they would arrive in plenty of time.

"Anyone asking about us?" Kendra asked, trying to sound casual.

"Stella's asking plenty," he said. *"We got a call from Threadville, but I didn't like the tone of voice . . . so I figgered you were none of their business."*

If he was telling the truth, Wales probably suspected where they were going, but would someone tail them so far if they didn't know for sure?

It was as close to an all-clear as they could have hoped for, but Kendra felt only dread as she and Terry prepared to board the bus for what she knew would be their last time together. They would all make it to Devil's Wake except Terry, and it wasn't fair. Meeting a great-aunt she barely knew couldn't begin to compensate for losing him.

Ursalina examined Terry's eyes with her flashlight.

"You sure you're good to ride?" she said.

"I want to see Kendra safe," Terry said. "All of you. It's probably the only thing keeping me alive."

Ursalina snickered. "Screw that, cowboy—keep *us* alive," she said. Unexpectedly, she wrapped her arms around Terry and hugged him tight.

Kendra clung to Terry's hand, trying not to notice how cool his skin was; his body temperature was dropping. He had stayed awake all night, but he wasn't the same. She could see the poison's work on the lines around his mouth and the hollow pockets under his eyes, already tinged red. Ursalina had missed it, but not her. His face was different.

"When we get to the plane," Kendra said, lingering in the bus doorway with him, "what happens after that?"

Terry shrugged, sighing. "Hard to see that far ahead," he said, "but Ursalina had a great idea about a six-pack and a gun."

Kendra cringed. "So you'd just kill yourself?" she said quietly.

"Don't you think I should?"

Kendra shook her head. "No. Because as sick as Wales is, he discovered the secret, Terry. The freaks we see around us aren't all there is. There's a fifth level, after rooters. Remember?"

"Yeah, we killed it," Terry said.

"He said if you go without fear"—Kendra struggled to remember everything Harry had said in Wales's Collections Room—"you won't be a monster. They weren't supposed to be monsters. You can be something else. It just takes time, and . . . faith."

Terry looked unconvinced. Her words sounded small and pathetic, even to her.

There was nothing left to say.

They boarded the bus.

Piranha drove, and an achingly tired Terry was glad to be free of the responsibility. If not for the cloud of gloom hanging over the bus and Hippy's constant whining from where he was tied in the back, the drive to Devil's Wake was perfect. Interstate 5, as Myles had been promised, was mostly clear. Once in a while, another vehicle passed going in the other direction, lights flashing, horn honking. Cheerful survivors.

Corpses were ceremoniously strung from trees and gallows every few miles with not-so-friendly reminders spray-painted on signs: PIRATES WILL BE HUNG. Not exactly law and order yet, Terry thought, but it was a start. Society was rebuilding.

At least he was luckier than most people who'd been bitten— too many had been wrenched out of their lives in chaos, with no reason to believe that the chaos might end. At least he had lived long enough to see the world fighting back.

By the time they passed Bakersfield, Terry was so tired that the world resembled one vast heat mirage. But just as before, Kendra always seemed to know. She literally sat with her arms around his neck, nudging and prodding, even pinching, until he felt alert again. He told her to move to her seat, afraid he might doze and bite her, but she always came back just when he needed her. He was having hot and cold spells, his body fighting the infection.

North of Santa Clarita, a lone female hitchhiker approached who looked just like Lisa, and Terry's heart jumped. But when he blinked and tried to see her again, she vanished like a heat mirage. Damn—a hallucination!

"Don't forget about Lisa," Terry told Kendra. "Everything I told you."

"I won't. I wrote it all down. I'll find her. I'll never give up."

Terry had thought about driving the bus into Los Angeles to find Lisa himself, but he fought the temptation. He wouldn't make it. Or worse, he just might. No way was he going to shamble up to his sister's doorstep and be the one to kill her.

No, he had to kill himself first, as soon as the others were gone.

But what about the other levels of freaks? Terry imagined the creature they had found with Kendra in Wales's mansion, and shivered. No thanks.

"How you doing?" Piranha said, standing over him. They were passing the burned and twisted remnants of an amusement park. Magic Mountain, the twenty-story, multicolored totem pole read. Someone had climbed all the way to the top and draped a sheet halfway across the sign reading STILL HERE. Were they? Was anyone? Burned industrial parks, shattered buildings, but cars pushed to the side of the roads. Someone still lived. Someone had cleared the roads.

Were they being watched, even now?

"Fine," Terry said, clipped.

"Really?" Without warning, Piranha slapped Terry's face— hard. Terry saw spots and thought his nose might be bleeding.

Kendra cried out in protest, but Terry's vision looked twice as sharp when he blinked. He'd been sleepier than he realized.

"Thanks, man," Terry said.

Piranha grinned. "I know you'd do it for me."

"Lean closer, and I'll do it for you right now."

Piranha only laughed.

"Next wake-up call's on me," Ursalina said. Everyone laughed. They had to laugh. There was nothing else left.

Kendra tightened her grip around Terry's neck, nestling her face against the back of his head. "I love you, Terry," she whispered.

Kendra's grip was far from comfortable, but nothing could have felt better. He wouldn't have asked her to let him go even if it meant he couldn't breathe.

The Blue Beauty slid through the remnants of downtown Los Angeles, a maze of shattered skyscrapers and lurching freaks. Kendra pressed her face to the window, looking for any sign of living, thinking human beings. *There* . . . on the rooftop. Someone waving to them, making a semaphore of his thin and desperate arms. *There* . . . another Still Here sign flagging out of a window. The window was smashed, the shards smeared with some dried and dark red substance. Dark, like the infinite space behind Terry's eyes.

When they crossed to the Harbor Freeway south to the 405, they hit two knots of freaks camped in the roadway. They looked incuriously at the Beauty but began to wheel their bodies in agitation when the faces of the occupants became clear. Piranha didn't slow or stop, just ground them under the snowplow, his hands locked in a death grip on the wheel.

Silence reigned on the Blue Beauty as they crossed the dead

city. Hipshot didn't bark, even when freaks passed within feet of their rolling fortress. He just laid his head between his paws on the seat and whined.

The Spring Street exit took them to Cherry Avenue, and from there they saw the signs leading to Long Beach Municipal Airport. The sight of the chained cyclone fence was welcome. A hand-lettered sign read DANGER: CHAIN FENCE BEHIND YOU EVERY TIME.

Ursalina and the Twins bounced down out of the Beauty, covering one another as Darius unwrapped a chain from the gate and swung the gate open. A freak lurched toward them, too slowly to be a threat, and their bus was in the airport and the fence latched again by the time the creature reached them. Ursalina didn't fire as the thing clawed at them, stretched its arms through the fence, and moaned.

She came closer to it. Female. About twenty-two. Black, in a blue Cal State Long Beach T-shirt with a McDonald's badge clipped above a torn pocket. According to the badge, her name was Tanya. Great red splotches of fungus matted her lips, almost obscuring her eyes. She was saying something. Whispering. Ursalina came closer, lowered her rifle, turned her head, listening.

Then walked away.

"What did it say?" Dean asked as they climbed back on the bus.

" 'Would you like fries with that?' "

"Probably poli-sci," he said.

"There it is!" Darius said, pointing toward a clutch of low buildings. They could glimpse a narrow strip of black pavement beyond. Piranha waited until they were all on the bus, then rolled it over onto a patch of grass next to the runway.

Dazed, a bit disbelieving that they had made it, they exited the bus.

Kendra Brookings, Darius Phillips, Dean Kitsap, Sonia Petansu, Piranha Cawthone, Myles Bennett, Jason Bennett, Jackie Burchett, Rianne Carter, Deirdre Bennett. A dog named Hipshot.

Survivors.

And of course a guy named Terry Whittaker. No one important. Just the first beloved of a girl named Kendra. What exactly was he? What were *they*?

They had no hope of carrying everything they'd brought, so everyone had gathered only their essentials and only what they could carry. Kendra had a duffel bag with fresh changes of clothes and her notebook, where she'd written her notes about Lisa—and where she planned to write about everything she had seen in Threadville.

What Wales had done would not be a secret. The fifth-level freak would not be a secret.

The rest they'd unpacked and stacked beside the bus, either for Devil's Wake residents to pick up later or for other lucky survivors to find on their own. Dean and Darius stroked their parked bikes like they were living beings, cooing good-byes.

Kendra and the others used belts, ropes, and scarves to secure Terry in his seat, all of them stone silent. They had run out of time for jokes and stories. They had run out of time, period.

Kendra stood outside watching while, one by one, Terry's friends from Camp Round Meadow stood beside him for private good-byes. Through the windshield, she saw each visitor share both smiles and tears. Even Hipshot stood on two legs in the bus doorway, staring curiously toward Terry. His last bark didn't sound hostile at all.

"I love you too, boy," Terry said, waving through the glass.

By the time it was Kendra's turn, the plane looked close enough to touch, ready to land. Myles and Deirdre stood twenty yards down the road, waving it down.

"You have everything you need?" Kendra said to Terry. "Food? Bottled water?"

"Nine millimeter." Terry avoided her eyes. The gun was on the dashboard. "I guess you know this already," he said. "But . . . I love you, Kendra, that's all. Before you, I never knew what that was like."

"Me neither," she said. Regrets seared Kendra's insides. Why hadn't she made love to him when she had the chance? Condom or not? Why hadn't she shown him how she felt?

"Thanks for saving my life," she said. "Again." Even her gratitude burned. If she hadn't been caught by that freak in the tunnel, Terry might not have been bitten. If she hadn't insisted on rescuing Rianne . . .

"Thanks for saving mine," Terry said, "making life matter more."

She squeezed his hand, which felt burning hot now instead of cool. "Remember what I said, Terry. Maybe if you're not afraid . . . If you find somewhere safe to root . . ."

"There's something good waiting for me on the other side?" he finished, gazing up at her with a sad smile. "Come on, Kendra. You don't believe that."

Irritation surged within Kendra's grief. Suddenly, she grabbed Terry's face and kissed him. Either he was too tired to resist or he didn't have the will, because he didn't pull away from her the way he had in the cabin before they left. He tasted like their blended tears.

"Hey," Ursalina said, knocking on the driver's side window.

Her voice was muffled. "What the hell are you doing? It might be in his spit already!"

Terry was startled, pulling away. Kendra's heart pounded while Terry stared at her, wide-eyed. He looked so stricken and worried, she was almost sorry she'd kissed him. But not quite.

"Why?" Terry said, his voice a husk. "Why'd you do that, Kendra?"

"Merry Christmas," she whispered. "All I have to give you is faith."

Kendra held him, weeping, for as long as she could. She left the Blue Beauty only when her friends dragged her away.

The pilot was annoyed about the number of passengers, but he allowed all of them to board—even Hipshot. Kendra barely noticed the haggling, only staring at the bus from her plane window, trying to catch a last glimpse of the only boy she had ever loved.

Soon after the plane took off, the Blue Beauty began driving east while the plane veered west. She watched as long as she could, but she fogged her window.

By the time she wiped the fog clean, Terry was gone.

Acknowledgments

The authors would like to thank Steve Perry, for overall sharp eyes, and Vivian Perry (no relation . . . I think!), for help researching the San Francisco Bay Area.

The first and second books in this series, *Devil's Wake* and *Domino Falls,* were originally conceived as two halves of the same book. Our editor, Malaika Adero, felt that it was getting . . . unwieldy, and she suggested we divide it into two novels. We hope our readers agree that this was the right move. We might consider Devil's Wake to be the name of the overall series, as the island itself will be a central character from this point forward. However, one consequence is that part of our previous acknowledgments applies equally to this work:

It would be dishonorable not to thank the artists who created the images and ideas most commonly associated with the "zombie apocalypse" notion, and the very shift from spellbound Haitians to something far more sinister and universal: Don Siegel, Daniel Mainwaring, and Jack Finney (*Invasion of the Body Snatchers*), Ubaldo Ragona and Richard Matheson (*Last Man on Earth* [*I Am Legend*]), George Romero (*Night of the Living Dead*), and Danny Boyle and Alex Garland (*28 Days Later*). Understanding our vast affection for these tropes will hopefully explain why we were eager to tangle these speculative threads together . . . winking at an audience that, we hope, is having as much fun as we are.

Equally true today.

Coming soon, the third book, *Freak Show,* takes our wanderers deeper into unknown territory. Can't wait to give you a clearer view of the strange and evolving world of Devil's Wake. It is hard to restrain that urge, but frankly, if we told you, we'd have to bite you.

Steven Barnes
Tananarive Due
September 28, 2012
Atlanta, Georgia